Can't Stop Loving You

BETTE FORD

AVON

An Imprint of HarperCollins*Publishers*

This is a work of fiction. Names, characters, places, and incidents are products of the author's imagination or are used fictitiously and are not to be construed as real. Any resemblance to actual events, locales, organizations, or persons, living or dead, is entirely coincidental.

AVON BOOKS
An Imprint of HarperCollins*Publishers*
10 East 53rd Street
New York, New York 10022-5299

Copyright © 2012 by Bette Ford
ISBN 978-0-06-172885-3
www.avonromance.com

First Avon Books mass market printing: February 2012

Avon Trademark Reg. U.S. Pat. Off. and in Other Countries, Marca Registrada, Hecho en U.S.A.
HarperCollins® is a reg'stered trademark of HarperCollins Publishers.

Printed in the U.S.A.

10 9 8 7 6 5 4 3 2 1

"I won't stop asking, not until I've sketched you. Please say yes."

Laura blinked, trying to ignore the way her cheeks heated at the sincerity in his voice. She was shocked to realize she was actually considering his offer. She should have been annoyed that he was softening her resistance with a few compliments. And then her gaze went to the nearby pool.

"You understand there can be no seduction? Nothing sexual between us?"

"I'm all business when I work," he said firmly.

"And when you're not working?"

"I will show you some of the most scenic places on the island, show you the best places to eat, to dance, and to hear the best Calypso, reggae, and blues on the island. This will be one vacation you won't ever forget. That's a promise."

She warned, "I won't pose in the nude or even a bikini, so don't bother asking."

"Agreed," he said. His slow smile softened his features, and his golden eyes never left her dark brown ones.

By Bette Ford

CAN'T STOP LOVING YOU
CAN'T GET ENOUGH OF YOU
CAN'T SAY NO
UNFORGETTABLE
AN EVERLASTING LOVE

ATTENTION: ORGANIZATIONS AND CORPORATIONS
Most Avon Books paperbacks are available at special quantity
discounts for bulk purchases for sales promotions, premiums,
or fund raising. For information, please call or write:

**Special Markets Department, HarperCollins Publishers,
10 East 53rd Street, New York, New York 10022-5299.
Telephone: (212) 207-7528.   Fax: (212) 207-7222.**

I can do all things through Christ who strengthens me.

Philippians 4:13 NKJV

CAN'T STOP
LOVING YOU

One

Wilham Sebastian Kramer didn't lift a brow when he stepped into the warmth of the waiting limousine and Gabrielle Martin, his highly efficient and beautiful personal assistant, handed him a stack of contracts. Aware that he didn't sign anything he hadn't read, Gabrielle had e-mailed him the contents the night before.

The bitter cold and crisp wind blew and the new dawn lit the cloudless sky as the car picked up speed, heading toward the private airfield on the outskirts of the city. Wilham was the president and coowner of Kramer Corporation, as well as the corporate lawyer for the international luxury hotels and resort complexes that had been founded by his older brother, CEO Gordan Kramer.

Despite their astounding success with hotels in the Bahamas, Martinique, St. Thomas, Austria, and South Africa, the brothers had chosen not to go public and reap even more financial rewards but to remain a family-owned company. Their headquarters remained in their hometown, Atlanta, Georgia.

Even though his nephew, Gordan Jr., now twenty-four, had recently joined the company, and his cousin, Kenneth Kramer, ex-FBI, headed their security team, Wilham handled the day-to-day operations, allowing his brother time to devote to his wife and family. Wilham was constantly on the move, jetting across the globe from one property to the next.

For the last few months, the hotel mogul had relocated to Chicago, where the newest Kramer acquisition, a luxury hotel and condominium complex, would be located. It would be their second stateside hotel, and it was rumored that it would rival Trump Tower in New York. It was their most ambitious undertaking and Wilham's pet project. He was overseeing the construction on prime real estate in downtown Chicago. The Kramer brothers had outbid and won the property from their chief rival, Tucker and Sons Realty.

Six-foot-two, forty-two years old, with deep bronze skin, a close-cut natural, and keen African features, the handsome confirmed bachelor turned female heads wherever he went. Although also a gifted artist, Wilham had to schedule time to indulge in that aspect of his personality.

"Anything else?" he said as the car turned off the interstate, onto a secondary road. He'd hired Gabrielle because of her efficiency, not her beauty, and was unconcerned by the rumors that they were intimate. He was no one's fool and didn't mix business with pleasure.

The car stopped at the security gate and entrance to the fenced-in private airstrip. They were quickly cleared and permitted to drive to the large hangar where the Learjet waited on the tarmac.

"That's everything." Gabrielle smiled, gathering up the stack of documents.

"Good. Unless there's an emergency where loss of life is imminent, don't call or e-mail," he said with a grin, slipping a gold pen into the inside pocket of his black leather jacket.

Tired, in need of some downtime, Wilham was looking forward to spending several weeks in the Caribbean, at his home on St. John Island. He said, "Gabrielle, I'm counting on you to hold everyone off."

"Including Mr. Gordan?"

"Especially."

She laughed. "Have a good trip."

"Thanks. Enjoy your time off as well. Bye."

Snowflakes were swirling in the weak light as he pulled up his coat collar before getting out of the car. Despite what he'd said, he boarded the sleek aircraft with his laptop inside his briefcase.

They'd been in the air less than an hour when Wilham's cell phone rang. "Yes," he said without checking the caller ID.

"How's the weather?"

"I have no idea, but it has to be better than the snowstorm I left in Chicago. What's up, big bro? Problems?"

Gordan Kramer chuckled. "None that I know of. If I didn't know better, I would think you didn't trust me to run the company without you for a few weeks."

Wilham smiled. "I have no doubts you can run it blindfolded. How's Cassy and the twins?"

There was no one he respected, admired, or trusted more than his older brother. After their father was killed in a car crash, their widowed mother had died suddenly when Wilham was eight, leaving him in eighteen-year-old Gordan's care. Having earned a full scholarship to Morehouse College, Gordan, determined to succeed despite the odds, took on a full course load while working nights to support them.

"They're well. I suggest you lock away your laptop for a couple of weeks and concentrate on enjoying your vacation."

Wilham smiled sheepishly, glanced down at the changes in blueprints for the new hotel he'd been poring over on his laptop. Closing the lid, he said, "That's the plan. Hopefully, I can settle down and get some painting done."

"Give our best to the beautiful Julianne. She was very gracious while Cassandra and I were on vacation in St. John. She hosted a very nice dinner party for us. Cassy really likes her."

Wilham smiled, thinking of his sweet sister-in-law, his brother's second wife after a disastrous first marriage. "I'll do that. But tell Cassy not to start picking our china patterns. Julianne is a good friend, very supportive of my artwork."

"That's all?"

"Yes."

"Besides being lovely, owning a profitable business, the lady's infatuated with you. What exactly are you looking for, Wil? Perfection?"

He teased, "You're married to her."

"You got that right. But seriously, bro, you are too picky."

"Did I ask your advice?"

"No, but you're in danger of becoming a workaholic. You're not a kid anymore, out to prove something to his big brother. You've done that years ago. Your knowledge of contract law has saved us millions, not to mention your ruthless approach to cutting a deal. I can't remember the last time you've taken time—"

Wilham interrupted, "Is there a point to this?"

"Yeah. I don't want you to miss out on having a family of your own. Don't get me wrong, I'm proud of you. Just as I'm sure Mom and Dad would have been equally proud of the strong man you've become."

The brothers had always been close despite the difference in their ages. Touched by the compliment, Wilham said, "Thanks, it means a lot."

"I want you happy. With the right woman . . ."

"I don't know what set you off, but I can manage my own personal life."

"I thought the same until I hit a rough patch when I realized how deeply I loved Cassy, but was stupid and willing to risk losing her rather than remarry. You gave me some much-needed advice back then and I'm glad I listened."

"I forgot about that," Wilham said.

"I haven't. Wil, while you're away think about the fact that there's a vast difference between a personal life that includes sex, but no love, and a loving relationship. Sex without love is meaningless. You deserve true happiness."

"What brought this on?"

Gordan confessed, "Cassy said something about you last night that got me thinking . . ."

Wilham laughed. "You're slipping if your lady's spending her nights worrying about me. Maybe I should be giving you some advice?"

Gordan chuckled. "My lady has no complaints. But I'll take the hint and drop it for now. Enjoy your time off."

"Thanks. Do me a favor? Forget this number for a few weeks. And pass the word to Gordy and Kenneth."

"Got it." Gordan laughed as he hung up the phone.

Wilham shut down his laptop and put it inside his briefcase and then leaned back in his armchair. His brother was wrong. Sure, he worked hard, but when he played he took off for weeks at a time.

"Workaholic? Hardly," he mumbled aloud. He was comfortable with his life. He adored women, enjoyed everything that made them feminine. Just because there wasn't a special woman in his life didn't mean he was lonely or unhappy. He had no trouble finding female companionship.

If anything, he was bored. The women he had dated over the past few years were flawlessly beautiful. Their makeup, hair, nails, and clothes all perfectly turned out. There was an artificial sameness about them that no longer held any appeal. A pity that natural, fresh beauty was no longer in vogue.

Julianne Shelby was sophisticated, smart, and a very successful businesswoman. She came from a prominent family in St. Thomas. Unfortunately for him, she had set her sights on him and had been after him for more than a year. While he appreciated her friendship and her support of his art, she wasn't right for him. They hadn't been intimate.

Unlike his brother, he'd never been in love. Although he hadn't exactly given up on love, he hadn't been searching for it either. If he ever married—and there was considerable doubt that he'd ever give up his freedom—he refused to settle just to have children. He didn't need to have a child of his own. He had a nephew and twin nieces. Besides, he had everything he needed, a job that he loved and that challenged him. Plus he was passionate about his art, which provided the creative outlet he craved. His brother was wrong.

"More coffee?" Penny Wilson, the attractive flight attendant, asked in a sexy voice.

When she served breakfast with a seductive smile, there was no doubt she was offering more than the meal. He ignored her overtures, aware that he wasn't what appealed to her. It was his wealth. Unfortunately, he had grown accustomed to women coming on to him because of his place in the world.

"No, but thanks," he said, turning to gaze out the window. He had also learned long ago not to play where he worked. Yet Penny had him thinking about how long he'd gone without a woman.

Casual sex had lost its appeal. Not one of the women he'd come into contact with in Chicago, both professionally and socially, had done more than tantalize his eye. Perhaps he had grown a bit cynical?

But he wanted real, not artificial, not a woman willing to say whatever she thought he wanted to hear. He wanted what his brother had with Cassy. And what their parents had had long ago. He wanted a woman who was genuine, passionate about something other than material things.

St. John, Virgin Islands

Sunlight filtered through the blinds, causing Laura Jean Murdock to stir and open her heavy lids. As her gaze slowly moved over unfamiliar furnishings, it took a moment before she recalled where she was.

"St. John Island!" the petite, single, African-American beauty exclaimed in delight. She smiled as she tucked a braid behind her ear. Despite her demanding schedule, she always found time to have her naturally curly, thick, dark brown hair braided into thin individual braids.

"I made it!" She giggled, unable to contain her joy and relief. She was on vacation and had spent her first night in the tiny bedroom of a small rented villa. Stretching leisurely, she raised slim, caramel-tone arms over her head.

Even though Laura was traveling alone on this trip, she was excited about leaving behind the brisk March winds and thick blanket of snow covering her hometown, Detroit, Michigan. Despite truly loving her work, she was delighted to be away from the demands of being a social worker at the Valerie Hale Sheppard Women's Crisis Center.

She had planned and saved a whole year for this trip. She was single, but had been so busy with her work that she hadn't been on a date in months. After working nonstop to clear her schedule, she felt she not only needed the break, but deserved it. More important, she expected to enjoy every moment of her three weeks away.

"And just think," she whispered aloud. She didn't have to do anything she didn't want to do, including getting out of bed. There were no meetings to attend and no cases to review, no court appearances to make, no battered or abused women and children waiting to be seen, no rape victims in need of counseling waiting for her at the hospital, or teenage girls in foster care needing to be rescued. What a relief knowing there was no one making demands on her time, and she had this beautiful tropical island waiting to be explored and savored.

A glance at the bedside clock radio confirmed it was already ten-fifteen. She couldn't remember the last time she'd slept so late. But then she'd been exhausted. Not from the long flight, but from spending the last three days and nights searching for seventeen-year-old Tasha Redman.

Tasha was one of the twenty-five teen girls involved in the mentoring program Laura had developed. All the girls in the project were in the foster care system and didn't have foster families. They lived in apartments, boardinghouses, and rooming houses throughout the city and were part of the state's independent living program.

If anything, Laura was surprised that she'd actually made the trip, especially after learning of Tasha's disappearance. Although living on a budget, Laura hadn't wasted time worrying about the money she'd lose if she had to cancel at the last minute. Immediately, she'd gone out looking for the girl. Finding Tasha had quickly become her number one priority.

She also couldn't stop worrying that the rumors were true, that Tasha had joined a female gang in a desperate effort to belong. Laura blamed herself for not trying hard enough to break through the girl's defenses.

The mentoring program was Laura's pet project. She was unwilling to risk losing even one of those precious girls to the streets. Having grown up in the foster care system, Laura knew the goals, the shortcomings, and the problems.

Plus she considered herself one of the lucky few who had been blessed by having been raised by a kind foster mother in a loving home with two other little girls, Jenna Marie Gaines and Sherri Ann Weber, her foster sisters. Even though Mrs. Frances Green had never adopted them because of her advanced age, she'd kept them safe, kept them together, and taught them to love and support one another, no matter what came their way.

Tasha had not been so fortunate. She had no extended family or siblings and had been in the foster system since her father was killed by a drunk driver and her young mother, unable to cope with the loss, had turned to drugs. Her mother died from an overdose, leaving Tasha alone when she was ten.

Although smart and a good student, Tasha was also painfully shy and withdrawn. She had been shuffled from foster home to foster home, unable to feel close to anyone. At thirteen, because she was pretty, she learned to fight to protect herself. Because none of her foster mothers believed her when she complained about unwanted attention from their boyfriends, husbands, or sons, Tasha didn't bother telling her teachers or caseworkers her problem. Instead, she gained a nasty attitude and had taken to using anything on hand—knife, fork, or spoon—for protection. She often had to stay awake nights and slept when and wherever she could, sometimes in school. There was no one she felt she could trust. Although she continued to get good grades in school, she was cranky, tired, and quickly labeled rebellious, a difficult placement.

Tasha was sixteen when she was put in an independent living facility. That was how she'd met Laura. Unwilling to trust, Tasha kept the pretty social worker at a distance. In spite of the girl's bad attitude, Laura believed she had potential and put her in the mentoring program at the women's center. After learning that Laura had also been in the foster care system, Tasha slowly began to let down some of her defenses—just before she disappeared.

Two

Four days earlier, Detroit, Michigan

When Tasha hadn't come back to her room, one of the girls in the program had called Laura very early the next morning. All the girls had her cell phone number. Laura began her search at the girl's high school. She talked to everyone who would listen, her teachers and classmates. Each new day without word from the troubled teen added to Laura's fears.

After Laura spent two nights searching alone on the streets, her foster sisters, Jenna and Sherri Ann, as well as her boss and friend, Maureen Hale Sheppard, began to worry about her. But Laura wasn't concerned about herself. Besides, she was stubborn, unwilling to give up even after the police and Tasha's caseworker were also involved. Her personal safety took a backseat, especially when Laura considered the dangers the girl was facing. Her goal was simple, find Tasha before she was permanently harmed by the mean streets of the metropolitan city.

By her third night out, Laura hoped that her fourth visit to the apartment of Monica Peyton, a female gang member, might prove useful. This time Laura didn't intend to leave. She planned to stay and annoy the girl until she revealed something, anything that might be helpful. She suspected the older girl had befriended Tasha in order to get her hands on what little money the teen received from the state.

After knocking repeatedly, Laura was shocked that Tasha eventually opened the door.

"Miss Laura, what are you doing here?" she asked anxiously.

"I came to talk to you. May I come in?"

"No! Monica's at her boyfriend's place, but she might come back at any moment! She won't like it if she finds you came back."

"Let me in, Tasha. We need to talk."

The girl hesitated.

"I'm not leaving until we have talked."

Reluctantly, Tasha unhooked the security chain, opened the screen door, and stepped back inside the sparely furnished, run-down, very messy one-bedroom apartment. Judging by the blankets and discarded clothes piled on the broken-down sofa, it looked as if Tasha had slept there. The flat-screen television sat blaring on an old table.

Dressed in faded jeans and old sweatshirt, Tasha picked up the remote and turned it to mute. Wrapping protective arms around her middle, she blurted out, "Why do you keep coming back? Why won't you leave me alone?"

"Because I care about you. Something is wrong. Tasha, you haven't been home or in school for days. Mrs. Campbell and your friends at her rooming house are worried about you. And you didn't come to the women's center last Saturday. Are you in trouble, Tasha? Are you using drugs?"

The girl's eyes went wide. But she shook her head vigorously. "No! I'm not stupid! Just because I'm staying with Monica for a couple of days doesn't mean—" She stopped abruptly, and then said, "How did you know I was gone, Miss Laura? It was Denise! That girl has a big mouth and is always in my business."

"Denise was afraid that something bad had happened to you. And so were Lakisha and Joanna, as well as the other girls who rent rooms from Mrs. Campbell. A lot of people care about you, Tasha. Your teachers and all the girls in the mentoring program, we all want you to come back. Miss Jenna may be away on her honeymoon but she knows what happened. She, like me and Miss Sherri Ann, we have all been very worried about you." She paused before she asked, "Can you please tell me what was wrong? Why you left?"

Tasha pouted, poking out her bottom lip. "You're wrong. No one has really cared about me since my family died. The girls in the mentoring program act like they're better than me because they're all so pretty and small, like you. Denise and Joanna made fun of my weight. I hate it! They're jealous because I get all A's in school and I'm on the honor roll. I'm sick of them calling me big and ugly because of the color of my skin. I'm here because Monica and her friends are nice to me."

Laura said, "It's not like you to miss school. Have you been using drugs with Monica and her friends? It smells like marijuana in here, Tasha."

"Not me! I don't take or smoke drugs! And I can't stop Monica and her friends from doing it! That doesn't mean I'm using. I'm not stupid, Miss Laura. That's how my mama died because she used too many drugs."

"I'm not trying to insult you. But if Monica was your friend, she wouldn't be using drugs around you."

"Monica and her friends are nice to me. They like spending time with me and going to the mall with me. I'm not like you or Miss Jenna and Miss Sherri Ann. I'm not light-skinned, or small. And I don't have long pretty hair like you, Miss Laura. Everybody knows your braids are not fake but your own hair. And we all know that you and your foster sisters made it out of foster care and into college because you're smart and beautiful. You three had each other for backup."

Tasha started to sob, accusing, "You lied to me when you said I could go away to college someday. How? There's not enough scholarship money in the world to make up for me not being small and not having pretty clothes! I don't have anyone to help back me if I mess up in those classes," she ended miserably, brushing away tears.

Laura wanted to hold her; instead, she settled for cradling her damp cheek. "Honey, this is not about your size or your clothes. You may not believe me, but I think you're a beautiful girl. More important, you're smarter than Jenna, Sherri Ann, and I ever were. We never got all A's in high school. We had to work hard and study like crazy to make up for not getting A in every class." She giggled. "I was never good in my science classes. I flunked biology in college. I had to take it again." With a sigh, she said, "There's nothing wrong with having curves, Tasha. You have beautiful skin and lovely cheekbones and long pretty legs, all the things I never had. But, young lady, this is not about the size of your jeans or your pretty dark brown skin or even the length of your hair. This is about you and how you feel about you."

Laura tapped the girl's forehead. "You've got it up here. And that's what counts. Nobody can stop you from being successful, nobody but you. Have you looked at our first lady? She's gorgeous, but she's also smart. Just like you, Tasha."

"And she had a family to fall back on," Tasha said unhappily.

"So that's why you're here with Monica and her friends?"

"I can't do it on my own."

"You're telling me that you've given up and stopped trying? Giving up puts you on a fast track to going nowhere. Honey, believe me, nobody's going to let anybody into a college in this country without good grades and money to pay for those classes. Why stay here with Monica?"

"She's my friend!"

"Are you sure about that? Think for a moment. You haven't known her very long. You say they like spending time with you and going places with you. When you go out to eat with them, do they expect you to pay for the food? When you go to the mall with them, do they expect you to buy things for them? What happened to the three hundred dollars you've been saving? Do you have any of that money left?"

"How did you know?"

"About the money you're saving? You told me. Both Denise and Joanna know about your savings, but didn't expect you to spend the money on them."

Tasha hung her head. "I know . . ."

"Honey, Monica and her friends are using you. When your money is gone, what then? What will you do? How long have you been hanging out with them?"

"Two weeks."

"Did you tell Monica about your savings?"

"Yes, but—"

"Do you have any money left?"

"A little."

Laura asked softly, "When that's gone, will Monica still want to be friends?"

"Yes!" she said defensively. "I'll get some money next month."

"What are you going to do in the meantime? How are you paying for the things you need? Food? Bus fare? Getting your hair done? You planned to graduate next year. How are you going to pay for senior pictures? Or your prom dress? Their friendship has already cost you your savings. What if they want more?"

Tasha whispered, "I didn't think about that."

"I'm not asking to be mean, but I want you to think. You've never had to pay Denise or Joanna to go out with you. Do friends keep each other from going to school? And what happens when they want more money than you have? What if they want you to sell drugs or use your body for cash? What then?" Laura kept asking questions. "And what if they want you to steal to get money? How far will you go to keep Monica's friendship?

"What about your dream of finishing school at the top of your class and earning a scholarship for college? What about going away to Howard University? Or someday teaching in high school like we talked about?" Laura gently reminded, "Friends respect and support each others' dreams. Tasha, you shouldn't have to pay anyone to be nice to you or to care about you. That's not friendship."

The girl's eyes filled with tears. "Miss Laura, you don't understand. I don't have anyone!"

"You have me. You have Miss Sherri Ann, Miss Jenna, and you have Denise and Joanna. Denise was so scared when you didn't come back to your room that she called me at five a.m. Joanna called me from school when you weren't there. My foster sisters and I have been close for over twenty years. We're family. You can have that kind of friendship if you nurture it by being a friend first. Be willing to really listen to the other person and support each other, be willing to forgive and forget past mistakes."

"But Denise teased me about my weight and Joanna said I was too dark to be pretty."

"So? You think my foster sisters and me always got along? You think we haven't called each other names? But that doesn't mean we don't care about each other or that we won't always be there when needed. Do you remember when Jenna was in that bad car accident on New Year's Eve? She and I had disagreed and she told me to mind my own business. But when she was hurt, I was there holding her hand and praying for her. Every day I went to see her in the hospital." Laura smiled. "I just got off the phone with Sherri Ann. She's mad at me right now because I wouldn't let her come with me tonight to find you. She told me I was just plain stupid and need my butt kicked."

Tasha gasped before breaking into a giggle.

"Foster sisters fight just like birth sisters. What matters is that we love each other and support each other no matter what happens. We adopted each other years ago. Do you understand why I'm saying this, Tasha?"

The girl nodded but then suddenly burst into tears. "Miss Laura, what am I going to do? I've made a huge mistake."

Hugging her, Laura soothed, "It's going to be okay."

"How? I'm in so much trouble. You probably already reported me to my caseworker, Mrs. Jones."

"I had to, but you know how the system works. That doesn't mean things can't be fixed or worked out."

Tasha moaned, "Mrs. Jones is going to kick me out of the independent program and put me back in a group home!"

"Maybe, but that's okay. Tasha, you may have to prove yourself all over again. You can get past this as long as you're honest with Mrs. Jones and the people who really care about you. Mrs. Jones only wants what's best for you. And I'll be there to help, if you want." She squeezed her hand before she cautioned, "But first you have to make a decision. Are you coming back with me or are you staying here with Monica and her friends? It's your life, your choice."

Worrying her bottom lip, Tasha thought it over. With a wobbly smile, she said, "I'm coming with you."

St. John, Virgin Islands

Although compact, the villa was bright and cheery, perfect for Laura's needs. The galley-style kitchen was so tiny that the round dining table sat in the middle of the room, separating the kitchen from the cozy sitting area with a small sofa and two armchairs. The major attraction was the lush garden shared by the four units. She had chosen the villa for its seclusion and peaceful setting. Her only disappointment so far was that there were romantic hot tubs, but there was no swimming pool. It was her dumb luck to rent the only villa in St. John without a pool. It was ridiculous, considering she loved the water even though she hated the way she looked in a bathing suit. But she refused to let it spoil her vacation.

This wasn't her first trip to the Virgin Islands. Last

year, Sherri Ann and Laura had spent a week in St. Thomas and stayed at the luxurious Kramer Hotel and Resort complex. The first-class hotel had all the amenities: lavish rooms, trendy boutiques, a fully equipped gym, a soothing spa, tennis courts, indoor and outdoor swimming pools, four-star restaurants, a casino, and a nightclub.

It was while she was in St. Thomas that Laura first saw and instantly fell in love with local artist Sebastian's paintings. His landscapes were spectacular. Laura thought his use of color was brilliant, perhaps as awe-inspiring as Monet's masterful water lilies.

She hoped to purchase one of his breathtaking vistas. Perhaps one of the island's lovely bays? Or a view of Bordeaux Mountain from Sebastian's artistic perspective and keen eye for detail? It would be something no camera lens could possibly reproduce, despite the most powerful zoom.

Laura was so eager to own a Sebastian signed painting that she'd already picked out the place on her bedroom wall. She wanted it to be the first thing she saw in the morning and the last thing she looked at before she closed her eyes at the end of a long day.

Unwilling to waste more time indoors on such a glorious day, she quickly showered and dressed in an ivory sundress splashed with bright pink and red flowers that she had sewn and embroidered herself.

Postponing a walk to the open-air market to purchase staples, she breakfasted on the blueberry muffin and banana she'd picked up at the airport's food court the day before.

After only one cup of fragrant hot tea, she returned to the bedroom and picked up her cosmetics case, then put it down. She didn't need makeup; after all, she was on vacation and had no one to please but herself. Instead, she smoothed on a rich moisturizer with high SPF level, and then applied her favorite shade of fuchsia lipstick and clear gloss, before lightly spraying her signature scent, D&G's Rose The One.

Next she tied a scarf in shades of pink around her head to keep her braids off her face, and began filling a roomy tote bag covered with an expensive designer's logo. Like her luggage, it was a birthday gift from her foster sisters.

The three, for the most part, were frugal, having learned early how to stretch a dollar until it screamed for mercy. But when their birthdays rolled around they'd spoiled one another, often pooling their money to buy the recipient one spectacular purchase. Jenna and Laura shared a love of designer handbags, while Sherri Ann preferred designer shoes.

As she slipped into a pair of gold, low-heeled sandals, she admired the way they looked on her small feet and her toenails painted a candy pink. Although she loved sandals, she hated getting her feet dirty.

Her foster sisters were always teasing her about her long list of quirks. For the most part, she ignored them since there wasn't a lot she could do about her strong and numerous likes and dislikes.

It wasn't as if she went around bragging about loving pancakes and waffles while hating the taste of maple syrup. Or that she broadcasted the fact she enjoyed swimming and being in the water, but hated the feel of saltwater as it dried on her sensitive skin and the gritty texture of sand between her toes.

Everyone had foibles, something that made them unique. Jenna and Sherri Ann certainly had shortcomings. She didn't pester Sherri Ann about being bossy and opinionated. Once the girl made up her mind, there was no changing it. It probably explained why Sherri Ann became an excellent lawyer rather than the teacher she'd once hoped to become. Nor did Laura nag Jenna when she had been determined to find her siblings. The girl could be relentless when she wanted something. It was no mystery why she was an exceptional college professor of economics.

She just wished her foster sisters would give her that same consideration when it came down to the way Laura felt about finding the right man. She knew what she wanted and had decided long ago that it was just as easy to fall in love with a rich man as a poor one.

Smiling, Laura hurried outside to the small red compact rented car parked beneath the carport. With sunglasses perched on her nose and the sunroof opened to allow the gentle breeze to caress her cheeks, she slowly backed out of the drive and headed toward Cruz Bay. She would start by exploring the shops she had spotted late the night before when she picked up her rental car.

She'd selected St. John because of the slow pace and scenic views. She was looking forward to exploring the island, hoping to get to know the locals and enjoy the Caribbean food while indulging in her top three favorite pastimes, reading, swimming, and shopping for art and colorful fabrics. Somehow, she would find a pool. How hard could it be?

The sun was high overhead when Laura entered one of the gift shops. After she'd been browsing for about an hour, her stomach began to feel empty. Back on the street, she spotted an art gallery a few doors down. She automatically quickened her step.

Air-conditioning immediately cooled her bare arms as she walked inside and removed her sunglasses. A variety of artists' works graced the walls, but Laura smiled when she saw Sebastian's paintings were prominently displayed. Mesmerized, she closely examined each one.

"They're lovely, don't you think?" The tall, attractive woman was flawlessly made up, every strand of her short, expertly cut and styled hair in place. She wore a costly sleeveless ivory dress that looked as if it was haute couture. Her feet were encased in well-known designer's white pumps. She also wore impressive gold and diamond earrings and matching bracelet.

Three

"*Breathtaking,*" *Laura beamed.* "I fell in love with Sebastian's work on my first visit to the islands last year. I saw a few of his paintings in a shop in St. Thomas. Unfortunately for me, it was my last day there and I had to leave without purchasing even one." Realizing she must be babbling, she blushed. "Sorry, I'm so excited I'm gushing."

"No need for apologies. I'm Julianne Shelby, the gallery owner." She offered her hand. "As you can see, I also adore Sebastian's work." She gestured to the wall above an elegant desk where two of his smaller paintings hung, without price tags.

The two women smiled in agreement and shook hands.

"I'm Laura Murdock. You have a lovely shop, Ms. Shelby. Did you say that you have more?"

Julianne nodded, moving toward the several oversize landscapes along an inside wall. "This grouping here is of Coral Bay and Salt Pond Bay. And this one, of Catherineberg Ruins' windmill, is a favorite. In this painting he has done his impression of our shops in Cruz Bay at sunset. And there are several very lovely pieces inside the national park on that far wall. Naturally, we only handle original works, signed by the artist."

"Goodness!" Laura exclaimed. "How am I ever going to be able to pick just one?"

"You simply must come back this evening. I'm hosting an informal showing and welcome home party for Sebastian. There will be some of his most recent paintings on display. Many arrived only this morning and haven't been uncrated. Think of it, all of them in one room. I'm sure you don't want to miss an opportunity to meet Sebastian. He has received international acclaim, yet he has a home in St. John Island."

Laura said excitedly, "I'd love to come. What time?"

"Eight o'clock. My father owns galleries in St. Thomas and St. Croix and has flown in for the event. All of our local dignitaries are invited."

Laura asked hopefully, "So it will be open to the public?"

"Invitation only," Julianne announced. "Not to worry. I will give you an invitation."

"Thank you, thank you." An avid art lover since college, Laura could hardly believe her good fortune. She was not only going to be able to study his paintings but would possibly meet her favorite artist. Awesome! Bubbling with excitement, she tucked the envelope into her tote before she said with a farewell wave, "Then I will see you tonight."

"Wow!" Laura said aloud as she hurried away. Eager to share the news with her foster sisters, she had her cell phone in hand before she recalled her situation, a single woman on her own surrounded by shops and strangers.

No, she would wait until she was back at the villa, where the reception would no doubt be better and she didn't have to worry about some thief looking for an easy mark.

As she walked, delicious smells came from the outdoor café across the street and caused her to pick up her pace. Her stomach growled, reminding her just how long it had been since she had a complete meal.

The street was busy, bustling with cars and tourists. Even though the café was crowded and all the tables were taken, that didn't deter her. Laura was hungry and willing to wait.

She ducked inside the small building next to the café and made use of the ladies' room. When she returned it wasn't long before she was led to a small table, close to the bubbling central fountain, surrounded by an array of potted flowers.

She ordered a tall glass of iced tea before she'd placed her tote on the chair beside her. The sun was high in the sky and the moist, tropical breeze barely stirred leaves in a nearby tree. The heat seemed to rise from the pavement. Using the menu as a fan, she smiled in relief when the waitress placed a tall, frosty glass in front of her. After taking a long sip of the cool, sweet tea, she finally opened the menu. Absently tucking sunglasses inside her bag, she carefully read the list of local dishes, unaware of the tall man seated a few tables away, busy studying her.

After ordering seafood salad, Laura looked around. She watched a waitress carry a pot of steaming hot coffee to a nearby table and fill an oversize mug with the brew. She shuddered, wondering how anyone could possibly want coffee in this intense heat. But then she detested the drink.

Suddenly, Laura's curious gaze shifted from the drink to the tall, very attractive man cradling the mug.

He paused, inhaling the fragrant brew before he lifted the cup to a set of full, beautifully shaped masculine lips. His strong African features were keen, his skin was a deep bronze tone, his black natural was touched with gray at the temples and cut close to his head.

She quickly decided that "attractive" was too mild a word to describe the man. Goodness, she sighed. He was gorgeous, but older than the men she went out with. He had clearly left thirty behind and was embracing forty, judging by his fine lines near his eyes and the brackets slashed into his high cheekbones. His tall, lean frame, powerful shoulders, and taut midsection spoke to a man in his prime.

"Good heavens," she whispered aloud. He had to be illegal or just too good to be true, she instantly decided. She was amazed at her disappointment when she saw the flash of gold on his left hand. Darn! The good ones were always taken.

"Good" in her estimation was not only good to look at or merely well-off, but a man with power and unafraid of opposition. Judging by his designer sunglasses, the very expensive watch strapped to his wrist, the quality of his navy silk short-sleeve shirt and well-cut navy chinos, and the designer loafers on his feet, he was either in hock up to his ebony brows or wealthy. Evidently, his wife was a fool to leave him on his own. The pretty waitress was not the only female smiling at him. The small group of young women who had been recently seated also were enjoying the view.

"There ought to be a law against good-looking, wealthy, married men being out on the streets," she mumbled as she reached into her tote bag and pulled out her guidebook. She was in need of a distraction. She wasn't about to sit there drooling like a hungry puppy out to find a tasty morsel. He was most definitely not for her.

Unfortunately, he proved to be too much of a distraction. When her seafood salad arrived, it had loss its appeal. She ate, but with little enjoyment. She was keenly aware that he'd removed his sunglasses and his eyes were on her. His eyes reminded her of rare golden brown topaz gemstones she'd seen in an exhibit. Her mouth tightened in disapproval.

Did the man have no shame? He didn't try to hide the fact that he was staring at her. The jerk! It would serve him right if his wife caught him up to no good. And what was he writing on that oversize pad?

When a couple stopped at his table to speak to him, Laura gave up trying to eat. She found her wallet in the bottom of her bag, quickly placed the money beneath her water glass, and then hurried away.

Pausing to look at a selection of St. John Island T-shirts on display outside a small shop, she moved on, rounding a corner. She went into a nearby gift shop and looked at an array of postcards. Moving on, she felt uneasy, as if she was being watched. Glancing over her shoulder, she didn't notice anything out of the ordinary. When she paused to gaze into a jewelry store window, Laura spotted the man from the café. She went inside the shop. The air-conditioned interior chilled her bare arms but she smiled at the clerk and pointed to a pair of gold earrings in the display case.

From her view of the door, she saw him glance in, but he didn't enter. He stood next to the door, waiting. She frowned, wondering why he was following her. She waited until she thought he'd moved on, then she left the shop and continued on. She was yards away when she saw him behind her.

Annoyed, she recalled that a former client had been molested by a good-looking stranger and decided not to take any chances. She darted into the center of a group of slow-moving tourists and then quickly ducked into the narrow alley between the shops. She didn't breathe easy until he passed the alley. For a reckless moment, she considered turning the tables by coming up behind him to ask why he'd been following her.

But she quickly dismissed the thought. In her line of work, she'd learned to use common sense and caution. She was on her own in the tropics, not in paradise.

Later that night Laura's excitement returned as she approached the brightly lit art gallery. She was running late for the reception. She wanted to look her best. It was silly, considering that she had no one to impress.

She wore a dark rose dress with a flirty ruffled hem that stopped at mid-thigh. It flattered her curvy, five-foot-four-inch frame. Her braids had been pinned up into a coil at her crown. Softly made up, she sparkled in faux pearl and diamond earrings, a single pearl hung from a gold chain nestled at the base of her creamy brown throat, and five thin gold bangles shimmered on her right wrist. Her hands trembled when she pulled out the folded invitation from her tiny ivory-beaded evening bag. Over her arm she carried the light wool ivory shawl that she had lavishly embroidered using silk ribbons to make green leaves, and roses in shades of blush pink, rose, and deep cranberry.

She had no idea why she was nervous as she looked around. The walls of paintings that greeted the guests were breathtaking. Pure Sebastian. The elegant shop was crowded, the walls had been draped in silk to showcase the featured artist's magnificent landscapes.

Soft Caribbean music flowed from the sound system while well-dressed people with a variety of accents echoed in the background. Uniformed waiters moved through the crowd, offering glasses of champagne and hors d'oeuvres.

"Ms. Murdock, so good of you to come," Julianne Shelby said. She was lovely in an ivory jacquard sheath that hugged her curves. There was nothing faux about the diamond earrings that sparkled in her earlobes.

Laura beamed. "Thank you for inviting me. The paintings are simply dazzling. I don't know where to look first."

"Look at everything. Enjoy yourself. Please excuse me," Julianne murmured before hurrying off to welcome the newest arrivals.

Rather than giving up her invitation, she tucked it back in her purse as a keepsake. She was terribly sentimental. Another small souvenir to add to her collection and mark her time on the earth. It was something she'd done since she was a little girl, gathering bits of her past. It was one of the reasons she loved quilts.

Laura slowly worked her way along the wall, studying each painting. She was drawn to an early-morning scene at the harbor in Cruz Bay. The place she was certain she'd seen just last night. It was exquisite, with the sun slowly breaking through the clouds, streaking warmth and beauty across the horizon. It was gorgeous.

"What do you think?" the deep male voice said from over her left shoulder.

"It's so vibrant. So real I feel . . ." She turned, lifting her head up to meet golden, topaz brown eyes. Her smile wavered as she stared into the deep bronze features of the man from the café. "Oh!"

"Aw, you remember." He smiled, displaying even white teeth.

"Of course . . ." She paused and then accused, "You followed me."

"I did. You left your guidebook on the table. If I'd known I'd run into you tonight, I would have brought it with me." Holding out his hand, he said with an engaging smile, "Wilham Sebastian Kramer."

She hesitated a moment before she slipped her hand into his, mimicking him by providing her full name. "Laura Jean Murdock."

"On vacation, Ms. Murdock?"

"Yes." She smiled, charmed by his Southern accent. "And you, Mr. Kramer?"

"Please call me Wil. Are you an art lover? Or just bored and have nothing better to do this evening?" he teased.

Laura laughed before explaining, "I'm an art lover. I adore Sebastian's work. I don't intend to return home without one of his paintings."

She blushed, embarrassed when she realized she not only was still holding his hand, but had been staring at him and not at the paintings on display. She quickly pulled her hand away and turned back to the painting.

Goodness! He was so good-looking. What was she thinking? Had she forgotten he was a married man? Suddenly, she was uncomfortably aware of the way his charcoal gray suit accentuated his broad shoulders, taut midsection, lean hips, and long legs. The expensive garment fit as if it had been custom-made for him. The top buttons of his white silk shirt had been left open to reveal his deep bronze throat.

Heaven help me! I'm losing it! she thought. For the

first time in her life, she was aware of a man with an intensity that was alarming. What was wrong with her? It was highly unusual for her, and completely unacceptable. She didn't steal and she most certainly didn't covet another woman's man.

"Champagne?" he asked in a deep, sexy tone.

She blushed, realizing she had been focused on the sound of his voice rather what he'd said. "What?"

"Would you care for champagne?" He pointed at the tray on a side table.

She nodded, reaching for a glass. Her skin tingled when she made contact with his hand. Then she quickly pulled back, causing the glasses to wobble. His quick reflexes steadied the glasses and prevented a mishap.

"Sorry." She blushed.

"No harm done," he said, holding a glass in each hand before he offered her one.

She stared at the gold signet ring engraved with a fraternity symbol. Flooded with relief that he was not married, she smiled. "Thanks."

Wilham's heart pounded as he savored her smile. She was incredibly beautiful. His entire body pulsed with awareness. From the first moment he'd seen her in the café, he'd been captivated by her natural beauty. There was nothing faux about her. A confirmed bachelor and admirer of women, he considered himself a connoisseur of femininity.

Everything about her was natural and thoroughly intriguing. Her thick, dark brown hair was in thin braids, her skin was as rich and creamy brown as the caramels he adored as a kid. Even her manicured hands and toenails were coated with clear polish. Tonight she'd brushed a hint of rose on her high cheekbones, and her lush, full lips were a lustrous dark rose, incredibly tempting. She had a small, determined chin and a long, graceful neck. Her petite frame was sweetly curved, all gifts from the good Lord that she had the good sense not to hide or enhance.

In the café, instinct took over, he knew he had to paint her, had to capture her rare beauty on canvas. His lunch had been forgotten while he sketched her. But his concentration had broken the instant her beautiful, dark brown eyes met his. In that moment, both parts of his personality vied for attention. The artist insisted he paint her in a field of wildflowers, while the hungry male suddenly went into full alert, urging him to learn all her feminine secrets. He wanted her, badly.

And even when he sensed she grew uncomfortable with his stares, he didn't stop. He couldn't, not until he had her on paper, but unfortunately for him, his hand was surprisingly unsteady. He could only attribute the tremors to an overwhelming need to take advantage of a golden opportunity.

He specialized in painting landscapes. He rarely did portraits, and then mainly due to requests from family. It was highly unusual for him, but that didn't deter him. He had just decided to introduce himself and ask her to pose when he'd been greeted by old friends. It wasn't until they left that he realized she was gone before he could get her name.

Alarmed, he nearly left the café without paying for his food. It was fortunate for him that he spotted her guidebook, and her waitress had seen which way she'd gone. He'd set out looking for her and found her, only to lose her again in a crowd.

She surprised him when she said, "Nice accent, Mr. Kramer. Where's home?"

"Please call me Wil. I was born and raised in Atlanta. And you, little Yankee?" he said with a grin.

"Detroit, Michigan."

They laughed as if sharing a secret.

"So you've met Sebastian," Julianne said, slipping her arm through his. "Laura, what do you think of how he depicted the harbor? Lovely, don't you think? Many of the locals believe he does his finest work here in St. John since his home is on the island." Julianne gazed adoringly at him, smoothing a hand over his. "Isn't that right, Sebastian?"

Suddenly, Laura realized this good-looking, handsome man from the café was the famed local artist. And she'd been right. He was taken. Apparently, the gallery owner and artist were linked professionally and personally. They were a couple.

Four

Laura forced a smile, struggling to conceal her disappointment. What was going on with her? They'd just met. She had no right to feel let down. She didn't even know the man.

"I didn't realize that you—" Laura began, but stopped, then lifted her chin before she went on to graciously say, "It's a pleasure to meet you, Mr. Kramer. I truly admire your work. You are very talented."

"Thank you, Laura," he said, smiling. "I've had a home on the island for several years. And I'm fortunate to have good friends like Julianne who support my art." He patted Julianne's hand before he gently lowered his arm.

"Mmm." Laura nodded, then said, "Julianne, I thank you for inviting me. But it's been a long day for me. My head is spinning with so many beautiful pieces to choose from." Even though she knew she was taking a huge risk of losing out by leaving early, since so many paintings had already been marked sold, she had to get out of there. "I must go. Good night."

She turned, pausing to place her nearly full glass on

the table, and began making her way through the crush of people.

"Laura, wait."

She preferred to keep on going, but Mrs. Green's lessons on ladylike behavior made her stop. She wasn't happy about it, but she knew that while being rude might feel good at the moment, later she would feel guilty about not doing the right thing. She couldn't bear knowing her actions reflected badly on the wonderful woman who had raised her.

Chin up and shoulders back, she stopped and slowly faced him. "Yes?"

"Please don't leave. You haven't seen all the paintings. There are some from St. Thomas and St. Croix."

When she firmly shook her head, he said quietly, "Julianne has been a great supporter of my art, but we're only friends." Before she could deny any personal interest in him, he asked, "Would you like to know why I followed you this afternoon?"

Thoughtful, Laura worried her bottom lip, unwittingly drawing his dark gaze to her full glossy, lips.

He confessed, "I was sketching you in the café. That's why I couldn't take my eyes off you even though I suspected I was making you uncomfortable, and it was why I followed you. Laura, will you pose for me?"

Shocked by the request, she searched his golden brown gaze with her dark brown eyes. "But I'm no model. Besides, aren't you a landscape artist?"

"Primarily. On occasion, I encounter a subject that's intriguing. That's what happened when I saw you in the café. I knew I had to paint you. Please just give it some thought. In the meantime, stay. We are auctioning off five paintings tonight and the proceeds will go to the pediatric wing of the local hospital." Then he smiled. "Surely you don't want to miss the auction. Come, let me introduce you to my friends and neighbors. If you leave now, you won't know how much we raised for the children."

Laura swallowed, her eyes lingering on his sexy mouth, the bottom lip fuller than the well-shaped upper lip. She could feel the gallery owner's glare from across the room. "I don't want to cause problems between you and Julianne. And she was kind to invite me here tonight."

"Does Julianne intimidate you?"

She blinked in surprise. "Of course not."

"Good. Then there's no worries, unless you have someone waiting for you at your hotel."

"No."

With a charming smile, he said, "Hopefully, we'll raise a great deal of money to help some very sick kids."

Warmed by his generosity, Laura smiled and let him introduce her to the governor of the islands and his wife. She also met the owner of the outdoor café and his wife and daughter. She was introduced to the owner of the gift shop she'd shopped in that morning and her husband and son.

Laura quietly acknowledged she not only was enjoying herself, but was flattered that he'd asked to paint her. Not that she really believed he was serious about painting her. It had to be a ploy to get her to stay. Nevertheless, she relaxed and forgot about the gallery owner. The locals were so friendly and welcoming that she had no trouble understanding why the Southern artist called St. John home, plus there was the island's unspoiled beauty.

She had saved for over a year to purchase one of his paintings and looked forward to the bidding. During the auction, she was outbid on the harbor painting and another painting of the sunset in the national park. Knowing the proceeds would go to the children's wing of the hospital eased her disappointment.

Laura found his willingness to donate his work very impressive, as well as his God-given talent. And she was thrilled when the proceeds from sales reached two hundred thousand dollars. Much to her dismay, nearly every painting was sold by the end of the evening.

Draping her shawl over her shoulders, she went over to him to say good night. He was conversing with a senator from St. Croix, but excused himself and came to her.

She said, "Thank you for encouraging me to stay. And congratulations. It's been a wonderful evening."

"Give me a moment to say a few final good nights and then I'll walk you to your car."

"There's no need."

"I insist. It won't take long," he said, squeezing her hand.

Her skin tingled from that brief contact. True to his word, it wasn't long before he escorted her out of the gallery.

They stood a moment, enjoying the warm, balmy night. They were steps away from the building when he asked, "Have you thought about posing?"

"Nope," she quipped.

"Aw, you need more time to decide," he surmised. He stopped when she used the keypad to unlock her rental car.

Laura laughed. "Time won't change the obvious. I'm

barely five-four and clearly not a model." She held out her hand. "But thank you. I had a great time. Your work is truly remarkable."

"That's high praise coming from an art lover. If you don't mind, I'll follow you back to your hotel. Can't have you getting lost in the dark."

"I know my way back to the villa."

"How long have you been here? Two days? Three?"

She smiled. "It's my first full day."

He chuckled. "Why take a chance on missing the turnoff in the dark on an unfamiliar road? Where are you staying?"

She told him.

Nodding, he opened her car door and waited until she was inside. "I won't be long. I'm parked behind the gallery."

He didn't move until she had agreed to wait.

She was unsure if it was due to good manners or old-fashioned chivalry; either way, she was surprisingly touched by his concern. She smiled when he pulled up behind her in a sleek, late-model sports car. She was aware of him as she drove carefully back to the villa. He parked behind her in the drive and was there to open her car door. At the door to her villa, she offered her hand. "Thanks again, Sebastian."

She nearly laughed out loud as she imagined her foster sisters' reaction when she told them her favorite local artist had a Southern accent. What was she thinking? He was not "her" anything.

He flashed a smile. "Call me Wil. Laura, you're welcome to drop by my studio. I'm home most mornings. If I can't persuade you to pose for me, I can at least return your guidebook. And I'll give you a peek at the calendar I'm doing of the island."

"I can't believe you're serious about me posing. I'm a social worker, not a model."

"Don't tell me my biggest fan is turning down an opportunity to see my studio? I noticed you bid on the painting of the St. John Harbor. I have a painting of Coral Bay at sunset you might like."

Before she could formulate a response, he reached in his jacket and pulled out a small card. He wrote on the back, then pressed it into her hand. "My address and cell phone number. I'm not far from Coral Beach. Turn right on Seaside Lane Drive." He leaned forward to turn her key and open her door. "Good night."

"Night."

Too excited to sleep, Laura went into the villa and called Sherri Ann.

"Hello?"

"Hi, did I catch you sleeping?"

"What else? What are doing calling so late? Having trouble sleeping?"

"I have a few things on my mind. How's Tasha?"

"She's doing well. As you know, they're keeping close tabs on her, and so far she's cooperating. She keeps saying she wants back in the mentoring program. Thanks to you, she realizes the advantages she'd be giving up."

"I hope she means it. She's so young, but it's vital that she thinks before she acts. I just hope she learned to stay away from those girls in that gang."

Sherri Ann sighed. "Me too. But I think she realizes how close she came to ruining her life."

Laura said, "I hope so. Those girls targeted her, made her think they cared."

"Well, it's over now. Thanks to you. So what's keeping you up? Wait! Hold on while I call Jenna."

"She's on her honeymoon."

"So? When she finds out about our talk, and you know she always finds out, she's going to be ticked."

"She should to be concentrating on her husband instead of worrying about us."

"She's not worrying about me. You're the one in the tropics with good-looking married men chasing after you. Now shut up and hold on a minute."

Laura waited. When Jenna's voice came on the line the three began catching up on each other's news. Laura, normally the most vocal, was quiet.

After Jenna finished exclaiming over the food and the tranquil beauty of Charleston, where she was honeymooning, she asked pointedly, "What's going on, Laura? How was the opening?"

Sherri Ann added, "Did you meet Sebastian? Did you find a painting?"

Laura sighed. "Remember the handsome, married man? He was there." She told them about the evening.

"That was Sebastian!" Sherri Ann exclaimed.

Jenna giggled. "The local artist by way of Atlanta?"

"There's more," Laura said.

"Start talking and don't leave anything out," Sherri Ann said impatiently.

"I'm not on the witness stand, Ms. Weber."

"Laura Jean, will you get to the point?" Jenna urged.

Laura rolled her eyes and then told them about Julianne Shelby, the charity auction, Wilham asking her to pose for him, his following her back to the villa, and ended with the invitation to his studio.

"I thought his name was Sebastian?" Jenna said.

"What difference does it make? She said no," Sherri Ann interrupted.

"His name is Wilham Sebastian Kramer," Laura said.

Jenna said impatiently, "I can't believe you turned him down."

"Call and tell him you changed your mind," Sherri Ann insisted. "You have to pose!"

"No, I don't."

"Yes, you do!" the foster sisters yelled into the phone.

Covering her ears, Laura snapped, "I heard you! And no, I don't have to do anything but stay Bla—"

Sherri Ann laughed. "Shame on you."

Chuckling, Jenna teased, "If Mrs. Green could hear you, I swear she'd send your fast behind to your room with no dessert. You know better!"

"Laura, this is not the time to be stubborn. You cannot miss this opportunity to have your portrait painted by a famous artist. If you don't do this, you're going to regret it for the rest of your life," Sherri Ann said.

Jenna pointed out, "Why are you holding back? Is there something about this Sebastian/Wilham person you haven't told us? Does he make you uncomfortable?"

"He prefers to be called Wil," Laura said softly. "And I enjoyed teasing him by using both names. The problem is that he's so smooth and sophisticated. Goodness, he practically oozes charm. The locals adore him, so much that they've adopted him as one of their own. I met the governor of the Virgin Islands and two senators tonight, but all I could think about was how Wilham Sebastian donated a small fortune in paintings to the children's wing of the hospital."

"Aw-oh," both foster sisters said at once.

"What?" Laura snapped.

"She's upset because she likes him," Jenna surmised.

"Of course! That explains her reluctance to pose and spend time alone with him," Sherri Ann said.

"I've known the man for, what, fifteen minutes? Heck no! I'm not taking my clothes off for a stranger! I don't care how well he paints."

Sherri Ann said, "He's an artist."

"Hold on. Did I miss something? Does he expect you to pose in the nude?" Jenna asked.

"I don't care what he expects. I'm not posing, end of discussion."

"It can't hurt to stop by his studio. You might find that painting you want," Jenna suggested.

"Well, I can't see anything wrong with him wanting to paint you. You're a beautiful woman," Sherri Ann announced.

Laura scoffed. "And there are artists lining up to sketch these fat thighs and short legs."

"Laura Murdock! Please tell me you're not letting the world dictate what's beautiful. There's nothing wrong with having curves. Evidently, Sebastian agrees. He didn't ask some skinny young girl to pose for him. He asked you," Jenna scolded. "What are you afraid of? Or have you forgotten Mrs. Green didn't raise no wimps!"

"Okay! Okay! I'll go to his studio. But I'm not making any promises about posing." Laura changed the subject. "Sooo, Mrs. Married Lady, how's the honeymoon? You and Scott get it right yet? Sherri Ann and I want to be aunties!"

The three broke into a fit of giggles.

The cottage that Laura was expecting turned out to be a large, sprawling seaside estate with an impressive view of the bay, on more than an acre of land.

Laura introduced herself when a smiling older woman answered the doorbell.

"Welcome, Ms. Murdock. Come inside. I'm Cora Chandler, the housekeeper."

Shaking hands, Laura smiled. "It's a pleasure to meet you, Mrs. Chandler. Have you worked here long?"

"Close to five years. Daniel, my husband, looks after the outside, garden, the grounds, and the pool, while I take care of the house and cook. We have a cottage on the grounds. Come this way. Sebastian's in his studio."

Laura glanced around as they moved through the house. She was left with the impression of gleaming hardwood floors; overhead ceiling fans cooled the interior. The furnishings were white, sleek and modern. Unable to linger, she caught only a glimpse of the artwork in the rooms on either side of the central hallway. There was a lush garden beyond the veranda. They turned down another hallway at the rear of the house.

Mrs. Chandler knocked on the open double doors at the end of the hall before she motioned for Laura to enter a large tiled room. The entire back wall was made up of floor-to-ceiling windows. There was an array of canvases in a variety of sizes and in various stages of completion stacked against the inside walls.

Wilham stood in front of a large easel intent on applying gray and blue streaks to what looked like dark storm clouds. He didn't look up or stop working.

Fascinated by his confident brushstrokes, Laura watched. There was no hesitation in his application of color onto the canvas. The sophisticated, debonair man she'd met the night before had been stripped down to an earthy male, dressed in paint-spattered jeans and tight black T-shirt. The shirt stretched over a broad chest and powerful shoulders and lean, taut midsection. His long, narrow, bronze feet were bare. He was as raw and elemental as the painting he was creating.

She had no problem keeping quiet, fascinated by her surroundings. Reluctantly, she admitted that she was flattered to have been invited into his sanctuary. She suspected very few people had received the honor. For a moment, she closed her eyes, absorbing the distinctive smells of oil paints and turpentine, the warmth of the sunlight pouring through the overhead skylights and onto the stark white walls while the cooling breeze circulated from open French doors.

Watching him work, she quietly became so immersed in the raw beauty of the painting that she jumped at the sound of his voice. "Good morning, Laura."

Her startled dark brown eyes collided with his and she blushed. "Hello. I hope I didn't come at a bad time."

Wilham placed his palette on the nearby table, dropped the paintbrush into a jar of murky solution, and wiped his hands on a cloth. "I'm glad you came."

His gaze slowly moved over her small features and petite frame, so thoroughly that she doubted he'd overlooked a single detail of the burgundy and pink, long, floral-patterned skirt that reached her mid-calf. Her crisp, white, sleeveless blouse was trimmed in pink, the wide, ivory leather and gold chain belt that encircled her waist, and the ivory high-heeled sandals with straps that crossed over her instep and circled her slim ankles.

Nervously, she licked rose pink–tinted lips before she smiled. "Sorry, I should have called first. You're busy."

"No worries. Would you care for something to drink?" He flashed a slow grin that caused her nipples to ache and her heart to race. He slid his feet into well-worn dark leather sandals that had been tucked beneath the padded stool beside the easel. "Coffee?"

"No, thank you." She shuddered with distaste, "I'd rather die of thirst. I detest the stuff. I can't understand why anyone can drink it, especially in this heat, or ruin something as perfect as ice cream with coffee."

He laughed. "Aw, that explains the grimace I saw on your pretty face in the café." He moved close enough for her to inhale his citrus-scented aftershave. "What do you like? Iced tea? Perhaps something stronger?"

"Iced tea would be wonderful. Thank you."

He nodded, then excused himself.

While he was gone, Laura used the time to look around. A large oil of a hillside scene caught her attention. It was propped against the wall. It was stunning! There was one of a meadow carpeted with pink roses and filled with an array of butterflies. Such simple beauty! There was another painting of the stark night sky rippling with deep shades of violet, plum, and crimson that was hauntingly lovely. There were so many. Some were complete and signed, while others remained unfinished. She marveled over what she believed was a God-given talent.

He returned with a tray. He gestured to the grouping of paintings in the far corner and explained about the calendar he'd been commissioned to do. "Well? Did anything interest you?"

"They are all so beautiful. I don't have to tell you that. You must be used to compliments."

"It's not something I take for granted, if that's what you are asking. But I'm not a fair judge of my work. I see what I've done but, unfortunately, it does not always match what's inside my head. But you didn't come to hear that."

She stared at him in disbelief. Everywhere she looked she saw beauty. There was no doubt of his talent. His eye for color, his superb compositions, and the details in his work were magnificent.

While she was awed by his work, she was also cognizant of his masculinity. He was incredibly male, so earthy and sensuous that she was unsettled. Her keen reaction to him was so far from the norm that it alarmed her and sent off warning bells deep inside.

What was this? Why was her reaction so strong? It was as if he threatened her. How? And why?

Five

"What do you think of my cottage?" He put the tray on the low table in the center of the room, in front of a taupe leather sofa and armchairs.

Laura was not uncomfortable around men. She had more male friends than female and most were wealthy, accomplished in their chosen fields.

Yet Wilham Sebastian Kramer unnerved her, made her conscious of her femininity in a pared-down way that was basic, elemental. He made her feel as if she must be on guard every second she was near him. It was so unusual. And she didn't understand or like the feeling.

"Hardly a cottage. You have a lovely home. Your studio is impressive and the view from here of the veranda, the pool, and the gardens is magnificent."

"Thank you, I got lucky," he said with a grin, folding his arms over a broad chest. "I found this place when it first came on the market. The location was an advantage. But this room was the reason I bought the place. In the morning when the sun comes up the light was fantastic, exactly what I wanted. The designer had intended it to be a breakfast room, since it's only a few steps away from the kitchen and opened onto the veranda, the pool area, and the garden."

Laughing, Laura said, "You mean you bought this house because of one room?"

Chuckling, Wilham said with a shrug, "There were other advantages."

"The pool." Unable to resist, Laura moved to the open doors. "Wow!" she exclaimed when she saw the Olympic-size infinity pool, bordered on three sides by chaise longues that were shaded by colorful umbrellas and flanked by palm and citrus trees. The setting was so tranquil, as rippling deep blue water sparkled in the sunlight. A private oasis mere steps away from where he worked.

"Aw, so you enjoy the water?"

Enchanted, she released a sigh. "It's the only thing wrong with the villa. It has a nice garden and hot tub right outside my bedroom, but no pool." She laughed. "Swimming is my kind of exercise, much more appealing than aerobics or grueling machines at the gym. I hate to sweat. I'd rather deal with the drawbacks of wet hair and having to wear a swimsuit than working up a real sweat." Realizing she was talking too much, she shrugged. "I've been told I have strong likes and dislikes. And it's true, I'd rather swim in a pristine pool than the sea. It may seem odd, but that's just me. Although I enjoy spending hours gazing at the water, walking along the beach, and collecting shells from the sea, I don't care for the feel of sand between my toes or saltwater drying on my skin. Growing up, I was teased about having a boatload of quirks and contradictions. I suspect everyone has a few, even you."

Grinning, Wilham absently rubbed his jaw. "I've never given it much thought. But at my age, people refer to it as being set in your ways. Of course, that can't apply to you. My nephew is probably older than you. Gordy is twenty-four."

"I'm older than your nephew. I'm thirty-one."

"A mere babe," he teased.

"Hardly a baby. I've been a social worker for over six years." Studying him closely, she said, "It's unfair. Gray at a man's temples and lines near his eyes are considered attractive, but undesirable in a woman. I answered your question. It's your turn to answer mine. How old are you, Mr. K?"

"I'm forty-two. Call me Wil. Please join me!"

Laura sat on one end of the plush sofa in the center of the room. "Thank you," she said, accepting a glass of iced tea.

She sipped the sweet drink, her eyes sparkled as they flitted around the room, constantly moving from one canvas to the next. She would never get used to seeing so much beauty.

He drank his coffee black. When he held up a plate piled high with homemade pastry, she shook her head no.

"Don't like pastries?"

She laughed. "Too much. I won't stop with one."

He talked about his art, enthralled she didn't interrupt.

"Would you care to see more of the house and grounds?"

"Yes, please," she said eagerly, not bothering to hide her curiosity.

The house was lovely, comfortable and simply furnished. There was a spacious living and dining area; a modern, fully equipped kitchen, three bedrooms, and a small library/den. The garden was spectacular and well tended.

She discovered they had something else in common. He too collected art and their tastes were surprisingly similar, a few of his choices took her breath away. His collection of African-American artists rivaled the Arthur Primas Collection. He had pieces by well-known Black artists Hale Woodruff and others dating back to the Harlem Renaissance, Aaron Douglas, and Charles White. But the one that left her speechless was a landscape by Robert S. Duncanson from the 1850s. Why was she surprised? Clearly the artist had studied and collected works from all over the world.

She couldn't help wondering if he'd been lucky enough to take advantage of the downturn in the global economy and picked up this piece of prime real estate for a song. Even though his paintings didn't come cheap, it was no secret that successful artists had to be dead or close to it before their body of work reached its full potential. How could he afford to live so lavishly?

Judging by his home, its location, and the popularity of his art, she suspected he was doing well financially. But was he as wealthy as some of the men she'd dated? Not that his income mattered, since she knew he definitely was not her type.

They were returning to his studio when fragrant smells from the kitchen enveloped them.

Suddenly aware of the time, Laura said, while tightly holding her guidebook, "I'm monopolizing the morning. I should go."

"Please join me for lunch. I can't say what's on the menu, but Cora's an excellent cook. I can guarantee it will be delicious."

She joked, "Aren't you afraid you won't be able to get rid of me? I came to see your studio and I'm still here hours later."

"Nonsense. We haven't talked about you posing for me. Did you think I'd forgotten?"

"I assumed you thought better of the idea," she quipped.

He threw back his head and laughed. "Not even close. Please say you'll stay for lunch?"

"I'd like that. Where can I go freshen up?"

"This way."

Moments later, Laura braced herself against the guest room sink. So many questions spun in her thoughts. Why did he have to be so good-looking? But even worse, why must he be gracious, generous, and thoughtful? It was unfair. She didn't want to like him, especially when he was wrong for her. Her fingers shook as she smoothed her braids before reapplying lip gloss.

She took her time. Untying her scarf and combing her fingers through her braids, she then gathered them into a ponytail. Unfortunately, she hadn't put on makeup because of the heat and there was nothing she needed to redo. And she was in no hurry to join Wilham Sebastian Kramer.

He was a major distraction. He was too attractive. His dark bronze features were flawless, his voice too deep and sexy. His body was both lean and muscular. Laura didn't doubt that there was no shortage of beautiful women eager to please him. Women just like the lovely gallery owner, Julianne Shelby.

Why did he want her to pose for him? He only had to open those gorgeous golden brown eyes to see she was not model material. And why did he keep asking?

Staring in the mirror, she reluctantly acknowledged that her unease was due to her obvious attraction to him. It was so unlike her, even outrageous considering she didn't enjoy sex.

Posing for him would involve spending a great deal of time with him. And it was bound to result in disappointment for him and awkwardness for her. It was a huge mistake for both of them. Her answer simply had to be a firm no.

Instead of staying on guard, she relaxed on the veranda under the shaded warmth of the sun listening to Wilham talk about studying art in Paris and his fascination with the Louvre Museum. It was almost as good as her dream trip come to life. She had chills. Going to Paris was near the top of her "someday" list, right after marrying the right man and before starting the large family she wanted.

Marriage for Laura was serious business. Marriage to a powerful and rich man was not up for negotiation. And it had nothing to do with money. Marrying well represented a depth of security that she'd craved her entire life. It was a necessity that stemmed from being abandoned as a baby. She realized most people could never understand and assumed her motives were monetary. She didn't care what anyone else thought. This was her life . . . her choice.

They had almost finished the meal when Wilham asked, "Explain to me, why are you so reluctant to pose for me?"

"It's not complicated. I'm not interested," she snapped. "I shouldn't have to point out my shortcomings, no pun intended, because my legs aren't long. Besides, I'm too hippy, and we aren't going to talk about my thighs. Yes, I have cellulite. And I'm over twenty-five." She said impatiently, "I'm here on vacation. No work allowed!"

He looked stunned. "You can't be serious? Laura, your caramel skin tone is flawless, your hair, body, and nails are gifts from God. You're a natural beauty that I couldn't help noticing. There is nothing fake about you. I was intrigued by you, fascinated from the moment I saw you in the café." Chuckling, he said, "You don't need me to point out there's nothing wrong with the length of your legs or your curves. You are bold enough to walk out the door without a lick of makeup or nail polish."

He shook his head. "You can't be worried about a few dimples on your thighs! You're a gorgeous woman. Last night you were dressed up for an evening out and you looked great. Judging by the natural movement of your body, I'd be willing to bet everything I own that your curves aren't enhanced by some skilled plastic surgeon. All I'm asking is for a few hours in the morning. You'll have the rest of the day free. I'm willing to pay you for your time. I won't stop asking, not until I've sketched you. Please say yes."

Laura blinked, trying to ignore the way her cheeks heated at the sincerity in his voice when he talked about her and glossed over her shortcomings.

"I'm on vacation," she repeated, refusing to let his flattery affect her.

"I'll volunteer to be your tour guide. I will take you wherever you want to go. You'll get to know the island and the locals in a way you'd never be able to do on your own."

Laura was shocked when she realized she was actually considering his offer. She should have been annoyed that he was softening her resistance with a few compliments. And then her gaze went to the nearby pool.

"You understand there can be no seduction? Nothing sexual between us?" she quizzed.

"Not a problem, I'm all business when I work," he said firmly.

"And when you're not working?"

"I will show you some of the most scenic places on the island, show you the best places to eat, to dance, and to hear the best calypso, reggae, and blues on the island. This will be one vacation you won't ever forget. That's a promise."

She warned, "I won't pose in the nude or even a bikini, so don't bother asking."

"Agreed." His slow smile softened his features, and his golden eyes never left her dark brown ones. "Now that that's settled, let's discuss payment for posing."

She shook her head. "Not so fast. You can't afford to pay me what I'm worth, but I won't say no to being allowed to buy one of your paintings at a discount. Nor will I turn down an occasional lunch by your housekeeper or the use of your pool in the afternoons while you're working. Deal?"

Chuckling, he held out his hand. When she placed her hand in his, he gently enveloped hers and then turned her hand over before he placed a kiss in the center of her small palm.

Laura shivered from the contact.

"Yes, we agree. I think I mentioned I'm working on a series of paintings for the chamber of commerce. Anyway, there are several harbor views you might like to see. The painting will be a gift."

"I couldn't."

"Yes, you can."

"No," she said firmly. "When do we start?"

"Eight, tomorrow morning. Please wear the sundress you had on at the café."

It was not until much later that she recalled he'd said he would be all business during work hours but had made no promises beyond that.

As Laura crossed his studio the next morning, Wilham watched in fascination the delectable sway of her lush hips and wondered how he would keep his hands off her. He didn't make promises lightly, nor did he usually have trouble keeping his word. And he hadn't been exaggerating when he said he thought she was beautiful.

Laura Murdock was sexier than any of the gorgeous models and actresses he normally dated. But then he hadn't known he had a foot fetish until he got a good long look at her shapely legs and small feet in those four-inch heels she seemed to prefer. And she had another pair on today.

Unfortunately, it was not just her pretty feet that held his interest. Her smile was downright captivating. When she'd smiled at him the night of the opening, he'd been mesmerized, unable to look away. For a few moments he feared his heart had stopped beating. He wanted her then, he wanted her now.

Frustrated, he swore beneath his breath. What exactly had he gotten himself into when he decided he couldn't rest until he had her on canvas? He didn't know why she fascinated him so. He soon realized that it went beyond her unspoiled looks when he discovered her effervescent personality. Instead of being turned off, he found her forthright demeanor intoxicating.

He had a hunch that the challenge of capturing her essence on paper would not be enough to get her out of his system. He wanted to know everything about her, longed to understand what made Laura unique.

"Where would you like me?"

In my bed, he instantly thought as his pulse quickened and his shaft hardened. "In"—he stopped, forced to clear his throat before he could continue—"front of the windows."

He'd set up an ivory chaise longue and small side table. On the table he'd placed a bowl of wild roses and an array of oversize art books.

Laura stood with her hand on the back of the chair, her spine ramrod-straight, and her head turned to one side. She pasted on a smile as if she were being photographed.

"You can't stand like that all morning. Why don't you sit, turn your head toward the window so the light washes over you. Yes, like that. Let me know when you need a break."

He moved to the easel, where a large sketch pad waited. "How was your evening? Did you go out to dinner?"

"Very nice. And yes, I went back to the outdoor café. The food was very good." Laura blushed, suddenly realizing she couldn't remember what she'd eaten.

She was relieved to be seated, as she'd had a bad case of nerves all morning and her knees were still shaking. She hadn't slept well, she'd been too busy wondering if she was making a terrible mistake by agreeing to pose for him.

"Relax, Laura. Try to forget I'm here." His voice was deep with a velvety tone.

Yeah, sure. How was she supposed to do that? She had thought of little else but him since his opening.

"And you? Did you go out to eat?"

"I had dinner at home. I finished another painting for the calendar. Laura, please try to relax. Take a few deep breaths and blow them out slowly."

She closed her eyes and did what he asked. It didn't stop the nervous fluttering deep inside her stomach.

"Did you grow up in Detroit?"

"Yes," she said, then quickly added, "How about you? Did you grow up in Atlanta?"

"I did." He surprised her when he confessed, "We had a small family, just Mom and Dad and the two boys. I'm the youngest. My dad was a truck driver, a good, hardworking man. He died much too soon in a crash on the interstate. My mom had to work hard to provide for us. We didn't have much but we were happy. All I wanted was colored pencils and a pad of paper and my old football. I was eight and my brother, Gordan, was eighteen when our mother died suddenly of a heart attack."

Laura forgot she was posing and turned toward him. "No," he said, "don't move. Hold still, please."

"I'm sorry about your parents."

"Me too. But thanks. Lift your chin. Yes, that's right. It was rough going on without her. But she and Dad taught us by example that hard work never hurt anyone. Education was also a big deal in our family. It was so important that both Gordan and I knew we had to go to college and finish. Neither of our parents had that opportunity."

"Did you?" she quizzed.

"Go to college? Or finish?" He chuckled when she sent him an impatient look. "We did both."

Laura started to nod, then stopped. "I imagine your mother would have been so proud of both her boys. Did you and your brother move in with relatives?"

"No. My father had only one brother and we didn't know how to contact him. Gordan took care of me while working full-time and carrying a full college course load. He worked nights at a small, family-owned hotel back then. I slept in the hotel office while he worked."

"He also finished college?"

"He did more than finish college. When the owner was ready to retire, Gordan bought the hotel. It was his first."

"Wow!" she exclaimed. "You had a very determined brother."

Wilham laughed. "He'd say he was too stubborn to give up. At any rate, he set the bar very high for me."

"Yes. He must be pleased with your success," she said, gesturing with her hand to his art.

"He's proud, but not because of my art."

"Wait a minute!" Laura said. "Kramer! Are you talking about Gordan Kramer, the hotel magnate? That's your brother!" Her eyes went wide.

"The same."

Laura stared at him, her lips parted to ask questions when his housekeeper, Cora Chandler, knocked on the open hallway door.

"Excuse me. Ms. Shelby sent someone to pick up some paintings. Should I ask him to come back later?"

"No, they're ready." He said to Laura, "Sorry about the interruption. Why don't you take a break?" He went over, easily picked up a large crate, and carried it out of the room.

Six

Laura was in shock. No wonder he lived so well. How could he not, being Gordan Kramer's brother? The man was reported to be a Black billionaire! It was a shame Wilham Sebastian wasn't her type.

Although tempted to take a peek at the sketch he'd been working on, Laura decided to wait until invited to look. Instead, she went to the French doors. She stared at the pool, imagining the cool water on her skin. Everything she needed for a swim was tucked inside her tote.

"Refreshments," Cora Chandler announced cheerfully, motioning for the heavyset older man to put the tray on the low table in front of the sofa and chair in the center of the room.

"Good," Laura said, pivoting.

The housekeeper said, "This is my husband, Daniel, Ms. Murdock."

"Please call me Laura," she said with a smile. "So you're responsible for all these lovely flowers and plants. The grounds are impressive."

"Thanks." He beamed, bobbed his head quickly.

"Just let me know what you like," Cora offered.

"You're a wonderful, cook, Cora. Everything looks good."

Daniel Chandler was a man of few words. He nodded again after centering the tray and then followed his wife out of the room.

Laura picked up a tall glass of iced tea and sipped. It was perfect, sweetened and with a touch of mint. Just the way she liked it. She peeked beneath the napkin covering warm, fragrant, homemade yeast rolls. Blueberry, mango, and strawberry jams were also provided. Although tempted, she managed to resist. Laura wandered around the room. When she returned to the small table near the windows, she read the names on the stack of oversize art books.

"Goodness!" she exclaimed when she saw a familiar title.

"Sorry about the delay," Wilham said when he returned. "Good. Cora brought in refresh—"

Laura interrupted, gushing, "I haven't seen this book in years," as she smoothed her hand lovingly over the cover. It was a wonderful tribute to the women of Africa, hallmarking their beauty. As a girl, Laura had been fascinated by the pictures and often pored over the book for hours. The women were dressed in their native costumes, some were adorned in bold gold or bronze jewelry, some were adorned with tattoos, and still others were adorned with enlarged lower lips or earlobes.

"The women are so beautiful. I'm just surprised that you have this book." She flipped to the copyright page and read aloud, "*Africa Adorned* by Angela Fisher, published 1984. Where did you find it?"

"In a small bookstore in Martinique. Like you, I thought the women were lovely, a unique display of tribal customs and traditions, and remarkable beauty."

She confessed, "This book was part of my childhood and the wonderful woman who raised me and my foster sisters."

Wilham had gone back to sketching, but paused. "Did you say foster sister? Your parents took in foster children?"

"Not exactly. I didn't grow up with my parents. I was only a few days old when my mother left me in a cardboard box on a church bench. Lucky for me it was August. The note pinned to my blanket said my name was Laura and that I was loved. She also said she was very sorry she couldn't keep me."

She didn't reveal that she was sentimental and had kept the blanket. Lost in thought, she smiled as she slowly turned the pages.

When she looked up at him, she said, "I was blessed to grow up in a wonderful foster home." Judging by his expression, she surmised, "I've shocked you. Don't you think I turned out okay?"

He stared at her for a few more moments before finally he said with a smile, "Laura, 'okay' is too mild a word to describe you." He walked over to the sofa and made himself comfortable. After filling a cup with coffee, he went on to say, "The only word I can think of to describe you would be 'remarkable.' I'd never guess your beginning was so humble. As for growing up with this foster sister—"

"Sisters, there were three of us. Sherri Ann Weber and Jenna Gaines Hendricks are my very best friends. We were six when Mrs. Frances Green opened her home to us and made us family. She was widowed, a retired teacher, with no children of her own. She forged a love bond with us and was our guardian angel."

"Was?" He sipped the hot brew.

Laura sighed. "She passed away, almost two years ago, from Alzheimer's." Absently stroking the cover of the book, she said softly, "I will never forget the wonderful stories that Mrs. Green told about growing up in the South. Stories about the remarkable women in her family, her grandmother, her mother, her aunts and cousins. People that are long gone, but they'd touched her heart and generous soul. Her stories made me feel connected to those women, the women in the book, and the past.

"I realized I had a rich and colorful history that dated back to the motherland and my African ancestors. Knowing the history of my people gave me the connection I yearned for as a young girl. That connection probably meant so much to me because I didn't know my personal history."

"So your braids are not an easy vacation style?" he said.

"My braids are a sweet reminder of being a little girl and having Mrs. Green all to myself. I remember sitting at her knee while she braided my hair and told me about her great-grandmother who was born a slave. She was six years old when slavery ended. It sparked my interest in reading. I used to love to check out books from the library about the courageous Black women and learn about their contributions that helped shape our country.

"Braiding of the hair was yet another connection to the past. I found the history fascinating. Perhaps because the African women in this book look like me. I felt as if I'm a tiny part of something much bigger. Even when the other girls wore curls, I still wanted braids. It's crazy considering I have no patience."

She laughed, admitting, "I hated sitting still, yet I

stubbornly insisted on wearing braids." She stopped and blushed with embarrassment. "Sorry, I'm going on and on."

"Your Mrs. Green sounds like you, a remarkable woman."

"Thank you." Laura smiled, warmed by the compliment. "She had such a generous spirit, always finding ways to help others. We lived with her until we graduated from high school and went to college. She was good to us and for us. We found both love and acceptance in her modest home." Then she said proudly, "Mrs. Green was a true lady, well educated, independent, and she expected no less from her girls."

"I'm glad it worked out well for you, Laura. You're right, you were very fortunate."

"No, Wilham Sebastian Kramer," she teased. "I was blessed."

He smiled. "Ready?" He gestured to the chaise longue.

She nodded, and soon she was seated and once more gazing out the window. As she studied the center courtyard, she decided she liked the way it had been laid out. A round wrought-iron, glass-topped dining table and chairs with green and blue cushions were positioned on a lattice-patterned area rug and were mere steps away from the kitchen. There were deep-cushion armchairs that faced a huge stone fire pit, plus there was an outdoor kitchen area for cooking and entertaining.

"It's lovely here, so serene," she mused.

"Mmm," he murmured, completely absorbed in his work.

She turned toward him. Laura couldn't see what Wilham was drawing but she could see him. She studied his keen male features, marveled at his high cheekbones, the thickness of his close-cut natural, and the length of his ebony lashes. She traced the lines from his strong nose and the grooves along his cheeks, the curve of a square-cut jaw. Her eyes lingered on his firm, beautifully shaped mouth; the bottom lip was slightly fuller than the top. Even his mouth was appealing, sexy. Suddenly, she blinked, realizing what she'd been doing.

Swiftly, she turned back to the window. Goodness! What just happened? Whatever it was, it had to stop now before he caught her staring at him.

When Wilham cleared his throat, her eyes were instantly drawn back to him. His dark bronze skin glistened with perspiration. Water dotted his forehead despite the open doors and the cooling motion of the ceiling fans mounted on sturdy beams throughout the room.

She watched as a bead of moisture slowly slid from his hairline to his forehead, down his temple and lean cheek to his chin, and continued down the length of his corded throat and finally dampened his cotton shirt. The top two buttons of his short-sleeve white polo shirt were undone. There was nothing to prevent her from seeing the dark shadow of chest hair covering well-developed pectoral muscles or his taut stomach. His jeans hugged his lean hips, muscular thighs, and long legs.

For heaven's sake! Why did he have to be so darn sexy? More important, why couldn't she keep her eyes off him? Something was wrong! She had no business imagining her lips trailing kisses down his bronze throat while inhaling his unique male scent. No! No! No!

She jerked her head around so fast she nearly lost her balance and had to brace herself. She balled her hands into fists as she stared out the window. The sun was warm. She slowly relaxed as she gazed at the water in the pool, watching ripples and imagining its cool welcome. She sighed and then shifted, restlessly moving her weight from her right hip to the left and back again. Her back and neck were beginning to ache from holding still.

Wilham said, "That's enough for today. Thanks, Laura. I appreciate your doing this." He flipped the pages down, covering the sketch he'd been working on. "Hungry? Can you stay for lunch?"

She stood, stretching. "No, but thank you."

She went over and grabbed her tote bag, then checked around to see if she'd left anything.

"Laura, you have to eat. Cora won't mind preparing something for you. What would you like?"

"No thanks. I'd rather go shopping. Good-bye, Wilham Sebastian Kramer," she said, enjoying the sound of his full name. "I'll see you in the morning." She walked out into the hall.

"What about your swim?" he called after her.

"Maybe tomorrow," she called.

Laura bolted out of the house like a scared rabbit with a pack of rabid wolves nipping on her tail. She didn't stop moving until she reached her car, even though she knew she was being ridiculous. Exactly who did she think she was running from? No one was chasing after her. Certainly not Wilham.

She had started off the morning shaking with a bad case of nerves, and ended it by leaving his studio with her heart pounding in dread. He'd been the perfect host, a gentleman, holding up his end of their bargain.

He hadn't come anywhere near her all morning. She was acting like a ninny, as if he'd propositioned her and invited her into his bedroom instead of for a swim and lunch.

Inside her rental car with the seat belt fastened, she sat. Her hands were shaking so badly she didn't dare start the engine. What was it? Why was she so afraid? What did she think would happen if she had stayed for lunch?

She covered her face. Mortified as she recalled the way she'd stared at him, unable to stop looking at him. It was a good thing she hadn't stayed, since he was not on the menu. She moaned unhappily.

She was a wreck! She was upset. She couldn't understand her intense sexual attraction to the man. She should be thankful she hadn't done something really stupid and acted out her fantasy.

Now that would have been hilarious, her trailing kisses along his throat. Especially when she didn't enjoy sex. What had happened to her? It had been so long that she couldn't remember the last time she had been sexually aroused!

"It must be this awful heat and humidity!" she complained, turning on the air-conditioning before she put the car into gear. Not only was it curling her hair but it was frying her brain cells. What she needed was a doctor! Clearly, she was losing touch with reality.

"Enough of this nonsense," she whispered aloud. She wasn't going to waste another second thinking about him. She'd kept her part of the bargain. She'd posed and fulfilled her obligation. She was free for the rest of the day.

Laura drove to her villa. She washed out the sundress that she was beginning to hate in the sink and hung it over the towel bar above the tub to dry. Then she changed into white walking shorts, a bright fuchsia short-sleeve top edged in lace, and white ballerina flats. She emptied her tote and repacked it with a guidebook, wallet, and cell phone before she headed back to the car.

She stopped at a roadside shack and enjoyed a shrimp and potato fritter covered with a delicious key lime mustard sauce and washed it down with passion-fruit punch. She'd asked for directions and was pleased that she had no trouble finding the Fabric Mill.

She spent the rest of the afternoon happily looking at and selecting fabrics. She also stopped at the market to pick up enough fresh fruit, bread, cheese, and eggs for a few days. The sun was setting by the time she returned to the villa.

Knowing she wouldn't relax until she had spoken to Tasha, Laura placed the call. Although surprised, Tasha was pleased to hear from her. The girl was back in school and was doing well. Thanks to her case-worker, Mrs. Jones, she was still in the independent living program. She was happy to have gotten her old room back. She also had made up with her two flat-mates and friends, Denise and Joanna. Both girls had apologized and begged her to stay away from Monica and her friends.

After hearing such good news, Laura was relieved when she hung up the phone. She'd just put down her cell phone when it rang.

"Hello?"

"Are you having fun yet?"

"Hey, Sherri Ann. Shouldn't you be in bed by now? Don't you have court in the morning?"

"I'm asking the questions. Are you having fun?"

Laura laughed. "Almost. I'd have more fun if you were with me."

"I wish, but I have this big case. I can't afford to mess up."

Laura scolded, "It's always a new case with you, Counselor. It never stops."

"We're not talking about me. Did you pose for Sebastian this morning or did you chicken out?"

"I kept my word."

"And . . ."

"Afterward, I had a delicious lunch, went shopping, and found some beautiful fabrics that are much too pretty to cut. You and Jenna can look them over and I'll make sundresses."

"I can't wait to see. But I was asking about your session with Sebastian. How did it go?"

"It went well. No problems."

"Good. I'm just glad you finally decided to do something for you. You needed to get away. I have to admit I was worried about you. It's been work, work, work lately with you. And I'm not the only one concerned. Maureen, your boss, remember her?"

"What about Maureen?"

"She was sure you'd find something to keep you in Detroit. You act like your body is a machine. You can't keep going and going without rest."

"It's not my fault that things have been crazy around the women's center for the last few months. No, it's been longer than that. Since Brynne married Devin Prescott and moved to St. Louis, we desperately need another counselor. Maureen hasn't found anyone who even comes close to having Brynne's understanding or talents."

"Crazy? Laura, that's a huge understatement. You've been so busy, I bet you can't remember the last time you've been out on a real date. You didn't have a date at your tree-trimming party this past Christmas, even after you went ahead and told everyone to bring someone. You invited Craig Owens, a coworker. Shame on you!"

"Craig and I are more than coworkers." She frowned, not liking the direction the conversation was headed.

"You picked him because he's a friend and safe. Admit it, sister girl, as far as men are concerned you're in a giant rut! You've been going out with male friends for more than a year. Why?" Sherri Ann didn't wait for a response, but rushed ahead to say, "Something has been bothering you. But you haven't talked to either me or Jenna about it. I'm hoping that when you're back from vacation and Jenna from her honeymoon, the three of us can sit down and talk seriously. Laura, I'm prying, but I'm worried about you. Something is wrong."

"Nothing's wrong. I'm on vacation and I'm fine."

"You're not fine. And this trip couldn't have come at a better time. While you're on that island forget everyone and everything. Promise you'll spend the next three weeks focusing on only you and what you really want. Laura, you're not the same person who decided in grad school that you would only date and marry a very rich man. You'd been badly hurt twice and you dreamed up this fabulous life. It sounded great at the time but it's not real. Why waste time choosing a fantasy?"

Laura didn't say anything. She didn't want to go backward. She certainly didn't wish to talk about past mistakes. Instead, she closed her eyes, leaned against the pillows, deciding to wait it out. Sooner or later Sherri Ann was bound to wind down or move on to something else.

"Laura, I hate to be the one to tell you, but you're not twenty-anything anymore. You're thirty-one years old. And lately you've been so caught up in fixing other people's lives that you've forgotten you even have a personal life." Sherri Ann giggled. "Did you find the sexy cocktail dresses and lacy underthings that I snuck into the bottom of your suitcase?"

"Yeah, I found them all right. At the airport while security was going through my luggage. I'd been meaning to yell at you for that."

Sherri Ann laughed. "Sorry. I wasn't trying to embarrass you. But at least you have something to wear when you go out dancing and actually have a little fun while in St. John. Girl, let your braids down, put on some makeup and perfume. It's time for you to unwind, get loose, and get rid of all that old stuff that has been weighing you down. Well?"

Laura laughed. "You've got some nerve. This coming from a woman as equally stressed and overworked. Do you hear me bring up what you always dreamed about as a girl, having babies and teaching kindergarten? No, I'm not rubbing that into your face. Nor am I telling you that it's not too late for you to take your own advice and hop on the next airplane headed for the Virgin Islands. The only thing you think and talk about, Sherri Ann, is making partner before you turn thirty-five."

"True, but unlike you, I do have a social life. I date. I'm going out on Saturday night with a good-looking attorney I met last week. What did you do tonight?"

"Shut up!"

"You're supposed to be having fun all day and into the night. Why are you alone tonight instead of out in some club dancing? Or out with that sexy Sebastian? Has he asked you out yet?"

"Why do you ask?"

"Answer the question."

"No!"

"Either he hasn't asked you or you turned him down. Which?"

Exasperated, Laura snapped, "Nosy, he asked me stay for lunch, not out on a date."

"Did you stay?"

Laura had never been good at lying, but right now she was strongly considering it. Eventually, she said, "No!"

"But why?"

Laura sighed. "I learned a long time ago I can't win an argument with you," before she reluctantly admitted, "I didn't want to get involved. He's not my type."

"You mean he's not tall, dark, and super rich?"

"He's rich enough. He's Gordan Kramer's younger brother."

"The billionaire?"

"That's the one. Must be nice to have rich relatives."

"We will never know," Sherri Ann said with a laugh. "How'd you find out?"

"He told me. He has an impressive art collection and very expensive, judging from what I saw."

"And he is not your type?" Sherri Ann asked.

"You already know that."

"Because he's rich, but not powerful. Talk about splitting hairs. Did you hear anything I said, Laura Murdock? You're stuck! You haven't moved from the decision you made at twenty-three. If you recall, Jenna brought this up at your Christmas party. I agreed with her! Why won't you admit she was right?"

Laura rushed to say, "Jenna has a big mouth, besides she was wrong. There is nothing wrong with a woman knowing what she wants in a man. Miss Thing didn't wait around asking what I thought of Scott Hendricks before she married him, now did she?"

Sherri Ann hooted with laugher. "Our dear sister didn't have to ask what you thought because you came right out and told her. Besides, we aren't talking about her, missy. We are talking about your love life or lack thereof. Jenna nailed it when she told you that if all you really wanted was a rich man you would have married years ago. And you flat-out refused to admit it's true."

"Of course I do because I don't agree with either one of you. My opinion is the only one that counts!"

Sherri Ann ignored the comment. She went on to emphasize, "You have dated some of the best-looking, wealthiest men on the planet. Yet, my sister, you managed to find something wrong with each and every one of them! Instead of trying to get close to any one of these remarkable men, you're busy trying to be his best friend. And we both know you haven't slept with any of them. So which part did Jenna get wrong?"

"All of it!" Laura snapped.

Seven

The problem, Laura Jean Murdock, was that you're too stubborn to admit what's right in your face. The reason the rich-man thing hasn't worked for you is because you're not really looking for money, power, or even love. What you want is a guarantee that he will always be there."

"Has it ever occurred to you that both you and Jenna might be wrong? I never said I didn't want love! I'm not stupid! I won't marry without love. And why can't you two mind your own business?" Upset, Laura brushed away sudden tears. Enough of this! She wasn't going there. Didn't want to even think about the old abandonment issue. Talking was out because it didn't solve anything.

"Honey, I'm sorry. I didn't mean to upset y—"

Laura interrupted, "Did you remember to pick up my mail?"

"Yes." Sherri Ann sighed. "But all I meant was that for a relationship to work, love has to come first. I don't want you to get hurt by falling for the wrong man for the wrong reasons. I love you. I'm sorry I upset you."

"I know." Unable to stay angry for long, Laura

sighed. "I keep wondering if I forgot to do something before I left town. I hated handing over my caseload to Maureen. She has enough to do just running the women's center, plus her own caseload. We have been stretched to our limit with only two other counselors. Yet I understand that dedication has to be number one in finding a new counselor. But I feel guilty because I'm away on vacation when I know how badly I'm needed at the center."

"You have no reason to feel guilty. Your only responsibility for the next few weeks should be to swim, read, relax, and enjoy yourself. Understand?"

Laura laughed. "Yeah. I get it!"

"Good. Do you have everything you need? Sunscreen, enough clothes and swimsuits, and your e-reader?"

"I have what I need, especially my e-reader. I've downloaded all the books from the book club that I haven't had time to read. I can't believe I missed so many book club meetings in the past few months."

"Laura, forget your life in Detroit and concentrate on vacationing."

"Have you spoken to Jenna today?"

"Yes, Scott took her out for a romantic dinner and a play this evening."

"I sure hope it means we get to be aunts soon!" Laura laughed.

"I know that's right, but we're going to have to stop teasing her about having a baby."

"Why?"

"She's worried about getting pregnant."

"But why? They were married on Valentine's Day! Barely a month."

"She's happy, more so than ever before. Instead of

enjoying it, she's worried about not being able to get pregnant and disappointing Scott."

"Why would she put that kind of pressure on herself?" Laura frowned.

"Who knows why? But she's scared."

"She's on her honeymoon. She's not supposed to be worried about one single thing!"

"I agree." Sherri Ann yawned. "Sorry! It's late and I'm due in court early. Still mad at me?"

"No. I'll talk to you tomorrow."

"Okay, but in the meantime, if Sebastian asks you out again, say yes. You went there to have fun. Get to know the locals and see the island. There's nothing wrong with taking him up on his offer to show you around St. John."

"Okay! Now good night, Sherri Ann."

After putting down the phone, Laura turned out all the lights. It was very late and she was tired. Sherri Ann was right. She was on vacation. She'd come all this way to have a good time. There was no reason that she shouldn't loosen up, let her braids down, and just chill.

Besides, Wilham had offered her the use of his pool in exchange for posing for him. She'd be stupid not to take advantage of his offer. Maybe stay for lunch? It wasn't like her to be so uptight or worried about a man. She was not about to let a little fear keep her from enjoying her vacation.

Wilham Sebastian Kramer was only a man. He didn't have anything that she hadn't seen already. She'd been around the block a few times and wasn't an inexperienced virgin. More important, she knew how to say no and mean it.

Tomorrow the man would have an argument on his

hands if he tried to back out of their agreement. They had made a deal and she was going to hold him to his part of their bargain.

The late-morning sun spilled across the room when Wilham admitted, "I've been thinking about something you said yesterday about your job. How can you like being a social worker?" he asked seriously. "The nature of the work has to be difficult and often unpleasant."

"I was very serious. I love my job."

"I'm sorry but I find that hard to believe." He looked up from his sketch to stare at her. She looked so lovely in her sundress. He never tired of looking at her. But he had been unable to sleep last night just imagining the harsh reality she faced daily. There was so much more to her than her natural beauty. He wanted to know all her secrets.

"I'm not saying it's easy. I don't like the unhappy, stressful situations I have to deal with, no one does. But I like helping people, solving problems."

For a time her dark brown eyes locked with his lighter golden gaze before she looked away. She began to tell him about the women seeking help from the women's crisis center and a few of the difficult cases dealing with violence, rape, and physical and emotional abuse, as well as child abuse that she routinely handled.

She confessed, "Even though I've been in social work for years, the one thing I've never been able to figure out has been why there's no end to the misery that some women are willing to suffer from the hands of the men who vowed, in front of God and everybody, to love and cherish them. I keep asking myself why. Love should never hurt."

"There is no answer to that question. At least, not one that makes sense to me," he said thoughtfully, carefully putting down his pencil. "I think we've all struggled to understand the impossible, to only end up with a headache. Laura, I really admire your dedication," he ended, meaning every word. She was unique. So unlike the women he dated. He enjoyed the way she challenged his mind, as well as tantalized his senses.

Laura said nothing, but blushed at the compliment.

Just then the housekeeper knocked on the open hall door. "Refreshments."

Wilham got up and took the heavy tray from her. "Thanks, Cora. I don't know about Laura, but I'm hungry." He placed the tray on the low table.

"If you need something, just yell," Cora said before she left.

Today Laura didn't try to resist. She came right over and lifted the napkin covering the pastries. It was hot almond-covered coffee cake.

Dropping onto the end of the sofa, she teased, "I hope you know that you have a jewel in Cora Chandler. What she can do with dough has to be sinful." Laura remembered her manners at the last moment and offered him the basket first. "Goodness, they smell so good."

He chuckled. "They are good, but ladies first." He'd been standing at the easel for hours. He sat on the opposite end of the leather sofa. After she'd placed a slice on a small plate, he helped himself to three slices. He grinned at her raised eyebrow. "I told you I was hungry. This morning I was in such a hurry to get started and only took time for some fruit and coffee for breakfast."

He watched her frown at the mention of coffee but she was soon moaning in pleasure. "Mmm, Cora knows what she's about. She's as precious as any gemstone. You'd better hang on to her."

He grinned and patted his flat stomach. "Her husband, Daniel, heartily agrees with you."

"Surely you are not referring to Mr. Chandler's waistline?"

Chuckling, he said, "Actually, I was thinking of the wide grin on his face whenever he catches a glimpse of her. They've been married for nearly twenty-five years. I'd bet her skills in the kitchen are a small part of the lady's appeal."

She smiled. "Aw, love. The magic and mysterious emotion that make the world go around. It's wonderful to see a couple who are devoted to each other after so many years. And very rare these days."

He studied her as she sipped her tea. "Do I hear skepticism in your voice, Ms. Murdock? Don't you believe in love? I thought all little girls were brought up on a nightly dose of fairy tales with happy-ever-after endings?"

Suddenly he realized how little he actually knew about her personal life. Was she seeing someone in Detroit? Was she serious about him? He frowned, detesting the possibility that she might care for another man.

"Not all little girls. I never said I don't believe in love. My foster sister Jenna recently married her college sweetheart on Valentine's Day after more than ten years apart. And two of my good friends in our book club, Brynne and Vanessa, are also newlyweds. They married first cousins."

"Keeping it all in the family," he said, then he asked, "Have you ever been in love?"

"Have you?"

He arched a brow. "I asked first."

"I've been in love twice. The first time while in high school and the next while in grad school. Two mistakes," she surmised.

"Sounds as if they turned you off love," he speculated, wondering how deep the hurt had gone. And what did it mean? Was she or wasn't she involved with some guy? More important, where was her lover? What man in his right mind would let such a rare beauty go off on vacation alone? Evidently, the man was a blasted fool, Wilham decided.

"Not at all. But just as your brother's success raised the bar high for you, my disappointments in love taught me not to settle for less."

"Aw. We've found something we agree on."

Laughing, she shook her head. "I seriously doubt that. But what about you? Have you been in love?"

"Never."

"Not even once?"

"Nope," he said, draining his cup. "I've been in deep lust a few times. But nothing that even comes close to what my brother, Gordan, and his wife, Cassy, share." Rising, he went back to the easel and flipped to a clean page. "About ready?"

Everything he said was true. He had never been in love. And suddenly the realization made him wonder why he had been content to settle for less than a full-blown love affair. He didn't know the answer. And surprisingly he couldn't stand the thought of Laura in another man's arms.

"Okay," Laura replied, before draining her cup.

"That's enough for today," he announced, closing his sketch pad.

Laura watched him put it on a nearby table cluttered

with art supplies. He picked up an unfinished canvas and propped it on the easel before he started squeezing oil paint onto a wooden palette.

"Is your offer to use the pool still open?" She stood stretching her arms over her head.

"Certainly. It was part of our deal." He didn't look up from the palette, busy mixing colors. "Give me a second and I'll show you where you can change."

"Don't stop on my account. I can use the hall powder room to change," she said quickly, retrieving a large pink floral duffel bag. She'd been looking forward to getting into the water all morning, even though she wasn't eager to traipse through his house in little more than her bikini and silk sarong.

"No trouble." He smiled, crossing to the French doors. Holding the screen door open, he waited for her to go ahead of him. They crossed the veranda and went down several steps to the pool level.

"If you don't have plans, you're welcome to stay for lunch," he said casually, and then asked, "What did I say to put that frown on your beautiful face?"

"There's no need to give me compliments. You've been very generous allowing me the use of the pool. Clearly, you're busy working and I wouldn't want to impose. Honestly, Wil. You really don't have to feed me."

He smiled. "I'm glad you finally decided to call me Wil. And we both have to eat sometime. I hope you don't feel as if I've kept you too long or been working you too hard the past two mornings."

She laughed. "Not at all. I didn't know what to expect, but posing doesn't feel like work to me. It's more like lounging in the tropics when I compare it to my normal schedule full of meetings, counseling sessions where I'm trying to solve problems on top of problems, or juggling court appearances in addition to staff meetings."

He stopped at a small building with a green and white striped awning. "You should find everything you'll need inside the cabana, a dressing room and full bath if you'd like to shower afterward. If you need anything, please just ask Cora. Enjoy your swim."

"Thank you." She surprised herself when she asked, "What about you? You're not going to take a break?"

He shook his head. "Not today. But I will stop for lunch, if you'll join me?"

Surprised by unexpected feelings of disappointment, she nodded. "I'll stay."

"Good. Enjoy," he said, before heading back toward the studio.

Everything she could possibly need had been thoughtfully provided. A stack of lush bath towels were neatly folded on an open shelf; a hair dryer, new containers of sunscreen, shampoo and conditioner, various shower gels, lotions, and variety of scented soaps all waited in wicker baskets.

Excited, Laura quickly changed into a blush pink bikini trimmed with a flirty red ruffle. There was nothing skimpy about the suit's underwire bra and full bottom that nearly reached her belly button. She tied a colorful floral-printed sarong around her waist and hurried out to the pool.

She took time to protect her skin with sunscreen while enjoying the tranquil setting. But she was a little sad, wishing her foster sisters could have shared this with her.

The three had never been able to take a long vacation together. They were either in college, graduate school or law school, and too poor to travel far. Any extra money had gone toward their schooling. Other than a few long weekends to New York to visit Jenna while she'd been in grad school, they had stayed close to home.

Last year Sherri Ann and Laura had taken their first trip out of country and flown to St. Thomas. They had a wonderful trip, but missed Jenna, who had been finishing up her doctorate.

Jumping into the water, she couldn't stop smiling. The water was perfect, caressing her skin as she swam the length of the pool. With a giggle, she decided it was more than worth the price of admission, a few hours of posing.

While floating on her back, she thought of the girls selected for the mentoring program. They were great kids who, through no fault of their own, had dealt with tough situations, often from very young ages. Unable to settle in a foster home, they'd been forced to grow up too fast. Most of the girls had developed protective shells in order to feel safe, unsure of whom to trust.

She considered lack of trust as an advantage because of the high number of predators out there waiting for vulnerable young girls to use and abuse for evil purposes and profit.

Laura and her foster sisters were working hard to ensure "their" girls not only finished high school but went on to college. The sisters were not about to give up because the odds weren't in their favor. Unfortunately, many of the girls didn't take advantage of the educational opportunities out there to make better lives for themselves. Pregnancy was a huge obstacle.

And Laura strongly believed it was loneliness, not love for some boy, that drove them into becoming young mothers before they were emotionally and financially prepared. The desperate need to connect and to belong to a family was the culprit.

The three foster sisters were trying to show the girls by example what they could accomplish if they just stayed in school. Although the sisters did their best, there never seemed to be enough time. The demands of their careers and personal lives cut into their good intentions.

For the next few weeks Sherri Ann would handle the mentoring program alone. Naturally, Maureen, the director of the women's center, could be counted on to step in if Sherri Ann needed help. But as much as Laura loved and appreciated her boss's kind and generous spirit, Maureen Hale Sheppard came from a very privileged background. The girls liked her but couldn't relate to her.

What they needed were more mentors. Successful women like the three of them who had been in the foster care system, willing to reach back with a helping hand and share their time and experiences. Laura planned to use some of her downtime creatively. She needed to come up with a way to draw attention to the problem and persuade more like them to get involved.

It was her empty stomach rather than her wrinkled fingers and toes that convinced her to get out of the pool. After a soothing hot shower, she changed into a white denim short skirt and crisp white ruffled blouse. Because her braids were not completely dry, she tied a long, colorful scarf around her head and twisted the ends into a decorative knot at her temple. A pair of white high-heeled sandals, pearl stud earrings, and her thin gold bangles completed the casual but chic style she aimed for.

Nerves reappeared when she walked out of the cabana, and she chided herself for being silly. It would be a simple meal with light conversation. And afterward she might drive over to Leinster Bay and tour Annaberg Plantation. She and Wilham were becoming friends. He wasn't out to seduce her. He didn't seem to be having any trouble keeping his word. Evidently, she was not his type. He hadn't made a single move on her.

When Laura approached she saw that a large, colorful umbrella shaded the dining table. There were two place settings on citrus-colored placemats. But there was no sign of Wilham. Cora's husband, Daniel, came out of the kitchen carrying a large tray of covered dishes. He nodded to her before placing the tray in the center of the round table.

"Hello," she greeted. "Something smells wonderful."

"Please, miss," he said as he pulled out a green cushioned chair for her.

Laura smiled her thanks as Cora hurried out with a tall pitcher of icy lemonade.

"Sorry, I didn't mean to keep you waiting," Wilham said as he came out of his studio. He took the chair across from hers.

Her heart had skipped a beat at the sound of his deep, sexy voice. "No, no. I just got here." To distract herself, she added, "Cora, the table is lovely."

Cora smiled. "Aw, but the food is even better."

Amazed by the amount of food, Laura asked, "Are you expecting company?"

He grinned. "No. I often start at first light and work up a healthy appetite by midday. Cora indulges me."

Laura giggled. "I'd sleep the afternoon away if I ate like this every day."

He joined in her laughter.

"Cora and Daniel won't be joining us?"

"They like to eat around noon, while I often get caught up in my work."

Laura was pleasantly surprised when he bowed his head and said grace before he held a bowl of crisp green salad topped with sliced green onions, tomatoes, mushrooms, avocado, and a creamy dressing. Wilham cut her a sizable wedge of the meat pie covered with a flaky, golden brown crust.

Wilham bragged that it was a West Indian dish that Cora had perfected and was filled with lean beef, onions, red and green sweet peppers, jalapeño peppers, and olives, seasoned with coriander, nutmeg, garlic, thyme, and cumin. The meat pie was to be topped with a habanero, hot sauce of vinegar and tomato paste, finished with grated cheddar cheese.

Arching a brow, he teased her, "Are you game?"

She smiled. "I'm willing as long as my glass stays full of ice water and lemonade as backup." After a cautious bite, she nodded. "Mmm, very good. Hot but delicious." She was giggling when she realized he held her glass for her, and eagerly took several sips. "Wow!"

"I'm glad you like it. Cora often makes it for me. More sauce?"

Laura firmly shook her head no while gesturing with the free hand that didn't have a stranglehold on her water glass. "You've got to be kidding me."

But she quickly saw he wasn't teasing. She watched as he tucked into a hearty slice of pie doused with the thick, creamy hot sauce.

Laura listened as he explained the scene he'd been painting was from Bordeaux Mountain, St. John's highest peak. When he asked if she worked with foster families, she nodded and then told him about the mentoring program.

"How many girls are in your mentoring program?"

"Twenty-five, but it's not nearly enough. We had to start small to make sure we meet each girl's needs. My foster sisters help me mentor the girls and volunteer on Saturdays at the center. It's not easy for them, especially with demanding jobs. But we try to show our girls by example that they can also be successful if they stay in school and help each other."

"But why aren't these kids living with relatives or in foster homes?"

She sighed. "Most have no family due to death, drug abuse, physical abuse, neglect, or even mental illnesses. The kids in the independent living programs have been unsuccessful in the foster home setting. Some kids resent authority. Some constantly run away because they've been taken advantage of by abusive foster parents, and some have been disappointed so many times that they aren't willing to trust any adults. A few of the girls have had to deal with sexual abuse in foster homes. Until they're eighteen, they have to live and receive services in either residential group homes or independent living programs."

Then she told him about her hope of getting more former foster care professional women involved. She confessed, "Because my foster sisters and I couldn't afford to join a sorority while in college, it has put us at a disadvantage."

Wilham admitted, "My brother encouraged me to join a fraternity. He was right. Becoming a Kappa Alpha Kappa cracked a few doors open for me. Have you and your foster sisters joined any professional women's groups since college?"

"Of course." She named the groups they'd joined to stay up-to-date in their fields.

"There you go. You ladies might consider attending the local conferences. It's an excellent way to get the word out there."

She beamed at him. "I don't know why I didn't think of it. Thanks."

Suddenly, she silently acknowledged she genuinely liked him. Despite his good looks and his wealthy relative, he was down to earth, understanding, and easy to talk to. Instead of the realization putting her at ease, it had the opposite effect. She was instantly on guard, acutely aware of the risk she took because of her strong attraction to him. Unfortunately, spending time with him hadn't lessened her awareness of him and his masculine appeal.

This persistent attraction to him was not only annoying but also becoming a problem, making her feel vulnerable. It was definitely not a part of their bargain.

Laura nearly choked on a piece of meat pie when he said, "Explain to me again why such a beautiful, sexy woman is vacationing alone. What's wrong with the brothers in Detroit? You won't find a Georgia boy leaving such a sweet peach on the tree. Or the Caribbean man walking past a ripe mango. Must be the bitter cold, apparently it damages the brain."

Eight

Speechless for a moment, Laura just stared at Wilham.

"Have you been out dancing yet?"

"Not yet," she hedged, uncomfortable with the conversation.

He went on to say, "You haven't lived until you've listened to good calypso or swayed to some island blues in one of the clubs in Coral Bay."

"Mmm, I'll keep that in mind," she said, eager to change the subject. Eyeing a piece of Cora's mango and coconut cream pie, she said, "I know I shouldn't, but I don't think I can resist."

He grinned, cutting into a fresh slice. He brought a forkful to her mouth. "You don't have to resist. Open please."

She glared at him but opened her mouth. "Mmm, goodness, it's so good. You're so wrong to tempt me."

He laughed. "Life wouldn't be worth living without some temptation."

"Shame on you!" Laura reached over and grabbed his pie.

"Hey!" he complained.

"That's what you get for being a big tease."

"What? You think you can finish both pieces?"

She nodded. To get back at him she ate both pieces of them. In the end she was moaning, holding her stomach and blaming him. "Look what you made me do!"

Wilham laughed so hard, he nearly tipped over his chair. "A man can't ever accuse you of being boring, Laura Murdock."

Later while she was preparing to leave, Wilham apologized for not keeping up his end of their bargain by taking her sightseeing that afternoon.

He asked, "Can I make it up to you by taking you out to dinner tonight?"

"Sorry, I've already made plans," she lied, then quickly headed for his front door. She called from over her shoulder, "See you tomorrow!"

Hours later propped up in bed, Laura started the tedious job of unraveling a single braid, brushing and coating her hair with her favorite hair butter, and then redoing the braid before she moved to the next one. Although she was quick and her work smooth, she was not nearly as fast as her stylist. Besides, she knew her limits. She was no expert when it came to evenly sectioning and parting the hair.

She still couldn't believe she'd lied to him! It was just plain wrong. She had no plans that evening, but that didn't stop her from sticking with the lie. To make up for it she had an early dinner at Chateau Bordeaux in Coral Bay. By the time she returned, she was relaxed and hoped to put the mistake behind her.

She'd followed her instincts and ran to put as much distance as possible between the two of them. It seemed a little crazy now that she was away from him and had time to give it some thought. She'd lost it, and overreacted. But it was okay.

On the job Laura had learned to pay attention to her instincts. They had saved her neck on more than one occasion. She never knew when she might have to deal with some angry, abusive male who was convinced that she was responsible for his wife or girlfriend leaving him.

She just needed to remind herself that he wasn't a threat. He wasn't her type and didn't fit into her plans. His enormous talent took him into the well-heeled, moneyed world, but that didn't make him right for her. He wasn't a power broker like his big brother. No matter how good he was to look at or how much he made her tremble because of his golden eyes and his ready smile, he was simply not the man for her.

She should be relieved that he couldn't take her sightseeing. Turning down his dinner invitation had been smart. She was using her head when it came to Wilham Sebastian. It was important to keep her wits about her. Just because she liked him didn't mean she would fall under his spell. She had set her course. And she wasn't changing it because she admired his artistic talent.

Besides, she didn't really know him. The novelty of posing and being around such an enormous talent would pass. Her wild thoughts probably had a great deal to do with the romantic setting.

Besides, it only proved she was human, not vulnerable. The only thing she was in danger of losing if she stopped coming was the use of his pool. She was not in danger of losing her head or her heart. Wilham Sebastian Kramer was no threat to her. He wanted to feed her, not bed her.

Wilham wasn't her type. Now if his brother, Gordan Kramer, was still single, then he should be worried. Something about a man in control was so appealing.

"Morning," Laura called as she pulled up to Wilham's place.

Engrossed in packing the jeep, Wilham paused when she parked behind him in the circular drive.

"Morning," he said, his eyes hidden behind sunglasses. He absently rubbed his brow, feeling tired and out of sorts. Last night he had drunk one too many beers, which was unusual for him. He also hadn't slept well because of a very sensuous, erotic dream of making love to Laura. He woke hard and hungry for her.

Around four thirty he'd given up even trying to sleep. He'd showered and dressed in his customary work clothes, a clean pair of paint-spattered jeans and a cotton shirt. He'd gone into his studio and started yet another sketch of her. Today's shirt was burgundy. He picked the dark pink because it reminded him of her.

Clearly, she favored pink. Not that he was complaining. The woman looked good in everything. But then Laura was incredibly beautiful. And he'd wanted her from the first moment he saw her. Unfortunately, that hadn't changed.

He'd spent the past few mornings studying her small features, yet he was no closer to understanding her than he'd been the day they'd met. What he'd learned about her, especially her passion to help others, touched him, and reminded him of his mother. She too had a generous heart. Laura was guarded about the men in her past, and why she was still unmarried. He had no idea why he longed to know everything about her. Or why she fascinated him.

"Going somewhere?" She turned off the car's engine, but didn't get out of the car.

He tucked a large cooler behind the driver's seat. "Why spend a beautiful morning inside? I thought I'd take you to one of my favorite spots on the island. I'll sketch while you take in the view." He arched a brow. "Coming?"

She gathered her things. "Where are we going?"

He waited until she was settled in the jeep before he fastened her seat belt and closed the door.

Climbing behind the wheel he teased, "It's a surprise," and started the motor. "Pretty," he said as he tucked the hem of her pink sundress, embroidered with white daisies across the hem and bodice, close to her leg and away from the gears.

"Thanks." She put on her sunglasses, then pulled off the scarf draped over her shoulders.

He watched as she folded the long cotton gauze— ombré in shades of pink, from a pale blush to a deep cranberry—lengthwise into a wide band, place it over her head and tied it at her nape. He fingered the soft cloth, saying, "Very pretty."

"Thanks." She smiled, explaining, "It was one of the projects my foster sisters and I did with the girls in the mentoring program."

"Lovely. Hand painted?"

She shook her head. "Hand painting is far too complicated. We filled squeeze bottles with fabric dye, we folded the white length of fabric in half, then sprayed across the fabric starting at the bottom, a few inches wide, then we added water to the bottle to dilute the dye and we sprayed the next section. Then we continued to add more water each time, refilling the bottle. We did this several times until we saturated the middle, the palest shade. Once the fabric dried, we hemmed the raw edge using the sewing machine. A simple project, but the girls enjoyed it and were proud of their efforts. They had to work in teams. The goal was to learn to work together, without arguments or bickering."

"You're amazing. You are smart, have a big heart, and are very creative," he said as he set the jeep into motion.

"Nice of you to say, but my artistic talents are limited. But I do enjoy sewing, quilting, and embroidery, but it is all done with a machine. There's no comparison when you consider your paintings. You take a handful of colored pencils and paper, or paintbrushes, oils, and a blank canvas and then you make magic. That's talent."

He shook his head. "Laura, you're too hard on yourself. There are all kinds of creative energy. Who's to say one isn't as important as another as long as it affects others positively. That's all any of us can hope to accomplish."

He slowed as they neared town and pointed out places of interest. He spoke to or nodded at nearly everyone they passed. Eventually, they turned off onto a narrow road and began to climb the hillside as they drove toward the national park.

She was in awe when they entered the popular park. He continued on until they reached a grove of trees.

"We walk from here." He paused, studying her pretty feet in high-heeled pink sandals. "I should have taken you back to your villa to change into something you can actually walk in."

She laughed. "No need. I always tuck a pair of flats in my tote just in case."

"Good," he said as he turned off the motor. "We've

a bit of a walk. Do you mind carrying the bag with the blanket and cushions?" he asked as he reached behind the seats.

"Sure," Laura said, changing into ballerina-style flats.

Wilham busied himself emptying the back. He didn't want to catch even a glimpse of her creamy brown thighs. He'd never suspected he was a leg man until he spent the time while she was in the pool daydreaming about her and her shapely hips and sexy limbs instead of finishing another canvas for the St. John's calendar. It had taken all his resolve to keep his promise and his hands off Laura.

He didn't have a clue what was going on with him. It was true that he'd always had a keen sex drive, but never to this extent. He'd been semi-aroused whenever she was in his home. Even though it had been a while since he'd been with a woman, he didn't just want to have sex. He wanted it with Laura.

Until recently, Wilham understood himself well, always knew his motivation. When he worked, he worked full-out. It was the same when he painted. But when it came to his love life, he'd always held a part of himself back. He made sure his current lady never suspected because he made a point to lavish her with his attention and money.

He hadn't exaggerated or lied to Laura. He'd never been in love, never even come close to wanting to open his heart to a woman. He had started to doubt that he was capable of loving deeply. That any one woman could hold his interest. That was until he met this petite beauty.

He wasn't shocked by his awareness of her, but he was surprised when it hadn't let up. The more time he spent in her company, the more he wanted to be with her.

Even more startling, she was never far from his thoughts. He'd been very disappointed when she turned down his dinner invitation.

He was a man who prided himself on always being in control. Around Laura, he was different. He felt compelled, almost driven to sketch her and get her every nuance down on paper. The most disturbing was the extent of his desire for her. His need was raw and unrelenting, unlike anything he'd ever experienced.

What he needed was to sleep with her, get her out of his system. But how was he supposed to accomplish that without going back on his word? He spent his mornings studying her and the rest of his day wanting her. Why was he surprised that she had entered his dreams?

Frowning, he tucked the portable easel and sketch pad under one arm along with a tackle box in the same hand. In his right hand he carried the heavy cooler.

"Ready?" he said, leading the way.

Smoothing her dress, she remarked, "If I'd known, I'd have worn walking shorts."

"You're fine. We're walking, not hiking," he said from over his shoulder.

They moved up an incline and into the trees that eventually opened into a meadow. He couldn't help studying her lovely face as she took in the thick carpet of lush green grass populated with an array of wildflowers. Her generous mouth tilted into a beguiling grin that made her dark brown eyes sparkle.

"Wow," she gushed in a near whisper. "God's been busy. It's beautiful here." She looked up into a clear blue, almost cloudless sky.

The sound of songbirds filtered through the peaceful glen as they perched high in the trees, encircling the lush sanctuary.

Wilham spread the blanket, plopping a pillow cushion in the center. Gesturing, he said, "My lady." While she got settled, he quickly set up the easel before opening a tackle box full of colored pencils and pastels.

When he looked over at her, she sat with her back stiff, her legs tucked beneath her, and her hands folded primly in her lap. "Laura, relax and try to forget I'm here. Would you care for something to drink? I have fruit juice, iced tea, and bottled water. Sorry, I forgot to bring the coffee," he added playfully.

She laughed, shaking a finger at him. "Shame on you, Wil. But no thanks. I'm fine. It's so lovely and peaceful here. Hard to believe we're in a national park. I can see why it's a favorite of yours. You used this place in some of the paintings you sold at the opening."

"That's right."

Leaning his shoulder against a tree, he flipped to a clean sheet and began working. He said absently, "The national park lands are a treasure trove of lovely vistas. I can't get bored. Tell me about your foster sisters. Jean and Sherri, right?"

Laura corrected, "Jenna Gaines Hendricks and Sherri Ann Weber. We decided to adopt each other while we were little girls. No matter what came our way, we would stick together. We got in trouble a few times. Sherri Ann was always the sensible and smart one. Jenna was determined to be a good girl, me, not so much.

"Despite Mrs. Green's best efforts I was a tomboy, always getting dirty or into trouble. I was curious, always wanting to play outside and be free like the boys. It wasn't until my twelfth birthday that I started noticing boys. Suddenly, I realized there were better things to do than climb trees and ride bikes. I've never told my sisters but I was secretly glad that we weren't adopted. I don't want to imagine my life without Jenna and Sherri Ann."

Touched by the honesty and warmth in her tone, he asked, "The three of you work at the women's center?"

"Heavens no. Jenna is a college professor. Once she completed her doctorate in economics she moved back to Detroit and started teaching at her alma mater, University of Detroit–Mercy. She has recently married and is honeymooning in the Carolinas with her new husband.

"Sherri Ann is a lawyer and works in a very prestigious law firm. She is determined to make partner before she's thirty-five. Although she is very pretty and dates, she's not about to let anything get in her way."

He smiled thoughtfully. He knew she had to be equally as bright and determined as her foster sisters, to not just succeed but thrive. "Aw, three resourceful and successful young women despite the odds against you. I'm impressed, Laura."

She shook her head before she said in earnest, "The credit goes to Mrs. Green. She made the impossible possible. She gave us the confidence to try. When she stressed the value of education, we listened. We were simply determined to make her proud."

"Hardly simple," he said softly as he studied the glimmer of love and devotion in her eyes. He sensed the wealth of emotions she kept hidden. He suspected that while she offered him a few of her beautiful smiles and laughter, she withheld her trust. He wondered if she had been hurt by some guy. And if so, it had to be recent. That would explain why she was traveling alone. Or was it an old wound that continued to fester?

Even though he hadn't known her long, he decided the guy must be a weak, heartless coward who didn't deserve Laura. She was special.

"Where did you go to college?"

Nine

Laura was busy studying the sensuous curve of his mouth. She found herself wondering if his lips were soft and yearned to know his taste.

"Laura?"

She blushed, embarrassed. "What did you say?"

"Where did you go to college?"

"Sherri Ann and I wanted to go away but we couldn't afford it. We stayed in the city, went to Wayne State University. We shared a small apartment."

What was it about him? He was intensely male. More mature than the men she normally dated. Why was she so drawn to him? He was only a man, like all the others. Yes, he'd exhibited a measure of control, but that didn't change his basic male nature. Once Wilham was aroused, desire would take over, and need would dominate. Under those circumstances, even a strong man could lose control. Hands that normally created rare beauty would harden and lose all gentleness as the artist vanished and the earthy, raw male part of him took control. Unfortunately, it had nothing to do with his degree of talent, creativity, or intelligence.

Unlike many of the women she counseled, Laura had never been raped, hadn't suffered that ultimate betrayal and abuse. Yet she cringed remembering the discomfort involved with intercourse. Experience had taught her sex was not pleasurable. While she enjoyed being kissed and held in a man's arms, she was one of the few females who didn't crave or yearn to have sex. She had read clinical studies on the subject and understood the data.

Some might find it unusual. But she knew she was a happy, healthy female who loved to flirt and spend time with men. But unlike most of her friends and sisters, she was not easily aroused. It wasn't a problem except when it came to finding a mate. She desperately wanted a husband and family someday.

"What is it?"

"Hmm?" She blinked, lost in thought.

"Something's wrong. You were frowning."

Her dark brown eyes collided with his golden gaze. She was the first to drop her lids. How could she have forgotten even for a second that he was studying her?

Forcing a playful laugh, she said, "What could possibly be wrong on such a picture-perfect day? This is a gorgeous spot. If I lived here, I don't think I'd ever want to leave."

"There's no such thing as heaven on earth. It's not always blue skies. We have storms and hurricanes too."

Laura quipped, "Aw, but your storms don't bring freezing rain, ice, or snow."

"True. But there's beauty in a crisp winter morning when the sky's azure blue, the sun's bright overhead, and the ground's blanketed by untouched snow. Do you ski?"

"Snow or water?" she teased. "It doesn't matter. I

have never skied on either of them. Not many opportunities for a poor girl like me to indulge in costly sports. I may have grown up in Michigan, but I've never been fond of the cold unless I'm in front of a cozy fire."

He grinned. "You haven't lived until you've been on the slopes in Aspen. There is nothing like taking a steep slope on several inches of powder. You have to give it a try, city girl."

Intrigued by the twinkle in his eyes, she surmised, "So you're an outdoorsman."

"I enjoy a challenge. But then I enjoy lots of things, including boating, deep-sea fishing, and snorkeling."

"How long have you lived in St. John?"

"About six years. It's a long way from Atlanta. Lift your chin, just a bit. Thanks. What did you do while I was busy working yesterday?"

Laura told him, unaware of the animation in her smile, the gestures of her hands, and the sparkle in her eyes.

"You found someone to braid your hair."

Surprised by the observation, she said, "I braided my own hair. You don't miss much."

He shrugged. "I'm curious about you. The more I know about you, the more I want to know, Ms. Murdock."

Laura blushed, warmed by the heat in his golden brown eyes. The man was not only easy on a woman's eyes, he was smooth and sophisticated. He knew the right things to say and how to make a woman feel special. Wilham Sebastian oozed male charm.

It was time he realized he was not the only one who knew how to flirt. Two could play this game.

She laughed before she purred, "Really, Mr. Kramer. And why is that?"

"Ah, so you like to tease, Laurie girl."

"You noticed, but I'm Laura."

"I like Laurie. It suits you."

She sobered suddenly, then said quietly, "Other than giving me life, my name is the only gift my birth mother ever gave me."

"Laura, I'm so sorry. I didn't mean . . ."

"No need to apologize."

"Laura, I enjoy your honesty. You're very beautiful, yet there's nothing pretentious or artificial about you. The day we met your skin was dewy, soft, and free of makeup. Even your hair is natural. I like those things about you."

She blushed, warmed by the compliments. "I may not be high-maintenance, but believe me, I have my share of faults. I'm quirky and full of contradictions. I'm very modern in my ideas but old-fashioned in other ways. I love vibrant colors that most people would never put together. I enjoy quilting and sewing. I probably belong in another era."

"Some people consider pastels, paintbrushes, and oils outdated compared to a digital camera. Naturally, I'd disagree."

Laughing, she said, "I'm hungry. What's in the cooler?"

"I have no idea. Let's find out." He closed the sketch pad, resting it on the easel.

They enjoyed pulled pork barbecue sandwiches on homemade buns, creamy coleslaw, a variety of sliced cheeses, and for dessert, lemon bars.

"Another lemon bar?" he offered.

She laughed. "I'll pop if I take one more bite," she said, sipping from a glass of Cora's iced tea.

Together they cleaned up, storing the leftovers in the

cooler and making sure the area was as pristine as they found it.

Laura watched him dismantle the easel. "We're leaving?"

"You're on vacation. And I promised to be your tour guide. Come on, daylight is being wasted. I thought you might like to see Catherineberg Ruins. It's an eighteenth-century sugar and rum factory. Interested?"

"You won't hear any objections from me." She folded the blanket and packed it away along with the cushion. After one last check to make sure that nothing had been left behind, they headed back to the car.

They were leaving the park when she said, "I know you're busy. I won't hold you to that promise."

"Too late, I'm looking forward to showing you my island."

Laura's heart picked up speed at the prospect of spending an entire afternoon with him.

They were at a traffic light when she caught him watching her from half-closed lids. Laura's cheeks were hot as she returned his smile. At that moment, she acknowledged she wasn't concerned about being alone with him. Wilham was a man, not a little boy. He wasn't going to make a move on her. Nor was he going to do anything she didn't want him to do. She was free to be herself.

It was after five by the time they returned to his place. She had just finished thanking him when he casually said, "I have reservations for dinner at a wonderful restaurant in the hills. Old friends of mine, Clark and Regina Gardner, own the place. The food is the best on the island and the music is vibrant with steel drums that can't be missed. Reynar, their eldest son, has a reggae band and plays there most weeknights. He plays in the big hotels in St. Thomas on the weekends. I'll pick you up at seven."

"I'll be ready," she said without hesitation.

Laura had dressed with care in a dark rose silk sheath that accentuated her curves. Her braids had been twisted and pinned into a knot at her nape. Only a few whispery thin braids were free to curl around and frame her beautiful face.

"You look nice," she told him as she took in his dark gray suit and dove gray silk shirt and striped tie. The compliment was an understatement because she thought he was devastatingly handsome and sexy in a custom-made suit.

He smiled as his golden eyes moved over her. "And you are enchanting in that dress." He draped her wrap over her shoulders. "Ready?"

She nodded.

Wilham expertly handled the vintage sports car as they wound their way up the tree-lined hillside. Awed by the mauve and gold colors in the sky as the sun set, she shivered when she gazed down to the long drop at the rocky coastline far below.

"Spectacular," she whispered, complimenting the natural beauty of the island.

"You ever afraid of burning out?" Wilham asked seriously.

"No, because it's not about me but the work. Child molesters and sexual predators don't take vacations. They continue to prey on the weak. Someone has to support the victims and help them fight back. Besides, I'm not afraid of a good fight, especially if it's for a woman or a child. My clients don't come to me for sympathy. They need solutions, and that's exactly what

I try give them. And hopefully, I find ways to improve their lives."

"I imagine you've been in some dangerous situations," he said with a frown.

"A few. I can't just walk away when a woman and her children are at the mercy of a heartless male who left them destitute or beaten, claiming he loved them. But I'm not foolish. I know my limits. I'm not out there trying to be Wonder Woman. Most important, I know who to call to get them out of a bad situation fast and before it escalates into something ugly. My frustration comes when I can't convince a woman at risk to leave and that she deserves better and has choices."

She changed the subject. "Tell me about the restaurant."

"It's owned by old friends Regina and Clark Gardner. They've worked hard to make it successful. He's the chef in the family and she runs the business." He grinned. "Just wait until you taste the food."

Wilham made a right turn and followed a long drive to what looked like a sprawling older home.

"It's lovely but it doesn't look like a restaurant."

"That's the idea. To make you feel comfortable and welcomed. The land and house have been in Clark's family for generations." He stopped in the wide circular drive.

A young man opened her door and she stepped out onto the gravel drive. Wilham greeted the man by name before handing over his keys. He cupped her elbow, guiding her up the walkway lined with solar lights, passing between thick columns that supported the wide wrought-iron upper balcony. Heavy double doors provided a grand entrance and were thrown wide to display a softly lit, impressive foyer.

A pretty older woman stood beside the archway at a podium making notes. She looked up and beamed. "Well, well. It's about time you showed your face, Sebastian." She was tall, with smooth, flawless brown skin. Her voice was sweet and lyrical.

Chuckling, he kissed her cheek. "Regina, you look ravishing. How's the family?"

"Flattery won't stop me from scolding you! Clark and the kids are well. Sorry we couldn't make the reception at the gallery. I heard you had a nice turnout and raised a huge sum for the hospital. Congratulations."

"Thanks. We did well." Smiling, he said, "Laura Murdock, our hostess for the evening and my good friend, Regina Gardner."

The women shook hands.

"Welcome to St. John, Laura. Are you enjoying yourself?"

"Very much. You and your husband have a charming place here."

"Aw, but you must tell me what you think after you've tasted the food." She laughed. She looked up at him speculatively. "The main dining room? Or would you prefer the privacy of the balcony?"

Wilham threw back his head and laughed. "The main dining room, please," he said quickly.

Smiling, Regina led the way. The former living and dining rooms had been cleverly converted into one large, very elegant room. The floor-to-ceiling wall of windows overlooked a spacious veranda and were draped in white sheer curtains, and the round tables were covered in a rainbow of pastel tablecloths and topped with small shaded lamps and fragrant fresh flowers.

Wilham paused to greet familiar faces in the crowd as they made their way to a table in front of screened double doors that led out to the veranda and the lush garden beyond.

"Good?" Regina asked.

"Perfect." Wilham squeezed her hand before he drew back a wrought-iron chair for Laura, the seat padded with a floral cushion. He took the seat across from her.

Two young men dressed in black slacks and starched white shirts removed the extra chairs and filled their water glasses before handing out menus.

"Cocktail? Wine?" Regina asked. "We have a very nice Chardonnay tonight from a local vineyard."

Wilham looked at Laura and waited, his golden eyes caressing her features.

She smiled. "Wine, please."

Startled by the heat in his gaze, Laura was careful to keep her eyes lowered. She didn't want him to guess how much she'd enjoyed his attention today. Or that she wondered what it would be like to feel his strong arms around her. She studied her hands clasping a small beaded evening purse, not wanting him to know she'd been charmed by his deference to her needs.

He'd made a point of opening her door, carrying the heavy items, complimenting her, but most importantly, he'd actually listened to what she had to say and was interested in what she thought. Wilham had done dozens of little things that made her feel special, as if she mattered to him.

She paused, startled by her thoughts. What was this? Was she falling for this charismatic man?

Wilham Sebastian Kramer was a suave man who knew how to treat a lady. She couldn't help wondering how he treated the special woman in his life. He was older than the men she'd been intimate with. Did that mean he was not a selfish lover? That he was patient? That he might not put his needs ahead of his lady?

Wait! What was she thinking? Wilham wasn't the one for her! She wasn't going to bed with him! This was not some wild island romance.

Goodness! She was letting her imagination get the best of her. Just because she thought he was charming, smooth, and very sexy didn't make him right for her. She wasn't weak, nor was she stupid. She knew what she wanted, and it was certainly not a good-looking playboy.

"Impressed?" he asked.

Laura nodded. "But I'm taking Regina's advice and withholding my judgment until I've actually tasted the food."

He chuckled, opening the menu.

Laura surprised them both when she touched his hand.

Ten

"Yes?" Wilham's heart skipped a beat and his flesh tingled from her soft touch. Refusing to let his imagination go wild and consider all the places he'd welcome her soft hands, he was forced to swallow a husky groan. Had he made a serious error by bringing her here? He'd been cautious for days, careful not to say or do anything to jeopardize their agreement. Yet his instincts warned him something had changed between them, and the shift had been so subtle that he was unsure of the new parameters.

There had been a hint of the change earlier in the meadow. She'd teased him, even flirted with him. Because of that change, his longing had intensified. He was hungry for a taste of her soft lips. But the yearning didn't stop there. And it was stronger than the simple male desire to make love to an attractive female.

He was no monk. He had known many beautiful women, but none like Laura. Wilham wanted to spend all his time with her, wanted to know her secrets. Laura Murdock was sweet femininity packed into a petite, curvaceous frame, with enough quirks and contradictions guaranteed to hold his interest. The lady would never bore him.

Her eyes told him she wanted him while her body language screamed for him to stay clear. She was like an exquisitely formed, richly hued butterfly. Although hungry, she was reluctant to take the nutrients her small body craved. Instead, she fluttered, flitted, always teasing yet careful not to come too close to him. Even though she sensed he had the nectar she needed to survive, she stubbornly held back.

From the first she'd fascinated him to the point he felt compelled to try and create her likeness. If he'd been a sculptor, his fingers would have ached to mold her unique beauty and not stop until he captured her essence. The creative force within him demanded he paint her, not in pastels or charcoal but in rich vivid oils. The artist within compelled him to include her subtle nuances, first on paper and then eventually on canvas.

The problem came when he was supposed to be working, totally engaged in sketching her. Yet his male needs would suddenly kick in and he found himself yearning to caress rather than draw her high cheekbones and instead of reproducing her soft, full lips, he ached to cover her mouth with his and to learn her sweet taste. He'd already committed her lush curves to paper, and he'd memorized each soft, full curve. His need was so acute that he'd started dreaming about her, imagined her naked beneath him, her body open to his.

Today he had taken her to one of his favorite places on the island, determined to get beyond the desire to bed her. Instead of concentrating on the work, he had been semi-aroused the entire time and focused on the subtle change in her demeanor. His shaft thickened and lengthened in response to her flirting. He was ready, all right. Ready to fill her soft body. It was good her gaze hadn't gone below his waist. Annoyed with the train of his thoughts, he swallowed down a curse word.

He'd always taken pride in his control. He'd learned early on to keep his head, no matter what temptation came his way. Wilham rarely had to ask a woman for anything, including sex. More often than not, it was generously offered and in some cases served up on a silver platter.

Laura's reaction to hearing about his family was unusual. Her demeanor hadn't changed when she learned of his connections to wealth and power. Her reaction was so rare that it surprised him and had him wanting to know why. Although she'd been open about her professional life, she had told him next to nothing about her love life. And he wanted to know why.

Wilham's teeth clenched, frustrated by how much he didn't know about her. Although curious, he hadn't had her investigated. It was a simple matter to call his cousin Kenneth Kramer, head of their security team. But then he had been acting out of character from the moment he'd met her. It wasn't like him to chase a woman down, and that's exactly what he'd done. The truth was he wanted her to open up and let him into her world.

His head had told him he was right to be cautious, that he didn't really know her. His heart whispered she was exactly what he needed and had been waiting for. His body told him that it would be different with her, special. But a callous part of him reminded him that once he had her he would quickly lose interest and move on to the next new conquest. Yet his instincts insisted this time would be different. That Laura was not out for personal gain. What if she was interested in the man and not all that came with the Kramer name?

He was floored by the mere possibility that Laura could be the one he longed for but had given up hope of finding. He had grown so jaded and might not recognize what was real.

"Why did Regina ask if you required privacy?" Laura asked, breaking into his thoughts.

His golden eyes darkened as he studied her. "You do look particularly beautiful in this soft light. Did I tell you how much I like you in that color? It's wonderful against your skin."

She blushed. "I wasn't angling for a compliment. Please answer the question."

"You didn't answer mine, little butterfly."

"Little butterfly?"

"You remind me of the butterflies we saw in the meadow, fluttering from flower to flower," he teased, his voice heavy with need.

"You, Wilham Sebastian, are good at not answering my questions while raising your own. I'm not that easily distracted."

He chuckled. "So my little butterfly has teeth."

"I not only have teeth, I have claws," she warned.

Wilham laughed, unable to contain the sheer joy she sparked in him. His heart pounded in sweet anticipation. He could barely wait for the band to start playing and the music to fill the night. The vibrant beat of the steel drum couldn't match the powerful beat of his pulse as he held her close and they moved around the dance floor. Had he ever wanted a woman more?

"Well," she persisted, "would you like me to repeat the question?"

"Regina's a married lady. She knows the difference between sparks and a cold hearth."

"That's not an answer. But that's okay. I have another question for you. Why does everyone call you Sebastian, yet you insist I call you Wilham?"

He hesitated, reluctant to admit that only his family and close friends called him Wil. When he first moved to the island he'd gone by his middle name for two reasons, to maintain a measure of privacy and to shield his family from embarrassment in case his work had not been well received. The name had stuck.

"Good evening, Sebastian." The young man quickly filled their glasses and placed a basket of fragrant rolls and a container of butter on the table.

"Raymond! Howard University can't be out this early."

Raymond laughed. "I'm only home for a week, spring break. Instead of letting me goof off, my folks put me to work."

"Laura, this is Raymond Gardner, Clark and Regina's middle son," Wilham said before he asked, "How are you doing in your classes?"

"Great. I made the dean's list. Any hope of us getting you out of your studio long enough to go out on the boat with me and Dad? You should have seen the size of the snapper he caught this morning! That baby was huge!"

Wilham grinned. "I'm glad you are doing so well, but I'm not surprised. And you're right, it has been a while since I've been out with your dad. So tell us about the menu."

Raymond sobered and said, "Chef Clark has prepared an excellent red snapper in a garlic butter sauce, we also have spicy curried chicken with gingered sweet potatoes, and the house special tonight, pork tender ribs in a mango-guava barbecue sauce."

"Laura?"

Her dark eyes sparkled as she held his gaze. "What do you suggest?"

"The seafood is always excellent," he drawled, fighting to ignore his body's base response to her.

They both ordered the red snapper.

Wilham soon had her laughing when he told how his twin nieces talked him into taking them deep-sea fishing in Martinique. They were only five at the time and claimed to love fishing. The girls insisted on throwing the fish back into the water, refusing to gut, clean, or actually eat their friends.

Laura laughed, surprising him when she said, "You'd make a wonderful father."

"Why? Because I enjoy spending time with my nieces?"

"I know you said you were a confirmed bachelor, but you clearly enjoy being around kids. I don't get it. I thought all men wanted a son?"

"Not all men. I'm content with my life." She looked stunned, as if she didn't believe he was serious. Curiosity got the better of him, for he asked, "Why are you frowning?"

"You really don't want your own family?"

"I have a family. Everyone is not cut out to be a parent."

"Yes, but—" Laura stopped, looking as if she wanted to argue the point. Instead, she said, "You still have time. Who knows? You might change your mind."

"I'm forty-two. A little late to start having a family. Cassandra, my sister-in-law, insists I'll change my mind once I fall in love. What do you think?"

"I haven't a clue. Are you one of those men afraid to make a commitment?"

"Afraid?" he repeated. "No, I don't think so. I'm happy, content with my life. Why change? Apparently, I'm not like my father and brother. I certainly haven't met the woman I can't live without. I take it you want children someday?"

"Very much. I want a large family. No less than five, maybe six kids. All I have to do is find the right man for me. I'm very particular."

Just then Raymond returned with soup and salads.

When they were alone he said, "Explain particular."

She quipped, "Particular means belonging to a single person or group."

He grinned. "Cute. You mentioned having a large family someday. What qualities are you looking for in Mr. Right?"

She lifted her chin. "I plan to marry a highly intelligent, very successful, confident man. Someone who will know I want him for him, not the elaborate trappings that come with his position."

"So you plan to marry for money?"

"No! I plan to marry for love. I just don't intend to love someone who can't afford or appreciate me."

Wilham just looked at her. He was keenly disappointed. She was just like the others! He should have known better, should have expected her to change once she learned he was a Kramer. But she had known for days who he was. Yet she hadn't warmed toward him, hadn't come after him with both guns smoking. But why had she come right out with it? What kind of crafty game was she playing? Finally, he said, "I appreciate your honesty. Have you met a likely candidate?"

"Several."

Doubtful, he quipped, "Any of them eligible bachelors?"

"Of course."

"Really?"

"That's what I said," she snapped. Then she told him about being asked to be a bridesmaid for her friend's wedding. She went on to say, "Brynne was engaged to Devin Prescott, star quarterback for the St. Louis Rams. His groomsmen were single and pro athletes."

"And? Was there a hookup?" he asked quietly, his body unexpectantly taut with tension as he waited for her answer, his meal forgotten.

"Yes," Laura said with a smile. "Vanessa Grant was Brynne's maid of honor. She hooked up with Ralph Prescott, Devin's best man. They married and are raising her twin siblings and her teenage sister together."

"You know what I meant," he said impatiently.

She smiled. "We had a blast that spring. Did a lot of partying. Brynne and Devin had a lovely wedding. If you're asking if there was a love connection for me my answer is no."

"You get a real kick out of teasing me, don't you?"

Laura laughed. "Yeah, I do."

Wilham relaxed and joined in the laughter. Apparently, she hadn't hooked up with any of those young, rich jocks since she was vacationing in St. John alone.

"Since then I've dated a very successful attorney and two prominent businessmen. I've made some very powerful male friends." She shrugged. "But I haven't given up on finding Mr. Right."

"What if Mr. Right comes with empty pockets?" he asked.

She shook her head. "Not possible."

Before she could say more, their waiter brought their main course.

"Mmm, looks good," Wilham said. Once they were alone he couldn't let it go. He prompted, "So you're determined."

She nodded before she admitted, "My foster sisters have stopped taking me seriously, insisting my actions speak louder than my words. If I really wanted a rich husband, I'd have one by now. I strongly disagree! Just because the wealthy men I date end up being my friends doesn't mean my sisters are right," she huffed indignantly.

"All of them?" he quizzed.

"That's correct."

"But why?"

"I told you. I know what I want. Unfortunately, we're shorthanded at work right now and I have been so busy that I haven't had time to date."

He leaned back. "Are you telling me that not even one of your good friends can cut the mustard? None of them meet your expectations?"

"I didn't say that."

"What then?"

"And why are you so interested? Don't tell me you're worried?" she teased. "There's no need. You, Mr. K, are safe."

Stunned, he blinked and then said, "Why am I safe?"

"You're not my type. Why aren't you eating?"

"I think I'm in shock," he said candidly. Picking up his fork, he resumed eating. Then he demanded to know, "How, Laura? How are you going to pull this off? How are you going to convince this guy that it's a love match?"

"Simple. Because he won't have any doubts about

my feelings for him. Why are you scowling at me, Wil? I don't see the problem. I'm honest to a fault. I'm fiercely loyal. And I'm not a liar or a cheat. He will never have a reason to doubt my love or sincerity."

"My instincts tell you mean every word," he said softly.

"Your instincts are correct." Laura noticed the activity on the veranda. "Oh look! The band's setting up."

Wilham stared at her while trying to make sense of it all. She was not playing a game. The lady was serious!

She whispered, "Will you please stop staring at me? It's rude."

"I'm enjoying watching you eat. You savor each bite," Wilham teased.

She laughed. "My curves prove I love to eat."

"Well, I have to say you are honest, straightforward, outspoken, and unpredictable. It's refreshing. Can I tempt you with dessert, my little butterfly?"

"Nope. I've done enough damage for one day. I don't plan on leaving this island carrying an extra five pounds on these hips and thighs."

"You can't pass on desserts. The chocolate cream pie and fruit tarts can't be missed." He signaled to a passing waiter and asked for the dessert tray.

"It's not fair to tempt me. Look at you, long and muscular. No fat. You probably wouldn't gain an ounce."

"You're on vacation. Who's going know? Your secrets are safe with me, sugar dumpling."

"My name is Laura," she scolded, even though she enjoyed his playful side. Most often he was intense and put in long hours.

She tried not to listen as Raymond described the sweet confections in mouthwatering detail.

Wilham crooned, "Tempted?"

"Beyond good sense. You order and I'll just have one bite of yours."

"No problem." Then he proceeded to order the entire tray.

"No you didn't! Have you no shame?"

Chuckling, he caught her hand and gave a gentle squeeze. "None whatsoever when it comes to you. You're pure temptation, Laura, with that captivating smile and those sparkling brown eyes."

A blush heated her cheeks she didn't dare look into his eyes, afraid she would do or say something to show how flattered she was by his attention. It was stupid! The man could probably charm the songbirds into singing just for him alone. He had her acting like a teenager.

"Enjoy." Raymond grinned as he placed the dessert dishes in the center of the table.

Laura tried to glare at Wilham but she felt like a child in an ice cream parlor, too busy sampling each forkful he aimed at her mouth. When she wasn't moaning with pleasure, she complained, "I'm not ever going out to eat with you again! You're a very bad influence on me."

"Why?" he challenged. "Because I encouraged you to let go and do exactly what you want without guilt? You should be thanking me."

"Not in this lifetime," she grumbled before pushing a forkful of chocolate pie toward his firm lips. She smiled as he savored the treat. When they finished sampling everything they both groaned.

After dropping a few large bills on the table, he grabbed her hand. "Come on. Let's go work off some calories on the dance floor."

He led her out onto the veranda, which was quickly filling with diners. Padded benches and chairs lined the perimeter of the dance floor while the sound of guitars, keyboard, and steel drums filled the night with the distinctive rhythmic sound of the Caribbean islands.

Laura discovered Wilham was an excellent dancer. She worried that she might not be able to keep up with him, but soon relaxed, and she was quickly swept up in the vibrant music. It was uncanny the way her body instinctively flowed against his. As if it wasn't their first dance and they'd been dancing together for years.

Caught up in the magic of the night and the music, she felt happy, carefree. She was secretly pleased by how naturally she seemed to sense his every move, their bodies melded on the dance floor.

Eventually, the music slowed and a deep male voice sang of lost love. Wilham pulled her close. She closed her eyes and inhaled deeply, glorying in his unique male scent. Her senses whirled as she rested her cheek on his chest, her breasts pressed against the hard contour of his lean torso.

Laura nearly moaned aloud when Wilham's long, hard-muscled thigh parted her legs as they swayed in time to the music. Eyes closed, her feminine mound pulsed, and automatically she tightened her inner muscles and began to ache. It was intense, unlike anything she'd ever felt before. Her nipples were unusually hard, so hard that they too ached. Goodness! Her heart raced and suddenly she couldn't catch her breath. She was light-headed, feeling faint. She had no idea if it was because of the dancing, the press of the crowd, or Wilham's closeness.

As if he sensed her distress, he said into her ear, "Need a rest?"

"No way!" she lied, not wanting it to end. "I could dance all night. How about you?"

His laugh was husky. "I might have a few gray hairs but I'm a long way from dead. Let's go."

He tightened his hold around her waist, pulling her even closer. Her body swayed with the beat of the steel drums until she brushed against his erection. She stiffened and would have stumbled, but he held her steady as he swayed with the music.

Somehow, she managed to keep pace with him while waiting for him to take advantage. But he did none of the things she expected from an aroused male. He didn't crowd her, didn't force her lower body into contact with his.

When the band stopped playing, he stepped away. "Come on. Let's get something cool to drink."

Laura nodded and allowed him to place an arm around her waist as he guided her through the crowd.

"What would you like?" He signaled a waiter.

"Fruit drink, please. No alcohol."

Once they had been served he led her to an empty bench. "Is something wrong?"

"No," she said quickly, using a cocktail napkin to blot her brow. "Why did you ask?"

"You went all stiff on me." He stroked a finger along her cheek down to her mouth, then he dropped his hand. He took a long swallow of his beer.

As she struggled to come up with a lighthearted comment, a male hand settled on Wilham's shoulder. He turned and smiled. "Clark! It's good to see you."

The older man grinned before he said in a deeply accented voice, "I hope I'm not intruding. I heard you were here with a pretty lady, man."

"Laura, this is Clark Gardner, our host and chef."

She smiled. "Hello. You have a wonderful place. And the food was excellent."

"Thanks. It's a pleasure to meet you." Clark beamed. "Just wanted to say hello and invite you out on the boat with me and my sons."

Wilham smiled. "We'll talk."

Before they could say more, Clark was called back to the kitchen.

"Another drink?" Wilham asked.

"Nothing for me." Then she covered a yawn. "Sorry. It's been a long day."

"An enjoyable one?" he asked.

Eleven

"Oh yes." She smiled.

They'd begun threading their way through the crowd. And they went down a few stairs and then followed the path through the garden and along the side of the house.

When Laura stumbled on an uneven patch of grass, Wilham caught her, placing a hand on her waist.

"Okay?" he asked, leaning toward her.

When she looked up to thank him Wilham lowered his head until his firm lips touched hers. His kiss was warm, a slow, tender caress. And it was over before she thought to protest.

He resumed walking as if nothing had happened, and kept a supportive arm around her. "You're awfully quiet."

She didn't know how she felt about the kiss or her response to him. Finally, she said, "I'm fine."

She hadn't expected him to kiss her. It happened so quickly, too quickly for her to . . . What? For her to stop him? Or stop her natural response to him? This was ludicrous! It wasn't as if she'd never been kissed. She was no virgin. So why then was she so rattled?

While she was used to going out with wealthy, so-phisticated, talented men, she wasn't used to them slipping beneath her guard. Wilham Sebastian had managed to do just that.

But how? It must be the allure of St. John Island. The sweet magic of the romantic, tropical setting, com-bined with her admiration for his enormous talent as a renowned artist, had weakened her resolve. Plus the delicious meal, the wine, and the power of the music and the steel drums had all clearly gone to her head. Now what?

Wasn't that why she came? To have a good time? She might as well enjoy herself because before too long she would be back in Detroit and dealing with life's harsh realities. Instead of worrying about a simple kiss, she should be busy collecting memories.

"Are you going to let me see your sketches?"

Instead of answering, he said playfully, "You have heard the one about curiosity and the cat, right?"

"Have you heard the one about vinegar versus sugar?" Laura quipped as they rounded the house and approached the entrance.

Chuckling, he signaled the parking attendant to bring the car.

The warm, fragrant breeze felt good against her skin as the car picked up speed. Her shawl was draped over her bare arms. She closed her eyes and relaxed. It had been a perfect ending to a perfect day.

"The Gardners have a lovely place. Thank you for inviting me."

"My pleasure. Regina and Clark pooled their money and their talents, put their large family to work, and created a gem. The place has thrived despite hard times," Wilham said. "I enjoyed dancing with you. You're quick on your feet and quite graceful."

Pleased by the compliment, she laughed. "You're an excellent dancer. I just followed you. It was pure fun."

"Good. Let's go dancing again, soon."

"I'd like that," Laura said without hesitation and reached out and lightly touched his arm. "Wil, I can't remember when I enjoyed myself more."

"I'm glad." He grinned, not taking his eyes from the road. He expertly handled the powerful car. It wasn't long before he slowed the car to take the turnoff to her villa. It was after midnight when he eased the car to a stop and parked behind her rental car in the drive.

It was true. She was happy. She was relaxed, not thinking ahead and dreading the end of the evening. Only once had she been uncomfortable, when she accidentally brushed against his arousal. But Wilham had not taken advantage of the situation. He was not self-centered. He had a generous spirit. And she liked that.

Laura's encounters with aroused men were not something she was eager to repeat. She routinely counseled rape victims whose experiences were traumatic in comparison to her two unpleasant attempts at making love. Unfortunately, those attempts to give and receive pleasure always ended in disappointment.

Wilham Sebastian was not a rapist or a teenage boy or a heartless young man playing at love until he found the best offer. Wilham had none of those hang-ups. He was a man in every sense of the word. He knew what he was doing and, no doubt, went out with experienced women.

Laura didn't hesitate to place her hand in his and let him help her out of the low sports car. When he encircled her waist, she didn't protest, but she relaxed, relishing the moment. She knew she was safe with him. She sighed softly, savoring his hug and inhaling his citrus-scented aftershave. He smiled and stepped back.

"Did you leave the light on?" he asked as they climbed the few steps to the porch and past her window. "Or should I go in first to check things out?"

"No need. I don't like returning to a dark room, especially in an unfamiliar place. I left the lamp on."

After using her key to unlock the door, he said, "It's late. And eight comes awfully early. Or have you changed your mind about posing for me?"

"Why would I change my mind?"

"I kissed you."

"I'm not complaining."

"Good, because I sense something has changed between us tonight."

"We've become friends. As far as I'm concerned nothing changed. Unless you've changed your mind and taken back my pool privileges?" When he shook his head no, she said, smiling, "Then I will see you at eight."

"Sleep well, Peaches," he said softly.

"Peaches?"

"That's right. Peaches are sweet, succulent, yet tangy. For me, irresistible."

"Are you comparing me to a piece of fruit?"

"It's a compliment. I'm a Georgia boy. We're very fond of peaches."

"Really," she hedged, surprised by her disappointment that he'd made no move to kiss her again. "First you've likened me to an insect and now it's a piece of produce. What next? A lamb chop?"

"You'll just have to wait and see. Interested in hearing some island blues tomorrow night? I know of a club near Coral Bay."

"You don't believe in wasting time, do you, Mr. Kramer?"

He shrugged. "A simple yes or no will do."

"There is nothing simple about me," she boasted.

He flashed a grin. "I've noticed. Your answer, Ms. Murdock?"

"Yes," she said quickly.

He surprised her when he dipped his head and placed a lingering kiss at the side of her throat close to her ear. Shivers of awareness raced along her nerve endings, and her nipples instantly beaded into twin aching peaks.

Tightening an arm around her, he pulled her close and crooned into her ear, "Kiss me . . ."

She surprised them both when, without hesitation, she lifted her chin, went up on tiptoe, and pressed her lips against his.

This kiss wasn't like the first one. It was a hot, gentle caress. And it was as different as moonlight from sunlight. Wilham's open mouth moved hungrily over hers. He teased her mouth, slowly following the shape of her lush upper lip with his tongue before exploring the ripe bounty of her fuller lip. He groaned as he took her bottom lip into his mouth to suckle. He teased one corner until her lips parted and she opened, allowing him full access.

There were no demands on his part, and nothing withheld on her part as tenderness fueled sparks of desire. Slowly, he caressed her tongue, stroking it with his. She shivered as new sensations rushed along her nerve endings.

"So sweet . . ." Wilham whispered, then stepped back,

dropping his arms to his sides. "Sleep well," he said before he walked away, leaving her to stare after him.

For the next few days Laura found herself reliving that last kiss again and again. She repeatedly asked herself why but found no clear answer.

She enjoyed her time on the island, so much that she started feeling guilty about the afternoon and evenings Wilham spent with her and away from his work. Soon, she gave in and simply enjoyed. They explored the other islands, often boating over to see the sights, or went out to swim, fish, or snorkel.

They took his boat to St. Croix, where red-roofed homes and stone windmills dotted the hillside. Wilham took Laura to see the old Danish fortress in Christianvaern. They lunched at an open-air Mediterranean restaurant before touring the botanical gardens and enjoying jazz in Frederiksted at sunset.

In St. Thomas, they went snorkeling at a deserted bay and later shopped in Charlotte Amalie, where Wilham bought her gifts of Belgian chocolates and perfume. He surprised her when he steered her into the cool, air-conditioned interior of an elegant jewelry shop.

When she arched a questioning brow, he whispered he needed a reprieve from the afternoon heat. Laura looked around, moving past the cases of diamonds, emeralds, and rubies to admire the ropes of cultured pearls. Engrossed, she barely noticed a young saleswoman's approach, it was not until an older woman of African descent, tastefully dressed, walked over to Wilham and greeted him warmly. "Hello, Mr. Kramer. Did your sister-in-law enjoy her birthday gift?"

"Hello, Mrs. Carter. Yes, she loved the pin you selected for her. How have you been?"

"Well, thank you. How may I help you?"

Laura expected him to say they were just browsing, but instead, he introduced Laura to the store's owner. Then he said, "Ms. Murdock would like to see your pearls."

Swallowing a giggle, Laura smiled and shook hands. She was impressed by the woman's knowledge of fine jewels, gemstones, and cultured pearls.

Mrs. Carter showed her a deep pink kunzite gemstone. The large square-cut stone was set in eighteen-karat gold and surrounded by round diamonds. It was an enhancer designed to be worn with a double rope of pale pink cultured pearls. There were also a six-carat square-cut kunzite and diamond ring and matching earrings.

Laura admired each piece in the set and was amazed at the workmanship and incredible beauty. When asked if she'd like to try on the pieces, she thanked Mrs. Carter but declined.

When Mrs. Carter excused herself to take a telephone call, Wilham said in Laura's ear, "Should we ask her to gift wrap the pearls and enhancer?"

Laura laughed. "Stop playing around. You aren't that rich and I would never accept such an extravagant gift from a man. I'm no gold digger."

"Then why bother looking for a rich husband?" he whispered.

"I told you," she whispered back, "it's not about what he can buy that concerns me, but what he can give me. There's a difference."

Clearly baffled, he said, "I don't get it."

"You don't have to. Be glad I'm not some money-hungry female using you to meet your older brother. What did you buy your sister-in-law?"

"A gold pin, shaped like a whisk and saucepan. She loved it. Cassy was a chef before she married Gordan." He surprised her when he said, "And if I want you to have the pearls? Would you accept?"

"Nope. Friends don't take advantage of each other."

"So sorry to keep you waiting." Mrs. Carter approached. "Is there something else you'd care to see, Ms. Murdock?"

Laura smiled. "No, but thank you. Bye." She grabbed Wilham's arm and raced for the door. Once they were on the outside, she scolded him. "Honestly, Wilham Sebastian, I can't take you anywhere."

To her chagrin, he started laughing and wouldn't stop.

Two days later, the afternoon sun was high in the sky while Laura relaxed beneath an oversize umbrella. She'd slipped on a pair of sunglasses and watched Wilham's strong, muscled body swiftly move through the water. Was there anything the man didn't do well?

After she posed that morning in the national park, they came back to his place. He'd gone into his studio and she'd enjoyed a leisurely swim. Evidently, he came out and joined her.

Covering a yawn, she asked, "Do you have any flaws?" She was exhausted from getting up early every morning, sightseeing in the afternoon and dancing every night. But she was having too much fun to worry about lost sleep. He was making sure she had the vacation of a lifetime.

"And you're expecting me to point them out?" Clad in tight swim trunks that rode low on his lean hips, he used powerful arms to lift himself out of the pool as water streamed down his superb dark bronze frame and long, hair-roughened legs.

Laura was grateful for her dark glasses. Unfortunately, they couldn't cover her burning cheeks or the hard tips of her breasts beneath her suddenly tight bikini top. She squirmed, squeezing her thighs, as her feminine core began to throb and moisten. Goodness! There ought to be a law against displaying that much male flesh. He was gorgeous! She nearly giggled at the thought of snapping his picture. No need. One look and she felt as if his image had been seared into her brain.

She should be relieved that his back was turned as he picked up a towel, for her eyes roamed over unbelievably wide shoulders, a broad back that tapered down into a taut midsection and firm male buttocks, to long-muscled thighs, strong calves, and narrow feet. Every powerful inch practically screamed, *Male in his prime*.

Just then he turned. Instead of covering up, he moved the thick terry over his legs, hips, deep chest covered in dark hair, across his shoulders. Frustrated because he'd buried his face in the towel, Laura tried not to stare at the damp fabric that outlined his thick shaft and heavy testicles. She inhaled so sharply that her breath caught in her throat and she nearly strangled when she swallowed incorrectly. She jerked upright, eyes watering as she coughed to clear her windpipe. Her heart raced like a bucking bronco when Wilham came and squatted down next to her so he could pat her back.

"You okay?"

Gasping for air, she nodded.

Twelve

"I'm fine," she finally got out.

"Here, take a sip." He picked up her bottled water.

"Thanks. How hot is it today? It has to be over a hundred."

She didn't dare ask the question uppermost in her thoughts. The same one that had gone unanswered since the first night he took her dancing. She longed to know how he remained in control when he was clearly aroused. Each time they slow danced, she'd felt his erection. She was no longer shocked by it nor did she pull away from him.

It was not as if she hadn't known he was a big man. But today she had gotten an eyeful. And here she was blushing like a schoolgirl, unable to meet his gaze.

"I should get changed." She scrambled to her feet, tying her sarong around her waist. She was shamed by her body's immediate response to his bold masculinity. It happened automatically, as if an internal switch had been left in the on position. It was odd because she'd never responded to other men that way. It was a first for her.

And to further complicate matters, she really looked

forward to the evenings he took her out dancing. Inevitably, Wilham would pull her against his lean, hard body for a slow dance. It could only be described as sweet torment. Whenever his body brushed against hers, sparks would fly. And when she felt his desire, she'd sizzle unable to control the tremors. Once the music stopped she would search his face, look for anger, frustration, or even impatience. But there was never even a hint of those emotions when they parted.

He hadn't kissed her since that first night. Yet, it hadn't stopped her yearnings for another kiss. Only she didn't hunger for the tender brush of their lips like the first kiss. No, she wanted the deep, hungry kiss he'd given at her door. To make matters worse, she was starting to crave his kiss, so much so she was shamefully close to asking him to kiss her again. Why? Why hadn't he kissed her again?

And when they would say their good nights, their eyes would lock and hold. Alarmed by her increasing sexual responses to him, Laura began to think that she might be the one to weaken and lose control. Instead of being cautious and keeping her distance, she was busy savoring the time they spent together. She was heading toward trouble and didn't know how to stop it.

"What's your hurry?" Wilham stepped into her path. When she remained silent, he said, "Laura! You're blushing!" Placing a finger beneath her chin, he lifted her face and pulled off her dark glasses. "What's going on inside your pretty head?"

Licking suddenly dry lips, she said, "It's nothing, just need to get back to the villa and get ready. But you know that."

"I also know you've been avoiding getting too close to me. You set the limits between us, Laura. I'm trying like hell to respect those limits. But I felt your eyes on me. Why the blush? We both know I want you. Every time we are together on the dance floor, you must feel my arousal and I can feel your body trembling in response. If the feelings are mutual, what the hell are we waiting for? If there's another problem, tell me what it is so we can deal with it."

Disturbed by his candor, she took a step back. "You're a talented man, Wilham Sebastian, but there's nothing to deal with. You've been very generous with your time. You've even rearranged your schedule to keep your promise to show me St. John. I have to admit you're a great tour guide. I've been enjoying myself."

"But . . ." he prompted.

She looked away when she said, "I didn't expect to be attracted to you. That's unusual for me."

"There's nothing unusual about a female being attracted to a male."

"Not with me. Generally, I'm not attracted to the men I date, but for some strange reason, I'm attracted to you. While I enjoy your company, you aren't the right one for me and I'm not the right one for you."

Frowning, he said, "But why bring that up now?"

"I don't want you to get the wrong impression. I don't do casual sex."

"Yeah, I know. If this was only about sex, I would have taken you to bed after the reception that first night. The chemistry between us was that incredible. And don't tell me you didn't feel it because I won't believe you."

Laura's eyes went wide but before she could comment, he asked, "Tell me, why am I so wrong for you? You've said it more than once. And since we're being honest, please don't hold back on me now." Suddenly, he smiled before admitting, "Your honesty is one of the things I admire most about you, Laura Murdock. You don't play games."

Shocked by the depth of emotions his compliment had caused, she blinked hard to hold back tears. Why should it matter what he thought of her? Why did she care? They were two strangers in paradise, teasing, flirting, and playing with each other. Both of them knew it could not last. It was an island fling, a little romance, a lot of fun, but nothing serious.

Naturally, she was flattered that he'd selected her to be his current muse . . . his inspiration. But she was not fooling herself into believing that she could mean more to him than temporary distraction. When the vacation was over they would both go back to their real lives.

Plus she must not forget that this was billionaire Gordan Kramer's little brother. Wilham Sebastian was a playboy who just happened to be a talented artist. He was born with a silver spoon in his mouth. He could afford to indulge in his craft. It was no secret that he could also have any woman he wanted. Right now he happened to want her. So what? It would pass.

"Why, Laura?"

She stared at him, suddenly angry. "You know why! You're too good-looking, plus you are a flirt and a tease. Half the women in St. John want to pose for you and go to bed with you. Come on, Wil! You're rich and talented. But you are not for me. I want to settle down and have babies, you don't."

"And if I wanted those things?"

"You don't! But it doesn't matter. We are here to have fun." She flashed a smile from beneath lowered lashes. "So why are you getting all serious on me, Wilham Sebastian?"

He laughed. "You are calling me a flirt and a tease? And you're full of quirks and contradictions. It's going to take a smart guy years to figure you out, Peaches."

"Stop calling me that!" She wiggled a finger at him.

Still chuckling, he said, "We'd better get changed. I'll meet you at the table in . . . fifteen minutes?"

"Make it half an hour. It's going to take at least that long to wash and dry my hair."

As she showered she told herself that it was good that he knew the truth. She did want more. After toweling off, she lotioned her skin with gardenia-scented cream.

She didn't have to be told that he was an experienced lover. It was evident that he was a man of the world. And it was there in his art. For there was a passionate depth, a raw, sexual earthiness in his work that was evident in every bold brushstroke. His use of color was phenomenal. Wilham's masculinity practically reached across the canvas to draw the viewer in.

Laura didn't doubt that other women would consider themselves extremely lucky to be on the receiving end of all that masculine charm and sex appeal. So why was she pushing him away? Acting as if he was a personal threat? She was no coward and could easily prove it. All she had to do was stand still long enough to play a little. He wanted them to go all-out and really have an island fling. Could she do it?

Her heart rate picked up speed at the thought of being intimate with him. Did she dare? Needing a distraction, she hurried into the dressing area and reached for the blow-dryer. This thing between them had started the moment their eyes met in the outdoor café. It came out of nowhere. Instead of diminishing over time, her yearning for him was intensifying.

Lately, she had taken to dreaming about him, wildly erotic dreams that left her trembling and aching for . . . for what? She didn't understand what was happening to her any more than she could comprehend her keen responses to Wilham. She hadn't felt this way when she fell in love with Johnnie while in high school or with Brad during grad school when she thought she wanted to spend her life with him, until things fell apart. This thing with Wilham was different, so intense.

And when she was out on the dance floor with Wilham, it was sheer magic. It had to be this place, this slice of paradise. When they danced, her body was fluid, swirling, dipping, turning to his slightest movement. It was uncanny the way she was able to completely let go, to become an extension of him as the pulse of steel drums and the island music flowed over them.

She didn't understand it, and couldn't possibly explain it. All she knew was that she suddenly felt free, able to let everything else go and allow her senses to soar. Out on the dance floor their connection was absolute. It made her wonder what it would be like to be intimate with Wilham. Would it be different? Would she be different with him? Eventually the music would stop and then reality would rush in, along with the doubts.

Laura had promised herself that she didn't have to have sex again, not until she was married. Besides, she was not fooling herself. She might be attracted to Wilham, but she couldn't hold on to such an earthy, virile man. It was crazy! How could she have an island fling when she didn't enjoy sex! Both times she'd been in love and it hadn't worked for her. She had only been a kid when she was involved with Johnnie. But she was older when she fell in love with Brad.

What was she thinking? Had she forgotten Wilham didn't have the qualities she was looking for in a husband? No way she was climbing into bed without a ring on her finger.

Thank goodness, there was no danger of her falling in love with Wilham. The man might look like a Greek god in bathing trunks, but his looks weren't the problem. She hadn't exaggerated when she told him she knew what qualities she valued in a mate. And he didn't even come close.

Laura pulled on black walking shorts and a sleeveless black and white blouse. When she left the cabana, she was confident that they had been candid with each other. Besides, she had learned from experience while still in her teens that the simplest and fastest way to get rid of a male was to sleep with him. Once he got what he wanted, he moved on to the next pretty face. Evidently, for each man who had been interested in her, the thrill was in the chase. Once the deed was done, he'd put on his athletic shoes and run as if the devil himself were after him.

It was late when Laura and Wilham left the nightclub and she expected him to take her back to the villa. Instead, they made a detour. He drove to the beach and parked. He kicked off his loafers and before he came around to open her door, he unbuckled the straps on her high heels and eased them off. Then held out his hand and she placed her hand in his.

They walked comfortably in the silence, the way illuminated by the crescent moon. Neither felt the need to fill the night with chatter. Hand-in-hand they strolled along the shoreline, their toes sinking into the sand still warm from the heat of the afternoon sun. It was a beautiful night; stars studded the sky. A fragrant breeze caressed their skin, and the sea rippled over an outcrop of rocks.

Wilham stopped, slowly encircling Laura's waist. While he stared down at her, her mind went blank. Laura couldn't think of a single thing to say, even an objection to their closeness. Instead, she inhaled and closed her lids to quiet her senses. It didn't work. She breathed deeply, focusing on the warm, citrus scent of his aftershave and the wonderful scent of his dark skin.

When he kissed her forehead, she slipped her arms beneath his jacket and wrapped them around his trim midsection. She savored the hard feel of his chest against her breasts. It felt good to be in his arms with only a few layers of cotton and silk separating their skin.

Wilham kissed his way down her face until he could cover her mouth with his. The heat of his mouth lured her into his solid embrace. One kiss led to another, each hotter, deeper, and more sensuous than the one before it. Laura shivered against him and Wilham soothed her by smoothing a large hand over her shoulders and down her spine to her hips.

Then he dropped his head, kissing her cheek before he whispered against the side of her throat, "Did I tell you how beautiful you are tonight in that sexy cream dress?"

She smiled. "You did, but I never get tired of hearing it. Thank you."

"You're welcome. I'd like to paint you just as you are now on a deserted beach, your lovely features bathed in the moonlight, your braid loose." He pulled out the pins that anchored her hair.

She smiled and shook her head, causing them to fall around her slim shoulders.

When she shivered and covered a yawn, he removed his jacket, placing it around her shoulders.

He ran a caressing hand down her back. "I should take you back to the villa. I've been selfish. You haven't gotten much sleep this past week."

Not wanting the night to end, she shook her head. "I can sleep when I get back to Detroit."

He chuckled. "I've monopolized your time, but even I can see that my unpredictable princess needs some rest."

Laura teased, "Are you my frog prince?"

"Aw, you've seen Disney's Black princess?"

"Yes, and she's lovely. Little Black girls have been waiting forever to have their very own fairy princess." She giggled. "I'm surprised you even know about it."

He chuckled. "I have twin nieces who keep me up on the important things in life."

She laughed, but wasn't ready to leave. She supposed she was being greedy, but couldn't help it. It was so peaceful here. No worries, just the two of them, alone on this quiet stretch of beach. A slice of heaven she desperately wanted to hold on to along with him.

But it was very late and they were both tired. She sighed heavily but she didn't protest when he escorted her back to the car. She tried to convince herself it was for the best.

"I can't believe how quickly this first week has flown by. I want to catch it and make it stop," she whispered. Then she closed her eyes for only a moment.

She must have fallen asleep because she gasped when he swung her off her feet and carried her up to the small front porch. "No, put me down. I'm too heavy."

"You won't hear me complaining. I like how you feel in my arms." He said, "Can you open those pretty brown eyes, Peaches, long enough to find the key and unlock the door?"

It took several tries before she completed the task. She steadied herself by looping an arm around his neck. She didn't think to protest when he pushed the door closed with his foot and carried her into the bedroom. The light from the lamp in the sitting room spilled over into the bedroom. Sheer curtains covered the windows and the blinds were open, letting the moonlight shine inside.

"Thanks for the lift." She giggled, suppressing a moan when he released her legs and her body brushed against his.

"Sweet dreams, Peaches," Wilham whispered, kissing her forehead.

Laura didn't want him to go, not yet. Tightening her arms around his neck, she stretched up onto her tiptoes, pressing kisses at the base of his bronze throat. She complained, "I can't reach your mouth to kiss you good night. Come down here, please."

His splayed hands rested on either side of her rib cage. He shook his head no, before he confessed, "Not tonight. If I kiss you, I won't stop, not until you're naked and beneath me." Resting his forehead against hers, he sighed, "I should go."

The protest rose in her throat as her arms tightened around him. Suddenly she realized, she'd gradually given him her trust. Dancing, she surmised. Evidently, she'd grown accustomed to the feel of his hard male contour against hers.

Wise or unwise, right or wrong didn't change what she was feeling. Laura wanted Wilham. She craved his touch, his kisses, his closeness. Her past, the doubts and reservations seemed unimportant compared to the overwhelming need to be with him tonight.

Although he held her, she grew frustrated because she couldn't reach his firm mouth. Sighing, Laura closed her eyes and tried to memorize this moment and this very special man. She felt his desire and suspected he wanted to stay, but was held back by the conviction that it was not what she wanted. Now what? How did she let him know she had changed her mind? How would an experienced woman seduce such a sophisticated man?

Drawing in his scent but not his taste, she was tired of waiting. She needed Wilham's kisses, wanted his caresses.

Laura smoothed uncertain trembling hands over his silk-covered, hair-roughened chest and waist, pressing her cheek over his heart. She listened for his heart's beat, and heard his uneven breath. Did he want what she wanted, needed what she needed? They were alone in this magical place as the hot flames of unspoken desire surrounded them.

Her breasts felt heavy, the nipples hard, aching peaks. Pushing doubts away, she did what she had been wanting to do. She rubbed her soft curves against his torso and pressed her mouth against his bronze skin, thankful that his shirt was unbuttoned nearly to his waist. It didn't matter that she was not good at sex. All that mattered was how he made her feel. And she wanted this. She wanted Wilham . . . now.

Encouraged by his husky groan when she kissed his hot and salty chest, she licked her way over to his flat ebony nipple. She sponged and sucked it. His response was immediate, a deep, throaty moan and tremor.

Looking up at him, she whispered, "Don't leave. I want you to stay with me . . . make love to me."

He groaned, dropping his head and covered her soft mouth with his. He slipped his tongue in and out of her mouth. He playfully bit her bottom lip and then drew it into his mouth to suck. She gasped at the heat, the magic, and opened for his deep, hungry kisses.

"Laura," he moaned, suckling her tongue. "I want you. You're so unbelievably sweet."

"Mmm," she purred deep in her throat, shivering from his kisses. He certainly had her knees shaking. Mesmerized by his incredible kisses, she was soon caught up in the magic of this place and the man. It didn't matter that it would end up being messy and unpleasant or that it would be over quickly. He would gain pleasure, and if she was very lucky, he wouldn't stop kissing her the entire time.

To her delight his sizzling kisses heated even more. They were deep and intoxicatingly sweet, even better than she'd imagined. When he lifted his head she begged, "Please, Wil. Don't stop kissing me."

His response was immediate. He covered her mouth and hungrily feasted on her lips as he gathered her tight against him. His hands stroked her hair, moving over her shoulders and down her back. Cupping and squeezing her buttocks, he growled deep in his throat and she trembled from his caress, never wanting him to stop.

Wilham surprised her when he pulled back, putting space between them. He took several deep breaths. Aching with longing, Laura also filled her lungs with air and waited. She hoped he wasn't disappointed, that she hadn't done something wrong.

"I'm glad you like my kisses because I can't get enough of your sweet mouth," he crooned. To her relief he kissed his way down her neck to the scented base. He lingered there, tonguing the hollow, before he slowly tongued the other side of her throat, below her ear. He sponged the lobe, taking it into his mouth to suckle.

Laura moaned as his hot tongue moved over her heated flesh. He kissed and licked the way to her soft nape.

He whispered, "More kisses?"

"Yes!" she nearly shouted, pressing her lips against his.

Engrossed in his hot, wet kisses, she was unaware of him unzipping her dress and pushing it off her body. She still wore a nude, lace strapless bra and matching panties. They soon followed the dress. After several more kisses, she trembled. "Oh, Wil. I can never get tired of your kisses."

His response was to leisurely explore the soft lining of her mouth, enjoying the smoothness of her cheek and the rippled roof of her mouth. She moaned when he rubbed her tongue against his and then began suckling. His hands tenderly moving over her breasts. But he didn't stop there. He tantalized her tender flesh by tugging an aching, engorged peak until she was breathless, a trembling mass of nerves.

When he pulled back so they could catch their breath, she stared up at him in wonder. She studied his full lips, which were swollen from their kisses. His forehead was beaded with perspiration and his breathing was uneven. But there was no denying the pulsating strength of his erection against her. She closed her eyes, not wanting to acknowledge that part of him.

It would hurt, but hopefully he would finish quickly. And then what? Maybe he'd return to kissing her and touching her breasts? Or would he be like Brad and voice his keen disappointment and then unfavorably compare her to other women? She shuddered at the thought. And her feverish body began to cool.

"Wil, . . ." She hesitated.

"What, Peaches? More kisses?" he crooned in her ear, before he kissed his way from her throat, to tenderly tease the outer curves of her swollen lips with love bites until she gasped at the sweet sensation before he licked her lips.

"Oh yes . . . more," she moaned, and shivered as the glorious heat returned in tantalizing waves and an unexpected ache deep in her feminine core began to unfurl. She took a deep, steadying breath. All she knew was she needed his heated kisses and she couldn't stop now. She wanted this . . . she wanted him. She could do this! She could!

Thirteen

Laura kissed the base of his throat and collarbone, quickly pushing away his shirt and accidentally brushed his shaft. He moaned, and she jerked back as if she'd been burned. Unfortunately she knew what came next. She fumbled as she tried to unfasten his belt buckle because her hands were shaking so badly.

"I'm sorry," she stammered, knowing what to do didn't make it easy. She read the sex journals and listened to girlfriends talk. The last thing she wanted was to freeze up and disappoint him.

"I'll do it," he said, placing her hands on his chest. Her startled dark brown eyes momentarily locked with his heated golden gaze. "There's no hurry."

"But . . ." She swallowed nervously. "You're . . ."

"Aroused," he said, trailing kisses from her nose, her cheek, down the side of her throat, causing her to shiver. "I've been that way for days. It will keep until you're ready, sweetheart."

"I'm ready."

Arching a dark brow, he shook his head. "Impossible. But we've got all night to play."

Play? She wanted him to hurry and get this part over

with so they could get back to the kissing. Before she could say more, Wilham covered her mouth with his.

Laura whimpered deep in her throat, her skin flushed with pleasure. "Oh my," she gushed as he kissed her again and again. Then Wilham nestled her breasts and then sponged the hard, aching tip repeatedly. Suddenly, her knees began to give way. As she reached out to steady herself, he encircled her small waist and lifted her off her feet. He dropped his head to tantalize the other breast and gave it the same druggingly sweet attention. He licked the engorged peak, gently scraped it against his teeth before he soothed and then tormented her with deep suction.

Laura could not believe it. Never had she been touched this way or handled with such exquisite care. Stunned by a sudden rush of pleasure, she quivered, gasping when he intensified that suction. He took his time, clearly savoring her soft breasts.

Laura barely caught her breath as blinding pleasure shot through her system. She felt the tug of his mouth all the way to her sensitive core. Instinctively, she tightened inner muscles, damp and pulsating with need. Suddenly dizzy, she felt as if her head was spinning and only then realized Wilham had placed her on the bed and was urging her to wrap her legs around his waist. Shaking from overwhelming need, she clung to him.

"You've heard the phrase 'sweeter than honey'?" Wilham said huskily. "You are my peach and I want more." He lowered his head and returned to her nipple, giving her more of the hard suction she craved.

Bombarded by the blazing hot sensations generating from deep inside her, Laura quivered as her racing heart picked up even more speed, while her nerve endings tingled and her inflamed senses soared. It felt so good that she cried out as she rode a wave of sheer pleasure. She was so consumed by that desire that she could no longer think, only feel as the hard persistent tugs of his mouth caused white-hot flames to lash at her flesh, shattering her control. She felt as if she was on the edge of something that felt so wondrous she didn't want it to stop . . . not ever.

When Laura moaned loudly, Wilham lifted his head. "Sorry, Peaches. It's too much. Your breasts are so beautiful, so sensitive. I got carried away. I didn't mean to make you sore," he soothed. "I know, more kisses." He shifted until he could reach her lips. "Good?"

Embarrassed, Laura nodded, rather than begging him not to stop as the seductive haze she'd been caught in receded.

He gave kiss after kiss, the first tender but slowly deepening as he stroked her tongue with his. Then he was there between her thighs, opening her legs. Laura stiffened, her body quickly cooling. It was time. His turn. How could she complain? He had been so generous, incredibly patient. Nervously, she bit her lower lip.

Wilham was ready for her. There was no mistaking the steel-hard pressure of his erection. And he was so big!

Trembling with nervous self-consciousness, Laura began to close her legs.

"Don't, Peaches. Let me see you, touch you." His voice was thick with need.

Perspiration beaded her brow and trailed down her spine. Her muscles were taut from dread of what came next.

"What is it?" he asked, smoothing a hand down her spine to her soft hips.

She shook her head, "Nothing."

"You are tensing up on me. Why?"

"I'm fine," she insisted, wrapping her arms around his neck. She stopped short of demanding he hurry and get it over with. "Kiss me."

"My pleasure."

After several long, tongue-rubbing kisses, she clung to him and pressed the aching tips of her breasts against his hair-roughened chest.

He groaned, cupping and squeezing her bottom as he stroked from her ankle to her soft inner thighs.

Laura moaned when he parted and fingered her damp folds. She was embarrassingly wet, but he didn't seem to mind, for he took his time, rubbing her plump folds, teasing her aching clitoris and circling her soft opening. Once more she was lost in the seductive haze that was so thick that she didn't think to protest that it was his turn or voice her shock that yet again she was on the receiving end of his unhurried caresses. This time the flames of desire took her higher and higher and yet again it abruptly stopped.

Her lowered lids flicked up and her questioning eyes met his golden hot gaze. He surprised her by announcing, "It's my turn." Then he slid down her body.

Suddenly bombarded with sizzling hot sensations, she forgot her disbelief when he kept on going until he licked behind her knee and her inner thigh.

"Oh! Oh!" Laura moaned. Those moans swiftly turned to whimpers when he boldly tongued her slick heat, slowly tasting her and plying her soft opening. Her cheeks burned and her heart pounded louder than a steel drum as her excitement bubbled upward. He slid a long finger deep inside while he sponged her clitoris.

"Oh! My!" she nearly screamed as what she thought was impossible happened. Her small, petite frame shook from the force of her release.

"Wilham!" Laura cried out again and again. When she opened heavy lids and looked at him in a combination of utter shock and wonderment.

He grinned as he kissed the side of her neck while holding her close. He tucked several thin loose braids behind her ear, away from her damp face.

"Wow!" she whispered, in a daze. Her heart still pounding while she struggled to understand what she had just experienced. "Did I clim—" She stopped, her face hot.

"Climax . . ." he finished for her. "You came apart in my arms. It was sweet, unbelievably sweet." He kissed her tenderly.

Before she could ask why he had ignored his own needs, he stood up and finished undressing.

His eyes smoldered with desire as he watched her watching him. Swiftly, he unzipped his trousers, shoving them, along with dark briefs, down his long, bronze legs. His heavy shaft boldly jutting away from his body captured her attention. Her eyes widened as she stared at his generous proportions.

Laura quickly looked away and swallowed with difficulty, recalling hurtful memories. Her doubts returned in an unexpected rush.

"Laura," he whispered. His gold-brown gaze practically sizzled with desire as he studied her soft curves in appreciation. "You are so beautiful, so lovely."

Nervously, Laura licked dry lips, reminding herself that she was with Wilham. He'd been so patient, already given her more than she could imagine. It was too late to back out now.

As if he could read her thoughts, he said quietly, "I won't hurt you, Laura. I promise."

"But you're so . . ." She struggled with the word, before she finally said, " . . . big."

He came down beside her. Kissing her temple, he said, "You haven't said much about your experiences with men, but from what little you revealed I assumed you were not a . . ."

Laura shook her head vehemently. "I'm not a virgin. I've slept with two . . ." She stopped, realizing she had nearly said "boys." Compared to him, they both seemed incredibly immature. Afraid of revealing too much, she hesitated.

How could she explain the profound relief she felt now that she knew there was nothing wrong with her. That she didn't have a problem. For so long she'd been harboring so many feelings of inadequacy. Thanks to him she was close to weeping with relief because of what she'd learned about herself.

She explained, "I've been in two relationships. Both ended badly."

Wilham stroked her hair. "Shush, no worries. You told me you've been in love twice. Your past has nothing to do with us." He grinned. "But I'm selfish enough to admit I'm glad I was able to pleasure you, make it special, sweetheart."

She surprised them both when she confessed, "I thought there was something wrong with me because I don't enjoy sex." Pressing her lips against his, she whispered, "Thank you, Wil. I'm relieved. I've never even come close to feeling like that before."

Beaming, he said, "Giving you pleasure and watching the sweet way you came apart in my arms was pure magic for me. He teased, "My sweet succulent peach."

Laura giggled. She couldn't help being pleased by the endearment. She stroked the hair on his bronze chest, needing to touch him. "Tell me how to please you."

Wilham smiled, pressing her hand over his pounding heart. "That's easy. Looking at you, touching you does it for me. From the moment I saw you in that café, I wanted to make love to you."

He slipped a hand under her braids, caressing her nape, before he stroked down her back and rested his hand at the base of her spine. Wilham shifted until he was behind her, kissing and stroking her neck and shoulder. Soon he was kissing his way down her spine.

Laura closed her eyes and gave in to the pleasure.

"I never get tired of looking at you," he said.

Once again she was the one on the receiving end. Feeling selfish, she pulled away. "No, let me touch you."

Playfully, he lightly bit her soft nape, and then quickly soothed the tiny sting with his tongue. Then he leaned back and laced his hands behind his head. Closing his eyes, he said, "I'm all yours."

With her heart racing and unsteady hands, she stroked him from his jaw down the side of his neck, over his wide shoulders and down his hard-muscled, long arms. His skin was hot and firm as she smoothed down to his taut stomach. Suddenly, she yearned to please him, as he had pleasured her. Laura dropped her head and placed a string of kisses along his throat, inhaling his unique scent.

She was pleased by his husky groan when she licked his flat male nipple. Encouraged, she tongued the other nipple and smoothed her hand over his hair-roughened chest.

She hesitated at his waist, her dark brown eyes momentarily locked with his. After he nodded his consent she took a fortifying breath and gingerly touched his manhood. She trailed a finger down the length of his shaft from the thick base to the broad tip and then she encircled his shaft, stroking him. She smiled when he groaned huskily.

He growled close to her ear, "I'm a patient man, but I can't take much more of your soft hands." Cupping her face, he moved over her and took her mouth in a heated exchange.

Laura was breathless by the time he lifted his head. Her heart pounded in a combination of anticipation and dread, she urged, "Hurry!"

Her fears returned as she watched him retrieve a foil packet from the nightstand and open it, covering his thick shaft. Tears that she refused to let fall burned her eyes.

"Now," she said urgently, closing her eyes and wrapping her arms around his neck.

Wilham kissed her tender lips and the sensitive place on her throat as he covered her soft body with his. She sighed, enjoying the way he caressed her hips and inner thighs.

"Relax," he crooned in her ear. "No worries. I've got you, sweetheart."

She closed her eyes at the sweetness of his body stroking her intimately. Hungry for more, she arched her back, opening her arms and legs to welcome his unrelenting hardness. Eyes closed, she gasped when he nestled against her breasts, teasing the sensitive nipples.

"Wilham!" She trembled, enjoying the hard pressure as he slowly pushed forward to fill her emptiness.

He whispered huskily, "Open your eyes, Laura."

When she lifted her lashes, he gazed into the depths of her chocolate brown eyes. "Am I hurting you?"

She shook her head no.

"Good," he said, moving inside her tight sheath. First, he used short, shallow strokes, giving her time to relax and adjust to his size. Gradually, he deepened his thrusts. Soon they were moving as one, both swept up in the ageless, deeply erotic dance of lovers.

Laura clung to Wilham, not wanting him to stop. He felt so good, so right deep inside her. Her body was burning from the blazing heat of desire and excitement. She clung to him, instinctively tightening around his pulsating length. As Laura's inner muscles stroked Wilham from his thick root to the broad crest, he shuddered, lifting her legs and wrapping them around his waist. They moved as one in rhythmic ease as the white-hot flames of passion caused their breathing to be quick and uneven, their heart rates to pick up speed, as they raced together toward the ultimate goal. Laura tried to keep pace with his deep even strokes but lost it when Wilham began to caress her clitoris. Suddenly, she felt as if she was hurling through space straight into a shatteringly sweet release. He issued a hoarse shout of triumph as his lean body joined hers, convulsing in a mind-numbing climax.

His voice was gruff when he asked, "You okay, sweetheart?"

She moaned, barely able to speak. Eventually, she managed to get out, "I had no idea it could be like this."

Wilham rolled onto his back but kept an arm around her waist. He rained kisses from her forehead to her small chin. "You are incredible." Then he chuckled deep in his throat. "And you screamed. I'd be surprised if the entire complex didn't hear."

Fourteen

Blushing, Laura covered her face. "You weren't supposed to notice," she said in a frantic whisper.

He laughed and gently kissed her swollen lips. "You won't hear me complaining. You were amazing."

"Wow!" She giggled. "It must be all this Caribbean moonlight. Or perhaps too much wine that caused us to end up in bed tonight."

He chuckled. "We didn't drink that much. But whatever the reason, I can't get enough of you."

Bemused, she said, "Let's not talk about it."

"So you can pretend it didn't happen?"

"I didn't say that. But we both know it wasn't supposed to happen," she insisted.

Wilham ran a finger down the bridge of her nose. "But it happened and we both enjoyed it. No worries, Peaches, especially not tonight. Come here and let me hold you."

She sighed and relaxed against him. *No worries*, she repeated silently. Covering a yawn, she said, "I'm sorry."

He whispered in her ear, "Close your eyes, and sleep."

As she succumbed, her last thought was that she was glad she had been wrong about him.

"Hmm." Laura woke to Wilham brushing his lips against her forehead. Lifting heavy lids, she saw that he was not in bed with her. He sat on the side and was fully dressed.

Predawn light was just beginning to peek through the partly closed blinds and a soft breeze ruffled the curtains.

"Good morning. Sorry I woke you."

She blinked in surprise. "You're dressed."

"I made tea. Would you like a cup?"

"You're leaving," she said with a frown. "What's the time?"

"It's early, not quite six. You were sleeping so peacefully, but I didn't want to leave without saying goodbye."

Why? she wanted to ask, but didn't because she already knew the answer. She had been so wrong about him. He was exactly like the others. Suddenly conscious of her nudity, she held the sheet over her breasts.

When she moved to sit up, he said, "No reason for you to get up because I have to work. Why don't you get some rest, go back to sleep?"

Suddenly hopeful because he said he had to work, she released a pent-up breath. Pushing her braids out of her eyes, she said, "I'll get dressed."

"No need. I have enough sketches to work from." He leaned down to brush his lips against hers, but she turned and his lips touched her cheek. "I have to go," he said absently. Physically, he was still there, but mentally, he was elsewhere. He didn't look at her when he said, "Go back to sleep. See you later. Bye."

Laura closed her eyes so she didn't have to watch him leave. She hated feeling weak and vulnerable. Unfortunately, it was nothing new to her. She listened to him leave the bedroom and cross to the door. She didn't cry when she heard the villa door close behind him.

"I was right all along!" she hissed in misery. Her hands were balled into fists. It had happened not once, not even twice, but three times! He was the third man to walk away after getting what he wanted from her. Maybe she should be grateful that he spent the night instead of leaving when he finished. She had even posed for him, but now that he'd slept with her, he was done. It was a pitiful pattern that happened repeatedly to her.

No, it hadn't started with the men she was stupid enough to share her body with. It had started long ago with the girl-woman who had given birth to her and then abandoned her. Laura's heart ached and her eyes burned with unshed tears.

Clearly, there had been no reason for him to stay. He had plenty of sketches of her. Somehow, she had managed to do the impossible. She had pleased him in bed. Now that he had what he wanted, it was over.

The anguish that she could no longer contain had her sobbing into the pillow. Awash in pain and disappointment, she wondered why she always fell for the wrong men. She'd been in high school the first time she'd fallen in love and in grad school the next time. Well, maybe she had learned one thing over the years. This time, she might have been foolish enough to have sex with him but was smart enough not to fall in love with him. Perhaps wisdom did come with age? Once again she'd made a terrible mistake when she let him make love to her. And she'd opened herself up to a brand-new kind of misery.

She'd been so caught up in basking in her favorite artist's attention that she was convinced he cared about her. It wasn't as if she expected to have a future with him. But she had expected more than a kiss on the cheek and the empty promise to see her later. He'd left as if she meant no more to him than a one-night stand. And it hurt, badly.

There hadn't been even a hint of hesitation when he said he no longer needed her to pose for him. Clearly, he was done. She had no choice but to accept she had been used and tossed away like the condom wrapper on the bedside table. How could she have been such a fool? She was supposed to know better!

Unable to find a tissue, she used the corner of the top sheet to dry her tears. "No more!" She wasn't going to spend the day crying over a man! She refused to waste any more of her time on him. She most certainly wasn't going to let the fear that she might have gone ahead and fallen in love with a man she'd known barely a week, keep her inside feeling sorry for herself.

She showered and dressed, refusing to dwell on the unbelievable pleasure she'd discovered in his arms. It was no secret Wilham was an older, sophisticated experienced, and sensual man. Evidently, he had good reason to be confident in his ability to please his lady.

So what if he'd shown her that when it came to sex, there was nothing wrong with her? Or that he'd made the two younger men she'd been with seem like two inexperienced boys playing at love? It didn't lessen the hurt she had to deal with knowing he had his fill of her after only one night.

Laura drove into town to go shopping for gifts for her foster sisters and friends. She realized she had nearly two full weeks left of her vacation. What was she supposed to do now? That meant she would be going home with not only a bruised heart, but also with a wounded ego. And she would leave without one of Sebastian's signature paintings. The low-life snake! She didn't need him to give her a painting. She no longer wanted one of his paintings. She needed no reminders that they shared a brief island fling. She was better off without him. News flash! Wilham Sebastian Kramer was not her type. It was a shame his older brother, Gordan, was married!

She picked up a pretty floral yellow and red patterned silk scarf for Sherri Ann and a lovely porcelain box shaped like a seashell for Jenna. She could use it to store her wedding rings while she was working in the kitchen.

Spotting a bookstore ahead, she thought of Maureen, Trenna, Vanessa, and Brynne, the ladies in her book club. Maybe, she could find something for them to read? They called themselves the Elegant Five. Back when they'd started the club, they were all single and proud of the fact they didn't need a man to feel good about themselves. They were five single, gorgeous, very elegant ladies.

Brynne had been the first to marry and drop out when she moved to St. Louis with her daughter and new husband, Devin Prescott. Vanessa had been next to fall in love and marry Ralph Prescott. Their husbands were cousins. The remaining three book club members were unmarried and hadn't bothered to change the name. They also hadn't recruited any new single members although Laura had really tried to convince Jenna and Sherri Ann to join them, but had been unsuccessful. Both foster sisters insisted they were too busy.

Laura left the bookstore, pleased because she had found five copies of a novel by a St. Thomas writer. She didn't mind having to send Brynne her copy. Determined to keep her spirits up, Laura decided to treat herself to dinner out. She could go back to Clark and Regina Gardner's restaurant. And she would have a better time on her own.

She put on a pretty pink and white floral silk strapless dress. Flirty ruffles edging the bodice and hem moved whenever she did, which made it perfect for dancing. So what if Wilham had seen her in the dress and complimented her? The man might be a jerk, but she couldn't fault his eyesight or his artist's eye for color and detail.

Because of its breathtaking view, the restaurant was situated high in the hills. Laura took her time navigating the narrow road and kept a tight grip on the steering wheel. She was nearly there when she started questioning her choice. How could she have forgotten the steep drop? Or the inadequate guardrails? It was frightening. But then Wilham had been behind the wheel.

She released a heartfelt sigh of relief when the road leveled off and she neared the turnoff to the restaurant. She frowned, realizing the return trip would be made in the dark. And it was too late for second thoughts.

Regina Gardner greeted her with a hug. "Laura, you look pretty tonight in that dress. I like your hair up like that."

She teased, "This old thing? Now, you look lovely tonight. Do you and Clark have big plans for later?"

The older woman laughed. "Maybe." Then she said, "Where is Sebastian? Is he parking the car?"

"I'm alone tonight. Unfortunately, I didn't listen to the weather report. I hope it doesn't rain." Laura glanced at the overcast sky, deciding not to stay long.

Regina patted her hand. "Hopefully, the storm will hold off until much later tonight." After checking her seating chart, Regina smiled. "Right this way."

Entering the candlelit room, Laura instantly noticed the restaurant was mostly filled with couples.

"How is this?" Regina asked.

"Perfect!" Laura smiled, accepting the menu.

"If I have a free moment, may I come back and chat?" Regina asked hopefully.

"Please." After Laura quickly scanned the menu, she ordered the shrimp scampi.

She sighed, upset because she had tried but couldn't hold back memories of Wilham and the special night when they were here. It was the first time they'd danced together. She'd never thought of herself as being a good dancer. Of course, she had never danced the tango. And it had been pure magic the way she had been able to let go of her inhibition and followed his lead, turning, stamping, and twirling to the vibrant beat of the steel drums. It was amazing the way his lean, strong body moved with natural ease and grace, almost as if the music flowed through his veins. And she hadn't missed a step. That night Wilham had kissed her for the first time.

"Your salad, miss." The waiter set the plate in front of her. She nodded her thanks but was no longer hungry and only picked at her food. She shouldn't have kissed him, or posed for him. More importantly, she never should have slept with him, knowing full well they were wrong for each other.

Laura was only fifteen the first time she'd fallen in love, twenty-three the next time. Both times, she'd loved deeply and it ended badly. She thought she had learned from these mistakes. In fact, she'd changed her entire approach to finding love because of those mistakes.

After she had taken time to really think and figure out what qualities she wanted in a mate she decided love was no longer her only goal. She was looking for an accomplished man who was unafraid of hard decisions or commitment. She wanted a very successful man who had proven himself to be a man of his word. She needed a wealthy man who had no problems shouldering responsibility. A man of conviction who would be in for the long haul and unlikely to walk away once the newness had worn off the relationship.

A man she could trust to always be there. Most important, a man willing to give her the large family she'd craved her entire life. She longed for a home filled with children and unconditional love. It wasn't a pipe dream or a childish fantasy.

She hadn't exaggerated when she told Wilham about the single, wealthy male athletes in Brynne's bridal party. She would be the first to admit she hadn't taken advantage of the opportunity. She had been fortunate in that she dated the crème de la crème—well educated, intelligent, and confident men who knew what they wanted out of life. There was no doubt she made some wonderfully long-lasting friendships. But as yet she hadn't found Mr. Right.

On the other hand, her good friend Vanessa, also in the wedding party, had used that time to get to know Ralph Prescott. The two had recently married.

Recently, Laura had concentrated on her career. Caught up in the demands of her work, she had allowed her love life to suffer. She had not made finding Mr. Right a priority. While she went out with men who were right for her, she also believed she wasn't like her girlfriends and she had stuck the "sexless" label on her own forehead.

Well, the one good that had come from sleeping with Wilham was that he'd convinced her she also had needs.

Laura was genuinely thrilled when her foster sister Jenna had finally married the man of her dreams. The wedding had been small, with mostly family, but very beautiful. Both Laura and Sherri Ann were very proud of Jenna and so happy for her. It had taken Scott and Jenna more than ten years to finally make their way back to each other again.

For Laura, the difficulty always came when intimacy entered the mix. And it seemed as if she was always forced to choose between remaining friends or becoming lovers. Unfortunately, she had never been tempted to sleep with any of the "right" men she dated. Until last night she had no problem saying no.

Truly, Laura hadn't asked for her foster sisters' views on her problems with men. Nevertheless, they'd given it anyway. And she didn't appreciate that they had pointed out that judging by Laura's record, she was more interested in collecting male friends than in marriage. It was not true!

Once Laura had discovered that most wealthy men had two essential qualities that other men lacked, she knew she was on to something. In her estimation, those two qualities—relentless determination to succeed and never giving up—were the key to what she needed in a matc and were worth risking her entire future. While other men might long for success, a self-made man would never stop until he had what he wanted. Nor would he ever let it go, not without major consequences.

She'd never been attracted to men who inherited wealth, but was fascinated by the man who fought for his dream. That type of male was never going to walk away or let go of a treasure. Laura desperately wanted to be treasured.

She didn't expect anyone to understand her personal grief or the yearnings of her heart. It was complicated. And not one of her many quirks, such as detesting coffee and loving tea or enjoying wearing sandals while hating to get her feet dirty. It stretched back to her beginnings, back to being left inside a cardboard box, with only a note stating her name and she was loved. As far as she was concerned, being abandoned had nothing to do with love.

Her goal to marry well might not make sense to anyone else, but it made perfect sense to her. To know she was valued was most important to her.

Unfortunately, she learned early the very painful truth. Love didn't mean forever. Nor was love the automatic cure-all that the romance novels, movies, and love songs strongly claimed. Love was only a part of what she longed for. And love was not even the first step toward laying claim to a man's heart. Both Johnnie and Brad had said they loved her. Yet, in both cases, love hadn't lasted nor had it made them stay.

It didn't matter what others thought of her desire to marry well. After searching her heart she knew her motives weren't mercenary or selfish. There was nothing wrong with going after what she wanted or vowing not to settle for less. She could do this! And she wasn't about to let another "handsome distraction" get in her way. She had her priorities straight. She would have a secure future. As far as she was concerned, security beat out love every single time.

Her goal was simple and her heart pure. And her man was out there! Somehow she would find that wealthy husband with relentless determination and unwavering loyalty. In return, she would gladly give her groom her heart, her devotion and loyalty, and if God was willing, lots of pretty brown babies.

With two weeks left on her vacation, she'd had her island fling. And she couldn't afford to forget that Wilham had never been in the running for a potential husband.

How had he managed to shatter her defenses? He was a playboy for heaven's sake! He was busy traveling the world, painting and out for a good time in the process. It was her bad luck to fall for an accomplished lover! Life wasn't always fair!

There was no shortage of beautiful woman eager to help him spend his billionaire brother's fortune. He'd boldly claimed he was over forty and had never even come close to falling in love. He didn't have serious relationships. And he had no intentions of ever settling down. How could she have been so foolish? How could she have slept with him? For a few hours, she was his entertainment.

Blinking away tears, Laura bit her lip to hold in a sob. She was not about to fall apart just because she'd temporarily lost her mind and crawled into bed with him. He used her. So what? She was a grown-up. It wasn't the end of the world.

For a few moments, she'd even considered that she might be wrong about him. But he had proven her wrong. He hadn't called her once during the entire day. She knew because she'd checked, several times. It was over for him the second he walked out her door.

Fifteen

There wasn't a spot on her body that he hadn't caressed, kissed, and licked. It was disgraceful the way she responded to his lovemaking. But then Wilham Sebastian Kramer was not ordinary. Apparently, the highly skilled artist played as hard as he worked. Why hadn't she paid attention to the warning signs? No man danced that well, moved so effortlessly, or made love that skillfully without tons of practice. He was a womanizer!

She had foolishly underestimated him. She should have been doubly cautious considering her unusual reaction to him. From the moment he looked at her in the outdoor café with those sexy gold eyes, she'd been keenly aware of him.

"Big mistake," she mumbled aloud.

"Miss Laura, did you enjoy the salad?" Raymond asked as he placed the entrée on the changer plate in front of her.

"Very much. Smells heavenly." She smiled.

"Please enjoy."

Intent on savoring every bite, she picked up her fork. *Mmm*, she thought, *Wilham would enjoy—* She stopped eating. Enough!

She should be trying to find a way of coping with the hope and longing their lovemaking had created. It was unlike anything she'd ever experienced in a man's arms! And she resented it. She didn't need or want it messing with her head or her heart. She had to find a way to fix it or at the very least to make it go away. She was fed up with constantly being reminded of her mistake.

His lovemaking had left her vulnerable. She couldn't afford to have feelings for him. She didn't want to recall the way he made her feel. It was pointless! What did it matter that for a few short hours, she felt she was finally where she truly belonged? She refused to care about a man who didn't value her.

"I'm so sorry!" Regina said, returning to the table. "We have been so busy tonight. How was your dinner?"

"Fabulous! Please tell your husband how much I enjoyed it."

Regina beamed. "I will. Would you like to see the dessert tray?"

She shook her head no. "I'd better not. I have to get moving. I don't want to get caught in the rain going back to town. Please may I have the bill?"

"Right away. If you would like, I can ask one of my sons to take you home?"

Laura pulled out her credit card and gave it to the older woman. "Thanks, but I can't impose. With a little luck, I'll miss the storm."

While waiting, Laura's gaze strayed to the table she'd shared with Wilham the first night. Her heart heavy, she realized it was a mistake to dine here tonight. For a moment, she was desperately afraid that she had made a bigger mistake . . . that she might be falling in love with Wilham.

"We're all set." Regina smiled. "I had Raymond wrap a little dessert for you to take with you."

Laura smiled, quickly rising. "That's so kind. Thank you."

No, not love, she hastily decided. It was more like a bad case of lust. No more playing with fire. She was moving forward with the plan.

"Good." Regina smiled. "Then you come back soon."

Laura nodded. "I had a lovely time," she said as they walked to the entrance.

"Are you sure you won't change your mind about driving? I can't imagine what Sebastian is thinking to let—"

Laura interrupted, "I will be fine." She nearly flinched at the sound of his name. She was not Wilham's responsibility. "Sorry, I have to rush. Bye." A quick wave and she was gone.

She hadn't gone far when the rain started. "Oh no!" she exclaimed, turning on the windshield wipers. "What else can go wrong?"

She did her best to ignore the nerves in the pit of her stomach as she approached the two-lane highway with the steep drop. After activating the defrost, she struggled to stay calm.

The day had gone downhill from the moment Wilham woke her to say good-bye. Why had he bothered? One look into his eyes told her all she needed to know. He was there physically, but mentally he had already left.

Gripping the wheel with both hands, she prayed for courage. The side of the road was way too narrow for her to consider stopping. She should have stayed in tonight. Better yet, she should have stayed in Detroit and canceled the trip.

"What was that?" Laura exclaimed after hitting something left on the road. It was dark and pouring rain. She couldn't see a darn thing. By the time she'd slowed the car to nearly a crawl, she knew she'd punctured a tire. Carefully, she pulled over as far as she dared to the guardrail.

Fighting tears, she pounded her fist on the steering wheel and promptly broke a nail. She felt like swearing but remembered Mrs. Green. She had raised a lady, not a sailor. Laura grabbed her phone from the bottom of her purse, only to discover there was no signal.

"Now what?" She couldn't just sit there. She had to either change the tire or hike back to the restaurant. With a frustrated moan, she located the lever to open the trunk and pulled. Just because she'd never changed a tire didn't mean she wasn't capable of learning.

Muttering to herself because she'd forgotten to bring an umbrella, she stepped out into the downpour. Holding her shawl above her head, she glared at the flat, left front tire. She frowned as several cars sped past.

She was wet and miserable by the time she managed to wrestle the spare tire and jack from beneath the floorboard and then out of the car. She let out a scream when she tripped, scraped her knee, and broke the heel of her favorite pink strapless sandal. Wiping away tears, she bit her lip, refusing to cry. She didn't need a headache on top of everything else!

She leaned on the car while struggling to put the jack together when another car pulled over and stopped. She debated the wisdom of remaining where she was or getting back inside and locking the doors and windows.

A man got out of the car. "Ms. Murdock?"

Surprised that he knew her name, she slowly straightened, using her hand to shield her eyes from the glare of his headlights. "Yes?"

"I'm Reynar Gardner. My mom sent me to make sure you got home safely."

"Thank Regina for me." She gave him a warm smile and hobbled over to him. "Hi, I'm Laura. As you can see, I'm having car trouble. I ran over something left in the road and punctured my tire."

"Are you hurt? Do you need to go to emergency?"

"Nothing serious." Laura quickly explained, "I tripped, broke my heel, and scraped my knee."

Reynar nodded. "Come, let's get you out of the rain and into my car. Then I'll see what can be done about that flat."

"Thanks," she said, thinking it was a shame Sherri Ann hadn't made the trip with her. Reynar was a bit young, but very handsome with those long, thick locks. Surprised when he picked her up and carried her to the passenger seat, once she was settled she said, "Forget about trying to fix my car tonight. I'm wet and cold. It can wait until morning and then I can arrange for someone to take care of it. Please just lock it up and give me a ride back to my villa."

"Certainly. Should I check the car? Do you have everything you need?"

"My purse! I left it on the console."

He nodded. "Be right back."

Wilham raised his arms over his head and stretched the stiff, tired muscles in his shoulders and spine. He'd been standing for hours, working nonstop. His eyes burned and his stomach growled. He swore, frustrated.

He'd done it again! He had been so focused on his work that he forgot all else. His concentration had been absolute and he lost touch with the world. Totally absorbed in the work, he didn't remember when he'd last eaten. And his throat was so parched, it hurt.

"What time is it?" Looking up through one of the glass skylights overhead, he studied the cloud-streaked night sky.

Evidently, he had been on auto-pilot, for he didn't recall turning on the lights that illuminated his studio. Determined to accurately get the image out of his head, and onto canvas, he had pushed everything and everyone away. Now he stood studying the work, struggling for a measure of objectivity. Finally, his weakened condition and physical needs forced him into action. Suddenly, he remembered eating an apple when he'd gotten home that morning.

That morning! "Laura!" She was bound to be annoyed. Had he said he would call? Had they made plans for the evening? Wasn't he supposed to take her out for dinner and dancing?

Wilham groaned and hung his head. He was so tired that he couldn't think, couldn't remember what they said that morning. His shoulders drooped as if he felt each of his forty-two years. His age was catching up with him. He wasn't a kid anymore. He couldn't stay out all night and work all day without feeling the effects.

He swore beneath his breath. Why hadn't he sent her flowers? It was the least he could have done, knowing he was going to be busy all day. She had to be upset because he hadn't called her today, especially after the night they shared. She had probably called him all kinds of names for neglecting her. Then he grinned as he imagined the very special, intimate way he could make it up to her.

He was beat but it would have to wait. First, he needed water and then food to recharge his body. Covering the canvas and switching off the studio lights, he headed to the kitchen. He also needed to shower and to change out of his sweaty T-shirt and paint-smeared jeans that would probably stand up on their own. Rubbing a stubbled jaw, he added a shave to his to-do list before he could see his lady.

"Laura," he said softly, smiling. He ached to see her, to hold her. What was this overwhelming need to be with her? Was this what Gordan felt for Cassy? Was this how his father had felt about his mother? He'd been warned that when the Kramer men loved, they did it full-out. But could this be the real thing? Could it be love?

They'd been apart only one day and yet he missed her. He needed to see her, kiss her, and hold her close.

Although keenly disappointed when he discovered she had gone out, Wilham smiled when he saw she'd left a lamp on. He frowned. He shouldn't expect her to sit inside and wait for him to show up. Laura was feisty despite her petite size. He loved that about her. Aw-oh, there was the "L" word again. He glanced at his watch.

It was nearly ten. Where was she? Who was she with? He scowled suddenly, not thrilled with the trend of his thoughts. Possessive? That had never been his style. Besides, Laura hadn't given him reason to question or doubt her.

They'd been together . . . what? One week! Yet, after only one night of making love to her, he was feeling as if she was part of him? Yet her absence reminded him of another time, another place, and another woman? Funny, he hadn't thought of his brother's ex in years.

Hell no! He was not about to let someone else's mistake trigger an old wound. Laura was nothing like Evie, his deceitful former sister-in-law. Nope, his lady was not one to sit back and let anyone dictate to her. Laura had a strong sense of right and wrong. She was her own person, unafraid to challenge or debate anyone, including him. Nor did she waste time playing manipulative games. If she had something to say, she said it. And he liked that about her.

Despite his old-fashioned views about women and honor, he knew he had no rights were she was concerned. What they'd started last night was brand-spanking-new. What they needed was time to be together. Time to get used to each other, time to understand their foibles. Time for trust and love, if they were extremely lucky, to take root and blossom.

Wilham grinned. He was more like his older brother than he realized. He was not afraid of what he was feeling. If this was what love looked like, felt like, and tasted like, then bring it on. He was willing to give it a fair shot.

At first he'd been bothered by her stance on marrying well. But that hadn't kept him away. Maybe because . . . he strongly suspected it had nothing to do with financial gain and something to do with growing up without a parent. Everyone had baggage, past issues. So what? He wasn't going to let his issues with trust or her need for security get in their way. Wilham made himself comfortable in a patio chair and settled back to wait.

Laura, his sweet peach, was special. He was glad

she wasn't like the other women he'd been involved with over the years. Despite what she claimed, Laura hadn't set out to trap him. He was deeply grateful that his lady didn't have a manipulative bone in her sweetly curved, sexy little body.

He smiled. She had given him the utmost pleasure. He wondered if she knew how deeply their lovemaking affected him. She was not like any other woman he'd encountered. And he was no monk. Yet he accepted she had touched a place deep inside him. She touched his heart. And he couldn't just walk away or pretend it wasn't significant. He hadn't been looking for love. But he was no fool. He intended on staying put until he could figure out what this was.

Shifting, he stretched out his long legs. He recalled his brother's exact words on the subject. "You'll know if she's the one. You will feel it in your heart."

Wilham remembered how upset Gordan had been when Cassy broke it off with him. Cassy wanted marriage and babies. Gordan had been there and done that. She wasn't wasting any more time on a man who flatly refused to remarry. Distracted by the glare of headlights and the crunch of a car's tires over the gravel in the drive, Wilham watched a beige SUV stop in the drive. It wasn't her small rental car.

Wilham suddenly heard the car door open and a deep male voice said, "Hold on a second. I'll be right there."

Assuming it was the couple in the next villa over, Wilham didn't look up until he heard Laura say, "All right, but it's not raining. Look, the ground isn't even wet."

He heard a door slam shut, followed by footsteps moving across the gravel. Filled with disappointment and deep hurt, Wilham quickly got to his feet. By the time they reached the walkway, his hands were clenched and balled at his sides. His normal cool, easy-going manner vanished, replaced by anger.

He couldn't see them until they emerged from the shadows into the low light spilling across the porch. He was outraged when he saw that Laura was in Reynar's arms, a slim arm around the younger man's neck.

"Reynar, Laura," Wilham said tightly, stepping into the light.

"Wil!" Laura gasped, pressing a hand over her heart. "Goodness! Why are you here? I didn't expect to see you."

"Yeah, I figured as much." Looking pointedly at the other man, he demanded, "What's going on? How long have the two of you been seeing each other? And why are you carrying her?"

The younger man swallowed, cleared his throat before he said, "Sebastian. It's not what you think. Laura had—"

Laura interrupted, her tone sharp. "You've said more than enough, Wilham! Reynar, thank you. You can put me down now. I can make it on my own from here."

"You're hurt?" Wilham had just noticed her bloody knee, bare feet, and damp clothing. "What happened?"

Once she was on her feet, she sent Wilham a sharp glare but didn't bother answering.

Looking uncomfortable, Reynar quickly told him about the sudden storm in the hills, his mother asking him to check on Laura, and finding her on the side of the road with a punctured tire.

Wilham apologized to Reynar, and thanked him for coming to Laura's rescue.

Muttering beneath her breath, she limped toward

the door, carrying her shoes, shawl, and purse. Wilham reached to take her arm, but she hissed, "Don't touch me!"

"Peaches . . ."

"Go away! I've said all I intend to say to you. Ever!"

Sixteen

Shaking with fury, Laura shifted to avoid him and nearly lost her balance. He swiftly lifted her off her feet.

Furious, she snapped, "Put me down! I don't want your help." If he thought she was so desperate for a man that she'd let him use and discard her like a broken toy, he'd better think again. How dare he just show up and pretend everything was fine? "I said . . . !"

Wilham didn't speak until they reached the door. "Your key."

Frustrated, she found the key in the bottom of her small purse.

He asked, "Why do women carry such small purses at night? You can fit next to nothing in them."

She concentrated on fitting the key into the lock in the hope of getting rid of him as soon as possible. "I'm inside, safe and sound. Now please put me down and leave."

To her relief, he put her down on the love seat. Even though she could feel his gaze when he straightened, she didn't so much as look at him.

Quietly, he said, "Laura, I'm sorry. I was wrong to

accuse you of seeing Reynar behind my back. I was jealous and assumed the worse. You've never given me reason to doubt you."

When she didn't respond, he reached to take her hand but she jerked away, and folded her arms beneath her breasts.

"Sweetheart, listen. The thought of you hurt and alone on the road at night makes me break out in a cold sweat. Why didn't you call me? If not for Regina, you could have been stranded all night."

When she remained silent, he sighed. "Laura, I know you're angry with me for jumping to conclusions. It was a stupid mistake. And I'm sorry." He asked, "Where's your first aid kit? Your knee's bleeding."

"I don't need your help."

"You might as well tell me because I'm not leaving until your knee has been bandaged and we've talked."

"It's in the medicine cabinet in the bathroom," she said tightly. She drummed her fingers on the seat cushion while she waited.

When he returned he had the first aid kit as well as a damp wash towel. Dropping down on his haunches, he placed the warm, damp cloth over her injury. "Does it hurt?" He gently cleaned the wound.

"No," she lied. Nothing he did now could make up for what he'd done that morning.

He wiped the knee with a premoistened alcohol cloth, causing her to hiss from the sudden sting. He covered the wound with an adhesive-edged gauze pad. "See, that wasn't so bad," he said softly, brushing his lips over her cheek.

"Don't!"

"Yeah, I know. You don't want me touching you. Yet you can't say you didn't welcome the pleasure I gave you last night." He sighed. "Talk to me, Laura. Tell me what's really going on here."

"You tell me! You're the one who ended things this morning, not me. What I don't understand is why you came back tonight. What? Did you get horny? Decide I might be good for more than a one-night stand after all?"

"What?"

"You heard correctly. Why did you come back?"

Incredulous, Wilham said, "Where did you get the idea that all I want was one night? Was that why you encouraged Reynar?"

Laura huffed. "Encouraged Reynar? Hardly! I went out to dinner alone. Leave him out of this. He isn't responsible for what you said this morning before you walked out on me."

"What did I say to make you think all I wanted was one night with you? Or that I wasn't coming back?" When she didn't answer, he said, "Sweetheart, you misunderstood."

"No, you were very clear. You got exactly what you wanted. I posed for you and we had sex. It's over. Feel free to leave. And don't let the door hit you on the way out."

Laura took several deep breaths in the hope of calming down. She silently reminded herself that she was a lady. She wasn't going to start screaming her head off like a banshee. He might not know it, but she did. She deserved better than this rich, spoiled playboy!

To her relief, he walked out the door. Instead of heading for his car, she watched him walk around to the rear patio, circling the villa, not once but three times. Before she thought to go close and lock the front door, his tall frame filled the entrance, a scowl creasing his dark bronze forehead.

Leaning a shoulder against the door frame, he said, "I've gone over everything I said to you this morning. And I can't figure out what made you think I wanted out." He shook his head. "We made love. I don't know about you, but it was the best I've ever had. Laura, we just found each other. Why would I want to let that go?" Although baffled, he held up a hand to stop her protest. "Let me finish. Laura, I care about you. I've done nothing but think of you the entire time we were apart. No way would just I walk away. No way!"

"You said—"

"I said I had to go. Then I kissed you and promised to see you later. I've been in my studio working. Yeah, I admit I forgot the time, but . . ." He took a breath before he said, "Sweetheart, you misunderstood. Hell, no! I'm not giving you up!"

"But you said we were done! That you didn't need me to—" Laura stopped. Was it possible? Could she have been wrong about him?

"I don't care what I said. I didn't mean it the way you thought." Suddenly, he straightened. "Come on. Let's go."

"I'm not going anywhere with you!" She folded her arms beneath her breasts.

"Sure you are. I have something to show you. It won't take long. And I promise to bring you back later, if that's what you want." When she didn't move, he asked, "What are you afraid of?"

"Nothing!"

"Then let's go." He held out his hand.

"I'll come but I won't stay long. Nothing you show

me is going to change my mind. But first I need to take a shower and change out of these damp clothes. You can wait outside on the porch."

"Take your time." He walked out and closed the door.

Although tempted to punish him by leaving him out there waiting all night, she hobbled into the bedroom and locked the door.

The steamy shower soothed her tired body and eased the pain in her injured knee. She was limping when she joined him, dressed in black shorts, a pink St. John's T-shirt, and a pair of pink ballet slippers. She hadn't bothered with reapplying her makeup, but she'd taken the time to blow-dry her braids. She still wore the pearl stud earrings and thin gold bangles.

She said tightly, "I'm ready."

He nodded.

On the way to his home, Laura silently brooded. It wasn't until they were nearing his road that her patience snapped. "I can't see what possible difference my coming to your place can make. Nothing is going to change what happened. I changed my mind. Turn around and take me back."

Much to her annoyance, Wilham continued on as if she hadn't spoken. By the time they stopped in his drive, she was furious.

"This is crazy!" she yelled. She got out and slammed the passenger door as hard as she could. With her chin high, her spine straight, and her cheeks hot with embarrassment because she'd completely lost it, she limped to the front door. She was so upset she was close to taking off her shoes and flinging them at his head.

Every step she took, she silently blamed him for everything that had gone wrong. If he had just kept his lips and hands to himself and off her, they wouldn't be here. To make matters worse, she knew Mrs. Green would have been mortified if she could see her huffing like an angry bull. He wasn't worth losing her dignity. No man was.

She didn't so much as look his way as she limped her way to his studio. She did glance at him when he stopped in front of a large covered canvas.

Wilham said, "Last night after we made love, you fell asleep but I didn't . . ." He paused. ". . . because I couldn't stop thinking about you . . . couldn't stop looking at you. You were so beautiful. I thought of the various sketches I'd done of you. None of them seemed right.

"I have so many sketches of you. I was frustrated because day after day I've tried and failed to put on paper what I see when I look at you. Laura, you're very special to me. Your energy and exuberance for life are like no one else. Then there is your deep respect and appreciation for the beauty of the land and the earth. You also have a wealth of compassion for others, all qualities that I deeply admire. As I watched you sleeping, my head was filled with images of you. Now that my body was finally sated from our lovemaking, I suddenly knew why the sketches and the pastels I've done this past week weren't enough. Something wasn't quite right. I knew then I could not get any rest until I got this image of you out of my head and onto the canvas. And I needed to do it in rich, vibrant oil colors."

Wilham lifted her chin until he could see her dark eyes, before he admitted, "I didn't want to leave, not after what we shared. I wanted to bundle you up and take you with me. I also know I've been incredibly selfish. I monopolized your time. It was my fault that you were exhausted from days of little sleep. You needed the rest. And I was burning to paint you. I almost left without waking you but I thought better of it. Laura, I didn't mean to hurt you.

"I admit I was very distracted. Mentally, I was going over the composition, the light, the shadows, what colors I needed, every detail so nothing would be overlooked. When you asked about posing, I automatically said no. I came straight home while the sun was at the right place in the sky. Once I started I couldn't stop, not until it was finished." Quickly removing the covering, he said, "Be honest. Tell me what you think."

Laura stared at the canvas until her eyes burned and filled with unexpected tears. She couldn't believe what she saw. The painting was so incredibly beautiful, rich with details. There was no doubt it was she. Her braided hair, her skin, even her curves were flawless.

Her heart began to pound as she looked at herself as he must see her. She marveled at what he had created. Was it true? Was this really what he saw when he looked at her? Impossible! She had never looked that good in her entire life.

Deeply moved and touched by what he'd painted, Laura slowly turned to look at Wilham. He wasn't looking at the painting. And he was far from calm. His shoulders were tight, his teeth clenched, even his hands restlessly opened and closed into fists. His unease touched something deep inside and forced her to acknowledge she had been wrong about him. He valued her and wanted her approval.

"Well?" he said.

"I can't believe it's me," she managed to say in a whisper, reaching out to touch the canvas but jerking back. She closed her fingers into a fist and rested it against her heart.

"Of course it's you. But do you—" He stopped.

Blinking away tears, Laura turned toward him and wrapped her arms around his lean waist. She rested her head on his chest. And she held on to him.

"Wil, it's beautiful. I've never seen anything so lovely. I still can't believe my eyes. I wished I looked half as good." Her laughter rose skyward, bubbling up inside her. "I was wrong about you. I'm so sorry. It hurt this morning when you said you didn't need me to pose anymore. It felt as if you were . . ." She hesitated, her throat clogged with emotions. She swallowed, knowing she owed him the truth. ". . . as if you were done with me. That you'd gotten what you wanted from me and I no longer interest you. All the old hurts came rushing back. I felt as if I'd done it again, slept with a man who didn't care about me. That I was reliving my past. I'd already made that mistake twice, once in high school and again after college, when I was in grad school."

"Twice?"

Laura nodded. She had held it inside for so long that she wanted it gone. "I was only fifteen when I fell in love with a boy who lived down the block from us. Johnnie had dropped out of school. He would meet me at the bus stop and walk me home in the evening after cheerleading practice. He was older, seventeen, good-looking. All the girls had a crush on him. He spent the days hanging out on the streets." She paused before she said, "My foster sisters warned me about him, but I wouldn't listen. He made me feel special. He flirted with me, told me I was pretty and that he loved me. I fell hard for him. I believed we were in love. He begged me to have sex with him. Finally I said yes. It was over for him once he got inside my panties. He'd won the bet. I didn't understand. I still thought we were in love until he'd bragged to anyone who would listen that he'd slept with me and how much he had won. I was devastated. And to make matters worse, for a couple of weeks I thought I might be pregnant. Mrs. Green was so disappointed in me. She told me that I picked someone who couldn't afford to buy me a hamburger, let alone diapers for the baby. She couldn't understand why I didn't realize I deserved much better."

"Wow! No wonder you were hurt."

She nodded. "She was right. I did deserve better. I was lucky that I was only late and not pregnant."

"You are too hard on yourself. You forget you were young and in love."

"I was a fool. Let me tell you the rest before I chicken out." When he nodded, she rushed on to say, "By the time I was in college I thought I knew all I needed to know about men. Most of them were willing to say and do anything to get a girl into bed. I dated but steered clear of love until I was out of college and working on my master's when I met Brad at a mutual friend's birthday party. We dated but it quickly spiraled into much more. He said the things I wanted to hear. He was part of a large, loving family. He was ambitious and on the fast track in his law firm. He started talking about marriage and a family. He pressured me into being intimate, even though I didn't enjoy it.

"He complained about my being too slow in my responses to him in the bedroom. But, I was sure this was love. And our problems would work out. He was ambitious and wanted a large family also. About that time, he won a big case, impressed the head of the firm.

He was excited because he was being groomed by the boss, invited to lunch and dinners with his boss and his family. He was making a new circle of friends that did not include me.

"By this time, I was busy, close to graduating, and working long hours. I didn't know there was a problem until a week before his engagement to the boss's daughter was announced he broke it off with me. He claimed I was the problem. I was cold in bed. He needed more. Once again, I was humiliated. Only this time it was much worse because I was older, supposed to know better."

She shuddered at the memory. "I seem to have a knack for picking the wrong guy. Last night, we wanted each other."

She didn't add that she evidently wouldn't recognize the right one unless he smacked her on the head. For self-preservation, she had written down what she wanted in a man and developed a plan. She had stuck to the plan until last night. "I don't know what happened last night. How we ended up in bed. But when you woke me, ready to leave, my issues with men all came back. So when you said you didn't need me anymore, I knew it was happening all over again. It hurt and made me furious. I'm sorry I assumed the absolute worst." She sighed heavily. "I'm not sure who I was most angry with, you or me. When you left, I knew you weren't coming back."

She confessed, "And then you didn't call all day. I refused to spend the evening here brooding." She touched his arm. "I couldn't believe my eyes when you stepped out of the shadows. I'm sorry, Wilham. I put the blame on you. It was wrong. You didn't force me into making love with you."

Wilham brushed his lips over hers. He teased, "Can I say something now?"

Laura smiled, nodding. "Anything you would like, sweet man. That painting is exquisite." She went up on tiptoes to kiss the base of his throat before she tongued the spot.

He shivered and tightened his arms around her. He leaned down and covered her lips with his. It was a deep, tongue-stroking exchange that left them both trembling with desire.

"I'm glad you like the painting. I made it for you to take back with you, a reminder of our time on the island."

Laura squealed with delight and threw her arms up to bring him back down so that she could kiss him again. "I love, love it. I don't know how to thank you!"

Chuckling, he arched a brow. "You don't have to thank me. I hope when you look at it you will think of our time here."

Unable to find the words to express her feelings, she caressed his cheek. She was bombarded with so many emotions that she was unable to sort them out.

"Come, let's go for a swim." He took her hand.

"But I didn't bring a suit."

His eyes twinkled when he said, "You won't need one."

She smiled but shook her head. "It's too far with this sore knee."

"No worries." He swept her up so quickly she giggled. "How's that for service?"

"Wonderful," she crooned, locking her arms around his neck.

He took her out the French doors down the few steps over to the pool.

The pool was lit by soft light around the rim. He carried her into the cabana and set her down in a chair. He quickly undressed them both.

She blushed. "But Cora or Daniel might see . . ."

"I gave them the day off. I didn't want to be disturbed while I worked. No one is here, just us. Ready?"

"Yes," she said, smiling, but her cheeks were hot.

He tossed several towels over his shoulder before he carried her out.

Laughing, they jumped into the deep end, feet first. Laura came up first and he clasped her around the waist.

"You okay?"

She smiled. "I'm better. The water is warm, soothing."

"Does it sting?"

"Not enough to keep me from enjoying myself." She laughed and started swimming.

"How old were you when you learned to swim?"

"We were little when Mrs. Green took us to the YWCA for lessons. In the summers we went nearly every day. How about you?"

"My brother taught me. Because he worked at a hotel, the pool was always available."

They swam laps until she urged him to keep going while she flipped onto her back and floated. When he finished his laps, he came up beside her.

"Enough for me. I'm turning into a prune," she teased.

To her surprise, he tossed her up and onto his shoulder and carried her out fireman-style.

"You are a caveman." She was still giggling when he put her down in the cabana bathroom. "With no shame!"

He chuckled, urging her ahead of him into the stall. Her eyes met his when he joined her a few minutes later. She did not see he'd put on a condom.

Wilham covered her mouth with his, pulling them beneath the warm spray of the wide multihead shower.

"Too warm?" he asked.

"Please don't stop," she said, locking her arms around his neck and urging his head down to meet her lips.

But he lifted her up until she was clinging to him. She moaned as desire raced throughout her system and into her nerve endings. She tingled, she ached. She wasn't thinking about the past or the future. All she knew was that she wanted him so badly she was shaking with need. She called out his name when he pressed her spine against the tile as he guided her down onto his erection.

Laura closed her eyes, wrapping her legs around his waist, taking him deep into her moist passage. She clung to his shoulders. She quickly lost touch with her surroundings. She moaned and cried out at as one release was immediately followed by another climax, even more poignant because it was shared. His hoarse shout mingled with her soft moans. They held on to each other until the storm passed.

It wasn't until afterward she started to worry as he moved his soapy hands over her.

She whispered, "We forgot to use protection."

He kissed her. "No worries. I remembered."

She let out a pent-up breath. "Thank you."

"No, thank you," he said as he dried them off with a towel. When she shivered, he said, "I'd better get you inside before you got a chill."

They dressed and he carried her into his bedroom. They made love again before he turned off the lights.

He held her. She was nearly asleep when he kissed her temple. "I don't know what's happening between us, sweet Laura. But I'm in no hurry for it to end."

She mumbled inaudibly before she fell asleep with her head on his shoulder.

Seventeen

She woke to the feel of his lips on her nape. She had rolled onto her stomach. "Is it morning yet?"

"Not yet. Your hair is still damp."

"No, don't go," she murmured when she felt the bed shift.

He placed a kiss on the back of her bare shoulder. "Be right back."

She smiled when she felt the warmth of the blow-dryer as he moved it over her braids. She was relaxed, snuggled against the pillow. When he was done, she thanked him.

"You are welcome, but there is no need, I enjoy spoiling you."

She turned her head toward him. "Can't sleep?"

"I slept for a few hours. But I'm an early riser. This morning I've been watching you and thinking."

"About?" she prompted.

"We're both guilty of letting the past influence the present. I was only a kid when my brother's first wife, Evie, taught me a hard lesson about love and relationships. I was young but it stuck. Relationships can be complicated."

"Really?" Laura teased, hoping to lighten the mood. "Let's make a pact. Not to take this thing between us seriously. We're having fun. Why not just enjoy the time we have? No worries about the future. Okay?"

"You didn't feel that way last night," he remarked.

"I know. And I was wrong. Come on, Wil. We only have two weeks, and then I'm going home, back to my real world. Besides, we both know you aren't interested in commitment, marriage, or babies. And I certainly don't want to fall for an international player who's busy leaving a trail of broken hearts behind." Laughing, she poked him in his ribs, saying, "Why not forget the rest of the world and go with the flow? Enjoy our island fling?"

Chuckling, he tightened his arms around her and brushed his lips against hers. "Island fling, hmm," he crooned in her ear. Then he warned, "It sounds good. But reality can sneak up and smack you upside the head if you are not careful."

He went on to tell her how Gordan met Evie while in college and they married quickly. "The marriage proved to be a mistake. Evie not only lied to my brother's face while cheating behind his back, but she tried to force me to keep quiet and help her conceal other men. My brother was working day and night to build the company and secure our future. Her scheme backfired when she badly underestimated my loyalty and keen sense of right and wrong. I was young but nobody's fool. It was the hardest thing I've ever done, telling Gordan the truth."

"She expected you to keep her secret?"

"My nephew was only a baby. I watched him while she was out prowling. For a short time I kept quiet because I couldn't stand to see my brother hurt. But she got too bold, brought some guy into our home. That's when I realized I had no choice. I had to tell."

"Wow!" Laura hugged him, and kissed his throat. "That's terrible. I'm so sorry."

"The experience made it hard for me to trust. Just as your past has made it difficult for you to believe I was coming back." He stroked her hair. "Laura, after we made love that first time, I knew what we had was special. What we shared doesn't happen every day. I care about you. And I suspect you care about me."

"Yes, but that doesn't mean . . ." Her voice trailed away. She trembled, afraid of what these feelings might mean. Her future was already planned out. He didn't fit into her plan, just as she didn't fit into his world. She warned softly, "Wil, please. Let's not go there. Let's not confuse the past with the present. It only causes complications we don't need. I want to relax and enjoy the moment, not worry about the future. Don't you see all we really have is the moment. The future is not promised."

"Relax, sweetheart. No worries," Wilham murmured close to her ear in a deep, gravelly voice. "We're together and that's all that matters. And you feel so good in my arms."

He soothed her with gentle kisses; he started at her forehead and continued down to her soft, kiss-swollen lips. He didn't stop until her curvy body was once again soft, pliable against him.

She sighed. "Yes, no worries."

Wrapped in each other's arms, Wilham and Laura made slow, sweet love, then slipped into deep, restorative sleep.

* * *

When Laura acknowledged it was her last full day on the island she was very upset. She was leaving the next morning, but didn't want to go home. The day passed much too swiftly. And she did her best not to think about leaving.

Much later, walking on the beach with her fingers laced with Wilham's, she sighed wearily.

As a breeze ruffled the hem of her long skirt she felt a dull ache in her stomach, but knew it wasn't a result of the romantic meal they shared at his home. And her heart wasn't pounding in anticipation of a night of lovemaking. What she was experiencing was a combination of deep sadness mixed with dread of their final parting, and she hated having to say good-bye.

She'd gotten so good at enjoying each moment that she'd ruthlessly pushed thoughts of the future away. She'd done an excellent job of forgetting her reasons for not getting involved with Wilham. Those reasons had returned to taunt her all day and hadn't eased even though it was their final night together in paradise. She also didn't want to recall how wrong they were for each other! Not tonight!

She was tired of rationalizing why her flying back home was for the best. No matter how good looking he was or how knowledgeable he was about the art world and how much she admired his artistic skills, that didn't change simple facts. Yes, they had fun together and their lovemaking was intense. None of those things mattered. She and Wilham didn't fit into each other's lives.

In the morning their idyllic days and nights would be behind them. And they both would go their separate ways.

For years she had known what she wanted but hadn't pursued it. She had allowed her job to become a major distraction and divert her attention away from her personal goal. It was time to change that and get serious about her future. She still wanted that big family she'd dreamed about as a girl. She needed to find her Mr. Right. An overachiever with ruthless intent, whose instincts demanded he fight to hold on to what he treasured most. A man who valued family above all else. As soon as she got back it would be time to get serious. No more delays.

In the meantime they still had hours left to enjoy. And she wanted to spend every second of it in her island lover's arms.

His steps slowed to a stop and he drew her against his lean length. He whispered, "A penny for your thoughts."

Laura teased, "My thoughts are worth a lot more." She tilted her head back so she could memorize his bronze face in the moonlight.

"Several million pennies," he crooned in her ear.

She laughed. "That's more like it," she said, and wrapped her arms around his waist. She gave him a squeeze. "It's such a beautiful night. A night for lovers. Kiss me, Wil. Please."

"With pleasure," he murmured, lowering his head until their lips brushed and then lingered. The kiss was heady, full of anticipation.

They had spent the entire day together. He'd taken her out sailing to a beautiful private cove, where they'd played in the surf, shared a romantic picnic on the beach. Then they went back to his place because they wanted to be alone. Cora had prepared a special dinner and left them to it, while island music played in the background.

Laura hid her sadness behind a smile, ignoring un-settled emotions. So what if she was a bit clingy? She refused to cry. Tears would change nothing.

Looking up at him, she was dizzy with longing, her legs a bit unsteady, and she tingled deep inside wanting him. She pushed aside his shirt and kissed his chest, briefly licked his skin. She smiled when he moaned.

Laura softly urged, "Wil, let's go to the villa."

He tenderly cupped her face. "Not so fast. I can't let this moment pass without telling you how much you mean to me."

Her face heated as she recalled the intimate ways he'd shown her that morning how much he wanted her, "I know you want me and I want you. Let's go back now and enjoy the night."

"Soon, Peaches. Our time on the island has been very special, but this final week seemed to have van-ished at top speed. Tomorrow you will . . ."

Reaching up on tiptoe to press a kiss at the base of his throat, she whispered, "Don't, my sweet island man. Please don't spoil it. Remember, we promised no talk about the past or the future."

He chuckled, just as he always did at the endear-ment. His kiss was slow and deep before he playfully bit her full bottom lip.

"I've honored that promise. Whether we talk about it or not, my sweet peach, the sun is going to rise in the morning. Perfection for me means to start the new day watching you sleep curled against me while the sun rises in the sky," he said huskily. Then Wilham surprised her when he vowed, "Someday I'm going to paint you that way, lying on your side, your back to my front and your cheek resting on my arm. You look so lovely, in nothing more than the sheet draped over your lush curves, your skin the color of delicious dark cara-mel, and your braids a cascading cloud around your shoulders."

Laura smiled, recalling waking against him. But then she frowned, heart suddenly heavy because she had to accept that tomorrow would be their very last sunrise together. She would be alone in her home the next time she woke to the sun.

Wilham whispered into her ear, "I love you, Laura Jean Murdock. I want to wake each morning with you beside me. Marry me. Be my heart, be my love."

With her eyes closed, she had been focusing on the rich cadence in his deep, sexy voice, and the unique scent of his skin, but not on the actual words. The in-stant the meaning of those words registered, Laura's large brown eyes opened wide, brimming with a mix-ture of incredible joy, shock, and utter disbelief.

For a time, she merely stared at him, too stunned to respond. She rejected the joy, instead concentrated on his question. She didn't realize that she was shaking her head no as she eased out from his embrace.

"Did you just ask . . ."

"Yes."

She scolded, "Wilham Sebastian Kramer! Don't play with me!"

"I know it's a shock, but, dear heart, you aren't the only one surprised. I can't believe it either. But it's true. I love you. I'm still reeling from the discovery." He said seriously, "I didn't see this coming. But the past three weeks have felt like being hit by a hurricane! Every single thing that has happened between us has been fast and furious. Believe me, I didn't plan any of it." After tucking a braid behind her ear, he said as he snapped his fingers, "Just that fast, it happened. Laura, I'm in love with you. And the fact that you are leaving tomorrow has left me no choice but to deal with it."

She was shaken and in the icy grip of fear and anger. "Wil! Didn't I just ask you not to go there? Now look what you've done! You've spoiled our last night together! Why did you say anythi—" Her voice trembled and broke.

"You're upset? Why? Because I'm in love with you? Or that I want you to be my wife? They are not just words, Laura. I mean it. I don't want you to go home tomorrow. Stay and marry me. When we leave this island, I want the entire world to know that we're married and belong together."

She shook her head vehemently, struggling for control of her emotions. She silently screamed, *No! No! This couldn't be happening.*

Struggling for control, finally, she hissed, "You can't love me because you don't know me. There are a million and one things that I'm not proud of. I can be terribly selfish. I'm bossy. I like having my way. And I detest the very idea of compromise."

"Doesn't matter. I love you."

"No, you don't! Did you hear what I said?" She threw up her arms, gesturing wildly. "It's this place! All this darn moonlight and these stars! It's this island. Beautiful beaches, only steps away from the Caribbean. It may look like paradise but it can be deadly to your emotions. It messes you up until you have no idea what you really think and feel."

"Laura!"

Frantic, she said, "Wil! This is crazy. You evidently drank too much wine at dinner! This place can be overwhelming. It has you saying and doing things that under normal circumstances you would never let out of your mouth. Believe me. In the morning, you're going to regret every word. Please, please let's pretend it didn't happen."

She turned so quickly that she nearly lost her balance. She managed to right herself before he could touch her. "I'm going back to the car."

She started walking, trying to fill the thick void with mindless chatter. "The sand looks so pretty, so white, but I've never liked the way it feels between my toes. And sandals are so flattering."

When she looked back she realized he hadn't moved. He stood as if frozen in place. "Wil, come on. It's getting late. And we've both said too much."

His voice was deceptively soft when he said, "Laura, stop. The car's the other way. And you're wrong. In the morning, I won't regret telling you how I feel."

She stopped but she didn't look at him. She couldn't, not without breaking down. Her emotions were too close to the surface. Even though she was uncomfortable with his silence, she preferred it to his vowing his love. It was their last night. And now they both were upset. He didn't love her any more than she loved him!

Wilham walked with her. She was shaking and would welcome his support but she didn't ask. For a long time, neither spoke. Instead, they listened to the soft roar of the sea rushing along the shoreline. The caressing warmth of the trade winds ruffled their clothes and the long, thin leaves of a nearby palm tree.

It was their last night. She longed to turn, press her body against his, and beg him to make love to her right then and there. She wanted him inside her, wanted to hear his steady heartbeat.

"You are right," Wilham finally said. "This place can be magical, even hypnotic. But it takes a hell of a lot more than a few glasses of wine or a beautiful night to get me to say the things I've told you tonight." He cupped her shoulders before he said close to her ear, his breath heating her throat, "Please, Laura. Just listen. Let me finish."

"But—" She stopped, choking from conflicting emotions, and her eyes burned from suppressed tears. No! She wasn't going to cry! Not now. Why was he making it so hard for her? He knew about her plan, her agenda for the future. No matter how many times he said it, she knew it wasn't true. He couldn't love her. He'd never been in love before.

They'd known each other only a few short weeks. Everyone knew true love took time to mature and had to be nurtured. Besides, love alone offered no guarantees. And love also hurt. She'd learned that hard lesson too early.

"Laura, stop and listen to me."

"No! Why are you doing this, Wil? You know about my plans. And you know how important it is for me to find the right man. My entire future depends on me getting it right. I'm not going to let you or anyone else stop me from reaching my goal. I want a home and babies. Family means everything to me."

"Yeah, I know all that, but—"

"No buts, Wilham Sebastian. Just because this wild, romantic thing started the day we met doesn't mean anything lasting can come from it." She lifted a hand and caressed his cheek. "It has been an incredible ride, my sweet island man. It was so easy being swept up in St. John's magic. But it has to end right where it started. When my plane takes off in the morning, I will be leaving you and paradise behind.

"If we're honest with each other, then we'll both

admit I don't fit into your world any more than you fit into mine. Tonight's our last night together. It's supposed to be special. Please, Wil. I don't want it to end badly."

"Laura, why can't you see that it doesn't have to end? Peaches, I'm the one. I can give you everything you want and so much more than you could possibly dream of. If you'll just give us a chance, trust me to love you."

She interrupted, "You're not listening!"

"No, Laura. You're the one not listening."

When she tried to put some distance between them, he tightened his hands on her shoulders.

"I know you're not ready to say yes tonight. I get it's too soon for you. But you're wrong about me. I won't ever regret anything we've shared these past few weeks." He teased, "Dear heart, you may be tiny, but you have so much heart and so much courage." He laughed before he said, "Plus, you're gorgeous and so smart. Laura, you've been through a lot and been hurt by *boys*, not men, who didn't know the first thing about love, commitment, and loyalty. Because of them, you've got your heart set on marrying some rich guy that you've convinced yourself can give you the security you crave. Laura, what about love? Where does love fit into your plan?"

She accused, "You don't understand!"

"I understand why you feel this way. You still haven't answered my question. Where does love fit into your plans? What if Mr. Right has all the qualities that you want but you don't love him? What then?"

"Stop it! There's nothing wrong with my plan. I'm not excluding love. It just may not be my number one consideration, but it's there. I have no doubts that once I find him I will love him. Marrying well isn't a game to me, Wilham. I'm serious about this. Stop judging me!"

"I'm not. Your path has not been easy or smooth. You grew up without parents to back you up. You did well for yourself. It's no accident that you're well educated, successful, and determined to give back. I'm proud of you, Laura."

Stunned by how much his approval meant to her, she mumbled a hasty "Thank you."

He smiled. "You're welcome. All I'm asking is for a fair shot at winning your heart."

Eighteen

Laura, all I'm asking is that you open your mind to the possibility. I'm in love with you! And I think you feel the same way about me. I wouldn't be pushing so hard if I didn't believe that. You're not the type to climb into bed with a man you don't care about."

"You're talking about sex. We slept together, so what? Wil, for goodness' sake, that doesn't mean we should start picking out china patterns."

"It means you have feelings for me. Please don't take this the wrong way. But the first time we made love I knew there was something unusual between us. I didn't call it love because I'd never experienced it before. It wasn't until later that I realized it was love."

Laura was doing her best to hold it together. Showing any signs of emotion would be viewed as weakness. Refusing to back down, she insisted, "You're talking about sex, Wil, not love."

"I'm saying your sweet body told me all I need to know about your feelings for me, Laura. You've made no secret that I give you pleasure whenever we make love."

She flung her hands out in a helpless gesture. "Fine.

Now that we've established you're an exceptional lover and you made me climax, can we drop it?"

Undeterred, he said, "Being together here on the island has been wonderful." He bent forward until his forehead touched hers and he clasped her hands. "Like a slice of heaven." He confessed, "I don't want it to end. I realize tonight is too soon to decide. That you need more time." Cradling her face tenderly, he whispered, "It has taken me years to find you. Maybe we can come up with a compromise?"

"What kind of a compromise?"

He rubbed his thumb over the bare finger of her left hand. "I don't want you to leave until we come to an understanding. Will you wear my engagement ring? Will you give us a chance, prove what started on the island doesn't have to end?"

Before she could answer, Wilham gave her a deep, tender kiss. "Please say you will give us a chance. You will never be sorry. You can trust me to honor you, care for you, and keep you safe . . . always. Please don't let some preconceived plan keep us apart. Trust me, Laura."

Her eyes locked with his while her heart pounded a combination of fear and hope. This was a huge risk. He was asking her to set aside carefully made plans for a secure future without offering any guarantees in return. Take a chance? Wear his ring? No! He was asking her to risk it all after knowing each other for only a few short weeks. He asked too much when she wasn't sure how she felt about him.

"I can't!" she said, fighting back tears. "A good marriage should last a lifetime. Wil, we barely know each other. We're so different. We don't want the same things from life. My answer has to be no."

"If you're worried about me being able to take care of you and our family, don't. I'm a wealthy man."

"That's not the point. Look, we both knew right from the start that you aren't the right man for me. There're a boatload of reasons why we can't make it work. The most obvious being, your home is here in the Virgin Islands while mine is in Detroit. You're a gifted artist who travels the world for inspiration. People are deeply touched by your work. My work with teen girls in foster care means a great deal to me, so does helping rape victims and giving abused women and children hope for a better future. I'm needed in Detroit. No, it can't work. We'd never see each other! Besides, my future has been planned. I refuse to settle for less."

Wilham said harshly, "Where is he? This ideal guy. Damn it, if you are so sure he's the one, then produce him!"

"He's out there!"

"He doesn't exist!"

"That's not true!"

"Did he hold you last night? Did he make love to you until you were so weak from pleasure you could hardly keep your eyes open? That was me deep inside of you last night. Me! Loving you until you screamed and climaxed in my arms."

"Shut up!"

"How can you be sure I'm not Mr. Right? What makes you think I don't have a multimillion-dollar portfolio to back me up?"

"I never said—"

"It's what you're thinking. But the crazy part of your plan, Laura, is that the money doesn't really matter to you. If money mattered, you would already have sunk your hooks into one of those millionaire pro ballplayers you met last year!"

She gasped.

"Laura, admit it. It's not about money! It has never been about money for you. I suspect it has more to do with trust than anything else," he surmised.

She pulled away. "You've said enough!"

"I haven't finished."

"It doesn't matter what you believe. You're not my type! And I can't make you understand without being crude. So let's just drop it now."

"Do us both a favor, Laura. Make your point. At least that way I'll know what you really think."

She hesitated, determined not to let her temper get the best of her. He was right about one thing. She cared too much about him. It was her fault. She'd let him get too close. Now he thought he knew her. But he was wrong.

"Go ahead!"

"I said no!" She walked away and didn't slow down until she reached the car. "Please just open the door and start the car."

They didn't speak as they got inside and clicked seat belts into place. The tension inside of the car was thick as they both waited to see who would break the silence.

When he didn't start the car she finally said, "We're totally unsuitable. Can we please leave it at that?"

"I deserve an answer! Tell me what Mr. Right has that I don't."

"Fine!" she hissed. "I'm looking for a self-made man, who's had to claw his way to the top. Not someone who had everything handed to him by a wealthy relative. Everyone knows Gordan Kramer built the

Kramer brand into a billion-dollar company. Given a choice, I'd rather marry your older brother."

He snarled in cold fury, "I'm sorry to disappoint you, Laura. But my brother's already married to the love of his life."

"See, I told you that you wouldn't like it."

Staring straight ahead, he finally said, "It's time you knew all of it. I'm aware of some of the false information that's been printed in the press, broadcasted by the media, and put online. Yes, Gordan built Kramer Corporation. I was only a teenager when he sat me down and explained that he wanted to mortgage the home we jointly owned and take that money, plus what our folks had set aside for my education. I was young but I understood the risk and I supported my brother. My name was also on that deed.

"Times were hard. First our father had died in a trucking accident and then we lost our mother a few years later to heart failure. Gordan was eighteen but he stepped up. He raised me while working nights at a family-owned hotel and putting himself through college. He worked and studied while I slept on a cot in the back room. It was a struggle, but he managed to get it done and earn his degree.

"When the opportunity came, he had recently married Evie, his first wife. She strongly objected to him risking everything. His boss and the owner of the hotel had to retire for health reasons. His kids weren't interested in taking over the business. Because he admired and respected Gordan, he didn't sell to one of the hotel chains. He sold that hotel to Gordan. It was a huge risk for our family.

"I knew Gordan could make it work. And I encouraged him to go for it. Even back then, we were close.

We are more than brothers, we're business partners. He worked, day and night, to make that first hotel profitable."

There was pride in his voice when he said, "You're right, Laura, about Gordan. He didn't stop until he turned that one hotel into a chain of luxury resorts and hotels around the world. I grew up in the hotel industry. When I wasn't in school, I was working beside my brother. I know how to repair toilets, mop floors, clean rooms, make beds, and do laundry. I learned how to cook in hotel kitchens making meals for our guests."

Chuckling, Wilham said, "Art was the one talent that I didn't learn from my big brother. It was a gift that I was born with. Art was something I did for me. I never expected to draw the attention of prestige galleries and auction houses or acclaim from art critics around the world. While I enjoy the work and the opportunities it offered me, I don't have the time to devote to it. Art has never been something I intended to pursue full-time.

"Like my brother, I have always been fascinated by the hotel business. I was only sixteen when I graduated from high school, barely nineteen when I finished college, majored in business and minored in art. I surprised everyone when I developed an interest in the law, specifically international and corporate law. I got my law degree from Harvard. I was barely twenty-one when I passed the bar on the first try."

"Wow," she said, fascinated. She was also glad to be discussing something else.

"My brother thought I was too young to know what I wanted to do. He was wrong, but I humored him. I took a year off and studied art in Paris."

"And?"

Wilham shrugged. "I loved it. I discovered I had real

passion for painting. I had a great time in Paris, burned the candle at both ends. Paris was where I earned the reputation for being a playboy artist. By the time my name really hit the tabloids, Gordan yanked me out of there so fast. He put me behind a desk, had me pulling my weight poring over contracts at our corporate headquarters in Atlanta. The more difficult the challenge, the harder I worked. I thrived on it. He kept me in Atlanta for over a year before I began traveling, studying the new hotels and relearning our older ones. I did some troubleshooting solving problems, that kind of thing. When there's a problem I can become completely absorbed in a project. And when that happens it leaves very little time or energy for my art."

Amazed, Laura just stared at him.

"Since my brother married Cassandra and they started their family, he has been semiretired, working mainly in our corporate offices. I've taken over running the company, the traveling and acquiring new hotels, in addition to my corporate law work. Our last two hotels have drastically increased the workload, making it harder for me to find the time to get away and paint. Gordan has been grooming my nephew, Gordy, to take over the majority of the travel and troubleshooting for the company. It has helped."

Wilham turned and looked at her before admitting, "I'm lucky if I can get to the island twice a year and escape the pressure of business and relax. It doesn't take long before I'm engrossed in painting. Lucky for me, it's always there waiting for me. It's hard to explain but art has always been an essential part of who I am. In the past six years, I've gotten in the habit of returning to St. John. Your portrait, I believe, is my best work."

He hesitated before admitting, "Laura, I'm not a playboy or a womanizer. And I don't work for my brother. We jointly own Kramer Corporation."

Stunned, Laura was still reeling from all the things he had revealed. It took her a few moments to accept she was wrong about him. Wilham Sebastian Kramer wasn't the man she thought she knew and had slept with these past few weeks. He might not have lied, but he'd certainly kept an important part of his life secret.

Furious, she asked, "Why are you just getting around to telling me the truth now?"

"I never lied to you, but like you I was on vacation. While I'm here, I focus on enjoying every minute of my time on the island. Here I can be Sebastian and be totally engrossed in my art. It wasn't until you revealed your plan and I realized how I felt about you that the details began to matter. My name may not be Gordan, but I'm closer to being your fantasy man than you realized."

"Very funny!" she snapped. "Don't you mean they were details that you decided to keep to yourself because you believed I'm a money-hungry gold digger?"

Outraged, Laura rocked back and forth, folded her arms tightly beneath her breasts. Caught up in a maze of feelings, uppermost shock, hurt, and betrayal, she was nauseous, sick with regret and disappointment. She was also mortified as she recalled the number of times she'd told him that he was wrong for her. The final straw was when she'd compared him to his beloved older brother and he came up short.

Her comments had not been designed to wound, but to keep him at a distance and her safe from the intense feeling he aroused in her. She was ashamed of those comments, they were crude and distasteful, but now she suddenly felt as if the joke was on her. Well, he must be pleased. She felt like a class-A fool! He had certainly humiliated her.

No . . . She paused. That was not exactly true. Yes, she was humiliated, but she was equally to blame. She had been too open about her plans to marry well. But then, she had nothing to hide. She had never kept secrets the way he had from her!

Close to tears, she said, "I'd like to go back to the villa . . . now."

"If you're thinking I deceived you—"

She interrupted, "All that needed to be said has been said. It's pointless to keep rehashing it."

"I don't agree. It's important."

She looked away, determined to tune him out. Why couldn't he just drop it? Couldn't he see she was hurting?

If only she could put all the blame on him. It would be so easy, but she couldn't. She'd been the one to open her big mouth and insert both feet. She'd volunteered her views on everything from oatmeal to love and marriage. She hadn't held back.

And it hurt knowing he had judged her from the first, he'd weighed and measured every sentence that came out of her mouth. But the humiliation didn't end there. Oh, no, she'd gone and jumped into bed with him.

What she couldn't figure out was why he'd asked her to marry him. He could not love her! What he enjoyed was having sex with her. His sexual appetite for her was something he hadn't bothered to hide. He didn't want that to end.

But why would he propose when he believed she was a money-hungry, scheming gold digger? Sex! It always came back to the s-e-x. Evidently it took a while, but she had finally gotten it right. He was the only man who kept coming back for more. It wasn't moonlight or the stars at work. No, it was male ego. He had been the one who made her come apart in his arms.

She was crushed. It was all she could do to hang on to her composure. He may not think much of her as a person, but that hadn't stopped him from sleeping with her again and again.

But why *marry*? They didn't belong together. They had nothing in common other than a deep appreciation of art. They had only spent three weeks together and didn't really know each other. She was right to turn down his proposal. Marriage would have been a huge mistake. Once he was back at Kramer Corporation, he'd laugh his head off, relieved to have escaped. He wouldn't have a problem finding someone else to share his bed.

Suddenly, Laura knew what was worse than never finding her ideal fantasy man. It was finding him so unexpectantly, only to realize *she* was wrong for him. Life wouldn't be that cruel, would it? He couldn't be her ideal mate!

Biting her lip to hold back her misery, she stared out the open window while her eyes burned from unshed tears. Silence stretched the entire drive back to the villa. She was so anxious to get out that she nearly lost her dignity and screamed at him when he held her passenger door closed.

"What?"

"We've both made mistakes. I should have told you sooner. Please don't compound the mistakes by turning your back on what we feel for each other and what we already have. Take the risk, Peaches. I have your ring right here."

Before she could blink, he pulled out the box and opened it. She gasped. The ring he'd bought was the large, square-cut kunzite solitaire, surrounded by diamonds and set in eighteen-karat gold, from the jeweler in St. Thomas.

He had offered to buy the pearls for her. Evidently, it had been a test and she had passed. But it hurt because it was also a slap in the face.

Head high, she said tightly, "My answer is still no. That ring confirms what I've been thinking since I learned the 'little details' you didn't bother mentioning until tonight. You've been testing me from the moment we met. But you're right about one thing. I'm not the only one to mess up. You failed! I don't want or need your name or your money. I'm not desperate enough to want a man who hasn't been honest with me. It's over. You and I don't have what it takes to build a life together."

"What about your painting?"

She kept walking. After mounting the steps, she paused long enough to say, "I don't want the painting. Keep it, sell it, give it away. I don't care." At her door she said, "Good-bye," and hurried inside.

She waited until she heard him drive away before she allowed the tears free rein. She collapsed in utter despair on the sitting room floor.

Nineteen

Laura didn't recall much of the flight back home to Detroit. When Sherri Ann and Jenna met her at Detroit's Metropolitan Airport, she was all smiles. She laughed and chatted about what a great time she had, boasted about the places she had seen and the thrifty shopping she'd done. She raved about her daily swims and bragged about the number of books she'd read. She'd even managed to mention Wilham's name with a smile on her face. She was determined to close the door on the hurt and disappointment.

A touchy moment came when Sherri Ann wanted to see her painting. Laura had never been a good liar, so she tried to stay as close to the truth as possible. She shrugged and told them she let him keep it and hopefully to auction it off, and the proceeds would be donated to the children's wing of St. John's hospital.

She was relieved when her foster sisters didn't question her decision. She was already on shaky ground, close to giving in to despair. By the time she pushed them out of her condo with their gifts from the island, she was exhausted. Most important, both Sherri Ann and Jenna believed she was a little tired but pleased by her trip.

It wasn't as if she was trying to keep secrets, but there was no point in unloading her problems on them. It might give her a quick sense of relief but it wouldn't change what happened on the island. No, it was best to bury it deep inside and pretend she had not made an utter fool of herself and lost her one chance at true happiness. She still had her family and friends and a great job. It was time for her to get on with the rest of her life and focus on what was right in her world.

By Monday Laura was eager to go back to work. None of her beleaguered coworkers had the time or energy to look beyond her laughter and quick smiles. Their caseloads were hefty. Maureen had good news. She introduced Laura to Heather Gregory Montgomery, the new volunteer counselor. Laura and Heather connected instantly. Besides admiring each other's braids, they understood the importance of giving back. Because Heather was a busy wife and mother, she was able to work only three days a week.

On Wednesday, after a staff meeting, Maureen pulled Laura aside and asked if something was wrong. Laura shrugged before admitting she had not been sleeping well. She blamed it on jet lag.

Later that same evening the doorman called to say she had a special delivery. Although baffled because she hadn't ordered anything, she asked him to send it up. Two deliverymen brought in a huge crate. Insisting there had to be a mistake, she looked at the invoice and realized there was no mistake. The crate had been shipped from St. John, U.S. Virgin Islands. Her legs suddenly weak, she had to sit before she fell. She watched as the men pried open the crate while her heart pounded with dread. She didn't have to look beneath the thick padding and careful wrapping. She knew what was inside and what it meant. Wilham didn't want her painting. Evidently, he no longer wanted her. And she felt as if her heart was crushed. Until then she didn't think she could hurt any more. She was wrong.

When asked where she wanted it, Laura motioned to her guest bedroom. She managed to hold herself together until the men were gone. Then she cried until she felt empty inside. His message was clear. There was no longer even a sliver of hope that he loved her. By sending the painting he had proven beyond doubt that all they'd ever shared was their bodies. There was no love.

On Thursday, during her lunch with Vanessa at her new design studio, Laura found it harder to hang on to her smile. Since Vanessa's marriage to Ralph Prescott, she seemed to be floating on a cloud of sheer bliss. When Vanessa showed off some of the bridal and evening gowns she had created, Laura's heart ached. She was not going to marry and have a family. That part of the fantasy was gone. She shuddered at the thought of being intimate with another man. Clearly, she had no alternative but to accept that she cared more for Wilham than she had first realized.

Laura asked Vanessa how she balanced her time between going to college, her bridal boutique, and her home life. Vanessa not only had a new husband, but she was also raising her young twin brother and sister and teenage sister. Laughing, Vanessa confessed that her main focus was on her family, everything else simply had to wait. But she was lucky to have a housekeeper and help from Ralph with the kids. The major problem was finding time for the two of them to have some alone time.

When Vanessa asked about her vacation, Laura gave her rehearsed answer and moved on to their upcoming book club meeting and the new author she had discovered from St. Thomas.

On the drive back to her office, Laura conceded it was getting harder to conceal her unhappiness from her family and friends. When Jenna called on Friday to remind her about dinner on Sunday, she'd asked Laura if something was wrong. And Laura lied again, insisting everything was fine, then quickly changed the subject. She didn't like keeping secrets, but she wasn't ready to talk about Wilham.

The highlight of the week was seeing the girls in her mentoring program on Saturday. She was especially pleased to see that Tasha was doing so well. They talked only briefly but Laura gave her a big hug. She'd brought back souvenirs for all the girls and they were excited. She threw herself into working with them and thought she was doing well—until afterward, when both her foster sisters asked what was going on. They were in Laura's office at the women's center. Sherri Ann complained she didn't seem to be herself. Jenna said she didn't look as if she'd been sleeping. Avoiding their questions, she started talking about arranging to take the girls to a play at the Fox Theater.

Later she turned down Sherri Ann's offer to treat her to dinner and a movie. Reluctantly, she admitted she was tired, and wasn't sleeping well. She didn't add that she was upset. She wanted her old life back, before she'd met Wilham. Most of all she was frustrated, wanted to sleep and forget. She cried herself to sleep wishing she had never gone on vacation, never heard of Sebastian or seen his work.

On Sunday instead of joining her family after church, Laura begged off, complaining of a headache. Unable to relax, she restlessly paced her beautifully decorated condo, not seeing the twin yellow-green sofas facing each other atop a floral-patterned rug. Or the two pale pink Queen Anne chairs sitting opposite the marble fireplace. Jenna had helped her recover the chairs and refinish the coffee table. She didn't look at the needlepoint pillows Sherri Ann had made for her or Mrs. Green's silver candle holders on the mantel. She walked past the framed photos of them, the last taken at Jenna's wedding, moving aimlessly into the dining room, where her laptop and notes for the week ahead waited for her attention.

How could she concentrate on solving other people's problems when her own life had fallen apart? She'd closed the door to the guest bedroom and hadn't gone near it since Wednesday night. And she hadn't unpacked her suitcases. She didn't want to see any reminders of her time in St. John.

The only true solace she found was when she managed to sleep. Unfortunately, she hadn't slept well since her return. And when she did sleep, her dreams were filled with Wilham. She didn't want to remember. She didn't want to recall the passion they shared or the painful way they parted. She sighed. What she wouldn't give for a night of uninterrupted, dreamless sleep.

When her doorbell rang she frowned and glanced at the clock. It was after six. She had changed into pink pajamas when she got home. She debated whether to answer the door as she was.

Grabbing the afghan from the back of the sofa, she wrapped it around her shoulders and went to the door.

The afghan was a graduation gift from Jenna, knit in a traditional African arrowhead pattern with the background in blush pink, the arrowheads in cranberry framed by ivory and white diamonds. Jenna was an expert knitter and had skillfully reproduced the bold Zaire pattern.

"Who is it?"

"Open up!" Sherri Ann called.

Before she could respond, Jenna said, "Hurry up, Laura Jean! I've got to go."

She unhooked the chain, released the deadbolt, and swung the door open. "What brings you two out on such a cloudy Sunday night?"

"Excuse me," Jenna said, hurrying past with a covered plate in hand. She stopped in the kitchen before heading toward the half bath.

Laura turned hopeful eyes to Sherri Ann. "Any news? Are we going to be aunties?"

Sherri Ann shook her head quickly. "No, bladder infection. She was so disappointed when they got back from the honeymoon and the old period started."

"Disappointed? But why?"

"The more he talks about having kids, the more she worries." Sherri Ann shrugged.

"Hmm." Laura closed and locked the door.

"We came to find out what's going on with you. You look exhausted. Have you eaten?"

"Not yet. How was the family dinner?" Jenna had invited Scott's entire family, his widowed mother, his older sister, Taylor Hendricks Williams, her husband, ex-NBA player Donald Williams, and their two children, plus her foster sisters.

"It was great. She showed off her cooking skills."

"We missed you," Jenna said as she returned. "I

brought you a plate, put it on the counter." She gave Laura's shoulder a gentle squeeze. "So what's bothering you?"

"Nothing. What did you serve? Did you pass the mother-in-law test?"

Sherri Ann boasted, "She did well. Baked ham, candied sweet potatoes, creamed spinach, and salad, and finished with a double chocolate three-layer cake, the top covered with pecans. Mrs. Green would have been proud. You should have been there, Laura. How are you?"

"Sherri Ann is right. Mrs. Green would have indeed been very proud of you. I'm sorry I missed it. Is this going to be a new weekly tradition, Sunday dinner around the Hendricks table?"

Jenna smiled. "More like once a month! It will give Taylor and his mother a break. You didn't answer the question. How are—"

"I'm fine!"

"You're not fine. If you say it again I'm going to smack you!" Sherri Ann warned.

"Who pushed your buttons, Counselor? Trouble with a new case?"

"Stop changing the subject. Getting an answer out of you is worse than having to sit through an entire NBA game with Scott. Something is going on. It's not like you to keep secrets," Jenna persisted.

"Don't you two have better things to do with your time?" Laura snapped.

Jenna said, "Clearly not. We're going to keep right on asking until you fess up. You're not the only stubborn one in this family."

Sherri Ann had taken a seat on one end of the sofa while Jenna was perched on the ottoman between the two armchairs. Slowly, Laura carefully folded her afghan on the end of the sofa.

"You might as well spill it because we aren't leaving until you do," Sherri Ann insisted.

Laura rolled her eyes. "I told you I was fine."

Both Jenna and Sherri Ann let out loud unladylike grunts of disapproval.

"You sound like two beached whales," Laura joked.

Jenna huffed. "Stop stalling. Why must you do everything the hard way? It's never simple or easy with you, Laura Jean Murdock. But then you're the queen bee of contradiction and unpredictable!"

"Thanks." Laura smiled as if she'd been complimented. "Why can't you two take my word—"

"Enough!" Sherri Ann said impatiently. She went into the kitchen, when she returned, she said matter-of-factly, "Exhibit A: There's nothing in your refrigerator. No milk, cheese, bread, meat, eggs, and fresh fruit or vegetables. We put enough food in there to last until you could get to the store this week. What happened? It's not like you, Miss Always on a Diet, to waste money, calories, and time by eating out. Shall I go on?"

Laura snapped, "Very entertaining, Sherri Ann! By all means, continue."

Next Sherri Ann walked into the dining room. She came back with the stack of file folders. "Exhibit B: You, Miss Always Prepared, have not made a single notation in any of these files this weekend or any notes in your planner. It's almost seven and there is nothing to show what you plan to go over with your clients. We don't have your schedule to go by, but I would be surprised if there is any wiggle room. The clients are coming. Do you plan to stay home tomorrow? Are you taking a sick day?"

Laura didn't respond until she noticed her foster sister was heading toward the bedrooms. She jumped up, shouting, "Stop right there, Sherri Ann Weber! You have no right to go into my guest bedroom!"

Jenna and Sherri Ann exchanged a look before Sherri Ann said, "What's in there?"

"It's none of your business!" Laura yelled. "Both of you go home now!"

"You're shaking," Jenna pointed out. "Laura? What don't you want us to see?"

Laura glanced up in time to see Sherri Ann disappear into her guest bedroom. "No!"

Jenna looked worried but she got up and followed Sherri Ann.

When they returned, Sherri Ann said, "What's that all wrapped up? Something you bought in St. John?"

Laura said nothing.

Sherri Ann asked, "Why are you so upset? What is it?"

All she would say was "I asked you not to go in there!"

"Is that the painting he did of you?" Jenna asked.

"I bet it is," Sherri Ann said, and headed back to the guest room. She called from the room. "Come look, Jenna. It has to be a painting!"

Laura didn't move. She was so upset she was shaking.

"Jenna! Hurry!" Sherri Ann called.

When they returned, Laura was furious. "I told you no but you wouldn't listen. You went too far! And I won't put up with it! Both of you get out of my house and leave me alone!"

Sherri Ann said, "Why aren't you thrilled? I don't get it. You scrimped and saved an entire year to be able to buy one of his paintings. He sent you one. And you haven't even unwrapped it. Why?"

Laura rushed out to the foyer and opened her front door. She yelled, "Go! I mean it! I don't want either of you here, especially when you can't respect my privacy!"

Following, Sherri Ann said softly, "I'm sorry, Laura. We didn't mean to upset you."

Jenna clasped her trembling hand. "You're hurting. And we aren't leaving until you tell us why. Please come sit down. Let us help."

Sherri Ann closed the door. "Please, Laura. Sit on the sofa with us. Remember when we were little and how we used to love to snuggle together under one of Mrs. Green's quilts? Your favorite was the one with the pink flowers. Jenna loved the one with purple lace, but mine was the one with the red hearts that she always kept on her bed. Do you remember that one, Laura?"

She merely nodded, suddenly exhausted, too tired to protest. She sat between her foster sisters, sharing her favorite afghan.

"We're sisters. Whatever you are going through, you're not alone. Remember when I broke it off with Scott. You helped me hold it together. And you were there with me at the hospital after my accident," Jenna gently reminded her.

"I know, but—"

"No buts about it, sis. We're family, we stick together no matter what, we love you. If you're hurting, then Jenna and I are also hurting," Sherri Ann said softly. "What went wrong in St. John?"

The fight had drained out of Laura. Laura rested her head on Jenna's shoulder while clinging to Sherri Ann's arm.

Finally, she sighed heavily before whispering, "I didn't mean to keep it secret, but—" She bit her quivering lip to keep from breaking down. "It hurts so much I couldn't talk about it."

"Sebastian, he hurt you, didn't he?" Jenna asked.

Sherri Ann surmised, "Evidently, he did a lot more than paint your portrait and take you out dancing."

"Shush up, Sherri Ann. Let her talk."

"Wilham Sebastian Kramer," Laura said, unhappily. "Evidently, Wilham was more than just an artist and Gordan Kramer's younger brother. I seriously underestimated him. And yes, he's tall, handsome, and practically oozing sex appeal." She said sadly, "I mean I *really* messed up this time. I thought we were having a wildly romantic island fling until I did something really stupid. I think I have fallen in love with him. I thought I knew what love felt like. I was so wrong. What I feel for him is nothing like what I felt in Johnnie or Brad. I've never cared this deeply for a man."

"I'm lost, Laura," Sherri Ann said urgently. "Back up. After you started posing for him, what happened?"

Laura recounted that first week filled with carefree days on the island. She told about her shock when she realized how much she wanted him before he ever touched her. She confessed that for so long she thought there was something wrong with her because she didn't enjoy sex. That Wilham showed her that she didn't have a problem with sex. She told them about the first morning after they made love, the misunderstanding and later making up. Her eyes were dry until she told about their last night on the island. She didn't leave anything out, including his claim to love her, his proposal, the ring, her refusal, and finally comparing the brothers.

"He didn't bother telling me what he did at Kramer

Corporation until after he proposed. I thought he was some rich playboy artist living off his big brother. I had no idea they're business partners and they coown Kramer Corporation. After I said no that's when he decided to share! The man has a degree in business and a corporate law degree from Harvard! When I challenged him, he said he didn't lie—he just 'kept it to himself'!"

The shock on her foster sisters' faces was how she felt when she had learned the truth. Any other time, she would be laughing at their stunned reaction. But not today . . . not with her heart feeling as if it had been broken into a million pieces.

Sherri Ann was outraged. "What? He didn't tell you this until after he proposed? Why? Does he believe you were only interested in money? How could he be so blind?" she said. "I'm so sorry. He doesn't deserve you."

"I'm also sorry," Jenna said. "And you kept this inside all this time? No wonder you weren't sleeping. You poor thing," Jenna soothed.

"No! You both have it wrong. I'm the one who opened my big mouth and told him about my plan to marry well."

"Laura Jean Murdock!" Jenna scolded. "No you didn't! You went and told him all that foolish stuff about only wanting to marry a rich man!"

Twenty

"It's not foolish! It's the truth!" Laura yelled back.

Jenna got up and began pacing restlessly. "Sherri Ann, did you hear what she said? She came right out and told him about finding Mr. Right and then turned around and fell in love with the man. I don't believe it!"

Sherri Ann was quick to say, "It makes absolutely no sense! And she even got the guy to propose after comparing him to his brother!"

"Will you two stop talking about me as if I'm not right here?"

"I've got to hand it to you, sis. When you mess up, you do it in spades! How did you manage it, Laura? You not only found your dream man, but you found him in one of the most romantic places on earth," Sherri Ann exclaimed. "And he's wealthier than even you could imagine! How Laura? How did you convince the man you're in love with that you only want his money? Girl, what were you thinking?"

Jenna snapped, "She wasn't thinking! She was just plain scared."

"Wait a min—"

"Shush, Laura!" they yelled at once, clearly upset

with her. They went on discussing her situation as if she wasn't there.

Tired of being ignored, Laura snapped, "Stop talking about me! So I made a mistake. I don't remember asking for your help!"

"You don't have to ask. You're getting it regardless. Someone has to talk some sense into you!" Jenna said.

Miffed, Laura scowled at her foster sisters. Just because they were right didn't mean they had to rub her nose in it. She had made a royal mess of things. She had been scared, terrified of loving and losing. The fear of investing her hopes and dreams in Wilham and then knowing that someday he could walk away was too much! It was too risky! She couldn't do that to herself. And she had no doubt that he *would* eventually leave! She had done what was best for her! She could get past this! All she had to do was figure out a way to stop thinking about him, stop caring about him.

She announced unhappily, "There's nothing to fix. It's beyond repair. It's over."

Jenna and Sherri Ann exchanged concerned looks. They came back and sat on either side of her.

Jenna said, "No, it doesn't have to be over. Not unless you decide he's not worth fighting for."

Quickly, she said, "Believe me. It's over. I messed up, big time. I just have to learn to live with it."

"But you love him," Sherri Ann reminded. "And if he feels the same way, then . . ."

"Then nothing. It has only been since I've been back that I realized how I feel about him. I don't know what he feels or wants, especially after the things I said to him before I left. It was so horrible the way we parted. I've got no reason to believe he still cares for me. None."

"He proposed to you. It has to mean something," Jenna reminded.

And then Sherri Ann said, "He sent a painting. He didn't have to do that."

Laura shook her head quickly. "No, he sent my portrait. I told him I didn't want it. But—" She stopped abruptly.

"What?" Sherri Ann prompted.

"He didn't want a reminder. He doesn't want me."

Jenna insisted, "He loves you. If he didn't, he would have left well enough alone. He would not have proposed. And why did he buy that particular ring?"

"I don't know why he proposed or bought that ring. It doesn't matter because I don't believe he loves me," she ended sadly.

"Would you mind if we look at the painting? It might not be your portrait. You haven't unwrapped it to see what's inside. Maybe it will answer some of these questions," Sherri Ann suggested.

Laura shrugged, staring at her nails. "Go ahead. It's not going to change a thing."

While they were in the guest room armed with utility scissors, she went into the kitchen. She didn't have to look. She knew.

She didn't want to think about what he'd said when he'd shown her the painting. Instead, she heated her dinner in the microwave. But after a few bites, Laura gave up, covered the plate, and stored it in the refrigerator.

Busy making notes, Laura didn't look up from the stack of folders when her foster sisters joined her in the dining room.

Jenna gushed, "It's so beautiful."

Sherri Ann quickly agreed. "Spectacular. How can you—"

Laura interrupted, "I can't talk about it. Please make sure you close the guest room door. I appreciate you coming, but it's getting late. Sherri Ann, you probably have to be in court tomorrow and at your best; for that you need sleep. And you, Jenna, have a sexy husband waiting for you to get home. No need to stay and baby-sit me."

"There she goes trying to get rid of us again," Sherri Ann told Jenna.

Releasing a frustrated groan, Laura said, "Can't you two find something else to do tonight besides bugging me?"

"We're going, but before we do, I have something to ask you." Jenna urged, "But I don't want you to respond now. I'd like you to really think about your answer."

Laura said impatiently, "Go ahead."

"You told him you wouldn't marry him, but did you tell him why it was so important to you that you marry well? Does he know that your decision to marry well has nothing to do with money and everything to do with your need to feel secure? Did you even bother to explain how important it was for you to know he's not the kind of man who will walk away when things get tough? Did you even bother telling him how important it was to you to be with someone who's willing to fight to keep those he loves? Are you sure he knows that this comes back to being abandoned? Did you break it all down for him?"

Suddenly agitated, Laura admitted, "I told him about being left in that church."

"But that doesn't explain how it made you feel. How is he supposed to know the possibility of it happening again is your worst fear?"

"She didn't tell him," Sherri Ann answered for her. "Jenna, you know she won't admit weakness. She's so busy trying to be Wonder Woman. Honestly, Laura, that man must be a saint, if he fell in love with you in spite of your crazy quirks and contradictions."

"Sherri Ann Weber! Who are you calling crazy? I may have a few quirks, but I'm not the one who went to law school because it paid well when all you ever wanted was to teach kindergarten and be a wife and mother. Just because you got all A's all through college and law school doesn't mean you know everything!"

"I can't believe you threw that in my face. I was twelve when I told you that, Laura Jean!"

"So? It's true!"

"Shush up, both of you!" Jenna snapped.

"She started it!"

"No, Sherri Ann, you started it when you went into my guest room! You always think you know what's best."

"For heaven's sake! It's a good thing Mrs. Green can't hear you two fighting like alley cats. She'd be disappointed in both of you!" Jenna stopped when she realized she too was yelling.

Several calming breaths later, Jenna said, "Sherri Ann, Laura said that to distract you because she doesn't want to talk about Wilham Sebastian. She's so busy trying to forget the man that she will say and do anything rather than deal with her feelings for him. Fear is what's driving her."

"Yeah, I know." Sherri Ann sighed. "Laura, I can't believe I fell right into that one."

Pleased with herself, Laura shrugged. "What can I say? A girl's got to do—"

"Do what, Laura Jean?" Jenna demanded. "Keep

running like a frightened child? You're letting fear consume you, make your decisions for you. I asked Sherri Ann earlier, now it's your turn. Where is your head, girl? How much longer are going to let the fear control you, decide what's best for you? When are you going to stand up and deal with this like a woman? Closing the guest room door doesn't change what happened between you and Wilham in St. John." Jenna paused to catch her breath before she said, "Laura, when you got into bed with him, you gave him your heart, as well as your body. Judging by that painting, he also gave you his. How long are you going to deny what you feel?"

"He doesn't love—"

"Stop it, Laura! Stop lying to yourself," Sherri Ann urged. "All you have to do is look at that painting. It's there in every brushstroke. He painted you without a single flaw. If it were me on the receiving end of that kind of love, I'd say give me a double dose, pretty please."

"Amen to that." Jenna laughed.

"He was willing to take a chance on you. You're the one who walked away without giving anything in return. You refused to take any risks, trying to protect your heart." Sherri Ann warned, "You will be a grade-A fool, if you leave things the way they are now. Fear won't hold you at night. Fear won't give you the babies you want. Just think about how he must feel. It had to have hurt him badly when you said no to marriage and then refused to accept his ring."

"She's right, sis." Jenna predicted, "The next woman who comes along, and believe me, there will be someone willing to stand in your high heels, if she's smart she won't waste time worrying about the foolish woman that let him get away. Miss Thing will be so busy soothing his poor ego with sweet kisses and giving him hot sex to help him forget about you. I bet he won't have to ask her twice. Not her! She will put your ring on her finger and sink her claws into your man while you are here denying your feelings for him and pretending that painting doesn't mean anything."

"That's right," Sherri Ann quickly said.

Laura moaned, "I get your point."

Unconvinced, Jenna said, "You said that too quickly for me to believe you mean it. Sweetie, you can't run from what's in your heart. Those feelings aren't going to just go away. Time and distance won't make it stop.

"Believe me, the pain from loss doesn't stop when you walk away. If anything, it gets worse. It's what you are feeling now. I had to find that out the hard way when I broke off my engagement with Scott the first time. And then, years later, I repeated the same mistake. I nearly lost him for good this last time, before I faced the truth. My feelings weren't going away. Married or not married, I'm still going to love Scott Hendricks. Maybe it will be different for you, but I doubt it."

Sherri Ann asked, "Think about how you are going to feel when he marries someone else and gives her those babies you desperately want? If you don't try and fix this now, there will be no guarantee that in six months or a year when you're finally ready to face him that he will be willing to listen to what you have to say. You have to decide if you are woman enough to go after your man."

Jenna said, "Which is it going to be, Laura? Are you going to take the easy way out? Are you going to stay here, where you feel safe solving other people's problems, and hold on to the fear? Or are you going to face him and tell him the truth? That you love him but you're scared. Are you willing to take your chances with him? Take a chance on a lifetime of love and happiness?"

Sherri Ann said, "Laura, you've already done the hardest part, you finally found your Mr. Right. Or do you plan to start over looking for someone new?"

Laura shuddered. The thought of being intimate with another man was reprehensible. The moment she looked into Wilham's golden brown eyes she had felt something for him. Something unlike anything she'd ever experienced with any man. And it scared her to the point where she couldn't run far enough or fast enough. She couldn't fathom caring so deeply for another man . . . not ever.

She surprised everyone, especially herself, when she confessed, "I don't need time to think. I've done nothing but think since I came home. I'm in love with Wilham. I can't help it, nor can I stop it. My feelings haven't disappeared because I'm scared. And I can't keep pretending they don't exist. Somehow, I have to deal with it." She sighed tiredly. "Clearly, I can't fix this with a telephone call. After the way I left, I owe it to him to face him and tell him how I feel. I just pray that he will be generous enough to hear me out."

Kramer Island, Georgia

A big party had been planned to celebrate the Kramer twins' ninth birthday and Gordan and Cassandra's tenth wedding anniversary. The long weekend celebration resembled a mini family reunion. Wilham, along with his nephew and cousin, had flown to Atlanta on the corporate jet and then took the helicopter to the family's estate on Kramer Island. The crown jewel of the Kramer hotels and resort complexes was also on the privately owned sea island, off the coast of Georgia.

Cassy's older sister, Sarah Mosley-Rogers; her husband, Kurt; their ten-year-old son Kurt Jr.; and their sixteen-year-old granddaughter, Mandy, had flown in from California. Plus there was a number of close family friends staying at Kramer House on the northern side of the island, overlooking the bluff.

Carla and Carmella were identical twins and thrilled by all the attention. Wilham smiled indulgently recalling his nieces' antics as they opened their presents at the big barbecue on Saturday afternoon. They had argued over which one of the gold diamond-cut, engraved lockets he had given them was the prettiest.

Later that same evening after a sumptuous meal, Gordan and Cassandra opened their gifts. Wilham had brought them a special anniversary gift.

But his smile vanished when he recalled his high hopes the day he'd gone back to the jewelry store in St. Thomas and purchased Laura's engagement ring. His heart was heavy with grief. He couldn't stop thinking about her. Laura. She had captured his attention from the moment he saw her walk into the café. He wasn't just attracted to her; he really cared about her. He quickly discovered she not only mattered to him, but she was what had been missing from his life.

Once they had gotten to know each other, she let her guard down enough to tell him about her plans to marry and have a house full of babies, fathered by some well-to-do stranger. His temper had flared. Instead of being taken aback, he'd been green with jealousy. He didn't merely dislike the concept, he downright hated it. That was when he realized he was in trouble because it didn't stop the wanting. But he couldn't stand the thought of her with another man.

As he got to know Laura, it wasn't long before he realized her plan to marry well was more complicated than financial gain. It stemmed from a deep emotional need. He suspected it was linked to being left by her mother. It also gave him hope, hope that, given time, she'd realize the two of them belonged together. And that someday they could have that large family she dreamed of and share a life filled with love. Because she gave him her body, he believed she had feelings for him. He believed it right up to the moment she turned down his proposal.

For the first time in his life, Wilham couldn't paint. Painting had always been a major source of solace and comfort to him, especially during hard times. Three days after Laura's departure, he'd closed up the house in St. John.

It was fortunate that he'd completed the twins' portrait a week before. He quickly discovered once Laura left the islands, he couldn't stay either. He couldn't stop thinking of her and remembering. Like a lovesick fool, he still carried her ring around in his pocket, a painful reminder of what he'd lost.

The worst had been when she refused his proposal without giving it even half a second's worth of thought. When she flatly refused to wear his ring, he'd felt as if he'd been punched in the gut. He'd been so wrong. She'd enjoyed their lovemaking but she didn't care about him.

Even with the party in full swing and the house full of family and friends, Wilham was holed up in his brother's study, near the back of the sprawling estate. Again and again, he'd gone over every detail, trying to figure out what went wrong between them. The pain of her rejection was just as raw as it had been the night they parted.

Wilham stood at the floor-to-ceiling windows, staring out across the well-manicured lawn and lush garden beyond lit by the soft glow of solar lights that lined the walkways. She'd thrown him for a loop. It still hurt when he thought of how she'd compared him to his brother and he'd come up short. Laura didn't love him. She never had. Now all he had left was his pride. He was not going to make an even bigger fool of himself by trying to change her mind. They were done.

He sighed wearily, exhausted from sleepless nights. He had his own wing of the house with a separate entrance. If he wanted privacy, he could go to his condominium in Atlanta. Unfortunately, none of his residences held much appeal; each seemed desolate, empty.

And for the first time in his adult life he was uncertain what he should do next. Should he stay in Atlanta? Go back to St. John? Or return to work in Chicago? The only thing he was certain of was that he couldn't stay here. He wouldn't subject his family to his restlessness and foul moods. He'd leave in the morning.

It was time to stop brooding. The sooner he accepted that they had no future, the better off he'd be. It was over.

"Wil, there you are," Cassandra Mosley Kramer said with a smile. "I've been looking all over for you."

Happiness radiated across her lovely brown face and was echoed in her dark eyes. These days, she kept her wavy hair cut short. She no longer worked as a pastry chef, but always found time to make special desserts for her family. She complained that her figure was a bit fuller than she liked, but his brother loved every curve.

Cassy came in and shut the door. "I've been trying to find the words to let you know how happy you've made Gordan and me. We love your portrait of the twins. It's so lovely. We treasure it. And the way you were able to capture the sparkle in our girls' eyes and subtle change in their faces, just on the brink of womanhood—remarkable!" She stretched up to kiss his cheek. "We can't thank you enough. I have no idea how you managed to bring out their differences while highlighting their similarity. Amazing! Wil, this has to be your best work!"

When Cassy said the word "portrait," his focus instantly shifted to another portrait. The one of the petite beauty who had stolen his heart. Laura. He recalled how absolutely beautiful she looked on a carpet of wild roses in the meadow. His anguish hadn't lessened as he recalled how she'd deliberately left without the portrait. She claimed she loved it, but that had been a lie. She didn't want it just as she didn't want him. He scowled.

Cassy said urgently, "What's wrong?"

Just then Gordan Kramer opened the door. At fifty-two he was still a very handsome man. His dark hair and well-groomed beard were both generously streaked with gray. His tall body was still muscular and fit.

"So you found him." Gordan's caressing gaze moved lovingly over his pretty wife. "Did she tell you—" He stopped abruptly. "Something wrong?"

"I just asked the same question. Honey, hurry and close the door so we won't be interrupted," Cassy said.

Wilham let his sister-in-law take his hand and pull him along with her to one of the bronze leather sofas positioned on the large area rug across from the massive desk and enormous built-in bookshelves.

"Wil, you've been on vacation for weeks. Instead of being relaxed, you've been down all weekend. Only the twins have been able to make you smile," Cassy said softly. "You aren't yourself."

Gordan asked, "Does this have to do with the young woman who posed for you?"

"Laura Murdock. She's a social worker and art lover from Detroit. She's a natural beauty. I knew I had to paint her the moment I saw her."

"And?" Cassy said impatiently.

"I fell in love for the first time in my life," he confessed candidly. He told them about falling under her quirky, sweet spell, but omitted the intimate details. "What? You didn't think I'd ever find love?"

Clearly taken by surprise, they stared at him for a time.

"It's not that. It's just . . . ," Gordan paused before he said, ". . . so sudden."

"But Wil, you don't seem happy. And why didn't you bring her along to meet your family?" Cassy asked.

Wilham's voice was gruff when he said, "You won't be meeting her." He told about their last night on the island. Then he confessed, "Laura turned me down. Evidently, in this instance any rich man won't do."

Wilham expected his brother to advise him to never give up as he recalled the way Gordan had chased Cassy from San Francisco to the island of Martinique after she'd broken it off with him. They had been in love for years. And Cassy's biological clock was ticking at full speed while Gordan flatly refused to remarry. Neither was willing to compromise.

Instead, Gordan surprised him when he said, "She doesn't sound like the best choice for you, Wil. Losing her might hurt now, but eventually the pain will subside. Someday, you will be glad she turned you down, considering her preference for millionaires."

Wilham protested, "You don't understand. She's not after money."

Gordan quirked a brow. "And if you're wrong?"

"I'm not wrong."

Cassy sided with Wilham. "I trust Wil. If he says she's not after money, then that should be enough."

Gordan persisted, "I don't want you marrying some gold digger. I don't care how pretty she is. Be glad you got out relatively unscathed."

Cassy pointed out, "If all she wanted was money they'd be married by now!"

"My brother deserves to have a woman who values him, not his net worth!" Gordan was not backing down.

"Honey, why won't you consider you might be wrong? They had known each other three weeks. I wouldn't be surprised if it happened too fast for her. She was probably overwhelmed. If she loves him, then all she needs is time to get her bearings." Cassy turned to Wilham. "Please, if you'd just call her, I'm certain once she hears your voice she will—"

"Will what, babe?" Gordan interrupted. "Recall the gold mine she let get away? You, my love, have a soft heart. You can't help seeing the good in others, even when there is none."

Cassy said, "Sweetheart, you're an expert when it comes to business. But when it comes to matters of the heart, take my word for it, you stink!"

Gordan insisted, "I can spot a gold digger miles away. You're wrong!"

Fed up, Wilham snapped, "Enough!" Changing the subject, he smiled at Cassy. "The twins definitely have that Kramer chin and topaz eyes, but their skin tone, their pretty features, and that twinkle in their eyes came from the Mosley sisters. I wanted to paint them before they move from girlhood into those teen years."

Gordan boasted, "You nailed it! That portrait caught them with one step planted in girlhood and the other becoming very beautiful young women." He shook his head. "Man, I'm not ready for them to be teenagers. I like it that they still climb on each knee and beg me to take time off to go horseback riding. And that they still love spending weekends skiing with us in Aspen. I don't want to give that up."

Cassy kissed her husband. "I hate to tell you this, darling. But they're already poring over fashion magazines and giggling about the boys in their class. It's only a matter of time until they want matching pink sports cars."

Twenty-one

St. John, Virgin Islands

When Laura reached Wilham's home in St. John, she found the house had been closed up. She walked over to Daniel and Cora's cottage on the west side of the property. It was there she learned that Wilham had left the island and wasn't expected back any time soon.

"Do you have any idea where he might be?"

Cora shook her head, but explained his mail was forwarded to Kramer headquarters in Atlanta. Cora suggested she call his cell phone.

Keenly disappointed, Laura went back to her hotel. She didn't waste time worrying about feeling like a world-class fool for chasing a man around the globe. Instead, she called the airlines. Once she was booked on the next flight to Atlanta, she called Jenna and Sherri Ann to tell them about her change in plans and for a much needed pep talk.

Atlanta, Georgia

By the time her plane touched down, Laura was feeling jet-lagged and cranky, plus her feet hurt. It was early afternoon when she climbed out of a taxicab on Peachtree Street in downtown Atlanta. She was dressed in a burgundy pant suit and black silk ruffled blouse, and three-inch black leather pumps. With a large black leather tote bag over one shoulder, she wheeled her suitcase.

She didn't want to waste time checking into a hotel. She needed to see Wilham as soon as possible. Once they talked, then she would be able to breathe, and release the tension from her taut muscles. She could do this, she repeated over and over to herself. He might be angry, but she would get him to listen.

She forced herself to breathe slowly and deeply as she stood for a moment in the bright sunlight, gazing up at the impressive glass high-rise. In bold, black lettering, "Kramer Corporation" was posted on the side of the building.

"At least this is the right place," she whispered aloud. She discovered that the executive offices were on the twenty-fifth floor. When she emerged from a bank of elevators, her heels sank into thick gold carpet. Lifting her chin, she approached the reception desk.

"Good afternoon, may I help you?" A smartly dressed, attractive blonde greeted her with a soft Southern accent.

"Yes, I'm here to see Wilham Kramer. I'm Laura Murdock."

"I'm so sorry, Ms. Murdock, but Mr. Wilham Kramer doesn't have appointments today."

Laura rushed to say, "It's important that I speak with him today. Would you please ask his assistant to get word to him?"

The woman said firmly, "I'm so sorry, Ms. Murdock. But if you would be so kind as to leave your card,

I promise to personally pass it along to Ms. Jones, one of his assistants."

Shaking her head no, Laura persisted, "You don't understand. It's important that I speak to Mr. Wilham Kramer today. Would you please just call and tell him that Laura Murdock is here to see him?"

"I'm sorry, but that's not possible."

"What are you saying? That he's not taking any appointments? Or he's not in Atlanta?"

The woman said firmly, "I am so sorry, Ms. Murdock. If you'd leave your card, I will personally see to it that Mr. Kramer's assistant receives it."

"You do not understand. What's your name?"

"I'm Donna. Donna Robbins."

"Ms. Robbins, I've just flown in from St. John. It's important that I speak to Wilham Kramer today. Won't you, at least, tell me if he's in the building?"

"I'm sorry but I'm not at liberty—"

Although the young woman hadn't come right out and said it, Laura strongly suspected that the reason he wasn't taking appointments was that he was not in town. The Kramers had property all over the world!

Suddenly exhausted, Laura had to hang on to the edge of the desk and lock her knees in order not to give in to overwhelming weakness while struggling beneath the crushing weight of disappointment.

Her heart sank as she accepted she might not have a choice. If she wanted to see him at all, she would have to use that cell phone number. Not quite willing to give up yet, she asked softly but firmly, "What about Mr. Gordan Kramer? May I speak to him, please?"

"Mr. Gordan Kramer is a very busy man. He may not have openings today."

Desperate, she decided to try another approach. Forcing a smile, she said, "I'm a friend of the family."

"Of course," Ms. Robbins said graciously and picked up the telephone. She spoke so softly that Laura couldn't follow the conversation. When she put down the receiver, she said, "I'm so sorry, Ms. Murdock. Mr. Gordan Kramer is out of the office, but he's expected back. Would you'd care to take a seat and wait?"

Laura nodded and sank into the closest chair. What had she done? Had she made it worse? What was she going to say to his brother? Gordan Kramer was a very powerful and busy man. And what if she couldn't get in to see him today? Then what? She'd just have to wait. He was her best hope of locating Wilham quickly.

An alarming thought entered her mind and nearly had her wringing her hands due to escalating nerves and fear. What if Wilham had left word not to accept her calls? What then? Fighting back a sudden onslaught of tears, she swallowed with difficulty and didn't look up when the elevator bell chimed softly and the doors slid open.

A tall man walked out, escorting a lovely woman. The sound of his deep, throaty chuckle captured Laura's attention and instantly took her back to St. John. He was lean and muscular, dressed in a custom-made three-piece, navy blue suit, crisp white shirt, and striped tie. He leaned toward the woman and listened intently, then threw back his head and laughed again.

Startled, Laura couldn't miss his resemblance to her island man. This must be Gordan Kramer. He was almost as good-looking as his younger brother. If not for the liberal streaks of gray hair and well-groomed salt and pepper beard and mustache, she could be looking at Wilham Sebastian.

Without hesitation, she stepped into his path and said, "Excuse me, Mr. Kramer. I'm Laura Murdock, a friend of Wilham's. Yesterday I flew back to St. John to see him and after finding him gone, flew here. I was told that he's not taking appointments today and to leave my card, but I really need to speak to Wilham. Please, can you help me?"

The couple exchanged a look before he said, "It's nice to meet you, Ms. Murdock. This is my wife, Cassandra. Please come into my office."

Laura smiled, quickly shook hands with first Cassandra and then Gordan, before she followed them down a short hall and into a large plush reception area with a small fountain. It was tastefully furnished, with several striking paintings of the tropics on the walls. A glance and Laura knew it was Sebastian's work.

"This way." Gordan opened the double doors, waiting for the ladies to enter a large, beautiful office. For a moment, Laura was captured by the large painting mounted on the wall behind the impressive desk. Another of his pieces. Laura's eyes filled with tears as she took in the beautiful and serene setting. She quickly blinked them away.

Cassandra said quietly, "That's our home on Martinique."

Overwhelmed with emotion, Laura managed to get out, "It's magnificent."

Gordan gestured to one of the visitors' chairs. Once his wife was seated, his hand lingered on her shoulder. He asked, "Ms. Murdock, how can we be of assistance?"

Laura swallowed nervously, folded her hands tightly in her lap. Suddenly, her eyes went wide and she jumped up. "What am I doing? I forgot my luggage."

"No problem. Sit tight, I'll get it." He didn't pass on the chore to another, but quickly left the room.

Cassy gestured to the side table against the wall that had been set up as a beverage bar. "Would you care for something to drink, Ms. Murdock?"

"No thanks. Please call me Laura."

"And I'm Cassy."

Laura nervously blurted out, "Wil spoke of you and your husband fondly. And your twins and Gordy as well."

"He mentioned you this past weekend. We had the entire family down to celebrate the twins' ninth birthday and our wedding anniversary."

Laura's eyes had widened in surprise. Before she could ask how he was, Gordan returned with her luggage. "Thank you."

"I was telling Laura about our weekend. We had a house full of family and friends." Cassy laughed.

Gordan said, "Ms. Murdock, as my wife explained, we were with Wilham over the weekend. You said you flew in to speak to him. Did he know you were coming?"

"No, he was not expecting me. We met while I was vacationing in St. John." She sighed before admitting, "It's hard to explain my reason for following him. I posed for him and we became close very quickly, but we did not part amicably. I flew back to the island only to learn he had left." Her hands fluttered restlessly. "Next, I came here, hoping to find him in Atlanta. Considering how we parted, I can't even say he'd be pleased to see me."

Gordan said dryly, "I still don't see how you think we can help. Do you have his cell phone number?"

Laura reluctantly said, "I do."

"Then why not use it?"

She shook her head. "You don't understand. It's important that I speak to him in person."

"Ms. Murdock. I don't make a habit of interfering in my brother's personal life. The only reason we are having this conversation is because Wilham told us how he feels about you and your refusal to marry him. Frankly, I don't see the point in you following him. The way he put it, he was not the right millionaire for you."

Both women gasped aloud at the brutally honest remark. Horribly embarrassed, Laura wished the floor would open up and swallow her whole. Her eyes shone with tears that she wouldn't let fall.

"Gordan!" Cassy scolded.

Laura said unhappily, "You're right. I deserve that and probably worse. It's complicated but I was never interested in him because of money. I have a lot of explaining to do. Most important, I need to tell him that I was wrong. And I'm sorry. It wasn't until I was back home that I realized how much I love him. It's not something I wish to explain over the telephone." Laura blinked rapidly, unable to hold back tears. She sniffed while asking, "Please, can you help me?"

When Gordan didn't respond fast enough, Cassy sent him an impatient look before she said, "Wilham's in Chicago, overseeing the construction of a new hotel."

"Chicago?" Laura whispered, stunned.

She didn't notice when Cassy went to her husband, placing a hand on his chest, and leaned in to speak to him privately. Lost in thought, Laura was unaware that Gordan picked up the telephone. Engrossed in trying to decide her next move, Laura jumped when Cassy touched her tightly clasped hands.

Concerned, Cassy asked, "Are you okay, Laura? Are you sure I can't get you something to drink?"

"No, but thank you." Laura admitted, "I'm a little tired. Is there a restroom where I might freshen up?"

"Of course." Cassy showed Laura to her husband's private washroom. "There are fresh towels in the cupboard, if you need them. And there's a shower stall. Take your time."

Laura offered a weak smile. "Thank you, Cassy."

She had not expected kindness, not after the way she had hurt Wilham.

Although tempted by the roomy, multihead shower stall and the stack of thick ivory towels, she took a few moments to use the restroom. After washing her hands, she splashed water on her face. Although she redid her makeup, there was nothing she could do about the damage from too little sleep and too much worry.

When she finally had her emotions under control, she quietly returned. It was obvious by the way the couple looked at each other and held hands that they were still deeply in love, even after years of marriage and children.

Despite his coldness toward her, Laura understood Gordan was protecting his brother. She really liked them both. Wilham was blessed to have a warm, loving family. She wished she'd met them under favorable circumstances. She wanted them to like and respect her. But under the circumstances it was too late for that now.

She would have liked to talk to them, learn more about Wilham, hear the stories of his childhood and teen years. She would have enjoyed hearing about their parents. She respected and admired Gordan for many reasons, though mainly for the care he had given to a much younger brother.

Saddened that Gordan didn't like her and upset that he believed she was after money, Laura knew she had no one to blame but herself.

Laura approached the couple with her chin up and her slim shoulders back. "I realize I have no way of proving to you that I'm sincere. Nevertheless, I'd like to thank you both for your time and willingness to listen to what I had to say. Even though I don't deserve it, I have one request. Would you tell me the name of Wilham's hotel? Please?"

Gordan said, "So you haven't changed your mind about speaking to him in person."

Laura nodded. "That's correct. Considering the way I hurt him, he deserves to hear my apology face-to-face. For what it's worth, I didn't plan to fall in love with Wilham. I never intended to hurt your brother."

Gordan went to the door and beckoned someone. A young man entered and closed the door. Gordan said to Laura, "This is my assistant, Mark Sanders. Mark will escort you to my driver. He's waiting to take you to the airport, where my pilot and plane are ready to fly you to Chicago. Once you touch down, a car will be waiting to take you to my brother. The rest will be up to you."

Gordan grinned for the first time. The family resemblance was remarkable but it was wasted on Laura. She was too stunned to notice.

"What did you say?"

"You heard correctly. Soon you will get your wish, a face-to-face meeting with Wilham Sebastian." He grinned. "You've got guts, Laura Murdock. Believe me when I say you're going to need them. Wil's a good man, but he's also stubborn." Suddenly he chuckled before saying, "Cassy would say he gets that honestly, from me. My brother won't welcome you with open arms. Frankly, I doubt you're going to convince him to listen to you."

Even though she knew she would be better off keeping her mouth closed, that didn't stop her from asking, "But why would you help me?"

"Because my brother cares about you and I trust his judgment. I'll admit, I was biased against you until we met. But you've been open and honest with us. Plus you didn't back down when challenged. I like that. You've earned my respect, Laura. Wilham's hurting. And you're the only one who can fix this."

Forced to blink back tears, she admitted, "I don't know how to thank you, Mr. Kr—"

"Call me Gordan. Cassy and I are pulling for you, but it won't be easy. Go in there prepared because Wilham's an excellent attorney. He won't back down, especially when he believes he's right."

Laura nodded, knowing the odds were not in her favor.

Cassy came over and squeezed her hands. "Laura, Gordan is right. Wilham might not want to see you, but he has a weakness . . . you. If the two of you really love each other, then you will have to find a compromise. One that both of you can live with."

"I still don't understand why you would—"

The couple laughed.

Cassy said with a smile, "Gordan and I have been there. Our path to finding and holding on to love wasn't exactly smooth, more like the roller-coaster ride from hell. We know what it's like when muleheaded folks fall in love."

Gordan glanced at his wristwatch. "You'd better get moving. That plane's only on loan, young lady. My pilot is waiting for clearance to fly. Plus the traffic out to Hartsfield-Jackson Atlanta International Airport at this time of day is a nightmare." He kissed her cheek. "Good luck."

As Laura studied the luxuriously appointed Kramer jet, she was consumed by shame. She recalled in nauseating detail the mistakes she'd made along the way, the worst being the numerous comments she'd made about marrying for money. She'd lost count of how many times she'd told Wilham he was not the right man for her. She hadn't hemmed and hawed, but come right out and told him that he couldn't afford her. If she had just stopped there. But no, she had gone so far as to compare him, unfavorably, to his older brother. It was not only wrong, but cruel. How could she even think to ask for his forgiveness?

She only had to look around to know the Kramers were wealthy beyond anything this poor foster girl could dream up, even in her wildest fantasy. And Laura was scared, now that it had finally sunk in that her island artist was really a powerful corporate owner and attorney. How was she supposed to convince him that she was there because she loved him? Or that her change of heart had nothing to do with his incredible wealth?

But money alone had *never* mattered to her. What she craved was assurance, security. She didn't want to go backward. She didn't want to end up the way she had come into this world . . . abandoned.

Weary, she rubbed her aching temples, knowing she was running out of time. If they were going to make it work, then she had to find a way of proving to him beyond all doubt that she didn't care about the money. That she was in love with him. Her future happiness depended on her finding the way, and quickly.

Twenty-two

Laura was fraught with anxiety by the time the plane touched down in Chicago. The late-afternoon sun heated the inside of the limousine as they made their way through rush hour traffic. It was nearly five by the time the driver stopped in front of a high-rise office building.

She thought she had been running scared when she turned down his proposal. She thought she had been upset when he sent the painting. And she thought she'd been stressed when she faced his relatives and asked for their help. She'd been wrong. They didn't compare to how she felt now as she waited for the elevator to take her to the forty-fourth floor of the Banner Building, where Kramer Corporation's executive offices had been temporarily housed.

After hours of traveling, she was a wrinkled mess. She'd been too busy trying to find a way out of the problems she created to worry about clothes. It was a fine time for her to remember Mrs. Green's advice, to always look her best when faced with a challenge. What she needed was a curve-hugging, pink strapless evening gown with a thigh-high slit. Now that would get his attention. Suddenly she gasped, struggling to suppress a giggle at the wild thought.

Knowing she was facing the fight of her life, she wondered if George Foreman had felt this nervous when he'd faced Muhammad Ali. She jumped when the elevator chimed, signaling she'd reached the top floor.

The elevator door opened onto a lobby. "Kramer Corporation, Executive Offices" was etched in gold lettering on the double glass doors.

Her heart was pounding by the time she entered and approached the desk. Two women were talking in hushed tones. The tall, attractive one seated in front of a computer monitor, said, "Hello, Ms. Murdock?"

Laura blinked, surprised, and quickly nodded.

"I'm Gabrielle Martin, Mr. Wilham Kramer's executive assistant." She rose and started walking. "This way, please." She moved down the hall, past several closed doors. She knocked briefly on the oak-paneled door at the end of the hall. "Mr. Kramer is expecting you."

"Thank you," Laura managed to say before the door opened. The first thing she noticed was that the paint-stained jeans and short-sleeve cotton shirt had been replaced by a dark brown, custom-made suit, crisp white shirt, and a gold and dark brown striped tie. He was seated at a large mahogany desk that was positioned in front of floor-to-ceiling windows. The drapes had been partly drawn, shielding the late-afternoon sunlight. He was on the telephone, but silently mouthed, *Thanks* to his assistant and motioned for Laura to take one of the cushioned chairs in front of the desk.

Wilham barely heard what his cousin Kenneth Kramer, head of security, said about the recent problems on the construction site. He was furious. All else failed to hold his attention. He couldn't imagine what Laura had said to his brother to change his opinion of her.

Gordan had gone from calling her a gold digger to offering her the use of his private plane and pilot. And his brother hadn't stopped there. He had asked for a personal favor. He wanted Wilham's word that he would at least hear her out.

Gordan was a fair man. A man of honor and integrity. If he didn't know how deeply Gordan loved Cassy and that Gordan would never betray him, Wilham would think Laura had seduced the man into helping her.

From the moment he learned she was on her way, Wilham had wracked his brain but couldn't figure out why she'd bothered to come—unless she was pregnant? Was that it?

Wilham swore beneath his breath, grinding his teeth in mute frustration. He didn't need this, especially not now. He was fed up with restless nights filled with dreams of her. He was sick of his relentless need for her. He couldn't control it any more than he could stop his heart from beating.

His hungry gaze feasted on the petite beauty. This woman had him tied in emotional knots for weeks. He tried to convince himself that she was just like the others, but despite his best efforts, it hadn't worked.

"Wil, are you still there?" Kenneth said in his ear.

"I'll get back to you," Wilham said, and put down the phone. "Laura," he acknowledged. "Why are you here? Are you pregnant?"

She gasped, then quickly said, "No, I'm not. Why would you ask such a thing?"

He arched a brow. "We slept together. It was a logical question. Why are you here, Laura? More important, why did you bring my family into this?"

He watched her glance around the room before she finally focused on her clasped hands. "I needed to speak to you. And I apologize for involving your family, but I didn't know how to find you. I flew to St. John on Monday, then on to Atlanta. I'm sure you've heard that I went to your corporate headquarters in the hope of talking to you." She paused before continuing quietly, "I was feeling a bit desperate when I asked for Cassy and Gordan's help."

Frustrated that she'd looked everywhere but at him, Wilham mocked, "Desperate? Hardly! You couldn't wait to get away from me the last time we talked. Why didn't you simply call my cell number?"

Finally, her beautiful dark eyes met his. But they were filled with . . . sadness? Regret? No way! She knew how he felt about her. And she had not hesitated when she turned him down. She hadn't cared enough to even consider his offer. She'd broken his heart without a backward glance. Fuming, he swallowed down a curse.

Yet, in spite of his anger, his body betrayed him. His shaft was hard and aching. Damn it, she'd rejected him. Hurt him. He had some pride. He wasn't about to beg her to reconsider. They were done!

Annoyed, he said tightly, "Do us both a favor and spit it out. I'm a very busy man."

She sighed before she said softly, "I didn't call your cell because it was important that I speak to you in person, face-to-face. That's why I flew back to the island."

He glanced at his watch. "You've got five minutes."

"Wil, please. I never meant to hurt you when I—"

"When you turned me down without giving it any

thought? Or when you refused to keep my ring?" he snarled.

"I don't remember you being this cold, so . . ." She hesitated.

"You left me, Laura! You wanted out. No problem. Are we done with the rehash?"

"I don't blame you for being angry. I imagine I should feel lucky that you were willing to talk to me!"

He snarled, "Damn it, just say what you came to say and—"

"—leave?" she whispered.

Wilham didn't answer. He didn't need to. His body language said loud and clear that he wanted her gone.

Laura frowned, struggling not to break down. She could see that he was not about to make this easy for her. He was acting as if he couldn't stand to be in the same room with her. Was it just anger? Or had love turned to hate?

Close to tears, she fought for control. She couldn't leave now, not until she said what she came all this way to say. Somehow, she had to find a way.

Taking a deep breath, she confessed, "When I returned home, I tried to pretend nothing had changed, nothing had gone wrong. I was back in my condo, working at the women's center and back to doing what I do best. I was only going through the motions, doing whatever needed to be done while trying to pretend that I'd never met you, never known your kisses, and never experienced your lovemaking." She rushed on to say, "My foster sisters suspected that something was wrong, but I denied it. I didn't want anyone to guess how I really felt. Wil, I was a mess." Then, she paused before admitting, "I didn't want anyone to know that I was miserable, crying myself to sleep night after night. I couldn't bear talking about what happened between us because it hurt too much."

"Hurt? Impossible. You got exactly what you wanted."

"I got nothing! But you can't see that. You don't understand." She hesitated, then said, "I thought I was doing fine, holding it together until I got that crate from you. Why, Wil, did you send it? Why couldn't you just keep it?"

"It wasn't mine to keep. It belonged to you."

"I didn't have to unwrap the painting to know which one it was. I was so upset, I had the men put it in my guest bedroom and close the door. I didn't want to remember that day in the meadow or you."

Restless, she began to pace between his desk and a large table with a stack of blueprints littering the surface. "I was home. Things were supposed to go back to normal. Yet I couldn't look at myself in the mirror. It was exhausting, pretending nothing was wrong," she said candidly.

"After the painting arrived, I was forced to deal with what was really going on inside of me. I was no longer the carefree Laura who flew out to St. John three weeks earlier. The bright, wonderful future that I planned so carefully for myself had lost its appeal. I couldn't figure out what I was going to do next, let alone understand how I felt about what happened to me. Wil, you're what happened to me. After I met you, nothing was the same for me. Everything I thought I knew about myself was wrong."

Laura turned to face him and pointed a shaky finger at him. "You crushed my plans! I might have been able to ignore you if you had done the decent thing. If you had just left me alone! No, you couldn't keep your hands and lips to yourself," she accused. "I'd be fine right now. More than fine, I'd probably be planning my wedding to some rich, wonderful man, instead of flying all over the place looking for you. I certainly would not have to explain myself to anyone. You, Wilham Sebastian, sure haven't made it easy for me. You crept into my head and then into my heart. Who knows how long I could have gone on pretending I didn't have feelings for you if you hadn't sent that blasted painting!"

Momentarily blinded by tears, she hastily wiped them away. "You did this me! You made me feel things I didn't want to feel. Thanks to you, my work, something I've always been able to count on, no longer held my attention. I couldn't concentrate because I couldn't get you out of my head! Instead of focusing on my girls in the mentoring program, I was busy remembering the husky sound of your voice filled with desire when we made love.

"When I should be consoling a rape victim, I'm remembering the scent of your skin and the feel of your body against mine. Instead of working on building a child abuse case against a dangerous parent, I'm daydreaming about something you said while we were together on the island. It was impossible to concentrate. I can't afford to make mistakes, especially when others depend on my clear thinking."

Overwhelmed by emotion, she glared at him. "Why did you have to go and ruin things? You're the one who got all serious on me. You forced me to think of the future in a new way. Now here I am like a lovesick puppy, following you all over the globe! I flew from Detroit to St. John and then to Atlanta and now I'm finally in Chicago." She narrowed her eyes. "We're going to settle this now! I want my life back!"

"Go home, Laura. Forget we ever met. It was not meant to be."

She sagged like a deflating balloon, forced to hold on to the edge of the desk. She said dejectedly, "I see. So you have changed your mind. You don't love me after all."

His laugh held no humor. "Why did you bother to come? A guilty conscience? Or to prove you didn't let the wealthiest one get away? Why aren't you chasing down some of those hotshot NFL players? It's not too late!"

She lifted her chin. "I came for an explanation! Please tell me why you sent the painting to me."

He rose, fists clenched. "You know why! It never belonged to me, just like you were never mine. I was wrong to touch you. I must have been out of my mind to let myself believe you cared for me the way I cared for you. Who knows!" He shrugged. "We might have made it if you hadn't had to fly back so soon. My mistake was confusing sex with love. My shame was not recognizing it until after you stomped all over my heart in your four-inch heels!"

When he turned away so she couldn't see his face, she followed. Although she ached to touch him, to once again feel his arms holding her, she didn't dare. She was acutely aware of the pain she caused him because she was such a coward, unable to admit the truth. She held her body so tight, her muscles hurt from the strain. He deserved the truth!

She forced herself to say, "Wilham Sebastian, you didn't confuse sex with love. I made love with you because I fell in love with you on that island. I'm sorry I didn't tell you, but I honestly didn't understand what I was feeling until recently. I didn't know it was love!

I'm so sorry. I didn't mean to hurt you. But I was so scared!" She took a deep breath. "And it was not until I got back home that I had time to really think about us and sort out all my feelings. You're wrong. It was so much more than just sex. We made love!"

He sank heavily into his chair, a frown creasing his brow. But he didn't say anything.

She moved to stand in front of him and reached out to caress his cheek. Laura confessed, "Until you, Wil, I'd never experienced a man's love. I didn't know what it was. I grew up without a father. There was not even a wayward uncle to teach me about men and love. My foster sisters helped me realize that I was in love with you and too stubborn and downright scared to admit it." Her lips quivered when she smiled tentatively. "When you asked if I was here because I was pregnant, I realized that I was disappointed that I'm not pregnant. There's nothing I'd like more, Wilham, than to carry your babies close to my heart. I love you. And I'm not going to stop saying it until you believe me."

For a poignant moment golden brown eyes studied dark brown eyes, yet neither moved or spoke. Her heart raced, filled with both dazzling hope and incredible fear. What if he refused to believe her? What then?

Finally, Wilham said Laura's name and reached out to bring her down into his arms. But she shook her head no, taking several steps backward.

Her eyes were filled with tears and her heart pounded like a steel drum when she said, "Do you still want to get married?"

A slow smile lifted his wide mouth and softened his features before he said firmly, "Yes, that's exactly what I want."

She ached for his touch, but stubbornly held back.

She didn't rush into his arms the way she longed to do. Laura said seriously, "Good, because I have two conditions. The first, we have to marry immediately, before my fears take over and I change my mind. Wil, I'm so scared this is just a dream and it won't last." She swallowed, then added, "The second condition is the most important. We must have a prenuptial agreement that says if the marriage fails and we separate, for any reason, then we each walk away with only what we brought financially into the marriage. Do we agree?"

Chuckling, Wilham went to her and wrapped her in his arms. He pressed deep, hungry kisses against her soft lips. When he pulled back, he whispered, "Laura, you are my love. You don't need to prove anything to me. Finally, I can see the love in your beautiful dark eyes. I don't need or want a prenup."

She held firm. "You, my love, may not need one, but I do. I must prove that it's you I love, not the money. I'm amazed how you and your brother have managed to make money in this dreadful economy but you have. I'm not only proud of your accomplishments, Wil, I also respect you. I want you to feel that way about me, someday. Now, please answer the question, Wilham Sebastian Kramer."

He teased, "You like using my full name, don't you?"

She smiled up at him, smoothing his lapel. "The folks in the Virgin Islands call you Sebastian because of your art, and your family and business contacts call you Wilham. I prefer using both names because you are everything to me. Are we in agreement, island man?"

Chuckling, he said, "Absolutely. I'll take you any way I can get you. Any other requests, Laura Jean?"

Laura squealed in delight, wrapping both arms

around his neck and pulling his mouth down to hers. They shared a long, hungry kiss.

"No more requests. You've made me so happy, my sweet island man. Thank you."

Laura was shocked by how quickly Wilham put their plans into motion. After speaking to his lawyer, he called his brother's pilot and told him their destination. Rather than waiting to get his plane ready, he was taking his brother's. Laura could not believe how quickly they were on their way to the airport and flying to Las Vegas. His assistant, Gabrielle, took care of the arrangements for a hotel and limousine.

She exclaimed. "So fast!" from the backseat of the limousine.

"Your number one condition, remember?" He pulled her onto his lap and kissed the tender place where her neck and shoulder joined. "Anything for you, Peaches."

"I don't need things, just you." She draped a slim arm around his neck.

"You may not need this, but I want you to have it." He reached into the inside pocket of his jacket and pulled out a small familiar box.

She gasped, "You kept it." Her eyes filled with tears.

"I've been carrying it around with me." He cradled her face in a wide palm. "Will you marry me, sweetheart and wear my ring?"

Blinking away tears, Laura nodded and whispered, "Oh yes."

He slipped the kunzite and diamond ring onto her left hand, kissed the stone, and then turned her hand over and placed a tender kiss in the center of her palm. She shivered at the sweet contact.

"Thank you," he said, giving her a hard kiss. "I promise to love you, always. Ready?"

The car had slowed as they approached the hangar where the plane and crew waited.

"I'm ready." She slipped her hand into his.

Las Vegas, Nevada

They agreed to have the ceremony at dawn, just for the two of them. But he also promised her a wedding reception in Detroit for their family and friends. His attorney, Grant Holmes, flew in and went over the prenuptial contract he'd brought with him. Laura nodded her understanding before she quickly signed the document without hesitation.

Laura wore an ivory silk dress with a fitted bodice and knee-length skirt of layers of chiffon, and over it a fitted lace jacket. Wilham wore a black tuxedo when they were married in a small, flower-filled chapel with a minister officiating. Grant and his wife, Liza, served as witnesses.

After the ceremony and wedding breakfast with the Holmeses, the newlyweds were eager to finally be alone.

"Happy?" he asked softly, a supporting arm around her waist when the elevator doors closed.

She smiled, looking up into his golden brown eyes. "Deliriously happy. How about you?"

He grinned. "I will be once I get you out of these clothes and into my bed."

Laura giggled. "You didn't have to marry me to do that."

"Yes, I did. I'm not willing to take any chances on losing you ever again." He kissed the tip of her nose. "Don't forget, I'm a lawyer. I didn't like loose ends."

"Once I realized I loved you there was no holding me back." She reached up to stroke his jaw. "I was scared but I knew I had to tell you. I just didn't expect I had to travel so far to find you."

He kissed her. "Sweetheart, I'm just beginning to realize how fortunate I am that you didn't give up."

She was trembling from fatigue when he swung her off her feet and carried her inside their suite. Resting her head on his shoulder, Laura said, "I'm so sorry, honey. All the travel on little sleep has finally caught up with me. I can't keep my eyes open any longer," she crooned tiredly. "My sweet island man."

He chuckled as he carried her into the bedroom. "Only the best for you, Laura Kramer."

"Mmm, I like the sound of my new name." She didn't open her eyes until he released her legs, allowing her lower body to slowly glide against his long frame.

The drapes had been drawn, shutting out the morning sun, and the room had been lit by flameless candles. There must have been hundreds of them because they were on every flat surface. The tall crystal vase on the nightstand displayed three dozen long-stemmed pink roses from the palest to the darkest hue.

"Goodness," she whispered, looking around. "Oh, honey, how beautiful. The roses are exquisite." She looked up at her beaming husband, her eyes shimmering with tears. "Thank you, Wilham. You make me feel like a princess."

"You're my princess, my love."

"You, Wilham Sebastian, make me so happy. I adore the way you take care of me. Now it's my turn to please you." She reached up and pulled his head down toward hers. She licked his lip, traced the full lower one with her tongue, causing them both to shiver with need. He groaned her name before he took her soft lips in a deep, tongue-stroking kiss.

"You have no idea how much I've missed you, sweetheart. I left the island a few days after you went home." He trailed a caressing finger along her face. "I was lost without you. For the first time in my life I couldn't paint. I closed up the house and just flew back to Atlanta because I could not bear being there without you." He kissed her tenderly. "I don't know how you did it so quickly, but you, Laura Jean Murdock Kramer, got under my skin and crawled into my heart. I was slowly going mad trying to do without you." He buried his face against her neck and whispered, "Never again. Promise me, love, that you will never leave me again."

Wrapping her arms around his lean waist, she held on tight. "Never again, my love. I promise."

They shared a tender, poignant kiss. "Tell me the exact moment when you knew it was love."

She shook her head. "I didn't know but I remembered the morning you took me to see the mural you painted in the children's wing of the hospital. It wasn't just your looks and your talent that made me realize you are a special man. I was touched by your generosity to those sick children. You took time with each one of them, showed them how to paint. I should have known then, but I refused to call it love. When did you know it was love?"

"I didn't know what I was feeling was love until the night we made love. Once I was inside you, then I knew this was unlike anything I'd experienced before. You touched my heart, you gave me joy. You took away the loneliness I had never acknowledged. But it wasn't until dawn the next morning when I had to paint you, I realized you mattered to me. I was just beginning to understand what was going on with me. My feelings were new, raw, and in that painting."

She nodded. "I saw the love but was too afraid to believe. I'm so sorry it took me so long."

He surprised her when he said, "I know exactly how I'm going to paint you next. You will be in this dress, standing in front of the colored glass window in the chapel. I don't want to ever forget how you looked this morning when you became my wife. You have never been more beautiful or precious to me."

She sighed, deeply touched. "Thank you." Then she spoiled the tender moment when she yawned. "I'm s-s—"

Chuckling, he said, "Time to put my sleeping beauty to bed."

Wilham began pulling the pins and wilting flowers from Laura's braided hair. He eased the lace jacket off her shoulders and unzipped the dress.

She was too tired to help. When he had her down to her white lace strapless bra and lace panties, he pulled back the creamy white top sheet and velvet coverlet.

"Wil," she protested when he lifted her and tucked her in. She clung to his hand. "This is not how I imagined our wedding night would be."

"Rest, love." He leaned over to place a kiss on her temple.

"Not without you," she protested, lids heavy.

"I'm right here and I'm not going anywhere. Now sleep."

Twenty-three

It was hours later when Laura woke. The drapes were still drawn and the room was still illuminated by the soft glow of candles. A glance at the clock told her it was seven-thirty, only she had no idea if it was morning or evening.

She shifted, immediately cognizant of the warmth radiating from her husband's bronze skin. Her cheek was on his bare chest, her arm around his waist, and one leg between his hard-muscled thighs.

"Hi," he said in a deep, husky voice. "Sleep well?"

She nodded. "I slept so hard I don't know if it's a.m. or p.m."

"Evening. Hungry?"

"Yes, but I have more urgent matters to take care of. Excuse me."

She dashed into the bathroom to use the facilities. While washing her hands, she frowned into the mirror. Her braids were all over the place and her eyes were smudged with black mascara and her lips were bare.

"I'm a mess," she whispered, and stuck her tongue out at her reflection. She unwrapped the hotel's gift basket on the counter and was thrilled to find small jars of expensive toiletries including facial cleanser, toner, serum and moisturizer, and night creams and lotions. She also discovered a wrapped toothbrush and sample tubes of toothpaste and bottles of mouthwash.

She quickly creamed her face. She was rinsing away the toothpaste when there was a knock on the door. "Come in."

Wilham carried her large tote bag and carry-on luggage. "I thought you might need these."

Laura blushed hotly, conscious of what they both were not wearing. She did her best to keep her gaze locked on his eyes as he approached her from behind. Keenly aware of the expanse of his dark bronze chest and his erection outlined in tight low-riding jeans, she couldn't control her burning cheeks or her rapid breathing. They studied each other in the mirror.

She trembled when she felt his lips on her nape and nearly lost her balance when he softly scraped his teeth over the sensitive spot. She shivered with awareness when he suckled the spot and gave her a love bite.

It was her very first and she loved it. She longed to turn around and return the sweet favor, but she hesitated. What she knew about pleasuring a man wouldn't fill a thimble. Goodness! She was woefully unprepared for marriage. And they were truly wed.

What had she done? Had she foolishly assumed because she loved him she would be enough to fulfill his desires night after night and year after year? What if she was not enough? He was a sophisticated, experienced man while she was a relatively inexperienced female who had never been able to hold on to a man. She hadn't experienced a climax until he'd shown her the way. Now what was she going to do to please him sexually? Could she keep him coming back for more?

"Peaches? Say something."

Nervously, she licked dry lips before blurting out, "How am I supposed to pleasure you?"

He looked into her eyes. "You have nothing to be concerned about. Everything about you pleases me," he said in a husky voice.

"You sure?"

"Positive. What would you like to eat? Breakfast or dinner?" he quizzed, as if they'd been married for years. Opening the black leather toiletry case on the counter, he pulled out a toothbrush.

Her stomach chose that moment to growl loudly. She giggled. "You decide."

Laughing, he said, "I'd better order something soon. But first we should talk."

"About what?" Realizing that she'd been staring at him as if fascinated by the way he put toothpaste on his brush, she searched in her tote bag until she found scented shower gel and body lotion.

"Do you like to eat in bed or out?"

"Out. I don't like crumbs in bed."

"Do you prefer showers or baths?"

"Baths when time permits. How about you?" she asked as she went over to the spacious tub and turned on the taps.

"Showers," he said around his toothbrush. After he'd rinsed, he grinned as he said, "You, Mrs. Kramer, may join me whenever you'd like."

She smiled. "Thanks, I'll keep that in mind." She was so busy watching the play of muscles beneath his dark skin that she squeezed out a lot more gel than she needed. "Goodness!" she exclaimed as a huge volume of bubbles appeared on the water surface.

"What?" he asked, as he used an electric shaver.

"Nothing really, I'm being wasteful, not paying attention to what I'm doing."

When he finished shaving and came over to her she surprised them both when she hopped in and sat down in the tub. Turning off the water, she was covered with bubbles. She unhooked her bra and then wiggled out of her panties. Her cheeks were hot as she washed them out.

Lifting a brow, he asked, "Do you normally bathe in your undergarments? Or wash them while in the tub?"

"Of course not!" She laughed. "It's you. You being here has me doing crazy things."

He grinned, watching as she dropped her soapy things on the floor. He picked them up and tossed them into the sink. When he returned, he unsnapped and unzipped his jeans.

Leaning against the side of the tub, she could not take her eyes off him. She watched as he pushed his jeans down long, muscular legs and stepped free. She gasped, nearly swallowing a mouthful of bubbles, when she realized he wasn't wearing briefs. Her entire body was suddenly flushed with heat. Good heavens! He was absolutely gorgeous and he was all hers. The wicked thoughts had her blushing like a schoolgirl.

When he slid into the scented water, her back against his front, she complained, "What took you so long?"

Wilham chuckled before kissing her nape and then moving until he covered her mouth with his and giving her the tongue-stroking kiss she adored. She moaned, opening for more of his wonderful, hot caresses.

She crooned, "Finally, I've got everything I want, Wilham Sebastian. Right here in my arms."

What she did not say, could not admit was now that she had him, her next step would be to figure out how to hold on to him. No matter how desperately she wanted to believe in everlasting love, life had taught her a hard lesson. One she must never forget. Love had never been something she could count on.

Releasing a husky groan, Wilham deepened the kiss. He both gave and received pleasure. Consumed by the need to be one with him, she moaned, turning to rub aching nipples against his hard, muscled chest. When the kiss ended, she licked his damp throat. Her eyes closed as he cupped and squeezed her plump breasts, and then took them between his fingertips, gently pinching the ultrasensitive peaks again and again, causing her to call his name urgently.

Laura was hungry for Wilham, so needy that her entire body trembled with longing. She burned to have him deep inside her, filling that empty place. Enjoying the feel and touch of his hot skin, she smoothed her hands up and down his back. When she reached the small of his back, she hesitated, suddenly shy and uncertain.

"Don't stop," he groaned, giving her the courage to freely touch him, to get to know his smooth flesh.

She slowly stroked down to his taut buttocks. She squeezed his firm flesh while marveling at their differences. When she caressed a hard-muscled thigh, she felt him quiver from her touch. She quickly realized that touching him also gave her pleasure. She arched her back and rubbed her aching mound against his thigh.

"Wil, please hurry. I need you . . . now," she begged, and gently sank her teeth into his fleshy bottom lip and then sucked it into the heat of her mouth.

He growled, deep in his throat. Then he shifted until she was straddling his hips. He kissed her urgently. Even though his voice was rough with need, he said softly, "Talk to me, sweetheart. Tell me what you need, how you want me to pleasure you."

Aching for him, she scolded, "You know . . ."

"Tell me . . ." he husked into her ear, tightening his arms around her until she could feel his erection. He was close but not yet touching her entrance.

Desperate to feel him deep inside her, she said, "Stop teasing. What I want is for you to make love to me." She moved her hand so she could caress the broad head of his penis. Encouraged by his heavy moan, she stroked down his hard length.

His breath was uneven, his skin felt hot, and his eyes were closed. Then he said, "Enough," and moved her soft hands to his shoulders. He rubbed against her cushiony soft mound and stroked her between her soft folds before he fingered her opening, and pushed a finger into her aching feminine core.

He said into her ear, "The water is hot but it can't compare to the way you feel deep inside. Laura, you're so wet, so tight." Wilham bit her lobe and then said, "I can't wait to be inside you. Is that where you want me, Peaches?"

"Yes, please! Now!" she begged.

With one strong arm around her waist he steadied her as he guided her over him and onto his shaft. Rubbing against her tender feminine folds with his pulsating length, he teased her sensitive opening with the broad crest of his sex, again and again. When she called out, arching her back, he moaned and quickly entered her, filling her moist, empty channel with his rock-hard shaft. She cried out his name as he stretched her. Shivering with pleasure, she locked her legs and arms around him.

"Am I hurting you, sweetheart?"

Now that she finally had him where she needed him most, she was not about to complain about a little discomfort.

"Honey?" he persisted.

"I'm fine . . . more than fine. Oh, Wil, you feel so good . . ." She trembled.

Lost in a haze of pleasure, she closed her eyes and enjoyed. She didn't think it possible but it was even better than she remembered. She instinctively tightened her inner muscles, unwittingly stroking from his thick root to the sensitive peak. Wilham groaned and pulled back, easing out of her, only to boldly thrust back again, tantalizing them both. He did it again and again. He stroked her deep inside, and soon she felt as if she was hurling toward completion. The burning sensation was quickly replaced by keen, intense pleasure. It was incredible! No, he was incredible! She knew that it was only the beginning, and the exquisite delight would build and build.

"Oh! Oh!" she cried out, clinging to him.

Her breathing was rapid and uneven while her heart raced with excitement. He quickened the pace even more, and then he was worrying her clitoris. He sent her tumbling into mind-numbing, unbelievable pleasure. Her climax caused her body to tighten around him, milking him, and soon had him shouting as he too climaxed. They clung together while their heart rates and breathing gradually slowed and the water surrounding them cooled.

Wilham was the first to recover. He smoothed a hand over her back and cradled her head. Kissing her softly, he asked, "You okay, babe?"

"Mmm," she murmured. Opening her eyes, she cupped his jaw and whispered, "I love you."

"Good." He sighed. "Because I love you. Oh, Peaches, you have no idea how much I missed you." He kissed her tenderly and then said, "I'm hungry. Let's get something to eat."

She smiled. "But I'm not sure I can move."

"No worries. Remember, it's my job to take care of you," he said, smoothing a hand down her cheek.

"And mine is to take care of you," she promised.

A little later, they sat side by side on the sitting room rug. They had shared a dinner in front of a fireplace that glowed softly from dozens of pillar candles in crystal hurricane glasses. They served themselves from an elaborate spread that had been wheeled in by waiters. The wide coffee table served as their dining room table and practically groaned beneath the weight of various dishes that had been piled on an ornate, heavy brass tray. Both wore thick white terry robes with the hotel initials monogrammed on the pockets. Her damp braids were wrapped in a thick towel.

"More?" Wilham held up a fork filled with lobster dripping in clarified butter.

Holding her stomach, she laughed. "I can't eat another bite."

"Delicious." He chewed slowly, his golden brown gaze caressing her features. "Come here." He patted his muscular thigh; his long legs were stretched out and crossed at the ankles.

"Better?" she said once she was seated in his lap, her head on his shoulder.

"For me. Happy?"

Laura nodded. She was beyond happy, so much so that it frightened her. Wasn't marriage supposed to make her feel safe? "You make me happy. How about you?"

"Very." He brushed his lips against her forehead. "Unfortunately, we can only stay a few days. I'm sorry, Peaches. I have to go back to Chicago. We've got a situation developing that needs my attention."

"What kind of situation?" She smoothed a finger over his creased brow.

"Problems with the new hotel. There's one construction irregularity after another. For some unknown reason, we can't get it under control. I'm really sorry, Laura. You deserve a long honeymoon."

She smiled, kissing his jaw. "We're together now. If you like, we can leave in the morning. You forget, I just spent three weeks in paradise, not doing much of anything but watching you paint."

He chuckled. "The best three weeks of my life. But you're entitled to a romantic honeymoon. Perhaps Paris? You decide where and we'll go later in the year. That's a promise."

"Okay."

"Okay, that's it? No other concerns? What about your work at the women's center and the mentoring program? We haven't even talked about your life in Detroit."

She confessed, "Before I left I told my boss that I didn't know when or if I would be coming back. I'm on an extended leave. I had a choice and I picked you."

He shook his head. "It's not going to work. You get a great deal of satisfaction from your work at the women's center. And those girls in the mentoring program mean the world to you. Why do you have to give anything up? You can do both. Chicago is less than a half-hour flight from Detroit. You can commute between the two cities, spend the weekends with me in Chicago."

She shook her head. "No. My job is too demanding,

and besides, I don't want to spend nights away from you. Neither one of us want that. I made a promise to you. And I meant it. No separation or sleeping in two different cities, states, or countries. When you have to fly to South Africa or wherever, I'm going with you. We're in this together."

"What about the mentoring program?"

"Sherri Ann and Jenna can take over. And I'll still help out when I can."

He didn't look convinced. "That will keep you happy for about a week, if we're lucky. What about your foster sisters? And your book club and other friends in Detroit?"

"I'd see them, just not every day."

He frowned. "I don't want you making sacrifices for me. I can't see how giving up your life will make you happy."

She leaned up until she could press her lips to his. When his arms tightened around her, she slid her tongue into his mouth, deepening the kiss. When he groaned huskily she slid a hand inside his robe, stroking his dark bronze hair-roughened skin. When she reached his stomach she felt his penis, thickened and hardened. Laura slipped off his lap and untied his robe. She stroked his taut stomach, running her fingers over the thick, coarse hair surrounding his shaft. When her eyes locked with his, she saw the need that he couldn't hide. He clearly wanted her to touch.

Conversation was quickly forgotten when she asked, "May I?" She waited for his nod before she caressed him, cupped and tenderly caressed the heavy sacs below the bold strength of his erection. She was thrilled when she heard his rough groans of pleasure. Knowing she was pleasing him gave her deep satisfaction.

When she moved a caressing finger over the broad tip of his sex, he moaned softly. But when she wrapped her fingers around his shaft, stroking up and down his length, he groaned and showed her how to use both hands to give him the firm hand strokes he craved. But after only a few strokes, he moved her hands away.

He said in a hoarse whisper, "Now it's my turn to explore."

He rolled her onto her back, opening her robe. He started at her small feet. He licked her heel, her instep, and suckled each toe. Shivers of excitement raced along her nerve endings as he trailed a string of open-mouthed kisses up her calves, parting them to linger on the softness of her inner thighs. Then he kissed and licked the tender seam where her thigh and hip joined. She moaned and trembled in response.

He took his time stroking the lush, dark curls covering her mound. Then he parted her softness, exposing her feminine core. He touched her folds as if she were an exquisite rose, caressing her dewy softness, and then he found her ultrasensitive pearl. She groaned with pleasure when he tested her readiness for him.

"You're wet and slick with need. I love making you hot for me, Peaches. But I want you even hotter," he crooned before he dropped his head to lick her softness, sponging her.

She cried out at the overwhelming pleasure as he slowly laved her, over and over again. But when he took the clitoris deep inside his mouth to suckle, Laura lost it. She screamed. He quickly sent her into an all-consuming orgasm. Before she could recover, Wilham covered her body with his and thrust deep inside her. His penetrating strokes were so hard and firm that he soon sent her into yet another pulsating orgasm. Only this one was so incredibly sweet because they reached completion together. They held on to each other, convulsing in each other's arms.

Chicago, Illinois

Three days stretched into five days of sheer bliss before the newlyweds had to fly back. Since she had only the one suitcase, it didn't take long that first night for Laura to get settled in Wilham's hotel suite. It was the penthouse, with three bedrooms and baths, complete with kitchen, living, and dining rooms.

Laura practically hummed from the pleasure when she woke that first morning to her husband's deep, drugging kiss. After making love, they shared a quick shower. While he dressed for work, she still in a robe ordered an elaborate breakfast, his favorites, French toast made from thick sliced brioche, creamy scrambled eggs cooked with cheddar cheese, and crisp strips of thick bacon. There was plenty of hot, strong coffee for him, and mint tea for her. As she thought about her first day without him at her side, she couldn't help wondering what she could do to fill the long hours until he returned from work.

Laura admired her handsome husband in his custom-tailored navy suit when Wilham walked into the dining room. He kissed her cheek and casually handed her a stack of invitations for upcoming formal dinners, receptions, and charity events to sort through. Pouring warm maple syrup on his French toast, he teased her because she had ordered waffles with sliced, sweetened strawberries but no syrup. She smiled, telling him he had the problem, not her. He laughed before settling down to eat.

Wilham admitted he didn't particularly enjoy the social functions he had to attend since moving to the Windy City. As she stared at the pile, her eyes widened in surprise as he predicted the invitations would triple once their wedding announcement hit the morning papers.

He casually mentioned they were scheduled to attend a dinner-dance at eight that evening at the Art Institute of Chicago. "Tonight?" she said. He nodded before matter-of-factly explaining how important it was to participate in the various functions. The new hotel's grand opening was planned for later in the year. Kramer House would soon rival Trump Tower in New York for square footage, plush hotel rooms, state-of-the-art conference rooms, luxury condominiums, five-star fine dining, first-class shopping, and entertainment. Black-tie events were necessary, part of his job.

He squeezed her hand. "You will quickly get used to it."

She frowned, "I have nothing to wear. My clothes are in my condo in Detroit."

He smiled. "No worries. Go shopping." Then he suggested she might as well get a new wardrobe that included a collection of evening wear. She swallowed a gasp when he gave her a credit card and a debit card, both in her married name, for clothing. He casually named a hefty amount that had already been deposited into her checking account to cover her general monthly expenses.

Laura had stopped eating because her mind was spinning at the drastic changes in her life as the wife of a major corporation player.

Wilham asked, "Peaches, can you start looking for a house? Something big enough for overnight visits from both our families, and with rooms large enough for entertaining. I'm tired of living in a hotel."

"Okay," she said, feeling a bit shell-shocked.

Wilham glanced at his wristwatch, quickly drained his coffee cup. "I've got to get moving. Can you meet me at the office for lunch around two?"

Laura nodded, remembering her promise to be the best wife. She wasn't giving him reason to regret their marriage.

"Good. I'd like to take you to one of my favorite seafood restaurants. It reminds me of being in the islands. Oh, I almost forgot. This is for you."

He surprised her with an iPad in a pretty pink, croco-leather case, and a high-speed pink laptop.

"But why? I don't expect you to keep buying me things. It's not why I married you."

"I know, but I like spoiling you. Indulge me."

Then he said, "I know I've given you a lot to absorb. But if you have any questions, call my cell or my assistant, Gabrielle. If I'm in a meeting, she's agreed to help out. And you have Liza Holmes's number, right?"

"Oh yes!" It took a moment to recall he was referring to his attorney's wife.

Wilham eased Laura out of her chair and into his arms for a hug and a lingering kiss. He whispered in her ear, "I love you." Then he explained he'd arranged for a car and driver to chauffeur her around the city until she had her bearings.

"How long are we going to be in Chicago?" she asked.

He said, "Indefinitely, since I will be handling our Midwest operations. There has also been discussion of building a Kramer hotel and ski resort in upper Michigan, or upstate New York, or Vermont."

"But which invitations should I accept?"

"Call Gabrielle. I'll have her e-mail the names of the best real estate agents in the city." He suggested she go online to read the Chicago newspaper society pages in order to put names with faces. His cell phone rang.

"Hello? Yes, Gabrielle." He frowned. "What?"

Although her head was still reeling from all the changes in her life, she studied her husband. Clearly, something was wrong. He was scowling.

"What is it?" she whispered.

"There's a problem with the hotel's latest building inspection. I have to go, babe." He placed a kiss on her cheek before he hurried out.

Twenty-four

Wilham often used a driver while in the city. Stunned, he reread the report that Gabrielle had e-mailed. There was a serious problem with the building inspection. The new hotel was not up to code, inferior materials had been used. His first call was to his cousin Kenneth, who was working from their South African property. Wilham relayed the problem and said he would send the corporate jet. He needed Kenneth in Chicago as soon as possible.

Determined and confident should have been his cousin's middle names. Kenneth was both ex-marine and ex-FBI. Unwilling to trade on the Kramer name, he'd earned the head security position at Kramer Corporation.

On the day Laura arrived in Chicago, Kenneth had been the first to bring to Wilham's attention the rumors that were circulating that someone was out to sabotage the project. Wilham's mind had not been on business. He'd been distracted by his problems with Laura. And because they were rumors and there was no proof, Wilham had not taken them seriously. His concession had been to beef up security at the construction site.

Apparently, it was too late and the damage had already been done.

Wilham's next call was to his nephew, Gordan Jr., who was working in Martinique. Gordy was twenty-four, an engineer, and had been acting as a trouble-shooter for nearly a year. His message was the same. Gordy was needed in Chicago.

By the time Wilham walked into his office he had also spoken to the builder, the contractor, and the architect, and had scheduled a meeting at the hotel's construction site. Wilham expected answers and quickly.

He was not looking forward to making the next call, but had no choice. He knew Gordan would drop everything and come to his aid. That was exactly what Wilham didn't want. When his brother had married Cassy, Wilham had taken on more responsibilities. He wanted Gordan to have time to enjoy his bride and growing family.

Wilham was proud that his brother trusted him to run the company and keep it profitable. And he made sure Gordan had never regretted the decision. Wilham could not forget that Gordan had stepped up when their parents had died. Gordan had not ever complained about the added responsibility. And he made sure Wilham had what he needed to thrive. Wilham might have been young, but he never doubted his brother's love and support.

"Congratulations," Gordan said when he came on the line. He chuckled. "I didn't believe it when Gabrielle said on Friday that she expected you back today. How's your bride?"

He smiled. "Laura's well. We've got a problem with the new hotel." He quickly switched to the reason for the call. From the first the Chicago project had been

Wilham's baby. Although Gordan wouldn't say it, nonetheless Wilham knew he'd let him down. There was no doubt he had been away too long, and when he returned he had let his personal life interfere.

Gordan offered his help, but Wilham refused, insisting the blame was his. And it was up to him to correct the problem and limit the damage. Gordan was concerned about the timing. Wilham and Laura were newlyweds and needed to focus on each other and establishing their new life together. Perhaps even start the family they wanted. Gordan cautioned him not to make the mistake of putting business ahead of family. Neglecting his bride was bound to cause a host of new problems. Wilham thanked his brother but insisted he could handle his marriage and the business. He ended the call with the promise that they would find the culprit and do it quickly.

Feeling a little homesick, Laura called her foster sisters. Unfortunately, she couldn't reach Sherri Ann because she was in court, but she was able to speak to Jenna before she left for the university. They hadn't talked since right before her wedding. Jenna wanted details on her dress, the wedding, and the honeymoon. Laughing, Laura filled her in and promised to e-mail their wedding picture. Sighing, Laura confessed their time alone had gone by too quickly. He'd only been gone an hour, yet already she missed him.

She told Jenna about their upcoming wedding reception in Detroit and warned she was going to need both her and Sherri Ann's help. She admitted she was looking forward to the delayed honeymoon he'd promised. Jenna laughed when Laura outlined all the things Wilham had dropped in her lap that morning, but assured her that she could handle anything, as long as she remembered she was loved. Before ending, Laura gave her a list of the things she needed sent from her condo.

Next, Laura called Vanessa. After scolding Laura for keeping Wilham a secret, Vanessa congratulated her on her marriage. Then they got down to the business of evening wear. Vanessa owned a boutique and designed both bridal and evening gowns. She had several dresses in her shop she thought Laura might like and promised to e-mail pictures. After passing along her measurements and discussing fabrics and colors, Laura was smiling when she hung up. She missed her family and friends.

After reading the Chicago society pages online, Laura came across an article about a middle school principal of a charter school with a high number of students in the foster care system without foster families, who had found innovative ways not only to keep them in school and out of trouble, but to help them thrive.

Fascinated, Laura learned the students were encouraged to earn extra credit by volunteering in the area soup kitchens, visiting nursing homes, and visiting sick children in hospitals, all while maintaining high grades. The students were unique because they had managed to gain entrance into the charter school because of their grade point average and without parental support.

She paid particular attention to the articles on teen drug abuse, high rate of teen pregnancies, lack of funding for community programs, female gangs on the rise in the low-income areas, as well as the rate of teens dropping out of schools.

Her new cell phone rang. It was Gabrielle, her husband's assistant, calling to say Wilham sent his apology because he couldn't keep their lunch date. Although disappointed, Laura was not surprised.

Gabrielle proved to be as efficient and well organized as her husband claimed. Laura liked Gabrielle and didn't hesitate to tell her how much she appreciated her help with their wedding, especially arranging for the bridal selection that had been sent to their suite.

Pleased, Gabrielle filled Laura in on the details her husband had overlooked. Gabrielle gave her a list of high-end shops and their specialties, her driver's name and cell phone number. She also told Laura what to expect at tonight's reception, what the ladies generally wore, some tidbits about their host and hostess. Gabrielle also gave her the names of two prominent real estate agents and the areas that Wilham might prefer.

After arranging to meet her driver in the hotel lobby at eleven thirty, Laura changed into a pair of dark, slim-fitting jeans, a crisp white blouse, and a short navy and pink tweed jacket, one of the few outfits she'd taken with her.

Her driver, Jack Connors, was holding a small sign with her name on it. The older man escorted her to the waiting dark sedan. Soon she was on her way to the well-known Magnificent Mile, four lavish malls along a stretch of Michigan Avenue running from Chicago River to Oak Street.

Although disappointed that she couldn't lunch with Wilham, she was satisfied with her purchases. Even though she had barely gotten started on what she would need, she was shocked by the amount of money she had spent in one day. She didn't want to remind him of why she had insisted on a prenuptial contract. It was still a sore point with her, one she'd rather forget.

She wanted to please her husband, wanted him to be

proud of her. She didn't want him to ever regret marrying her. He was never far from her thoughts. She hoped he liked the dark wine, silk knit evening gown. The dress had a pleated bodice, a long, slim skirt, and a wide sequin-covered belt. There was a matching sequined coat. She'd even found shoes to complement her dress.

They'd been married barely a week. It was the first day they hadn't spent together, and she missed him so much. She was a little disappointed that he hadn't found time to call her.

It was close to six by the time she returned to their suite. She hurried inside, eager to see him, only to find the penthouse was empty.

"Is there anything else I can do for you, Mrs. Kramer?" the bellman asked politely after taking her purchases into the master suite.

She forced a smile. "No, but thank you." She reached into her purse for cash to tip him.

Once she was alone she dropped into an armchair and kicked off her heels. There was a knock on the door. Thinking Wilham had forgotten his key card, she rushed to open the door. "Yes?" she said when she found a uniformed employee in the hall, holding a crystal vase filled with pink rosebuds and a pink cellophane–covered gift basket.

"Mrs. Laura Kramer?"

She nodded.

"A delivery from the hotel's florist and gift shop. Where would you like them?"

Gesturing toward the coffee table, she retrieved her purse to look for more cash. "Thank you."

She waited until she was alone before she looked at the card. She smiled when she saw her husband's name. The pale pink roses were perfect. The basket was filled with perfume, soap, shower gel, and lotion, all in her favorite fragrance, Rose The One by D&G. Just then her cell phone rang.

"Hello?"

"Hello, Peaches. How was your day?"

"Wil." She smiled. "It was busy. Honey, why are you calling? It's after six. We're going to be late."

"Did you get the gifts?"

"Yes. They just arrived. It was very sweet. If you hurry home I'll show you how much I like them," she teased.

His deep chuckle caused goose bumps to rise on her arms. "I'm glad you're pleased. They're a peace offering."

"Why would you need to bribe me?"

"I'm sorry, Laura. I won't be able to take you to that dinner and reception tonight. I've been in meetings all day trying to figure out what went wrong. I'm at the office waiting for Gordy and Kenneth to arrive. We'll be working all evening. I'm so sorry, sweetheart. Say you understand."

Laura sighed softly. "You don't need to bribe me with gifts. I'm not upset, just disappointed. I missed you today."

"I missed you too. Tell me about your day. Did you find a dress?"

"I did, but it will keep until the next event."

"No, Peaches, I don't want you alone in the suite while I'm working. I want you to go to the reception and enjoy the evening. You're going to love Chicago's Art Institute."

"I know, but I was looking forward to seeing it with you, and your wonderful eye for color and detail. No, I can't go on my own."

"You won't be alone. I spoke to Liza. You remember my lawyer and his wife. They're going tonight and will be happy to pick you up. If you'd like, I can ask Gabrielle. She has filled in when I had to have a date for a function."

"Really. I didn't realize you dated your assistant."

"Never dated," he quickly explained, "It was completely innocent. There has never been anything between the two of us. I don't believe in dating my employees. Besides, she's not you. You're my type, Mrs. K."

"Good. I like Gabrielle. She's beautiful and has been so helpful. Wil, I don't need a babysitter. I'll go with Liza and Grant. But it won't stop me from missing you, my sexy island man."

"Yeah, I feel the same." The regret in his voice went a long way toward soothing her disappointment. "Until later, my love."

"Yes, later," she echoed.

It was after eleven when Laura returned to the penthouse, and she was pleased to see her husband. Wilham was working in the dining room, poring over blueprints, his laptop open. He was missing his suit coat and tie, and his shirt sleeves were rolled up. And he was not alone. Two men with the same deep bronze skin tone were also working. Briefcases were open, papers spread out, while empty dinner dishes were piled onto the wheeled cart.

"Hello." Her dark brown gaze locked with his golden eyes.

He smiled, quickly rose from his chair and crossed to her. He brushed his lips against her. "You're back."

"Yes. Am I interrupting?"

"No." With an arm around her waist, he urged her

forward and made introductions, "Sweetheart, my cousin Kenneth and my nephew, Gordan Jr."

"Laura, it's a pleasure to meet you," Kenneth said; instead of shaking hands, he gently squeezed hers. He was a few years younger than Wilham but his demeanor was serious, although he gave her a warm smile. "Welcome to the family."

She was swallowed up in a gentle bear hug by his nephew. "You are gorgeous. No wonder Uncle Wil flew you out to Vegas without delay." Grinning broadly, he kissed her on the cheek. "Clearly, he wasn't taking any chances of you getting away. Welcome to the Kramers. Call me Gordy."

Smiling, she decided good looks must be in their DNA. The Kramer men were tall, very attractive, and well built. "It's nice to finally meet you both. Our wedding was hasty." She blushed, and her gaze moved to her husband.

Wilham boasted, "Quick, but no man has a lovelier bride."

Laura's eyes were lit with happiness.

The newlyweds were so busy looking at each other that they didn't notice the men packing their briefcases.

Wilham kissed her cheek. "I promised Laura that we would have a wedding reception with our friends and family."

"When?" Gordy asked, pulling on his sports jacket.

Grinning, Wilham asked, "Yeah, babe. When?"

"Soon." She laughed.

"Good night," the two men called as they went out the door.

"Where are they staying?"

"Penthouse across from ours. Our executive team and their assistants who came with me are all staying here. How was your evening? How does Chicago's Art Institute compare to Detroit's?"

Encircling his waist, she rested her cheek on his chest. "I was impressed, although I'm going to have to take the tour before I can compare the two. The dinner and reception went well. Grant and Liza introduced me to everyone. Mrs. Kimball, our hostess, was very nice. Judging by the crowd, she raised a great deal of money for Cook County's homeless shelters and soup kitchens."

"Great." He hugged her.

She complained, "But I missed you. I didn't like going without you."

"I'm sorry, babe. You look very pretty tonight. I like the dress and your braids pinned up and twisted fancy," he said as he kissed the side of her throat.

She shivered with pleasure, but confessed, "I was worried that I spent too much and you wouldn't like it."

"You're wrong on both counts." Covering a yawn, he said, "Time for bed."

Later when they were snuggled in bed with her back to his front, she said, "Tell me about your day. Did you find out what went wrong?"

"No, it's more complicated than we realized. I can't believe the problems that have been ongoing since we broke ground. It started small, nothing to slow down production. Things have progressively gotten worse. I was forced to stop construction today until I know exactly what we're dealing with. It looks like it's going to take a great deal of time to assess the damage and a lot of money to correct the mistakes. Unfortunately, it's going to put a lot of people out of work until we can get to the bottom of it."

"Oh, Wil, I'm so sorry. You must be terribly disappointed."

"The worst part for me was calling my brother, having to admit that I'd messed up," he said candidly.

"No, Wil. Why are you blaming yourself?"

"I dropped the ball. I should have stayed on top of things, should have seen this coming and stopped it before it got out of hand," he said tightly.

"That's crazy talk." She turned toward him, smoothing her hand over his bare chest. "You didn't cause this."

"It was my project! I had no business going off to paint and play in the sun," he said bluntly.

"You took a vacation, for heaven's sake!"

"Yeah, and look what happened. The blame is mine."

"Stop that! No one talks badly about my husband, not even you." She placed a series of kisses on his cheek and nose and lingered on his firm mouth.

He caressed her hips. "Don't start something I can't finish."

Giggling, she kissed his throat. "There's no doubt in my mind that you can finish, island man. Although you might be too tired to get out of bed come morning."

Chuckling, he cradled her cheek. "Our first day back in town didn't turn out the way I'd hoped. And our first night wasn't supposed . . ." He paused. "Sorr—"

She stopped him by pressing her lips against his. "No need to apologize. We'll have other nights. But, Wil, I think you're wrong about Gordan. I'm sure he doesn't hold you responsible for someone else's mistake. You're an executive and a corporate lawyer, not a contractor or builder."

He tucked a braid behind her ear. "Thanks, Peaches. I like it when you take my side." His voice was flat and cold with fury when he said, "Someone has targeted us and was willing to spend a lot of money to make sure we didn't find out until it was too late. We were lucky we caught it when we did. I won't stop until I find out who's behind this and why."

"You will find them," she soothed, caressing his shoulder and upper arms while inhaling his masculine scent. Unable to resist, she kissed and then licked the sensitive spot where his neck and shoulder joined.

Trembling from the sweet contact, he tightened his arms around her until their bodies touched from chests to hips. "Are you sure about that, Mrs. K?"

"Absolutely. Once you set your mind to something, you don't stop until it's done." Her soft lips returned to worry a tender spot before she worried his nipple.

"Did you have to kiss me there?" he moaned.

"What do you mean?"

He rolled until his hard body covered her soft curves. His erection throbbed against her stomach. "You know exactly what you're doing. Now behave. It's late and we're both tired."

"But of course," she agreed while she laved his throat repeatedly.

He growled huskily. Then he slid a hand down to cup and squeeze her soft mound. She moaned in pleasure as he stroked the dark curls covering her sex.

Laura was unable to control her shiver of desire as they raced up and down her spine while Wilham parted her damp folds, opening her for more of his hot caresses. There was no way to conceal how wet and needy she was for him. She was a heartbeat away from begging him to make love to her.

She kissed him, sponged his other nipple. "I can't help it. You have no idea how badly I want you tonight." Then she moaned, "Ohhhh . . ." as he used his thumb to worry her ultrasensitive pearl. Her lids were suddenly too heavy to remain open, her entire focus on his firm but tender strokes.

Heat licked at her inflamed flesh, and Laura moaned his name when Wilham caressed her with the hard tip of his sex. She cried out, pressing forward until she was completely open to him, soon moving along his long, hard shaft. Quickly, they were caught up in the most sensuous, erotic, dance as sparks of passion flared into hot flame that soared beyond their control. Their breathing was rapid and uneven as his hard thrusts quickly took her with him over the edge. With hearts racing, they reached completion and shared one intense, breathtaking climax.

Wilham cradled Laura as their breathing slowly returned to normal.

He said into her ear, "Unbelievable! I love you."

"I love you more," she whispered.

They were nearly asleep when he told her the next couple of weeks were going to be hectic but he didn't want the problems at work to interfere with their plans. He urged her to go ahead, schedule and plan their wedding reception.

Twenty-five

Laura's days were busy planning their reception, looking at houses, shopping, and learning all she could
about the Windy City while the evenings were filled
with dinner parties and charity events. Although she
talked to her foster sisters nearly every day, she missed
them, her friends, and her old life back in Detroit.

She didn't see enough of her busy husband and
couldn't help feeling as if she was merely marking time
until she could be alone with him. It was only when
she was wrapped in his arms that her doubts disappeared and she felt secure in her new role. There was
so much to do, so much more that demanded her attention. She worried constantly about spending too much
and giving him cause to regret their marriage.

During the rare times when he managed to steal a
few hours away from the office and was able to accom-
pany her to an event, she realized that looking pretty
on her husband's arm didn't give her the sense of ac-
complishment that came from her work at the center
and working with teen girls.

Her foster sisters encouraged her to be patient, give
herself time to adjust to the changes in her life. And she

agreed with them. She was hopeful that once the difficulties with the hotel were resolved, she would get her island man back and then her doubts and fears would disappear.

Much of her unease stemmed from seeing few signs of the man she had fallen in love with back in St. John. The carefree artist had been replaced by a corporate mogul consumed with business. She tried very hard to be supportive and never complain that they didn't spend nearly enough time together. But it was extremely difficult, especially on the days when he had no time for her. She felt as if she was the only one trying to make their marriage work.

Wilham's work ethic was remarkable. He never asked anyone to do more than he was willing to do. Even though he brought Kenneth and his security team in to find the culprit and Gordy in to assess the structural damage to the hotel, he worked tirelessly. Laura couldn't help wondering why he insisted on overseeing everything. She wouldn't be surprised if he put on a hard hat and started ripping out concrete.

They had been married only a few short weeks, but it wasn't unusual for them to go days without talking. He worked such long hours and he was often gone when she woke or he worked late into the night and didn't wake her when he came to bed.

She was ashamed to admit the less she saw of him, the more she worried about her ability to make him happy. What if they'd married too quickly? Was he secretly regretting their haste and dissatisfied with both their marriage and his lack of freedom? And if so how was she supposed to know? They shared the same suite, the same bed, but they were hardly ever together. She hated it!

She couldn't help being concerned that once the problems with the hotel were resolved and behind them, he would move on to the next new challenge. There was no disputing that Kramer Corporation meant a great deal to him. Perhaps more than she did?

Laura had plenty of reasons to doubt her ability to hold on to a man or to love. Her history was proof that she didn't know the first thing about either one. She loved him and didn't want to mess this up.

Laura struggled to hide her doubts. But deep down, she was just plain scared that he might be staying away because he'd changed his mind and no longer wanted her or a family. The possibility kept her reeling, feeling as if she was teetering on the edge of uncertainty. Would they make it last? Or were they steps away from his voicing disappointment and walking away?

Determined to distract herself and keep busy, Laura bought fabrics and sewing supplies and set up her sewing and embroidery machines in the smallest bedroom. She made bright, colorful, child-size quilts for the sick children in the hospitals, to hopefully lift the children's spirits and to occupy her time. Sewing quilts by hand had been something she grew up doing and enjoyed, especially with her foster mother and sisters. For practical reasons she used the machines to sew and decorate the small quilts.

Laura took advantage of the charity events to get to know wealthy sponsors and to learn about their causes. She tracked down and contacted the middle school principal she had read about in the newspaper online and visited the school to learn more about the foster children and the school. She wanted to learn and understand the needs of her new city. Also, she'd gone to visit a women's shelter run by one of Maureen's acquaintances. She read as much as she could about the problems women and children faced in the Windy City. She made notes and was formulating ideas of how she might be able to contribute to the community.

Wilham and Laura were attending a black-tie dinner the night she met Jessie Tucker. Her husband had introduced them. The two men had attended Morehouse at the same time and were fraternity brothers, as well as business rivals.

Almost immediately, she recalled the article she'd seen online about the community activist and real estate mogul. Tucker had recently taken over his late brother's foundation, which focused on rehabilitating gang members. Since that first meeting, Laura often saw and spoke to Jessie at other charity events. She was impressed by the way the divorced tycoon gave back despite the demands of running a successful business.

The pediatric cancer benefit dinner-dance was being held in their hotel's ballroom. All week, she had been looking forward to dancing with her husband on Friday evening. She had found the perfect dress. It was a pale pink, long silk evening gown with one covered shoulder and long sleeve, slit high on one side.

Just before they were supposed to leave, Wilham called to say he was running late, but promised to meet her there. Laura, along with Liza and Grant Holmes, took the elevator down to the sixth floor.

Dr. Joanna Rutherford, a pediatric heart specialist, was being honored for her charitable works throughout her long career. Dr. Rutherford had trained at Howard University and been an intern in the forties at Chicago's well-known Providence Hospital. She was eighty-seven, never married, and devoted her life to improving poor children's health care. Laura was delighted to meet Dr. Rutherford, tall, dark brown skin with a radiant smile.

Wilham hadn't arrived when they started to serve dinner. By the time her dessert plate arrived, Laura was struggling not to be hurt because once again, he had let her down and put business ahead of his promise to her.

No matter how many times she told herself there was no point in getting upset, her feelings were hurt. She already knew what he was going to say before he opened his mouth. He would apologize and ask for her understanding while promising that only for this short period business must come first in their lives.

Laura was really trying to be understanding. Despite her best efforts, her spirits sank a bit more each day. She hated thinking she was getting used to being neglected. Nor did she like feeling as if she was last on his list of priorities.

Laura managed to smile when Jessie took the seat next to her. By the time the award ceremony was over and the band started to play, her spirits began to lift. Jessie answered all her questions about his facility and volunteered to show her around.

She looked up and saw Wilham walking toward them. Even though he wasn't formally dressed he was in a black suit and still looked pretty darn good to Laura. She quickly excused herself and went to him.

"Hi, sweetheart." He kissed her. "I'm sorry I missed dinner. We got new information from—" He stopped and then said close to her ear, "May I have this dance, Mrs. Kramer?"

Laura forgot about scolding him for being late, forgot about telling him about Jessie Tucker's ideas about expanding her mentoring project in Chicago. She smiled and put her hand into his.

They danced until well after midnight. It was fun. She enjoyed herself. They danced until the musicians stopped playing and it was time to say their good nights. She was dragging by the time they entered their suite. So tired she nearly fell asleep in the tub. She barely recalled Wilham drying her off, slipping one of her gowns over her head, or sliding into bed with her.

She woke late the next morning and he had already left for work. Hugging his pillow, she inhaled his scent. She grabbed for the bedside telephone when it rang.

"Honey, why didn't you wake me so we could have breakfast together?"

"Hi, honey!" Jenna and Sherri Ann teased.

Laura laughed. "Good morning. What's the news from Detroit? Jenna, did you talk to Anna? What did she say about the changes I wanted on the wedding cake? Sherri Ann, did you get the okay from the Detroit Art Institute on using one of their private rooms for the reception?"

"Slow down, sister girl," Sherri Ann urged. "Take a deep breath. Everything is right on schedule. We got the private room."

"Oh good!" Laura exclaimed.

Jenna said, "And Anna is fine with the changes for the wedding cake, but insisted she needs to speak to you first. Anna Prescott Mathis is a pro who knows what she's doing. What about the invitations?"

Laura said, "Yes, she's the best. I'm all set with the invitations. Gabrielle is helping with those."

Jenna said, "Folks in Detroit have never seen anything like this fancy wedding reception. The girls are beyond excited to be invited. They can't stop talking about it."

Laura laughed, leaning back against the pillows. "I can't wait to see them. Are their dresses ready?" She had insisted on inviting all the girls in the mentoring program.

Sherri Ann said, "Yes, thanks to Vanessa, we're taking them for their final fitting on Saturday."

"Great!" Laura beamed. "I need to call and thank Vanessa for hiring extra seamstresses to get the job done. Just seeing our girls happy will be worth the inconvenience."

Sherri Ann teased, "It doesn't hurt to have a rich husband willing to pick up the tab!"

Jenna joined the laughter. "You got that right. We could never have arranged a reception so quickly and so elegantly without the Kramer name behind us. Speaking of rich husbands, when are we going to finally meet him?"

Laura winced, wishing she had never linked "rich" and "husband" in the same sentence. It still hurt knowing she had come into the marriage at a distinct disadvantage because of those foolish words. She was always careful about money, determined not to overspend. She wondered if the day would ever come when she would truly feel as if it was behind them.

"We're flying in Thursday, the twenty-fifth. That gives us a long weekend to get acquainted. But I still have a million and one things to get done here. We went to a benefit last night.

"Oh, do you two remember me talking about Jessie Tucker and his work with ex–gang members? He was there last night and we talked. He volunteered to show me his facility."

"Fantastic! You must be so excited. What does Wil think about your plans to expand the mentoring program?" Jenna asked.

"I haven't found the right moment to tell him."

"What?" Sherri Ann asked.

"Why haven't you told him?" Jenna cautioned. "Secrets aren't good in a marriage."

"I'm not keeping secrets!" Laura huffed. "What do you know about marriage, Jenna Gaines Hendricks? You've been married about, what, five minutes longer than I have! And Sherri Ann, don't even start! I'm going to tell him! I'm waiting until things settle down with the hotel."

"Laura, why are you so upset? Jenna was only trying to help and you jumped all over her. That's not like you. What's wrong?"

"Nothing. I'm sorry, Jenna. I'm stressing over the plans for the reception. It's coming quickly and I want everything to be perfect."

"Relax. It's going to be fine," Jenna encouraged.

Sherri Ann said, "I can't wait to see you. But I've got to run. I'm meeting a client."

Jenna said, "And I have a staff meeting this morning. We miss you!"

"Me too," Laura said. "Bye. I love you both!" She slowly put down the telephone.

What was wrong, what she and Wilham needed was time alone, just the two of them. The long weekend in Detroit celebrating their marriage with family and friends wouldn't be as nice as a long honeymoon but it was a start. Maybe she could convince him to take a few extra days off after their reception and fly back to St. John.

She called his office. "Morning, Gabrielle. It's Laura. How are you today?"

"I'm great. How about you? How was the dinner-dance last night?"

"The food was good but more important it was profitable. I suspect they raised close to a quarter of a million. So what's on Mr. K's schedule today? I was hoping he would be free for lunch."

"I'm so sorry, Laura. He's on his way to the construction site and he will be tied up in meetings most of the day. You might catch him between meetings on his cell."

"Thanks, Gabrielle. While I have you on the phone, please indulge me. Will you please check his schedule for Thursday, the twenty-fifth?"

Gabrielle laughed. "I don't mind double checking for you. Give me a second. I'm bringing it up now. Nothing on Thursday, the twenty-fifth; Friday, the twenty-sixth; Saturday, the twenty-seventh; and Sunday, the twenty-eighth. His plane and the crew are all set to fly both of you to Detroit. The flight leaves O'Hare at two o'clock in the afternoon. A car and driver will be waiting when you touch down."

"Thanks, Gabrielle. You're the best!"

"You're welcome. Call if you need anything. Bye, Laura."

In the bathroom Laura found a note taped to the mirror over the vanity. She smiled when she read, "Hi Peaches, You looked so peaceful, I let you sleep. I'm going to be busy all day but I've ordered a special dinner for tonight at eight. Just the two of us. There are two requirements. We both wear a bathrobe with nothing underneath. I promise not to use the words 'hotel' or 'business' if you promise not to use the words 'charity' and 'event.' "

Laura giggled. "You got a deal."

Two weeks later, Laura was alone when she boarded the Kramer jet. She was trembling with keen disappointment, anger, and hurt. She was flying back to Detroit without her husband. He had broken yet another promise, because business always came first with him. It wasn't as if he hadn't known their plans. He had approved every detail. His schedule was clear for the entire four days. He was supposed to be with her!

Biting her bottom lip to hold back a sob, Laura silently watched the flight attendant secure the cabin door while the jet's engine hummed in the background. He'd said when the plane returned that evening he would be on the next flight and she would sleep in his arms. When she protested she could wait for him, he insisted there was no point in them both being late. Besides, her foster sisters would be waiting at the airport. He had a few last-minute things that needed his attention. But he would be there. He'd promised, just before he kissed her and left for the office. She'd been so upset that she hadn't said good-bye.

That had been hours ago. All morning she had been experiencing a terrible sense of dread. The feeling had hung over her like a dark shadow and had not eased up regardless of how often she silently repeated, *He loves me.* The old fears had reared up and refused to let go.

"How could he!" she muttered beneath her breath. Her head was starting to pound and her stomach was knotted with tension. How dare he do this to her? How was she going to explain his absence to her sisters? It wasn't fair!

"Mrs. Kramer? Did you need something?" the flight attendant asked, hurrying over.

Laura forced a smile. "Nothing, but thank you. Jennifer, right?"

The other woman smiled. "Yes. We will be taking off very soon. The flight is so short there's no point in turning off the seat belt sign."

"Mmm," Laura murmured, automatically fastening the safety belt. She stared out the window, but didn't see anything. Had she made a terrible mistake? Perhaps the biggest mistake of her entire life by rushing into marriage with a man she barely knew. What was the old adage? Marry in haste, repent at leisure? She needed to face facts. She'd married a stranger. Did she even know this powerful business tycoon and corporate lawyer she'd been living with these past few weeks?

She felt as if Wilham Sebastian, her island lover, the gifted artist, had vanished and been replaced by a Mr. Kramer, relentless corporate mogul intent on finding and punishing those at fault. He would stop at nothing to make sure those responsible for sabotaging the hotel were caught. He might look the same, smell the same, sound the same, and even make love the same way as her island lover. Still, there was one major difference. Her island man had limits. Yes, he was busy but he always made time for her. He kept his promises. There was no guesswork involved. She knew beyond all doubt that she came first with him.

As the Learjet's wheels touched down, giving her a small jolt, Laura had no choice but to accept the truth. She'd married Wilham Sebastian Kramer, but she didn't know if she could count on him. Would he be her soft place to fall, no matter what?

Regardless of circumstance, in her book love should

always come first. Evidently, he had read a different edition! If he truly loved her, then there could be no doubt that she was first with him. How many dinners had he missed? How many promises had he broken? Would the neglect ever end? Or did he expect her to get used to it?

Well, she was fed up, knowing she was last on his list when she should be his number one concern. Forget about it! She'd had enough. She was not going to be overlooked, again!

Detroit, Michigan

Laura concentrated on the joy of being back with her family. Her foster sisters talked nonstop, laughing and trying to catch up on everything. It felt good being back in her home. She found comfort in the familiar. For a few moments her heart ached when she gazed at her painting, now prominently displayed on the living room wall where she asked her sisters to hang it. Along with memories, it brought with it a yearning to go backward to that special time and magical place when all had been right with them. She had loved and been loved in return.

They had dinner at Jenna's. Laura was pleased to see that Jenna and Scott were happy in their marriage. Jenna's job was going well and Scott had completed his classes, earned that long-awaited degree and had graduated. Jenna was planning a huge party to celebrate. The couple's only disappointment was that Jenna hadn't yet gotten pregnant.

Sherri Ann was focused on her career goals, determined to make partner before her thirty-fifth birthday. She was certain she could do it in three years. There was no talk of a special man in her life. Laura was shocked to learn Sherri Ann had stopped dating. Laura insisted that was not healthy. That working 24/7 was a great way to burn out fast. What she needed was balance in her life.

Sherri Ann argued she didn't work all the time. Not being in a relationship gave her time to devote to what was important, her career and the girls in the mentoring program. Sherri Ann pointed out how she was only following in Laura's footsteps. Until her vacation, Laura had been just as driven and goal-oriented. Teasing, Sherri Ann promised that when the next good-looking millionaire rang her doorbell, she would take a long, hard look.

Suddenly, Laura burst into tears, "I wish I'd never met Wilham Sebastian Kramer! It was the biggest mistake of my life, rushing into marriage with a man I barely knew! A man who doesn't love me!"

Shocked, her family tried to soothe her.

Scott gave her a hug. "It's going to be okay."

"He's right," Jenna soothed. "It's going to get better. You know deep inside that man loves you."

"I'm so sorry," Sherri Ann said. "I know you're extremely disappointed that he couldn't come with you. But I'm sure it's bad timing and nothing more."

Laura sniffed. She was miserable, but it was a relief to get it out in the open. "I didn't plan to ruin the evening by letting go like that."

"Being married to the love of your life is incredible, a dream come true. But it's not easy. It takes time, lots of time to get it right. Jenna and I are still working on it. Aren't we, sweetheart?" Scott said.

"That's for sure. Marriage is complicated. Some days it's wonderful and other days it's very stressful.

Just because Wilham isn't here tonight doesn't mean he stopped loving you. Try to be patient. He'll get here," Jenna said, squeezing Laura's hand.

Sherri Ann shrugged. "I don't know beans about marriage but I know you. You would not have married him if you didn't believe he loved you. He's not going to miss the reception."

Laura nodded. "Thanks. Now let's talk about something else. Jenna, dinner was great. Did you make dessert?"

Jenna smiled. "Lemon meringue pie. I'll get it."

"Please let me help," Laura volunteered.

Everyone took the hint. Sherri Ann told them about her latest victory in court. Jenna teased Scott into telling them about his getting them lost on a side trip they took while in Charleston.

Laura thought she was doing better until she returned to the condo and found it empty. Furious because he had done it again, broken another promise, she switched off the cell phone, turned the ringer off on the landline, and let the answering machine take the messages. She really appreciated her family's attempt to help. Unfortunately, Wilham had proven her right. He didn't love her. She ended up crying herself to sleep that night.

Twenty-six

Early on Friday morning, a florist delivered a crystal vase filled with long-stemmed pink roses at the same time her foster sisters knocked on her door, intent on finding out why she wasn't answering her phones. Both Sherri Ann and Jenna had received a call from Wilham. He was worried when he couldn't speak to her. Laura shrugged, tipped the deliveryman, and let them in.

Jenna and Sherri Ann were supposed to be on their way to work. Laura was preparing to leave for an appointment to have her hair braided. They stayed long enough to scold. Sherri Ann asked what if there had been an emergency, while Jenna found her cell phone and turned it on. Laura didn't bother arguing the point as the three left the condo and walked to the parking lot.

She was starting her car when her cell rang. When she saw Wilham's name she turned it on vibrate and dropped it into the bottom of her purse.

It was late afternoon by the time Laura left the salon. She dropped in at the women's center to see her coworkers and visit with Maureen. Determined to conceal her problems, she asked if Maureen had any luck finding her replacement. Maureen said no, but she was hoping to convince Heather to take a permanent position. Heather, the wife of a prominent judge, Quinn Montgomery, hadn't worked full-time since her twins were born. So far, Heather hadn't agreed, although she was working on convincing her best friend, Diane Rivers Randal, also a busy wife and mother, as well as a former teacher, to volunteer at the center. Both Heather and Diane had worked on several charity committees with Maureen's grandmother.

The high point of her day was when Laura drove over to Vanessa's boutique. The second she entered the shop, Vanessa greeted her with a big hug. Laura apologized for being late. The two friends teased each other, recalling when they were bridesmaids in Brynne's wedding, and Vanessa needed to know how Laura felt about Ralph. It had all turned out well since Vanessa and Ralph were happily married.

While Laura tried on evening gowns, Vanessa confessed Ralph wanted to start a family but she was holding back. And Ralph was not giving up. Recalling that Vanessa and Donna Prescott, Ralph's aunt, were close, Laura wondered if Vanessa had asked Donna for advice. Vanessa shook her head.

It seemed Donna had problems of her own. While she and her husband, Lester, had raised four very successful children and nephew Ralph, they were going through a rough patch. Donna was very upset. Since his retirement from coaching, Lester hadn't slowed down as planned. He was busy, working long hours at the new youth sports and education center. Then Vanessa confessed that long hours weren't the only problem. Donna feared Lester was having an affair with his much younger and very pretty assistant. Shocked,

Laura insisted that was impossible. Donna and Lester
had been happily married for more than thirty-five
years. Why would he cheat now? Vanessa shook her
head before she revealed that Ralph and his male cousins were convinced it wasn't true, that Donna was over-
reacting. But Vanessa and Anna didn't agree. Anna was
the only girl in the Prescott family, and grew up with
two older brothers, a male cousin and a much younger
brother.

After smoothing the gown, Vanessa stepped back,
asking what Laura thought of the dress. Laura laughed
and told her it was perfect. She predicted that once the
society ladies in Chicago saw her in this dress, Vanessa would be flooded with calls. She asked for some
of Vanessa's business cards, suggesting she consider
opening a boutique in Chicago.

Laura was behind schedule by the time she arrived
downtown for a quick dinner with her foster sisters.
Afterward, they drove over to the Detroit Art Institute. Anna Prescott Mathis greeted them and showed
them the private room for tomorrow's wedding reception. Although Laura was impressed, she was far from
happy, not when she didn't know if her husband would
bother to show up at their reception the next evening.

Early Saturday morning Sherri Ann and Jenna took
Laura to a salon. While Sherri Ann and Jenna had their
hair washed and styled, Laura's freshly braided hair
was gathered and pinned up and studded with pearls.
They also had manicures and pedicures.

Her foster sisters took her to a new restaurant. When
they arrived they were shown into a private room where
all her friends and family waited to shout, "Surprise!"

Sherri Ann and Jenna had arranged a bridal shower.

·

Thrilled, Laura was happy to see everyone. Laura scolded Vanessa for keeping quiet, hugging Trenna McAdams and Maureen. She was pleased to see the girls from the mentoring program. She hugged each one and told them how much she missed them.

Laura warmly greeted Taylor, Jenna's sister-in-law; and Scott's mother, Mrs. Hendricks. Laura was overjoyed that Brynne had flown in from St. Louis. She hugged her tight and kissed Brynne's little daughter. Laura's biggest surprise came when she saw Cassandra, her new sister-in-law, was there with her twin daughters, Carla and Carmella. The girls giggled, kissed her cheek, and called her Aunt Laura.

Surrounded by so much love, Laura couldn't help being emotional. Knowing Wilham's family had come so far made it even harder to appear happy when her heart was so heavy.

They hadn't been married two months and already it was falling apart. Why was he doing this to her? To them? How was she supposed to face these people tonight at the reception? What could she say? That her husband didn't care enough to come to their wedding reception!

How many more promises did he have to break before she got the message? Clearly, he no longer wanted to be married. He was not giving her anything to hold on to. What happened to all that love? It wasn't supposed to end so abruptly.

This was hardly her first lesson in love. That painful lesson had come from her mother and it was one she should never forget. Being abandoned had proven that love didn't last.

Suddenly overcome by emotion, she desperately needed privacy. Laura quickly excused herself and went looking for the ladies' room. Struggling to hold it together, she made it inside one of the stalls without breaking down. She took slow, even breaths, hoping for calm.

One glance at her cell phone confirmed the worst. He'd sent a text message. He was still in Chicago, telling her why he'd been delayed. Her eyes immediately filled with tears. She didn't care why! She wasn't interested in excuses.

Furious, she turned the phone off and flung it into her purse.

"Laura? You okay?" There was a knock on the stall door.

Laura sniffed. "I'll be right out." She used the rolled tissue to dry her eyes and wipe her nose. Tossing the wad into the toilet, she flushed. She took a few slow breaths before she came out. "Cassy." She smiled. "I'm glad you came. Are you enjoying yourself?" she asked as she washed trembling hands.

"You're the one I'm concerned about. How are you really doing?" Cassy touched Laura's arm. "I know how difficult it can be when Gordan's engrossed in business problems. It keeps him away from me and the children, and I hate it. But that's nothing compared to what you must be feeling. This couldn't have happened at a worse time. I'm so sorry. How can I help?"

Laura laughed, but it lacked humor. "You can't help," she said candidly. "This trouble with the hotel has been very hard to cope with, especially with Wilham working such long hours. I rarely see him. I attend most social functions without him. I thought that this weekend away would be good for us." She struggled for control. "I tried to convince him to postpone the reception but he wouldn't hear of it. Now he's in Chicago and I'm here. And I'm fairly certain that he won't be at our wedding reception." She hesitated before she confessed, "Cassy, I'm not sure I can forgive him if he doesn't make it."

Cassy squeezed her hand. "I'm so sorry. I wish I could tell you not to worry and assure you that no matter what he will make the reception. But I can't. Multibillion-dollar business demands can't just be ignored. It cuts into family time. Both Gordan and Wilham are good at completely blocking out everything and everyone when a problem arises. But when the dust settles, you must remember he does love you."

Laura nearly shouted, *Love's not supposed to hurt!* Instead, she said, "Thanks, Cassy, for trying to help."

Jenna dashed inside the restroom and grabbed Laura's hand. "Hurry! Everyone is waiting for you to open the gifts."

Sherri Ann was right behind Jenna. "They're getting restless now that they've eaten."

"Have you two met my sister-in-law, Cassandra Mosley Kramer?"

"We did"—Sherri Ann smiled—"but we only had time to say a quick hello."

"That won't do." Laura quickly told Cassy their history.

Always efficient, Sherri Ann checked her watch. "Ladies, I hate to break this up but we have to be out by three. Then we need to get Laura home to hopefully relax for a little while before she has to get ready. This bride will be rested and beautiful for the wedding reception at eight. Let's get this show on the road."

Seated at his desk, Wilham glared down at his cell phone. Nothing! No calls or text messages. Laura knew he needed to talk to her! Needed to hear for himself that she was all right. He swore heatedly. From the first she'd been told how much this project meant to him. And he'd made a point of keeping her abreast of the problems and his progress. How could she?

Just then, his cell phone rang. He grabbed it. "Laura . . ."

"No, Wil. It's Cassy."

"Hi, Cassy." He struggled to hide his disappointment. "How are you? Everyone checked into the hotel? What time did you all touch down in Detroit?"

"We're all here and accounted for. What's your excuse? Please tell me that you're on your way to the airport and not at the office."

He rubbed his unshaven jaw. "I realize I'm cutting it close, but it can't be helped. We're almost done. We finally know who's behind this mess. We just have to prove it. Have you seen my Laura? How is she?"

"How do you think she is, Wil? She's a strong lady, but she very upset that you're not here. And she is struggling not to let it show." Cassy went on to say, "Wil, I hate to tell you this, but I wouldn't be surprised if she never spoke to your sorry butt again. Do you realize that you're risking your future by choosing the hotel over your bride?"

"Wait! Cassy, what are you talking about? Didn't Laura explain? I've sent her enough text messages to keep her updated on our progress. She knows I'm working! I'm not neglecting my wife."

"Wilham! What's wrong with you? You are in Chicago! Or have you decided you no longer want Laura?"

"Cassy, stop! Laura knows how much I love her. This delay has nothing to do with how we feel about each other. I'm working! A couple more hours and—"

"Wil! Will you shut up and listen? You are so focused on business that you've completely missed the
point of this call. Laura's hurting!" She took a quick
breath, but before she could say more he interrupted.

"Cassy, you don't understand."

"No, you're not getting it. Laura is hurting badly!
First you rushed that poor girl off to Vegas and married her without family or friends. Now you expect her
to face hundreds of people at your wedding reception
alone!"

"Even if for an unforeseeable reason I don't make it
tonight, Laura will understand. We're solid. She knows
I love her."

"Are you absolutely sure about that, Wilham
Kramer? Because I just spoke to your wife at her surprise bridal shower. She was in the ladies' room fighting back tears." Cassy hesitated, then said, "Wilham,
you're a wonderful brother and a great uncle to my
kids. We all love you. And I appreciate all the extra
responsibility and work you've taken on so that Gordan
and I can have more family time. But think back a few
years. I've never forgotten that you encouraged me not
to give up on Gordan after we'd broken it off. Things
were so bad between us that I'm not sure I would have
come to him even after his plane crash, if you hadn't
called and convinced me he needed me.

"I'm sorry, but I can't sit quietly and do nothing
while you're about to lose your wife. Kramer Corporation can absorb the loss of a hotel. Can you absorb the
loss of the love of your life? Think about it. She could
walk away for good if you don't make that wedding
reception tonight. Are you prepared to take the risk?
And if she does leave you, I won't blame her," Cassy
said before turning off her phone.

* * *

It hadn't been easy, but Laura had convinced her foster sisters to go home and that all she needed was some rest. She was a big girl and could get herself made up and dressed without help. Although both were upset that Wilham was late, surprisingly, they hadn't uttered a word of criticism against him. They either believed he'd be there or they were doing their utmost not to upset her. Either way, Laura decided to keep her thoughts to herself. Losing control would change nothing.

She sat in the recliner in the living room rocking back and forth. Her eyes burned from unshed tears as she periodically checked and rechecked the small clock on the side table.

By six, Laura finally accepted the bitter truth. He was not coming. The hotel meant more to him than she did. Wilham wasn't late. He'd made his choice. Unfortunately, she didn't have that same luxury. She had to go to their wedding reception, and she had to go alone.

"No!" she said aloud. She still had friends. She would call one of them. Of course, Craig Owens! He was an old friend and one-time coworker. The seasoned police detective was someone she liked and respected. They'd worked on several rape cases.

She called and asked if he had planned to come tonight. When he said yes, she quickly explained that her husband was delayed and asked if she could ride along with him and his date. He didn't have a date, but would happily take her. Laura thanked him, asking him to pick her up at seven thirty.

With that settled, Laura showered, taking care not to wet her hair. She carefully applied makeup, using concealer to cover the shadows beneath her eyes from so many restless nights. She put on the dress she had worn to their wedding, smoothed it over her hips, and then pulled on the long-sleeved lace jacket.

Her gaze lingered on the black tuxedo and the white silk shirt and black bow tie that she'd carefully packed and brought with her. That morning, she laid Wil's things on the opposite side of the bed, in the vain hope he would come. She had remembered his diamond and onyx studs for the shirt and his diamond cuff links. They were on the nightstand, his polished shoes on the floor. Foolishly, she'd let her guard down, and believed that the years ahead could only bring a deeper love and happiness. How could she have been so blind?

She blinked hard, holding in the tears. The marriage was over. After the reception there would be plenty of time for tears. But first she had to get through this ordeal. So what if everyone saw through her forced smiles? She refused to ever try to explain why he wasn't there. Nothing she said could take away the heartbreaking truth. Kramer Corporation meant more to Wilham than his bride of less than two months. She'd been wrong to trust him and believe those empty promises.

She would get through this! She would face their friends and family with her head held high. But afterward, she was done. She was never going back to Chicago and didn't care about the things she left behind. All that mattered was that finally she knew the truth and accepted it. The man she fell in love with wasn't real. He was part of some wild romantic fantasy that had never been real.

It might take a while but eventually, she would pick up the pieces of her broken heart and shattered pride. Maureen would be thrilled to let her come back to work. And she would go on with her life in Detroit as if she'd never been a love-sick fool and married in haste.

Wilham Sebastian Kramer was a gifted artist, excellent lawyer, and talented businessman, but he made a lousy husband. She deserved better.

Somehow, she would get through this ordeal tonight and hopefully make Mrs. Green proud even if it killed her. No one need know until their gifts were returned that the marriage was an abysmal failure.

Laura had just put a pearl stud earring in her ear when the buzzer from the lobby sounded. Seven fifteen! Craig was early. She went into the foyer while fumbling with the other earring. She pressed the intercom button but the static was so loud she couldn't hear the doorman clearly. She shouted to let her visitor come up. A glance down at her bare feet had her dashing back into the bedroom for her high heels.

A few minutes later her doorbell rang. She opened the door with a warm smile. "Craig! You're—" She stopped, looking up into golden brown eyes.

Twenty-seven

Wilham leaned down and gave Laura a hungry kiss. He kissed her twice before he straightened, walked in and closed the door. He placed his leather duffel bag on the floor in the small foyer. "Who is Craig?" he said tightly. "And why in hell haven't you returned any of my calls or text messages?"

"Don't swear at me." She hadn't answered his questions, just stared at him in disbelief. "What are you doing here?"

"I live here with you, wife," he said evenly. He understood why she was upset, even angry. What he didn't understand was her distance and coldness. She was acting as if he'd set out to hurt her.

Folding her arms beneath her breasts, unwittingly drawing his eyes to her sweet curves, she glared at him. "Really? Well, you're late . . . too late!"

He frowned. "I know. And I'm sorry. But I explained why I was delayed. Everything was in the text messages and on the answering machine. You haven't answered my question," he said pointedly. "Why haven't I heard from you?"

"I didn't want to talk to you! I was upset because you broke your promise!"

"There was good reason, Laura. I thought you understood the problems we were having with the hotel."

"And I thought you kept your promises. Evidently, we were both wrong."

Fighting not to lose his temper, he asked, "Who's Craig?"

"Aw-oh!"

"I'd like an answer," he snarled.

She turned and walked past him into the next room. "Craig's an old friend and coworker, a detective with Detroit PD. I didn't think you were coming and I didn't want to arrive alone, so I called and asked him to escort me to the reception."

"Say what?" Incredulous, he glared down at her.

The doorbell rang.

"I thought this was a secure building. First the intercom's not working, then the doorman let me up, and now they are just letting anyone come to your door! I don't like it," Wilham snapped.

"The intercom normally works fine. But that's not the problem," Laura said in an urgent whisper. "Craig's doing me a favor. It's my fault, not his. Please be nice."

Wilham's temper had been simmering since she hadn't opened her lips and welcomed his kisses. Now it flared, very close to a full boil. He couldn't remember being so angry. The woman he loved had just told him her old boyfriend was on the other side of the door, expecting to take her to their wedding reception. And he was supposed to be nice! For days she had refused to take his calls or respond to his messages but she freely admitted to calling another man to take his place. Outraged, he swore beneath his breath, his hands balled into fists.

"Wilham, please . . ."

He hissed, "Open the damn door."

"No!" she whispered. She walked right up to him and poked him with her finger in the middle of his chest. She said in a soft but firm tone, "I've never slept with Craig, never even thought about it. I'm in love with you, Wilham Sebastian, even though you make an incredibly lousy husband." She flicked away tears and said in a tight whisper, "If you'd been here like you promised, I would never have called Craig in the first place. I was dreading having to face our families and friends without you! Do you have any idea how much it hurt me knowing you didn't care about me enough to show up at your own wedding reception? Do you?" She gave him a reproachful stare. "If anyone is at fault, it's you. I must have been out of my mind to marry you!"

The doorbell chimed again.

Wilham ground his teeth, his jaw tight. His anger unexpectedly shifted, turning inward. Suddenly, he was furious with himself. She was right. If he had kept his word they wouldn't be arguing now. He had insisted that she go ahead with the plans for the reception rather than wait until after the problems with the hotel were resolved. He was responsible for the unhappiness he'd seen on her face when he arrived. He had caused the shadows beneath her pretty eyes.

As he watched her open the door and let the other man in, he couldn't get beyond the label she had given him . . . "an incredibly lousy husband." It hurt, especially when he knew she believed it was true. He had vowed to love her, yet his actions hadn't matched those words. He was wrong because he had not put her first, nor had he kept his promises. He should have been on that plane with her on Thursday afternoon.

Distracted by business problems, he ignored his wife's tender feelings and her needs. He failed her and then he compounded that mistake by expecting her to understand why he put her last on his list of priorities. How had he let his pride in a chunk of concrete blind him to the point that he could no longer even see the woman he pledged to love and treasure always?

Cassy was right. He couldn't blame Laura if she turned her back on him and their love. He had been the one who put their marriage and future in jeopardy. Laura deserved so much better. Yes, it was his fault that she felt she had turned to someone else for help tonight. His fault she regretted marrying him. He'd messed up royally.

His brother had warned him, but had he listened? No. Like an egotistic fool, he thought he knew best. Wrong! Wrong! Wrong! And if he valued his wife and wanted to keep her love, then he'd better get busy and figure a way out of this mess. More important, he'd better pray she gave him a chance to repair the damage.

After Craig left, Laura was uneasy, uncertain what to expect. Wilham hadn't embarrassed her, nor had he created an unpleasant scene. He'd shaken Craig's hand. He hadn't been warm, but he had been civil, which was about all that she could have expected under the circumstances. He hadn't said a word while she apologized to Craig for the inconvenience.

His body was taut with tension and his firm mouth was tight when he surprised her by saying, "Laura, I owe you an apology for . . ."

She cut him off, too upset to listen. "We're going to be late. You should change."

He was casually dressed in jeans, gray shirt, and navy tweed sports coat. He turned and grabbed his brown leather bag from the foyer. "Which way?"

Laura pointed to the master suite. She didn't follow him inside or urge him to hurry. She stayed in the living room, so upset she was unsure what she was feeling.

Now that he was finally here, she didn't know if they had anything left to save. Yet they were getting ready for their reception, getting ready to celebrate their marriage with family and friends and toast the future. For the next few hours they had no choice but to go through the motions, pretending everything was perfect and they were a happy couple.

In truth, she had been hurt by his neglect and he had been hurt by the way she ignored his calls and asked another man to escort her to their reception. And he'd tried to apologize.

Was it too late? Was the trust gone? Did they have something worth salvaging? In their mad dash to marry, had they made a terrible mistake? When the evening was over and the guests had gone home, the two of them had to sort it all out. They had to either find a way to fix what was left of their marriage or let it go.

"Ready."

Startled, Laura jumped and then glanced at the clock. He had been gone only fifteen minutes.

Wilham came up behind her. "So that's where you put the painting." When she merely nodded, he turned her to face him. He placed a familiar jeweler's box in her hands. "For you. A wedding gift."

When she hesitated, he lifted the lid. She gasped.

Inside on a bed of velvet was the double rope of pale pink cultured pearls, the large pink kunzite and diamond enhancer, the pearl bracelet with a pink kunzite clasp, and a pair of pink kunzite and diamond earrings, all of them in eighteen-karat gold. He given her the entire set to go with her engagement ring.

They had first seen the pieces in the jewelry shop in St. Thomas on that long-ago day when they had been so happy and in love.

She whispered, "I don't know what to say."

"They remind me of you and a happier time. I hope you'll wear the necklace and earrings tonight. Please, Laura."

Deeply touched, she managed to nod. He opened the gold clasp, and placed the pearls around her neck. He fastened the enhancer on the left side, close to her heart.

Wilham leaned down and kissed her cheek. "Thank you."

Then he held out the earrings. She removed the pearl studs she'd put on earlier and replaced them with the kunzite and diamond earrings.

She touched the necklace. "Thank you, Wil. They're so beautiful. I'm surprised that you remembered—" She stopped, unable to finish.

"I remember everything about our time in the islands. I wish I could take you away tomorrow for a long honeymoon, but . . ."

"Please . . . I don't want to talk about the hotel . . . not tonight."

"I was wrong. I should have put you first. I never meant to hurt you. I'm so sorry, Peaches."

"I know."

He searched her eyes but she instantly dropped her

lids. After a lengthy pause, he said, "You are such a lovely bride, Mrs. K. Shall we go?"

"I'll get my purse and wrap."

Laura knew Wilham wanted her to accept his apology, but she was hurting so much she couldn't. Instead, she hurried away from the man she still loved but no longer trusted to love her back.

Laura's eyes filled with gratitude when they arrived at the beautifully decorated private room. Sherri Ann and Jenna hadn't overlooked a single detail. They had gone to great lengths to make this night special.

The tables were draped with blush pink cloths and adorned with small centerpieces of pale pink and white roses, and cream flameless candles. She had no idea how they managed it but several of Laura's favorite pieces of art from the museum's vast collections were prominently displayed on the walls. She hugged her sisters.

Heaping on praises, Laura also thanked Anna. The talented chef did not disappoint. The three-tiered wedding cake that Anna had created was covered in a creamy white swirl pattern, each tier brimming with the most incredibly lifelike pink and white sugar roses. No one would guess that the white butter cream covered rich, dark chocolate. It was spectacular.

The newlyweds were quickly surrounded by family and friends. Laura introduced Wilham to her foster sisters, Sherri Ann and Jenna. Then he met Scott, and his family. It turned out that Scott and Wilham had met briefly years earlier while Scott had been playing in the NBA for the Lakers.

Laura couldn't help smiling when she introduced Wilham to each of the giggling teen girls in the mentoring program. Maureen and Trenna received warm greetings from Wilham, along with Laura's other book club friends, Vanessa and Brynne and their spouses, cousins Ralph and Devin Prescott.

Laura met Cassy's older sister, Sarah, her husband, Kurt; their young son, Kurt Jr., and their pretty granddaughter, Mandy. Laura received hugs from Wilham's twin nieces, Carla and Carmella.

Laura was touched by the sisterly hug she received from Cassy and the supportive kiss on the cheek from Gordan. Kenneth and Gordy were also there and greeted her warmly. Wilham must have said something because there was no mention of the problems with the hotel.

Then her foster sisters ushered her into the ladies' room for a private word. Both watched her closely when they asked if everything was really okay. Laura insisted that she was better now that Wilham was finally in Detroit. She knew she would break down if she brought up her doubts and fears about the future, so she didn't elaborate.

The newlyweds had requested that instead of wedding gifts, donations be made to the Valerie Hale Sheppard Women's Crisis Center and the teen girls' foster care mentoring program.

After the customary toasts were made, they enjoyed a delicious dinner of prime rib and lobster. The chocolate fountain with an array of fruit for dipping was a hit with young and old alike. After the meal and before they cut the cake, Maureen went to the podium and proudly announced that their guests had donated one hundred thousand dollars to the women's center and fifty thousand dollars to the mentoring program. Both Laura and Wilham cheered.

When Maureen revealed the mentoring program had been renamed the Laura Murdock Kramer Mentoring Program and would continue for years to come, Laura had to wipe away tears of joy.

Next Gordan announced that both the Kramer Corporation and he and Cassandra were donating matching funds to the women's center and mentoring program, which brought the grand total up to three hundred thousand dollars for the center and one hundred and fifty thousand for the mentoring program. Laura and Wilham, like everyone else in the room, were on their feet clapping and cheering.

Laura thought the high point of the evening was when she and Wilham went up to thank their guests, but she was wrong. The pinnacle came when Wilham revealed that each of the twenty-five girls who kept their grades up and stayed in school and in the mentoring program would receive a full, four-year-scholarship to the college of their choice. And a tutoring program would be available to the girls who needed help with their studies. Their guests broke into laughter and cheered when Laura threw her arms around her husband's neck and kissed him enthusiastically.

It was a wonderful night that she would never forget. And thanks to the photographer and video cameraman Wilham hired, she didn't have to worry. During the limousine ride back to the condo, she couldn't stop thanking him for his contribution to the girls.

It wasn't until she was in the bathroom preparing for bed that she sobered, recalling that their problems hadn't disappeared. Their problems hadn't really changed. Just because tonight was in a sense their wedding night didn't mean . . . Surely, he didn't expect them to make love? Did he?

When she walked into her bedroom, she recalled the nights when all she wanted was for him to be with her. Well, she had gotten her wish. Wilham was in her bed, leaning back against her white lace-edged pillows and brass headboard. His broad chest was bare. The colorful patchwork floral quilt on the bed was bordered in shades of pink. It was one of handmade quilts that she had made with her family.

Each foster sister had a special handmade quilt that the three of them, along with their foster mother, had spent hours sewing as they laughed, talked, and shared.

He said quietly, "Your quilt is beautiful. I can see why you treasure it."

As she approached the bed in a floor length cranberry lace-trimmed nightgown, she was glad that his lower body was covered.

"Thank you, it was made from our old dresses with lots of laughter and love. Mrs. Green was old-fashioned, she didn't think a machine-made quilt could compare to handmade. Last summer my foster sisters and I enlarged our old quilts to fit our king-size beds." Uneasy, she confessed, "Nowadays, I cheat and use the sewing machine. It's a lot faster, especially when I make small quilts for the children in hospitals. I go for bright and cheerful to hopefully provide a little comfort."

Instead of getting into bed, she reached for a small jar of hand cream on her nightstand. After coating trembling hands, she quickly turned off the bedside lamp, plunging the room into near darkness. The night light in the bathroom glowed softly but Laura remained, standing beside the bed.

She heard the rustle of the top sheet, the blanket and quilt that he pulled back. He quizzed, "Not tired?"

Reluctantly, she volunteered, "Exhausted. I haven't been sleeping well."

"Then rest, Peaches. It's late and we're meeting the family for early service and then brunch before everyone goes their separate ways."

With a tired sigh, she slowly climbed in and turned her back to him. "Good night."

"Night," he murmured, pushing her braids aside in order to press his lips against her nape. He put an arm around her waist, easing her back against his front.

She stiffened when she felt his erection, uncomfortably aware that she had never refused to make love to him.

"Relax, I just want to hold you, babe."

"Okay." She was nearly asleep when Wilham brushed warm lips against the side of her throat. Desire raced like wildfire over her skin. Her nipples beaded while her feminine core grew moist in readiness. Annoyed by her traitorous body's responses, she held his arm.

"Peaches, there's no need to sink your nails into my arm. Nothing going to happen that you don't want to happen. I'm sorry I hurt you, and I can't undo what's wrong between us. It may take a little time, but I intend to prove to you that you come first with me. I won't ever neglect you or give you reason to doubt my love for you again. In the meantime, we will wait until you let me know when you're ready to make love again. Agreed?"

"Agreed." She closed heavy lids and slept deeply for the first time in days.

Laura didn't like saying good-bye. Nor was she eager to return to Chicago. As they waited on the tarmac for their plane to take off, she flipped through the current issue of *Ebony* magazine. It was a struggle not to show her resentment as she listened to Wilham, Kenneth, and Gordy talk business. Her heart was still heavy and she had a full load of doubts about their future despite her husband's late-night assurances things would be different. Different how? And starting when?

They hadn't left Detroit and already Wilham was absorbed with work. Judging by what she'd seen so far, very little had changed. She really wanted to believe he was serious and would not waver. But words came easy and were not enough. The issues with the hotel were still there and his determination to complete the project and find the person responsible had not changed. What was different this time around?

Kenneth said, "Tucker must have paid Murray to—"

Laura interrupted, "Kenneth, are you talking about Jessie Tucker? The real estate developer?"

Kenneth glanced at Wilham, who nodded briefly, then Kenneth said, "That's right. I believe he's responsible for the problems with the hotel."

"There has been a mistake," she said firmly. "Jessie can't be involved. He's a fine man. Despite his busy schedule he finds time to give back."

The three Kramer men exchanged a surprised look.

Wilham said, "I didn't realize you knew much about Tucker."

She nodded. "I haven't known him long. But we have talked a few times. He sat next to me at Baldwin's charity event last week. Jessie is a friend."

"A friend?" Wilham repeated.

"Yes," Laura said firmly. "I admire the work he has done with former gang members. I understand that he took over the family company as CEO after his older brother died suddenly in a skiing accident. Despite the demands of running a profitable business, Jessie has taken over his brother's foundation. That alone, I find impressive. The Tucker youth facility was written up in the newspaper. I first read about his work with teen boys online. It's amazing the way he has reached out to troubled boys. Many of those kids were in gangs." She shook her head, "Kenneth, I don't know what you think he has done, but I'm positive you are mistaken about Jessie."

Kenneth asked pointedly, "Has Tucker said anything to make you think he might resent Wilham or Kramer Corporation?"

Twenty-eight

"No!" Alarmed, Laura's eyes went wide. Then she looked into her husband's eyes. "When you introduced us you said you met at college and were fraternity brothers. Wil, I don't understand. Why would Jessie resent you?"

"We're both Morehouse men." He was seated with the others around a small conference table. Unbuckling his seat belt, he quickly crossed the narrow aisle and took the armchair beside her. "Tucker and I have been business rivals for years," he explained, automatically buckling the seat belt. "Jeffery Tucker, the father, started the business in the mid-seventies and built it into a formidable company. Jeffery has been semiretired for ten years. The article was correct. After his older brother died, Jessie has been at the helm for nearly two years. Tucker and Sons wanted the site where we're building the new hotel. They lost the bid. It's prime real estate and they planned to build an upscale new shopping mall, restaurants, and a movie theater complex with HD and 3-D. It wasn't the first time Tucker and Sons came up against us. They have lost to Gordan several times." Wilham revealed, "But due to recent financial problems because of the economy and the market, if the Chicago project had gone forward, I imagine they could recoup losses. It was the first time Jessie and I had buttted heads." Wilham frowned. "But it's not personal. Tucker has no reason to go after me, especially in such an underhanded manner. That's not his style."

She perked up. "You see. I'm right about Jessie."

"Maybe not you personally. But Tucker has a few million reasons to go after Kramer Corp.," Gordy said, siding with Kenneth.

"Until recently Norton Construction's reputation was first-rate," Kenneth said. "We suspect that someone at Norton was paid to replace good-quality material with inferior materials. We also suspect the city inspector was paid to overlook the problems. Problems that could eventually put hundreds of innocent lives at risk."

"Wait!" Laura said. "I don't understand. If the city inspection didn't show problems, how did you know something was wrong?"

Gordy answered, "We have a long-standing company policy of bringing in an independent team to inspect our buildings. Whoever made the payoff to the city inspector had no way of knowing that."

Wilham said, "Kenneth, Laura has a point. We've gone over this from every angle and always come back to there's no logical reason for Tucker to be behind this. Even though it looks as if the money is coming from Tucker and Sons, we still don't have a reason. A lot of people suffered losses in the market. That doesn't make them guilty of sabotage. There has to be something else. Perhaps someone with access to Tucker's accounts has a personal grudge against me."

Laura chimed in. "I don't believe Jessie's behind this. He has been so kind to me, even listening to me going on and on about my ideas for adapting my mentoring program."

Wilham remained silent.

Gordy interjected, "Someone's responsible. I've studied the reports and gone over the site, compared the two. The structure's not sound. I've talked to the crew, met with David Miller, the young foreman overseeing the foundation. A few of the men reported their concerns about the grade of the concrete to Miller. And then there were the reports from the independent team about the weakness with the beams. The bottom line, there are major concerns. It may be more cost-efficient to tear it down and start over."

"You trust this foreman?" Laura asked.

"David Miller," Gordy supplied. "He's young, hasn't worked for Norton long. Yes, I believe him, but more important the men trust him. They came to him one by one to report their suspicions. Miller promised to check into it. He went to his supervisor. When his complaints were ignored he went to the boss, Donovan Bringer. Bringer took over Norton Construction while Thomas Norton, the owner, was away due to family problems. According to Kenneth's reports, Norton's wife was terminally ill and he took her back home to southern California to be with family."

Kenneth said, "My sources reported that when Bringer ignored Miller's complaints, Miller threatened to personally contact Norton. That's when Bringer fired him. Miller has a young wife and two small boys to support. He needed the job. Lucky for us, Miller couldn't let it rest. He brought his concerns to Kramer Corp. Unfortunately, both Wil and Gabrielle were away on vacation. He didn't know who to talk to and left only his name with a receptionist."

Kenneth said, "Joy Dooney, the receptionist, remembered David Miller because he came back several times, insisting on talking to Wilham. She told Gabrielle."

"Did Mr. Miller say Jessie was behind the problems with the hotel?" Laura asked.

"No," Kenneth said. "But Miller pointed out the problems on the site, some we weren't aware of. He went out of his way to do the right thing. He helped us."

Laura nodded. "Well, I hope you had the good sense to give the receptionist a big raise and helped Mr. Miller get his job back."

Wilham chuckled. "Joy got a promotion and I hired David. He's going to be working with Gordy, troubleshooting. Kramer Corporation needs good people, honest people."

"So there's nothing to connect Jessie," Laura said with satisfaction.

Kenneth sighed. "No, we don't have proof. Recently, I found out Bringer has a serious gambling problem. Then he suddenly came into enough money to clear up his debt. I'm convinced Tucker is behind all of it."

"Laura," Gordy said, "has Tucker tried to get close to you?"

"What do you mean?"

"Has he done anything to make you uncomfortable?" Gordy asked.

"Of course not. I explained, we've only spoken a few times. But he has been very supportive and interested in my ideas. He's giving me a tour on Wednesday."

Kenneth and Gordy said at the same time, "You can't meet with him!"

Laura bristled. "This is my chance to learn. I'm

bound to gain some insight that might help me with the foster kids." She announced stubbornly, "I'm going. I won't miss this opportunity."

"But—" Kenneth said.

Wilham interrupted, "Laura won't be alone. I'll be there."

"But . . ." She paused, her eyes locked with his. "How will you find time when you have—"

"I'll make time." Wilham assured, taking her hand into his. "It's time Tucker realized you aren't alone. His reaction when he sees us together should prove interesting. Perhaps we can find the link."

Just then the seat belt sign flashed and bells chimed and the plane started rolling along the tarmac.

Laura braced her feet and checked that her seat belt was fastened. The plane continued to pick up speed.

She said softly, "So you agree with Kenneth. You believe Jessie paid off those people."

"I have some doubts. But that's enough about Tucker." Wilham lifted her hand and kissed her knuckles before he said, "I want to hear about your ideas for adapting your mentoring program. Tell me what you have in mind."

Wilham seethed with anger beneath a calm exterior. While he had been working long hours Tucker had been busy getting to know his wife, encouraging her to start a mentoring program in Chicago. He was outraged, but with himself for putting their future at risk. Tucker had been privy to her thoughts and her ideas. He also had no trouble recognizing the ugly green monster. He couldn't help it. He was jealous.

Also he was disappointed that she'd shared something with Tucker that she felt she couldn't share with him the man she loved. That knowledge hurt, but he fully accepted the blame.

As soon as the seat belt sign was turned off, he freed Laura and pulled her out of her seat and onto his lap, unconcerned that his nephew and cousin looked on. Wilham's focus was on his wife and he encouraged her to tell him more.

Her smile was lovely as she explained her hope of going beyond what she had done in Detroit. She wanted to continue helping foster kids, especially teenage girls without permanent foster families. She was excited by what was being done in Chicago by some of the charter schools. She had also been working on compiling a list of ways to persuade those former foster kids who are now professionals, to get involved in mentoring.

As Wilham listened to Laura, he saw the excitement in her eyes. And he knew he had a lot of work ahead. He silently acknowledged the depths of his love for her. Laura was more important to him than any brick and mortar building.

Chicago, Illinois

Wilham was secretly amused, the surprise on her beautiful features when he didn't go to the office with the others was priceless. Clearly, she didn't know what to make of his bringing her back to their suite and spending the entire evening with her.

Later that same night, true to his word, he didn't attempt to seduce her into making love to him. Instead, he focused on his gratitude that she allowed him to hold her during the night. Regaining and keeping her trust had become paramount. He had to be patient, had to give her the time she needed to fully accept that he was in it for the duration.

In the ensuing days, he remained true to his word. He limited his meetings to business hours. When he needed to work late, he brought the work home with him. After dinner he'd joined her in the living room. He'd work at the desk while she worked on whimsical child size quilts or read. They breakfasted together every morning, regardless of the demands of the day ahead.

Laura tried not to get too excited when Wilham left the office early on Tuesday afternoon and came with her to look at the four potential homes she'd picked out. Afterward, he took her out to dinner at his favorite Caribbean-style restaurant.

She struggled to push aside worries that he would get bored with spending so much time with her and that he was bound to lose patience with her because of her reluctance to make love. She tried not to read too much into the changes, and was careful not to expect too much. She couldn't help speculating on how long she had before things reverted back to normal.

Believing in love had always been difficult for her, but trusting in that love had taken on mountainous proportions. Laura grew up never losing sight of her humble start in this world. Remembering kept her grounded. She'd tried but never fully understood why her mother had abandoned her. Nor could she forget it, or forgive it. And it was always there in the back of her mind.

On Wednesday she was delighted that Wilham was at her side when she toured Tucker's youth facility. Clearly Jessie Tucker hadn't expected her husband to join them. But he recovered quickly and was the perfect host, introducing them to his staff and some of the young men.

The annual breast cancer dinner-dance was held that Saturday evening at the Lakeshore Country Club. Laura wore one of Vanessa's designs, a figure-hugging, floor-length, ivory silk dress trimmed with beaded organdy pleats around the square neckline, hem, and sleeves.

Laura thought Wilham looked incredibly handsome in a charcoal gray tuxedo, white pleated shirt, and dark gray tie. She was starting to wonder how much longer she was going to be able to resist him. Each night spent in his arms, lying against his lean, hard body, weakened her resolve to hold out until she was certain he wouldn't renege on his promise and resort to old habits.

They shared a table with Grant and Liza, and Kenneth and Gordy. Both Kramer men were very attractive in custom-made tuxedos and came without dates, which had Laura trying to figure out why they came. They were so absorbed with business, if she hadn't known better she'd think they were working. During the meal, Laura silently speculated which of her single friends she would fix up with Kenneth which could be difficult since he was such a loner. Gordy was too young to appeal to her thirtysomething friends.

The band was just starting to play when Jessie Tucker came up to them. For a few moments, he made polite conversation. Then Jessie smiled at Laura and asked what she had thought of his facility. Wilham was silent, listening to her response. When Jessie asked his permission to dance with her, Wilham quickly said it was her decision. Jessie turned to her and she smiled and nodded. Laura wouldn't dream of being rude to Jessie. One dance couldn't hurt. She appreciated Jessie sharing his knowledge and time.

Once they were out on the dance floor, Jessie asked why Wilham had come on the tour with her. Then he asked pointedly why Wilham didn't trust him. Laura's smile didn't waiver when she said her husband had come because she'd asked him to, then she changed the subject by asking about Ron, one of the young men on his staff, who had mentioned being in the foster care system. She asked if he knew how many others might have been in foster care.

When the band continued to play, moving into another slow melody, Wilham walked up, tapped Jessie on the shoulder. Soon she was in her husband's arms.

Once they were alone, she teased, "What happened to it was my decision?"

He smiled sheepishly, "Tucker can't complain. He got his dance. We may not have proof he's responsible for our problems, but I don't trust him. Do me a favor, Peaches, promise you will be careful around him? When possible avoid him."

Touched by his concern, she caressed his cheek and smiled up at him. "I promise."

"Thank you." He brushed his lips against hers. "I love you. You are an incredibly beautiful woman in a lovely dress."

She smiled. "How sweet."

He tightened his hold around her waist and led her into a series of intricate dance steps and graceful turns, reminding her of their time in St. John. When the music stopped they were both laughing. Other couples applauded their efforts.

When they returned to their table, Liza gushed,

"You two were really good out there." She tapped her husband's arm. "Why can't you dance like that?"

Grant grinned. "Two left feet."

Wilham smiled. "Nonsense, all it takes is a few lessons."

Everyone laughed at Grant's horrified expression. Then Kenneth and Gordy joined them and the conversation switched to business. The men were in deep discussion when Laura and Liza excused themselves and went off to the ladies' room.

Liza asked about Laura's dress. Laura revealed it was designed by a good friend. Busy chatting about Vanessa's boutique, the women didn't notice that Kenneth had signaled one of his men to follow them.

The ladies' room was crowded. It took longer than expected to use the facilities. After washing her hands, Laura accepted a paper towel from the attendant on duty. While turning away from the sink, she caught her heel in her hem, and ripped out the stitches. "For heaven's sake!" she exclaimed, using the counter to steady herself.

"Are you hurt? What happened?" Liza quizzed.

"I'm fine." Examining the back of her dress, she said, "My heel caught in the hem and I almost fell."

"Oh no! Don't tell me that lovely dress is ruined."

Laura examined the bottom. "It's only the hem. That can be repaired. Vanessa worked so hard on this dress. I would hate to have to give her bad news. I've received so many compliments tonight that I'm glad I talked her into letting me take some of her business cards." She giggled. "And I'm so relieved that I remembered to tuck them into my evening purse. Vanessa's going to have more business than she can handle."

Liza said, "You saved one for me, didn't you?"

"Of course." Laura laughed when Liza yanked the card out of her hand and tucked it inside her purse. She asked the attendant if she knew where she might get a needle and thread. The older woman nodded and hurried off.

"You're going to repair it?" Then Liza laughed. "Laura, I forgot you sew. If you can make quilts, repairing a hem would be a snap." She confessed, "I have so much time on my hands, especially in the evenings when Grant has to work. I've been thinking about you making those quilts for sick kids. There must be some way I can also help. I'm considering taking sewing lessons. I'd like to make something special, like a stuffed toy to go along with the theme of the quilt. Like a little turtle, or teddy bear." She asked nervously, "What do you think?"

"What a wonderful idea! The children would love having a new, soft friend to cuddle with. Liza, if you'd like to learn to sew, I can teach you to use the sewing machine," Laura offered.

"You mean it!" Liza squeezed her hands, excited.

"Of course, I've been sewing since I was a little girl. We can start next week. You can come by and try out my machine. If you like it, we'll go out shopping for all the things you'll need. It will be fun." Laura glanced at the clock. "This is taking forever. Liza, you don't have to stay with me. I'll be along soon."

"I don't mind waiting. What do you think I need?"

The attendant returned with a small sewing kit. "Wonderful, thanks." Laura smiled. "Liza, there's no need to wait."

"You're sure?"

"Positive. I won't be long."

"Okay. I'm so excited, I can't wait to tell Grant about

the sewing lessons. He's going to be shocked! He has listened to me, but he didn't think I was serious."

"Then he's in for a surprise. You're going to have to show him you mean business. We'll get started on Monday. Around two?"

"It's a date!" Liza clapped her hands and with a wave she was gone.

Laura turned when the attendant said, "This way, please." The older woman showed her to a secluded area behind a privacy screen. There were a chaise longue, small table, and lamp.

Laura went behind the screen while the older woman stood in front blocking the entrance. She removed the dress and went to work. The women chatted.

Mariam Ellis was raising her six-year-old grandson and had been out of work for more than a year. Just recently she started temporary work for an agency. Mariam was a seamstress, but had lost her tiny shop when the economy went down.

By the time Laura snipped the last thread and Mariam zipped her into the dress, Laura had told her about making quilts for sick children. Mariam explained she didn't have extra money to buy the materials for the quilts, but she volunteered to help with the sewing when she didn't have to work.

Touched, Laura gave her a hug. The ladies exchanged contact information before Laura pressed a generous tip into her hand.

The hallway was nearly empty when Laura started back. She liked Mariam, and if she sewed well, Laura would hire her to help. Working together, they could do even more and help more children. It would benefit both the . . .

Suddenly, Laura was grabbed from behind, lifted

off her feet, and swiftly pulled backward through the exit door. When she realized what was happening and opened her mouth to scream, a large hand was clamped firmly over her mouth. Fighting to get free, she tried to regain her footing, but was shoved hard against a concrete wall in the stairwell. Her cheek and upper body pressed into the cold, rough pillar.

"Don't say one word," he said into her ear.

She stiffened with terror when she felt something sharp against her neck, pricking her skin.

"Do you understand?" The arm around her rib cage squeezed hard, nearly cutting off her breath.

She managed to nod her head before she was dragged down a flight of stairs and then another. When they paused on the second landing, she lost a shoe trying to get free.

"Be still and don't say one word," he said into her ear, holding her firm. "I'd hate to have to cut your pretty face."

Badly shaken, Laura trembled with fear. Somehow she had to find a way to calm down so she could think. She needed to remember those self-defense moves she'd learned in class. But he held her so tight she could barely breathe and her head was pounding.

"Don't force me to hurt you," he warned.

She managed to remain still while balancing on one shoe. She wanted to scream but didn't dare. Her neck stung from where he'd pricked her with the knife. She couldn't see her attacker's face. She had no idea why she'd been taken.

Suddenly, they were moving. Laura's heart was racing as she was pulled backward through another exit door into an empty corridor. Then she was shoved inside a pitch-black room.

* * *

Wilham's gaze returned yet again to the entrance of the ballroom. He had a bad feeling. And Laura had been gone far too long. He was only half listening as Grant summarized his recent talk with Thomas Norton, owner of Norton Construction.

"Norton dismissed the independent report, insisting the city inspection was correct. He's convinced his VP's a good man. He's prepared to take us to court for shutting the site down. He's flying in from San Diego and not happy about having to leave his wife at such a critical time."

Just then Wilham saw Grant's wife across the room alone. Instantly, he crossed to her. "Where's Laura?"

"She was delayed, a problem with her hem," Liza explained. "She should be along soon."

Kenneth came up to Wilham. "Why isn't Laura with Liza?"

Suddenly alarmed, Liza said to her husband, "Grant, what's going on?"

"You had a man with them, right?" Wilham said to Kenneth.

"Of course. Where's Laura?"

"Still in the ladies' room."

Gordy joined them. "Where's Tucker?"

"He left the ballroom right after he danced with Laura," Kenneth answered. "Bill Hunts followed him to the men's room."

"What's wrong? Why is everyone so tense?" Liza demanded to know.

Wilham took her hand and started toward the restrooms. "I'm not sure if anything is wrong. But Liza, I may need your help. Would you please go inside and check . . ."

"Of course." Liza hurried ahead and went inside.

Kenneth spoke into his headphone as he, too, followed them. He verged to the left and entered the men's room.

Anxious, Wilham rechecked his wristwatch, unaware of his nephew's reassuring hand on his shoulder or the taut muscles that jumped in his cheeks as he clenched his teeth.

Kenneth was still talking on his cell phone when he emerged. His face was grim when he said to Wilham, "Tucker's long gone." While they waited Kenneth questioned one of the men on his team.

Liza emerged from the ladies' room clearly upset. She was with an older woman, dressed in a starched uniform. "I checked every stall. She's not in there. Wilham, this is Ms. Ellis. She was the last to see Laura."

Twenty-nine

In the dark, Laura managed to keep from falling by grabbing on to a smooth, hard surface. Momentarily blinded when the lights were turned on, she'd closed her eyes. She realized they were in someone's office. She was clinging to a desk. She quickly swirled to face her attacker.

"Jessie! What are you doing?"

His ebony eyes were cold; his coffee-tone features were surprisingly calm. "Simple. It's called payback. And it's long overdue."

"I don't understand." She could feel the rage that seemed to surround him.

"It's his time to suffer. He took what was mine. Now I have what he values most."

"What?" she said, shocked by the sheer hatred burning in his eyes.

"You're a gorgeous woman, Laura. Not as tall and slender as my Dana, but still gorgeous. Kramer's responsible for her leaving me, just as he stole the bid on the Burlington Street property." He frowned. "I don't know why the old man blamed me. He said nothing I've done has been right, not since my brother Greg died. But the cold bastard has always compared me unfavorably to Greg." He grumbled aloud, "And now he has thrown Wilham Kramer's name in my face. Called him a real man!" He snarled in an angry hiss. "I'll be damned before I put up with that!" he yelled. "Not after Dana left me because of him." Tucker's large frame shook with fury, blocking the door and only exit.

Confused by his rants and struggling not to show her fear, Laura said, "You're angry with my husband. So why did you grab me?"

"Wilham Kramer has never had to work for a damn thing in his life! Everything he has, his big brother gave to him! He's spoiled, selfish, and egotistical. And he has lived well thanks to his brother's accomplishments. Even back in college, he was lucky like a damn cat always landing on his feet. He was prelaw back then and popular with the ladies. He always had money. Dana couldn't help noticing. While I had to work like a dog to keep my grades up, he skated by. Because Gordan was also a Morehouse man all the professors always gave Wilham straight A's. The Kramer name and money meant generous donations for—"

"Who's Dana?"

"Dana is my wife. Ex-wife, now, thanks to Wilham. We met while in Atlanta. She was at Spelman. She didn't tell me until after we married that she'd been in love with Kramer but he wasn't interested in marriage. She never let me forget that she settled for second best when she married me." His voice vibrated from the force of his rage. "I loved her! I thought I could change her mind, make her love me. We were fine until Kramer moved to Chicago."

Laura forced herself to ask, "What does any of this have to do with me?"

"It's not complicated, Laura. The minute I saw the two of you together, I knew he married you because he loved you. That's when I knew what I had to do. It was simple. If I hurt you, Kramer bleeds." He laughed, thumped his chest, boasting, "I'm more man than Kramer will ever be. And it's not just talk, I'm going to prove it to you." He chuckled darkly. "After you've had me, Laura, you won't let Kramer touch you again."

Alarmed, Laura slowly began to inch her way behind the desk. "I don't understand. How can a man who has done so much good for the community do something . . ." She struggled to find the right word but settled for ". . . like this?"

"Working to help troubled kids was Greg's thing, not mine. I was forced into it. I only did it because it was good publicity and kept the old man off my back."

Apparently, Wilham and Kenneth had been right about him. Jessie Tucker had deliberately set out to hurt Wilham. His reasons were simple . . . jealousy and revenge. He hated Wilham and blamed him for dissolution of his marriage.

She forced herself to take slow, deep breaths. She had to get control of the panic and fear and start using her head. It was her only hope of staying ahead of Tucker. He was right about one thing. His plan was simple, but deadly. Hurt her, hurt Wilham. No! No! No!

She knew that it was only a matter of time until Wilham recognized something was wrong and came looking for her. In the meantime, she had to stay sharp and remember the self-defense techniques. She'd taken the classes because she never knew if a client's irate husband or boyfriend might target her. She also must stay calm and keep him calm and hopefully rational.

She said evenly, "You're an attractive man, Jessie.

You don't need to go after another man's wife. There were plenty of single ladies here tonight. Dana was a fool to let you get away."

"Dana," he snapped, "wanted Kramer. When he moved here it was her chance and she took it."

Instantly, Laura realized she had said the wrong thing.

"I gave her everything she wanted. She loved pretty things." He looked pained when he said, "But she said I didn't satisfy her in bed. She slept with Kramer in college and started comparing me to the bastard once he came into town."

Enraged, Tucker stared at Laura for a time and then he began slowly moving toward the desk and Laura. "Dana never gave us a chance. She was . . ."

"Yes, she was wrong," Laura quickly agreed with him, as she slowly backed away from him. Her goal was the door on the other side of the room. She said, "You have every right to be upset. But you can't blame Wilham for the problems with your marriage. Dana—"

"Why are you defending him? Kramer was a fool for leaving you on your own while you were still newlyweds, but he was distracted by his precious hotel. He was busy trying to fix my mess." Jessie chuckled as he inched toward her. "He gave me a chance to get to know you." He smiled before he lunged and yanked her against him.

"No!" Laura yelled, pushing at his chest. He wasn't tall, but very strong. She struggled to break his hold.

"Don't fight me, Laura. I can make it good for you," he crooned, tightening his hold on her and pressing his mouth against hers. He gave her a hard kiss. "Very nice. Let me . . ."

Outraged, she yelled at him, "I said no! Let go! I

love my husband." Deep inside she fully accepted what had been in her heart for some time. It was true and she meant every word. She loved her husband! She loved Wilham without reservations or qualifications.

"No! You deserve better. I won't leave you alone at night." He gripped her chin, angling her face up to his.

Laura turned her head, trying to evade his kiss. When she opened her mouth to protest, he shoved his tongue inside. She gagged before instinct took over and she bit down hard on his tongue, not letting go even when she tasted his blood.

Tucker bellowed with rage, gripping her jaw to pry her loose. She was thrown with such force she hit her head on a file cabinet before she fell to the floor. Momentarily stunned, she moaned in pain, but did not take her eyes off him. He groaned loudly, pulling a handkerchief from the inside pocket of his jacket, and applied pressure to the wound.

Although dazed, Laura yanked off her shoe, before scrambling to her feet. She clutched it, intent on using the four-inch heel as a weapon. Screaming for help, she dashed for the door.

Tucker grabbed her from behind and lifted her off her feet while dodging her blows to his head. Moaning in pain, he managed to overpower her and wrestled her to the floor. Struggling to get away, Laura kept on screaming for help over and over again. Tucker flipped her over, covered her mouth with his hand, using his weight to pin her beneath him.

"Shut up, damn it!" he snapped.

Her heart pounded with fear as she frantically fought for air. His large hand also covered her nose. Knowing she only had mere seconds, she butted him with her head, poking stiff fingers in his eyes.

Howling in pain, Tucker rolled away, covering his tearing and stinging eyes with one hand while holding his bloody nose. Enraged, he called her a series of foul names.

Gasping for breath, she wearily struggled to get to her feet and then ran for the door. Tucker grabbed a fistful of braids and dragged her backward. Her eyes filled with tears as she screamed, her scalp stinging with pain until he finally let go. She bit her lip to keep from dissolving into a heap of tears.

"You're a weak, pitiful coward! Dana was right. You're nothing like my Wilham! Nothing! He would never stoop so low to treat a woman this way! I can see why she left! Your touch makes my skin crawl!"

"You stupid bitch!" he snarled. His breathing was heavy, blood dripping from his nose, his face dotted with bruises where she'd hit him with her heel, his eyes bloodshot.

She sighed, realizing she'd lost her temper and made things worse. Weak and covered with bruises, she fought panic, concentrating on breathing deeply and conserving her energy. She had to be ready for the next attack.

When she opened her mouth to scream again, he clasped her hands and yanked them above her head. Holding them with one hand, he balled the other one into a tight fist. "Shut the hell up! Or I swear I'll knock your teeth down your throat!"

Shaking with fear, she silently began to pray while fighting to stay alert for the smallest opportunity. He clamped down hard on her small wrists, using his upper body to pin her down. She stiffened in outrage and shuddered with revulsion when she felt his erection.

Jessie told her he wanted her and then outlined in

detail what he intended to do to her. He squeezed her breast and boasted that he was more man than Kramer. He rubbed his sex on her thigh.

Repulsed, Laura took a fortifying breath and prayed for courage before she screamed for help as she rammed her knee up between his legs. Her total focus was on making what was round flat. The instant he let go and curled into a tight ball while cupping his groin, she scooted away and scrambled to her feet. Screaming and blinded by tears, Laura hurled herself toward the door. She bounced against a man's chest.

Suddenly, she felt strong arms gently close protectively around her and heard her husband's deep voice saying her name. Exhausted, her entire body immediately went limp. Her strength was gone as she sagged against him. As he cradled her and stroked her hair, she sobbed his name and she wrapped her arms around Wilham's waist. She clung to him. Overwhelmed with relief because she knew she was truly safe.

Thirty

Laura couldn't remember Wilham ever being so upset and angry. Nor had she experienced such tenderness as when he looked at her bruised face or when she moved suddenly and winced in pain. She'd lost count of the number of times she tried to reassure him, insisted she was fine.

Determined to keep her safe, his protective instincts were in high gear. Intent on shielding her, he argued to hold off questioning her until the following day, insisting she needed a little time to rest, to heal. She was equally determined to answer the authorities' questions and give her statement while the details were still fresh. Jessie Tucker was a wealthy man who probably had some high-priced attorney on his payroll. She was ready. She told the police exactly what happened. She was going to see this through to the end, make sure that Jessie Tucker would be held accountable for his crimes.

Later, despite her protests and the late hour, Wilham arranged for his physician to meet them at the hospital. The examination and tests seem to take forever. But Wilham persisted. He seemed to need the confirmation that she was on the mend and would recover.

It was very late when they returned to their suite. They were both exhausted. But Laura was too wound up to fall asleep. She couldn't control the tremors in her hands and limbs, even after a soak in the tub and a cup of her favorite hot tea. It wasn't until she was in bed, wrapped in her husband's arms, that she finally felt safe and could close her eyes and rest.

Hours later, she wasn't sure what had wakened her. But when she realized she was in bed alone, she got up and pulled on a robe over her pink satin nightgown. She went in search of her husband. She found Wilham in a bathrobe on the couch in the living room. The drapes were partly opened. The low light coming through the window was from the streetlights far below. Laura was shocked to find him staring at the bottom of a squat crystal glass of scotch cupped in his hands.

Disturbed by his silent brooding, she said his name. When he lifted his head, there was no mistaking the anguish in his golden topaz eyes.

"Honey, what's wrong?" she said urgently, placing the glass on the end table.

"Nothing," he said quickly. "What's wrong? You can't sleep? Are you in pain?"

Laura curled up next to him and slipped her hand into Wilham's. Shocked by the level of despair she'd seen in his eyes, she whispered, "Please talk to me. Tell me, why are you upset?"

There was a lengthy pause. Instead of answering her question, Wilham gently touched her swollen cheek, before asking, "Would you like one of the pain pills the doctor prescribed?"

"What I'd like is for you to be open with me," Laura said. "Wil, please stop trying to protect me, and talk to me. You have every right to be upset at the way that hateful man deliberately targeted the hotel. Why aren't you relieved now that he's behind bars and will stay there, at least until his arraignment in the morning? He will answer for all he has done. Honey, you should be celebrating that it's finally over."

His tall, lean frame was stiff from suppressed rage and his bronze features were taut with tension when he snapped, "Forget the hotel! You're what matters to me. I'm your husband. It's my job to keep you safe. I failed."

He felt raw from the anguish that he just couldn't shake. He looked away when his eyes filled and his vision blurred. He'd failed, and the shame and guilt from that disappointment ate at him. He didn't want her to see him weak like this, so he'd left their bed.

"No, that's not true!" she said firmly.

"I failed," Wilham said through clenched teeth. "If it hadn't been for that self-defense class and being able to keep a cool head, the bastard would have raped you. All of it was because he hated me. You're the innocent one in this." Lifting their joined hands, he tenderly brushed his lips over her small swollen knuckles. "I'm so proud of you, sweetheart. You never lost your head. You stayed a step ahead of him and brought the lowlife to his knees."

"Thank you. I'm proud of myself. Taking those self-defense classes was part of my job. I worked long hours and had to be prepared to go out alone late at night to counsel rape victims and battered women." After studying his face, she said softly, caressing his cheek, "Please, Wil, don't do this. Don't blame yourself. It wasn't your fault. You had no way of knowing that he was capable of snatching me. Or that he had been nursing a nasty grudge against you because of his greedy ex-wife. No, this was all Jessie Tucker's doing."

Wilham closed his eyes, heartsick he said candidly, "I love you, but marrying me was a mistake. You left your family, your friends, and job to be with me. From day one, I messed up. I rushed you to the altar. Once there, I vowed to love, to protect and honor you . . . always. Yet for weeks, I was so caught up in the problems with the hotel that I neglected you. I wasn't there for you. Even worse, I didn't make you my priority. I haven't been the kind of husband you need or deserve."

"Don't say that . . ."

He pressed fingertips to her lips. "Shhh, I need to say this." He waited for her nod of agreement before he went on. "I messed up badly. But I'd hoped to make it up to you. And I thought I was holding my own until tonight. I've never known such overwhelming fear or helplessness until I realized Tucker had taken you. Even with Kenneth's security team watching out for you, somehow he managed to get his filthy hands on you."

Wilham shuddered, before whispering, "I felt powerless. I couldn't think clearly, not until I held you and knew you were safe. And I'm ashamed to admit that I was jealous of Tucker when I learned that he'd gained your trust and envious when I discovered he knew about your plans for a new mentoring program. Hell, I didn't know there was a plan. My working so many hours left you open, vulnerable to a predator like Tucker. Love is not supposed to hurt." His hungry kiss stopped her protest. "I love you with my whole heart, but I'm selfish. I don't want to ever live without you. I'm so sorry this happened. And I can't help feeling partly responsible for the hell he put you through tonight."

"No! Wilham Sebastian, you're being too hard on yourself. The timing of all this couldn't have been worse. It started on our first morning back from our wedding trip. I was already feeling insecure, scared about starting a new life with you away from my friends and family. Suddenly, you were thrust into containing the damage Tucker had created. No, Jessie Tucker was the only one responsible for trying to destroy our lives. Why can't you see that you are letting that awful man win by continuing to blame yourself? We can't give him power over our lives. He doesn't have the right."

Resting her head on his shoulder, she stroked his hair-roughened bronze chest. "Sure, we had problems adjusting to married life, but other couples go through it. What matters most to me was as soon as you realized he'd befriended me, you warned me to be careful and stay away from him. Honey, you took time off to go with me to tour Tucker's facility. More important, you've kept your promise. Since our wedding reception, you've cut back your hours, and every night you've been with me, whether it's a charity event or at home. Honey, each day you've put me first and proved to me that you love me. I can't ask for more."

She paused, pressing on his chin until he lowered his head and they were gazing into each other's eyes. The last thing he wanted was for her to see his despair. When he started to pull away, she wasn't having it. Laura pinched his chin to gain his attention. When he finally gave up and really looked into her eyes, Wilham's breath caught in his throat because her love was clearly visible in the dark brown depths of Laura's beautiful eyes.

She whispered, "Honey, we've both made mistakes.

You're not holding mine against me. So why should I hold yours against you? No way am I going to let that evil, sick man come between us." A tear slipped past her lashes and down her cheek. He caught it with his thumb.

Suddenly, Wilham realized that was exactly what he'd been doing—allowing Tucker to change them. Holding on to the blame and guilt served no purpose. It must stop here and now. No more.

"I love you, Wilham Sebastian Kramer. You're my man, my wonderful island man. No matter what comes our way, we're in it together. Right?"

"Right," he echoed, smiling as he stroked her braided hair. "Have I told you lately that I love you, Laura Jean Murdock Kramer?"

She laughed. Her heart filled with sweet relief. "Mmm . . . not in, what, two whole minutes?"

He chuckled, but soon sobered. "Gordan tried to warn me not to get so caught up in business demands and forget what truly matters. He offered to help but I refused that help. The trouble happened on my watch so that meant I had to be the one to fix it." Full of regret, he shook his head. "And I actually thought I had it all under control. I was so wrong, so focused on business that I overlooked my beautiful bride, the most important person in my life.

"Thank goodness, Cassy got my attention, made me realize exactly what I was risking. Our entire future was at stake, and I didn't even realize it. I didn't have a clue how close I came to disaster, to losing you. You are my precious love, Laura. You're my entire world. I can survive anything as long as you're at my side. I sent Cassy a dozen roses the Monday after our reception to say thank you."

* * *

Laura confessed, "I was really hurting, busy trying to hide it from everyone at my bridal shower. And Cassy was so kind. Both she and Gordan have been wonderful to me. They believed I really cared about you and flew me to Chicago to see you." Releasing a heavy sigh, she admitted, "I too have regrets. Wil, I love you so much. I wish I had made love to you after our reception. Rather than trusting in you and our love, I held back. I was afraid to hope that we would work things out. I was so afraid that I kept you at a distance. I'm so sorry. I was wrong, especially when I saw that you were really trying to make things better for us. And I'm sorry I doubted your love."

"Shush . . . Peaches. There's no need to apologize."

"No, it's important to me that you understand. It has never been easy for me to trust, especially considering how I came into this world. For me, it always goes back to being abandoned by my mother. Because she didn't love me enough to keep me, I was afraid of love. I always felt I had to protect myself from it happening again.

"I came into marriage loving you and believing your love was a precious gift. But I was unsure if I could depend on that love. In my experiences, love didn't last. When you were so busy with work that you didn't have time for me, unfortunately, that was all the proof I needed to be convinced love didn't last. On the night of our reception I had already made up my mind that if you didn't come I was done with our marriage. I was going to stay in Detroit, picking up the pieces of my life, and move on."

He said, "I suspected as much, but I'm so glad I didn't take that risk."

"Me too. At the time, I didn't believe it was possible that anyone could love me for a lifetime. I kept going back to my mother. But you see, outside of my foster family, I hadn't experienced real love. It was a fantasy, something written about in a romance novel. It wasn't something I could depend on.

"While I was busy falling in love with one wrong man after another, I was convinced there must be something inherently wrong with me because I couldn't hold on to a man. I went into our marriage afraid to hope. Because I grew up without a positive male influence in my life, I didn't know how to deal with men. I never had a father, a brother, not even a wayward uncle. Surrounded by females, it was tough. So I came up with this crazy idea that a rich man was the best man. He would be the one who didn't give up and let go when things got rough."

She laughed, stroking his face. "And I was right. You haven't given up on me. But it has nothing to do with your income." She placed her palm over his heart. "You've opened your heart and shown me your love. Every day by your actions you've made me realize that we're in this together. Remember the lyrics from the song, 'You're All I Need to Get By'? Your love, Wilham Sebastian, is all I need. You've shown me that I was wrong about you and love. Through the good and not so good times we are not going to stop loving each other."

Laura kissed the base of his bare throat, then moved to the tender spot below his ear. She lingered there, warmed it with her tongue. She was rewarded by his indrawn breath and soft groan. Smiling, she slipped her fingers beneath the terry-cloth robe, smoothing over his chest, and then he moaned when she worried a flat ebony nipple with her fingernails. She trailed kisses down from his throat, over his pectoral muscle.

She was surprised when he stiffened and eased away but undeterred, she brushed her lips against his. "Make love to me, my sexy island man. It's been too long since I've felt you inside of me or I've shown you how I feel about you."

"Laura." He groaned huskily, but instead of taking control of their lovemaking, Wilham said, "I've missed making love to you, Peaches. But not tonight, my love. You've been through enough. You're bruised and sore. I won't risk hurting you."

"You're sweet, but you can't hurt me by loving me."

Then Laura leaned forward and gave him a hungry kiss. He moaned when she deepened the kiss by sliding her tongue over his and then into the depth of his mouth. His tongue felt like wet velvet when she rubbed against it. His skin was firm and incredibly hot when she wrapped her arms around his neck. Laura teased him, stroking Wilham's tongue again and again until she felt him tremble.

"Not tonight—" He lifted his head, stopping her from drawing his tongue into the heat of her mouth.

But Laura didn't want to stop. She pulled back enough to push her way out of her robe, to yank her short nightgown over her head. Both Laura and Wilham moaned when she straddled his firm thighs. Wilham's topaz eyes were hot with need as they slowly moved over her lush, caramel-tone curves, lingered on her hard nipples. Impatient, she tugged at the tie encircling his waist and pushed at his robe until his dark bronze flesh was bare and she could move her hands over the wide expanse of his hairy chest. She leaned forward and placed a series of kisses across his shoulders and collar bone.

In a raspy voice, he accused, "You're making it impossible for me to say no."

"Then say yes, island man." Laura tilted her head, flirted with him, giving him a sensuous smile as she teased his nipple with one hand while caressing his taut midsection and hard stomach with her other hand. When she reached the ebony thicket surrounding his sex, he husked her name, his voice brimming with need.

Using the soft pads of her fingers, she traced down his thick shaft. His bronze skin was both satiny smooth and steely hard. His erection twitched in response to her touch. He was hot, pulsing beneath her fingertips.

When she circled the broad crown he released a husky groan, but continued protesting, "Don't, babe. You're covered in bruises. I won't hurt—"

Wilham stopped talking when Laura flicked his bottom lip with her tongue and gave him a playful bite. Then she kissed him hard, despite her bruised, tender mouth.

"Why are you objecting when we both know you want what I want? I need you to touch me, Wil, all over. Please, babe." She pleaded, "Please, I need you to erase his hurtful touch from my body, remove it from my memory. When I think of this night, I want to remember you, loving me. Make me yours, again."

He lightly kissed her bruised cheek, her cut, swollen lip, and the bandage that covered where she'd been pricked with the knife. "I'm so sorry, my love. So sorry you were hurt. I wish I could take away the pain."

"You are healing me with your kisses," she insisted.

"If only it was true," he said quietly. And then he proceeded to kiss all her hurt places despite his denial.

Laura sighed, arching her back. She pushed her breasts forward, shamelessly offering herself to him. In a hoarse whisper he repeated her name again and again as he cupped and squeezed her breasts, relishing their softness. Dipping his head, Wilham took her hard peak into his mouth, easing the ache and warming it with his tongue. He laved the firm nipple repeatedly and she whimpered deep in her throat.

Drawing on the aching peak, Wilham applied the sweet suction Laura craved and her excitement quickly spiraled. She trembled as he intensified the exquisite sensation, sending shards of pleasure mixed with sizzling hot desire racing through her nervous system and dampening her feminine core.

Heat simmered, slowly bubbling, building as he pinched her other nipple between his fingers. She called out his name, feeling as if she'd reached a full, rolling boil. Instead of easing up, he cupped and squeezed her sex while he continued to suck her incredibly sensitive nipple.

Her entire body quivered in response, her breathing was rapid and uneven. Again and again she clenched and unclenched the muscles deep inside her feminine passage. She needed him . . . now! Suddenly, he gently bit her aching tip as he rubbed her clitoris and Laura screamed, reaching a climax.

She was still gasping and trembling in response, when she said urgently, "Wil, I want you now. Hurry, please hurry."

Wilham's tall, lean frame shook with need as he easily lifted her onto his throbbing shaft. Bracing her hands on his shoulders, she slid down his hard, pulsating length and welcomed him into her unbelievably moist and hot body. They had both held their breath as he reclaimed her, making her his alone.

It didn't take long. A half-dozen deep, hard strokes and then they were flying. And when they soared they reached completion as one.

Finally, they were where they belonged. Together, locked in each other's arms, sharing an amazingly swift and unbelievably sweet release . . . one heart and one love.

Laura was cradled in her husband's arms when he vowed, "I will never repeat the mistake of not putting you first. You, Laura Jean Murdock Kramer, are my heart, my love, and my wife. And I promise you and the children we will have someday will always come first with me."

She laughed, then whispered in his ear, "That's good, because you, Wilham Sebastian Kramer, my love, my lover, and my husband, may be a father very soon."

"What?"

"I'm not absolutely certain. While the doctor was ordering all those tests at the hospital, I asked him to include a pregnancy test."

He squeezed her tight. "Oh, sweetheart. That's wonderful news."

"Not exactly news. I wasn't going to tell you until I was certain, but I couldn't keep quiet. Are you pleased?"

He grinned. "Incredibly pleased." He kissed her tenderly. "No worries. If we don't get it right this time, we can keep on trying. What do you say to flying down to St. John for a few days of R&R and then to Paris for that honeymoon we talked about?"

"I say yes!" She giggled. "I love how you think, Wilham Sebastian. My sweet island man."

He chuckled before he said, "I didn't know what

it meant to truly live until I met you. And I certainly knew nothing about love. You changed all that for me. You make my life worth living. I love you, Laura mine. And I plan to keep right on loving you. Forever."

"Forever is a long time." She kissed him sweetly.

He kissed her back. "Count on forever," he promised.

At Avon Books, we know your passion for romance—once you finish one of our novels, you find yourself wanting more.

May we tempt you with . . .

- **Excerpts** from our upcoming releases.

- Entertaining **extras**, including authors' personal photo albums and book lists.

- Behind-the-scenes **scoop** on your favorite characters and series.

- **Sweepstakes** for the chance to win free books, romantic getaways, and other fun prizes.

- Writing **tips** from our authors and editors.

- **Blog** with our authors and find out why they love to write romance.

- **Exclusive content** that's not contained within the pages of our novels.

Join us at
www.avonbooks.com

AVON

An Imprint of HarperCollins*Publishers*
www.avonromance.com

Available wherever books are sold or please call 1-800-331-3761 to order.

FTH 0708